Praise for *The Language of Light*

"Richly atmospheric, gorgeously written, and filled with characters so real they breathe on the page, Clayton's first novel is as luminous as a perfect photograph shimmering with true light."

—Caroline Leavitt, author of *Girls in Trouble* and *Pictures of You*

"An engaging and compassionate portrait of an artist learning to embrace the full potential of her power. Meg Waite Clayton writes with a photographer's precision, clarity, and care."

—A. Manette Ansay, author of *Good Things I Wish You*

"*The Language of Light* has what readers want in a book—the believable kind of humor and pathos that makes for a terrific read."

—Katharine Weber, author of *The Music Lesson* and *The Little Women*

"*The Language of Light* shines on, a wonderfully knowing action photograph that has emerged from the darkroom as words."

—Baltimore *Sun*

"Will delight readers searching for a story with meaning, character and drama."

—Bookreporter.com

Praise for *The Wednesday Sisters*

"This book reminded me why I love to read."
—Lolly Winston, author of *Good Grief* and
Happiness Sold Separately

"This generous and inventive book is a delight to read, an evocation of the power of friendship to sustain, encourage, and embolden us. Join the sisterhood!"
—Karen Joy Fowler, author of
The Jane Austen Book Club

"If you've ever had a best friend, buy a copy for her."
—Masha Hamilton, author of
The Camel Bookmobile

"Move over, Ya–Ya sisters!"
—Amanda Eyre Ward, author of
Love Stories in This Town

"Readers will be swept up by this moving novel about female friendship."
—*Booklist*

"A heartwarming novel about the joys and complications of friendship, and an inspiring story for anyone who has dared to dream big."
—Michelle Richmond, author of
The Year of Fog

"I read *The Wednesday Sisters* in one delicious gulp."
—Lalita Tademy, author of *Red River*

"Clayton captures the evolution of a decades-long friendship in a highly accessible narrative. She grabs the reader's attention early on, introducing compelling and quirky characters that are easy to identify with."

—Salt Lake City *Deseret News*

"*The Wednesday Sisters* . . . poignantly [illustrates] the way it really was back in the days when the glass ceiling was more like the roof of a marble tomb. . . . Though all their hopes aren't realized, the friendship these women share provides a haven for each one anyway—and for the readers of this novel."

—*The Nashville Scene*

Early praise for *The Four Ms. Bradwells*

"It's rare that I come across a book that I immediately want to give to my best friends. This was one of them: a heartwarming page-turner about smart women and the complicated nature of female friendships. By the end you'll wish that you could join the Ms. Bradwells for lunch."

—Katie Crouch, *New York Times* bestselling author of *Girls in Trucks* and *Men and Dogs*

"In *The Four Ms. Bradwells*, Meg Waite Clayton introduces us to a group of extraordinary women. This is a fine, smart, compelling novel about the deep friendships that guide and nurture our most difficult choices."

—Elizabeth Brundage, author of *A Stranger Like You* and *The Doctor's Wife*

ALSO BY MEG WAITE CLAYTON

The Wednesday Sisters

The Four Ms. Bradwells

THE
LANGUAGE
OF
LIGHT

THE
LANGUAGE
OF
LIGHT

A Novel

Meg Waite Clayton

Ballantine Books Trade Paperbacks

New York

2011 Ballantine Books Trade Paperback Edition

Copyright © 2003 by Meg Waite Clayton
Reading group guide copyright © 2011 by Random House, Inc.

Published in the United States by Ballantine Books, an imprint of The Random House Publishing Group, a division of Random House, Inc., New York.

BALLANTINE and colophon are registered trademarks of Random House, Inc. RANDOM HOUSE READER'S CIRCLE and colophon are trademarks of Random House, Inc.

Originally published in hardcover in the United States by St. Martin's Press in 2003.

Library of Congress Cataloging-in-Publication Data

Clayton, Meg Waite.
The language of light / Meg Waite Clayton.
p. cm.
ISBN 978-0-345-52664-9
1. Parent and adult child—Fiction.   2. Fathers and daughters—Fiction.
3. News photographers—Fiction.   4. Single mothers—Fiction.   5. Horse farms—Fiction.   6. Maryland—Fiction.   7. Widows—Fiction.   I. Title.

PS3603.L45L36 2003
813'.6—dc21   2003046884

Printed in the United States of America

www.randomhousereaderscircle.com
2 4 6 8 9 7 5 3 1

Book design by JoAnne Metsch

For Don Waite and Anna Tyler Waite
and for
Mac, Chris, and Nick

We find beauty not in the thing itself
but in the pattern of shadows,
the light and the darkness,
that one thing against another creates.

—Jun'ichiro Tanizaki,
   from "In Praise of Shadows"
   (translated by Thomas J. Harper and
   Edward G. Seidenstricker)

THE
LANGUAGE
OF
LIGHT

I lie awake, studying the moonlight spilling over the foot of the bed I slept in as a girl. The soft splash of light is carved through with hard edges of shadow, vacillating lines of light meeting dark. I try to imagine capturing the image with my camera—how long could I leave the lens open to the subtle light before the crisp silhouettes of the bare branches outside the window blurred to murky gray? The image isn't possible to capture in this light, but I can't help thinking my father would have caught it anyway.

At two fifteen I slip from the bed, feeling on the nightstand for the brass skeleton key Dad gave me when I was ten. The key is small and hard and cool in my fist, and the house is dark, the wood floors cold on my bare feet as I make my way to his study. The room is drafty—it always has been—but sitting at Dad's desk, I feel warmed. When I try to remember what he looked like sitting here, though, no image comes to mind, and I panic, the way I sometimes panicked after my husband, Wesley, died and I couldn't remember some small detail about him—what color tulips he liked best or how he marked his place in a book or whether his crooked smile tilted to the right or to the left. But then I remember Dad in motion; he was always in motion. I feel his fingers gently squeezing my shoulders as he stands behind me in the Communion line. I smell the coffee on his breath as he whispers to me to move in closer for a better picture. I see his large hands wrapped around Ned's and Charlie's little ones as Wesley's casket is lowered into the ground, his lips whispering that it's okay to cry, that he was a grown man and still he cried when his daddy died.

Though I don't remember that; my father's father was dead before I was born. I don't remember ever seeing Dad cry except in the darkness of his darkroom, and I'm so young in that memory that I'm not even sure it's real.

On the paneled walls around me, framed magazine covers and photojournalism awards—all my father's—hang everywhere. Others rest against the books overfilling the bookshelves or lean against the walls. Some simply stand in stacks on the floor. A package with a New York postmark sits on the desk in front of me, addressed to my father. It arrived the day after he died. Inside it I find another framed magazine cover, this one showing a line of refugees walking down a dirt road. It's a haunting photo, the endless line of exhausted, starving people carrying mattresses on their heads, babies on their backs. I find myself wondering what Dad had been thinking as he took it, and whether there are other photographs of these people, ones Dad might have kept for himself in his box.

Across the room, the closet where Dad stored his cameras and gear is nearly empty—only a single film canister and his metal file box, which I pull down from the shelf and set on the hearth. I start a fire in the fireplace and sit on the floor in my pajamas, rolling the key between my fingers. First the newspaper, then the kindling burns.

The logs are hot, glowing red by the time I unlock the box and pull out a thick stack of photos. A large envelope at the back holds the negatives, all sheathed in polyethylene. As I take a fistful and lean forward to the heat of the fire, Dad's words come back to me, the words he spoke years after he first gave me the key, when he asked me to use it to open his box and burn the photographs in it after he died: "Those photos were never meant to be published," he'd said. "I don't ever want them to be."

But his photographs are all I have of him now. In some ways, they're all I've ever had.

"A glass of wine would be nice right now," I whisper, as if Dad can somehow hear me, as if he were here. In the bookshelf cabinet, I find a few glasses and an old brown ice bucket with no lid, all covered with dust, and Dad's scotch, too, though Mom's sherry is gone. Dad must have removed it sometime after she died. But I find an almost empty bottle of it on the top shelf of a kitchen cabinet, next to the serving platters and bowls we used on holidays when I was young. They were Grandma's, and then Dad's. Now probably they'll be mine.

With the last of the sherry in hand, I sit down to burn the pictures as I promised Dad I would. I begin to look through them first, though; Dad never asked me not to, and I never volunteered. Maybe I'll even keep one or two, keep some part of him for me. Surely he'd indulge me that. I'll make my boys promise to burn them when I die so that, in the end, they'll all be destroyed, as Dad wished.

The first photo is of a young man—a boy really—in uniform, army fatigues and a helmet, in a trench next to some type of large gun. He holds a letter in his hand, yet his eyes stare blankly. What could provoke a look like that? A lover gone? A brother killed? A mother dead?

I force myself to set the photo on the fire. Its center turns black, then melts.

The second photo is of a child, all ribs and bones and swollen belly. Huge, haunted eyes stare out from her dark face, her hair in tufts, patches. Her mother curls up on the dry, hard dirt beside her, eyes closed. She might be sleeping, but this photo is in Dad's box; the mother is dead.

Staring at the child, the mother, I try to imagine why my father kept these photographs only for himself. I close my eyes, trying to remember the sound of his voice, some few forgotten words that would give me the answer. I can remember the feel of my eyes adjusting to the red darkness in the darkroom; I can smell the chemical smell—that distinctive acid smell; I can see the ghost of a picture seep out of the submerged paper in the tray. But I hear only the pop and sizzle of flames.

I put the second photo on the fire and watch it melt.

The third photo is of a young woman—nineteen or twenty, barely more than a girl—in black-and-white. She sits at a cluttered wooden table, in a pub perhaps, surrounded by half-empty glasses, full ashtrays, empty chairs. She leans forward over the table, her arm stretching to grasp something just out of reach. The camera? She does have that self-consciously rigid posture of someone who doesn't want to be photographed. And then something catches my eye and I move the picture closer to the fire, to see the woman's face. The look in those eyes. Humor. Delight. But with some melancholy, something unforgettable underneath. I move closer, study the picture more carefully: the arch of the brow, the shape of the lips, the set of the chin. Some part of me wants it to be someone else. But even so many years younger, I know that face. It's Emma Crofton's face.

PART ONE

1

Emma Crofton was sixty-nine when I first met her, in the autumn of the year Wesley died. I'd just packed up our belongings and moved to Maryland with my two sons: Ned, who would tell you he was not just eight but rather eight and a quarter, and Charlie, who'd just turned six. We'd come to live in a simple stone house my great-grandfather had built on a hundred acres of horse country ninety years before. The farm belonged to my father by then, and though he hadn't visited it in years it was full of warm memories for him: swimming in the muddy-bottomed pond and following deer tracks through the woods, capturing turtles and frogs and snakes my great-grandmother allowed him to keep in large pickle jars when he spent summers there. For me, though, the farm was an empty place, full of other people's histories, surrounded by other people's friends living other people's lives, a thousand miles away from the life I knew. A life that had seemed to close in around me in the wake of Wesley's death.

That afternoon I met her, the sky was overcast, dreary, but the boys were outside anyway, down by the pond skipping rocks, Boomer, our golden retriever, barking at their heels. I was inside, sitting at Wesley's old desk, sorting through a messy pile of my photographs. Just as I glanced up to check on the boys, the sun peeked through the clouds, shooting rays out, fanlike, through the gap, and that's when I saw her: a stranger riding across my bridge on horseback, wearing a hat.

Emma wore hats generally, not just at St. James's Church, where all the ladies still wore hats in the old-fashioned way—and, quite frankly, not that kind of hat. You'd never catch Emma Crofton in a timid little pillbox or a floppy sunbonnet. She sported bold hats that marked her approach from some distance: men's felt bowlers in bright colors with feathers tucked into the ribbons; wide, strong-brimmed hats that blocked your view from behind; or, when she was perched on her tractor cutting her fields, the old brown suede hat that, Willa later told me, had belonged to Emma's husband before he died. When Emma was riding, though, she wore a simple black riding cap with a hunting coat and black britches, as she did that day. Her back was straight, her head motionless, as she bobbed smoothly up and down on the chestnut horse. She made her way up the gravel drive, looking as if she belonged a hundred years back in time, on an English country estate. Only the spatters of mud on her polished leather boots seemed to belong in my life.

I watched her through the window with a great deal of curiosity and a small measure of hope, and when she'd ridden nearly to my front porch, I came outside to greet her. She dismounted, moving as gracefully as a young girl though her face was weathered and deeply lined. She brought the reins over the horse's head and tied them to the lowest branch of the maple next to the drive. The horse snorted lightly and stepped forward a few paces, leaving horseshoe shapes of compressed grass where his hooves had been. Emma clicked her tongue twice and tapped him with her crop, coaxing him back up onto the drive. The animal smell of him mingled with the smell of decaying leaves.

"I'm Nelly Grace," I said, offering my hand, realizing only then that I still held one of my photos.

Emma nodded twice, sharply, and in a voice not quite perfectly American—English, I thought, or something English-like—she said, "Yes, of course you are."

She'd come to welcome me to the neighborhood, a "country neighborhood" that stretched across five square miles of land. Her place was one hill over to the south and slightly east, she said, and I wondered where that was in terms of streets (which only later did I come to call roads) but for fear of appearing ignorant did not ask.

I pointed out Ned and Charlie, their skinny bodies no taller than the remains of the pussy willows at the pond's edge, only their nearly black hair—my straight, thick hair—setting them apart, and she said she had a son, too, though he was grown now. He lived in a house on the farm they worked together, she said. That was done a lot there: siblings of families that had been in the area for generations lived on farms that bordered each other, family compounds in which the eldest child moved into the parents' house when the parents died, one of their children in turn getting their house, the cousins growing up together, leaving for whatever Ivy League college their family had attended forever (Princeton, generally), but always coming back. "It's rather nice," Emma said, "grandparents hunting with their grandchildren." Foxhunting, she explained; she was master of the hounds then, the first woman ever to be master, though she didn't tell me that.

"Nearly everyone here rides," she said. "We put them on horses even before they're your Charlie's age."

She said she hoped I'd consider leaving my farm open to riders; the hunt club had taken care of clearing the paths through the woods for years, and would be happy to continue to do so if I'd let them ride through. "Why don't you join us at the races Saturday, and I'll introduce you around?" she said. She had a spot at the finish line, and we'd have a tailgate party with my neighbors, Willa Jenkins, who lived up the road on the left, and Kirby and Joan, who had that pretty yellow house on the right.

"You'll enjoy Kirby," Emma said, "though you may not know it at first. He's an architect, but he designs sailboats, writes music, and plays the cello just as well as he builds buildings. He sings light opera in a local theater troupe, Gilbert and Sullivan and that type of thing, and he makes the most marvelous scones, though he's not even English." She leaned toward me and lowered her voice. "But he's rather odd-looking, to be honest. I'm afraid his features don't quite go together somehow."

"Don't—"

"Not quite symmetrical, I suppose. But don't let his looks scare you off. Or his manner either. He tends to be a bit flamboyant, but it's all for show and he's quite a fine sort underneath.

"Now, Joan . . . well, she is what she is. A lot of people don't like her—they say she's opinionated and bossy. And she is. But I like her anyway. She was kind to me when I first came here with Davis, when . . . when she might not have been.

"You'll love Willa," she continued as I shot a quick glance at Ned and Charlie, still skipping rocks.

"Everyone does," she said. "Particularly the married men, though even their wives can't seem to help liking her."

I said I'd love to go.

Emma, glancing toward the photograph in my hand, suggested I might bring my camera. I pulled the photo closer to me—almost a reflex—then made myself look at it with forced nonchalance. It was an old photo: a bell-bottomed, sign-carrying woman shouting angrily as she marched in a teacher's picket line. I'd thought when I'd taken the photo that I would submit it to my school newspaper, but on developing it, I'd seen I should have looked for a better angle or moved in closer—something about the shot wasn't quite right.

"That is *your* photograph?" Emma said. "I thought at first it was one of your father's, but it's yours, isn't it?"

Perhaps it should have struck me then that she knew my father's work, but so many people did that it never surprised me. Or perhaps I was simply too wrapped up in wishing I'd moved in closer for that shot, or in realizing how much that woman's angry face looked like Wesley's that last time we'd argued, I do remember thinking that. In any case I only nodded reluctantly and said yes, the photo was mine.

Emma smiled warmly, showing slightly gray teeth. "Yes, do bring your camera," she said.

She pulled a small Mason jar from her jacket pocket then, one with a plain, white sticker on the top that read EMMA's PEACH in barely legible blue ink. "I don't know if it's good," she said. "I've never made it before."

"I'm sure it will be wonderful, Mrs. Crofton," I said.

Emma hiked her boot up into the stirrup and swung her free leg easily over her horse. "Please, Nelly, won't you call me Emma?" she said.

"Emma, then," I said, and I stood on my front porch, waving a little half-wave and watching her ride off.

I had to peel Charlie off my legs when the baby-sitter arrived the morning of the races. Ned, older and braver, looked droopy and didn't say a word. They weren't clingy children, but ever since their father died they didn't like me to go anywhere.

I would rather have stayed home myself, to be honest. The thing about losing someone is that the fear becomes real, or at least it did for me; I knew that everyone could disappear from my life in the single moment it took for any one of a million things I couldn't even imagine to occur. For months after Wesley died, after his car skidded off that icy road, I would pull my pillow and blanket into the boys' bedroom at night and lie on the floor, listening to the deep, easy rhythms of their breaths.

Some nights I still did.

I went to the races that day, though, walking up the hill to Kirby and Joan's farm, where we settled on driving together in Joan's station wagon; we had only one parking pass and we couldn't all fit into Emma's beat-up old truck without riding in the truck bed, an opportunity Kirby declined for us on the excuse of his sport coat and his white shirt and tie.

"These will be point-to-point races," Kirby told me, as if I might have a clue what that meant. "Hurdles and timber races and steeplechase." Terms he was clearly sure I understood. I said, "Right, sure," as if I did understand, feeling uneasy under the focus of his dark eyes and bushy black eyebrows set in a crooked, Dudley Do-Right–chinned face. He was ugly, as Emma had suggested, but in a fascinating sort of way. Part of me wanted to zoom in for a close-up; part of me wanted to cap the lens and back away.

Not that I'd brought my camera—I hadn't. A fact Emma noted as she settled a broad-brimmed red felt hat on her head, the reflected sunlight casting a warm glow on her face.

"You forgot your camera, Nelly," she said.

"I—Yes," I said. "I forgot."

And when she offered to swing by and get it on the way out, I found myself admitting it was still packed. "I'm afraid I haven't even uncovered the box quite yet," I said.

Emma looked at me oddly, as if I were speaking an unknown language but she somehow understood my meaning from the tone of my voice, the expression on my face. Well, next time, she said after a moment, and I said yes, next time.

She handed us each a ticket then, a small square pink thing with a horse logo and the words RESTRICTED ENCLOSURE printed on it, with a green string attached. Following Willa's lead, I busied myself tying my ticket to a button of my blouse, and we loaded the picnic basket into the way-back of Joan's station wagon and drove to a large stone home perched upon a high hill, with views all around and a mile-long lawn stretching down to the road. There were cars already parked in their spots on the lawn, and we, too, drove right across the grass, to our space.

The place was festive, people mingling, drinking champagne from crystal flutes, and eating stuffed mushrooms and pasta salads and caviar. We spread our own picnic on a red-checked tablecloth on the tailgate, and Emma poured champagne and we began to discuss the races: who was riding which horse in which race and who'd been running well lately and who'd won these same races last year. Or rather, the others talked and I listened. I heard the name Dac come up again and again, and finally I caught on that he was Emma's son. I looked in the program and there he was, Davis A. Crofton V, named as the trainer for a number of horses running that day. Even, on one page, two in the same race.

We visited that way for a while, together with a stream of visitors who came and went, subjects paying homage to Emma. And as the race starting time (post time, Willa said) drew near, Kirby proposed a small betting pool.

"Winner takes all," Emma insisted.

"You want your horse, or are you feeling overinvested in this one?" Kirby lifted one eyebrow and we all laughed, and I looked down at my program to see a horse named Foolish Heart, owned by Emma and trained by Dac, running in the first race.

"You might as well hand me the money," Emma said.

Joan chose a horse named Regal's Q, whatever that meant, and Kirby took Double Barrel, saying that with a name like that, he'd better come out fast. Willa put her money on Tom's War, saying it fit her violent mood these days, and everyone laughed, including Willa, though I didn't understand why, not yet knowing the difficulties of her divorce.

I put my dollar on Newsbeat, thinking of my father, from whom I'd received a quickly jotted postcard that morning, a photo from the Archbishop's Palace in Lima with apologies for not having made it back to help us move. The boys had been so looking forward to his visit, too, to having Grandpa Pat show them his farm. And I wondered then how they were doing with the sitter. I hoped she liked playing Monopoly, or Clue, or Crazy Eights.

Behind us, two green-and-white striped tents that had been filled only with white folding chairs when we arrived began to fill with men in coats and ties and women in skirts and hats—one stooped old woman was dressed all in horses, on her skirt and sweater and even on her hat—while below us, along the post-and-rail fence marking the edge of the course, people in all manner of attire collected: men in blue jeans with babies in backpacks strapped on their broad shoulders, teenage girls with red lipstick and bright dresses, beamy women with big hair and pastel pants. Some brought along lawn chairs or picnic blankets, and some just stood or sat on the ground along the fence. Some brought binoculars. Some brought cameras. Some brought children, who ran around like trapped ants until their mothers or their fathers made them stop. It was wonderfully chaotic, spirited, amusing in a way that our enclosure, with its champagne-drinking, pink-ticketed patrons, was somehow not.

A man's voice came across the air announcing the first race, and a trumpet sounded, or a recording of one. The crowd turned in unison and focused across the field on the horses making their way single file to the starting line, circling there. And my program had prepared me for the colors each jockey would wear, bright primary colors on their shirts and hats, but it had not really prepared me for the grandeur of it all. A brief shiver shook my shoulders as we stepped up to the fence right at the finish line.

I wished I'd brought my camera, after all.

I wished Ned and Charlie were with me; I wished I could share this with them.

The horses came off the circle one by one at the starting line, and in an instant, some flag must have been raised or dropped or something, some signal that meant go, because they broke out fast, legs stretching forward and jockeys sitting tightly, compacted into the air above their mounts. It was the most furiously pounding graceful thing I'd ever seen.

The two lead horses went over the first fence simultane-ously, like a team, so that you might have thought it a syn-chronized event, and even I could see that jumping was the thing. Shoot the Loop was out in front, the announcer said, but how he could tell I didn't know. Foolish Heart was in sec-ond beside him. And they were all over the fence, with Regal's Q in third and Newsbeat in fourth, then Spellsinger and Tom's War and Happy Friar and, finally, Double Barrel at the back—so much for Kirby's name theory—all jumping smoothly. The pink-ticketed crowd applauded lightly, politely, as if it were a speech. I wanted to shout *Go! Go! Go!* But I could see it wasn't done. Even Emma stood quietly, just beside me, and though she chugged her fist like it was a piston, it barely moved. She did cheer her horse on, saying, "Go, Foolish Heart! You can do it, love!" But she spoke in a voice that, though filled with passion, was only a whisper to herself.

The horses took the second jump, a wooden coop, and a few seconds later they went over the third, a high hedge, and they were going over the fourth jump, a huge hurdle, when Shoot the Loop, still in the lead, took a nosedive, sending his red-jacketed rider sprawling, rolling, coming to rest as a bright lump on the green grass.

I reached instinctively for my camera. It wasn't there.

I held my breath as the other horses took that jump, waiting for a thousand pounds of horse to land on that red rider, crushing his leg or his rib cage, even his skull, who knew? My stomach went queasy, but I couldn't take my eyes off the scene. Finally Double Barrel, still in last place, cleared the jump, and I breathed out.

An ambulance, lights flashing, careered mutely across the field, its eerie silence more arresting than sirens would have been. At the same time, red-coated officials sprinted after the riderless horse. The chaos didn't distract the remaining racers, though. They'd already cleared the fifth jump, were hammering on to the sixth, bursting over the post-and-rail fence without pause. They stormed by us for the first time, almost close enough to touch, and my nausea began to ease, my body again moving in the rhythm of their step. I was alive with it, mesmerized.

The horses headed out toward where they'd started and around again, this time inside the circuit they'd just covered, over new jumps, but I didn't know that yet. I looked to see where the rider had tumbled, fearing once more for his life. He was gone, the ambulance pulling off the field onto the road. Even his horse had been contained, surrounded and held in place by a circle of red-coated officials.

And the horses sprinted still. Foolish Heart was holding first place now, the announcer said, but Newsbeat was moving up, and Regal's Q had dropped to third. Then Spellsinger and Happy Friar and still Tom's War and Double Barrel at the back, a good ten lengths behind. Shoot the Loop was out of the race, the announcer said.

"Looks like you can pick 'em," Joan said to me. "Look at Newsbeat go!"

The horses cleared the last jump and headed up toward us, all pounding hooves and stretching legs and cracking whips. Newsbeat, the announcer said, was challenging Foolish Heart. I could see him moving up on the outside of the turn, so close now that they traded the lead each time one of them reached his neck out with his step. And I was saying, aloud but not loudly, "Go! Go! Go!" But I wasn't even sure which horse I was rooting for anymore—my father's Newsbeat or my new friend Emma's Foolish Heart. And when the horses flashed past us at the finish line, I couldn't say who'd won, but I could feel the throbbing of the earth beneath my feet, the adrenaline in my blood.

"It's Newsbeat by a nose!" the announcer shouted. "Ladies and gentlemen, what an exciting race!"

The crowd around me applauded with some enthusiasm, but they kept their reserve.

The horses slowed and headed back out from where they'd started, to the trailers that would take them home, defeated, with weeks or even months of hard training before they could compete again. Only Newsbeat and his rider turned back toward us, the horse sweating from his lovely roan withers, the jockey straight-backed, proud. They rode right up to the announcer's tower, where they collected the trophy, the prize check, the wreath. They turned toward the crowd, then, the jockey raising the trophy high over his head, the horse lifting his head as if he, too, relished the victory.

Sweet victory, my father always called it.

All around me, cameras snapped and snapped and snapped.

As we were repacking the picnic basket, I gathered two last champagne glasses from atop the fence post—mine and Emma's—pausing for a moment to lean against the rough wood of the fence slats, to look out over the thick green of the winner's circle, the chalky white of the finish line, the deep shadow of the announcer's tower in the golden light of the late afternoon. When I turned back toward the car, my own dark shadow casting out in front of me, I found Kirby watching me, and Emma too.

"I'd like to ride like that someday," I said. "I wouldn't even care if I won."

Kirby's bushy eyebrows pulled together in the oddest of expressions, his eyes cutting to Emma. Joan, sealing a Tupperware lid, smiled as if I'd just said something incredibly naïve. Willa, too, who'd been rolling the silverware up in a cloth napkin, paused to look at me, then at Emma; she was, I thought, trying hard not to laugh.

Was it a laugh? Or some other emotion she was trying to suppress?

And Emma? Emma squinted into the low sunlight, her expression not so much amused or surprised as startled, almost angry. She took one of the crystal flutes from me finally, and tucked it carefully—too carefully—into the basket.

"That's an American thing, you know, that nonsense about how you play the game," she said. "You have to ride to win."

She nodded twice, sharply, the crisp silhouette of her head

on the car behind her echoing the gesture, as if even the golden sunlight wanted to be like her. I handed her the last champagne flute, envying her the self-confidence that seemed to ring from that gesture, Emma's certainty that she was who she should be.

2

Willa came down with her two boys the morning after the races to say hello and to offer me two of the necessities of country life by her telling: a place up the road where I was welcome to stop by any time I needed company, and geographically suitable playmates for Ned and Charlie in the form of her Matt and Craig. It wasn't long before we practically lived together and I couldn't tell you where our property ended and hers began, but at the time Willa was an unfamiliar species to me: comfortable with cocktail parties, horses, reptiles, large insects, and herself. We were in that middle space before true friendship breaks through; I knew her well enough to see her strengths but not well enough to know her secret weaknesses, and so was slightly in awe of her. Still, when, about a week after the races, Emma invited me for cocktails Saturday afternoon—"Not a party, just some people from the neighborhood. And do bring the children; I have puppies to amuse them"—I herded Boomer and the boys up to Willa's to find out what she planned to wear. In the few short weeks I'd been in the Maryland horse country, I'd learned that the rules of attire were quite different—

immensely complicated, uniformly followed, and impossible for me to understand. Just that morning, the boys and I had gone to the Hunter Trials in button-front cotton shirts and smart leather loafers, only to find ourselves the only ones not wearing moth-eaten sweaters and Wellington boots.

Ned and Charlie found Matt and Craig on the swing set in the yard, where Boomer found Ginger, their female golden and his new love. Not finding Willa in the house, I poked my head into the barn, where the smell of leather and hay and horse manure and Willa's cheerful voice greeted me—"Hey, stranger!"—as if she'd known me for ages. She dug her pitch-fork into the dry dirt of the barn floor with one swift jab, pulled her rubber gloves off, then rubbed the top of her head as if she had a ferocious itch so that her hair, sweaty-wet from her work, looked mussed in a pleasing sort of way. She had that sort of random energy about her, all crisp motion and acerbic wit not completely controlled, so it seemed at any moment she might clear off a cluttered countertop with a sin-gle sweep of her arm if no one were looking.

She answered my question about what to wear to Emma's in a comical, nasal voice, like a student mocking a professor. "An invitation to a cocktail party out here in the country generally means coats and ties for the gentlemen and a skirt at a minimum for the ladies. A dress would be the superior choice." Underneath her air of sarcasm she was speaking the truth. "Unless, of course," she continued in her own deep voice, "the invitation says 'No Ties Permitted,' which some of the 'young people'—meaning those under fifty—will some-times do. In that case, you can wear nice slacks and any gen-tleman who might accompany you can don a polo shirt." She threw some hay into the rack in the stall she'd been mucking, then dragged a bag of cat food from a corner and ripped it open. "But this affair at Mrs. Crofton's is cocktails, not a party, which is more complicated, and varies from hostess to hostess."

"Or host to host, as the case may be?"

"Not out here." Willa spilled cat food out across the top of her feed bins, and cats began appearing from the hayloft, from the tops of the stall walls, from every crevice of the barn. "Men don't throw parties out here, not if they're married, anyway. Though their names will appear on the invitations. 'Mr. and Mrs. Man's-Name Last-Name invite you to . . .' "

"Engraved, not printed, on plain ecru paper with a panel," I said, "in Stuyvesant type."

"And nothing but black ink unless it's the holidays, in which case a discreet sprig of holly, green with red berries, may be tastefully tucked into one corner, generally the bottom left."

We laughed, hers a deep laugh, as unrestrained as those of the boys playing on the swing set, and I said this was a social custom she was quite fond of, I could see.

She still got invitations addressed to "Mrs. Michael Jenkins," she said as she stepped into the tack room, a small, heated space lined with metal brackets and big wooden pegs. "We've been separated for a year and, God willing, the divorce will be final any day," she said.

She hoisted a saddle onto one of the higher pegs in the tidy room, the tendons of her neck standing out under the weight. Outside, the boys were laughing, the dogs barking, everyone having a ball.

"Makes you understand why so many women keep their names now," I said, wondering if she felt as odd at social functions as I did, being suddenly without a husband.

She told me her maiden name, Waeringawicam. "No one

could pronounce it. I gladly gave it up, and despite everything I don't want it back."

I said it sounded Indian.

"Like it should mean 'great dancer who brings the rains'?" Willa laughed. "Well, it's English, if you can believe it. The only complicated English name I've ever heard. All other English names are simple, straightforward: Cooke or Smith-wick or your hostess-to-be's maiden name, Whitfield. Mrs. Crofton is straight from England, of course. A direct import. She came over after World War Two." She picked up a plastic currycomb and a hoof pick and set them on a shelf. "Joan said it was quite the scandal at the time, Davis going off to study in Europe and coming back a war hero with this English wife and child."

"That's scandalous?"

She yanked on the faucet of an old sink in the corner, picked up a sliver of soap and stuck her hands under the sput-tering water. "This place is pretty inbred—people here prefer to die in the houses they were born in. A spouse imported from New York might be okay if you met at your summer place in Maine—Mike Hayley jokes that we do have to di-versify the gene pool now and then—but Mrs. Crofton came from quite another world."

"England?"

That was part of the thing, she said, the reason for the scan-dal: They met and married in England before anyone in Bal-timore ever knew. And then she came "with no apparent family and no apparent history"—Joan's words, not hers—and she never talked about herself or her life before she came. "And no one asks, of course, because it just isn't a topic she discusses," Willa said. "And she is a Crofton, after all."

"Joan told you all this?"

"Well, right." Willa dried her hands on her britches, set a bucket under the running faucet, and popped open a tin of saddle soap, filling the room with its soapy-sweet smell. "So you have to consider the source. Because the other thing I do know is . . . well . . . before Davis left, Joan and he had been tight."

"Engaged?"

"It's probably all nothing. It doesn't take anything to start lips flapping wildly out here." She swabbed the saddle soap with a sponge and began to clean the plaited leather of a bridle, her hands moving easily.

I asked how long ago Emma's husband had died.

"Davis?" Willa paused for such a long moment that I thought she'd lost her train of thought. "Davis died three years ago. Three years last week."

I nodded, watching her, wondering what had happened back then that she remembered so exactly when Davis Crofton had died. Something to do with her marriage maybe; I would always remember the date of Gabe Myers's birthday, not because it was his birthday but because Wesley and I had fought that night after his party, our last fight.

Willa, swabbing the sponge across the tin of saddle soap again, said there was a juicy rumor there too: Since Davis had died, Emma had taken to disappearing. "Just for a few days at a time," she said, her hands scrubbing again at the leather she had just cleaned. "The rumor is she has a secret lover stored away somewhere. It's ridiculous, really. I mean, Mrs. Crofton is nearly seventy. And who cares if she does? It might have been interesting if she'd been slipping away while Davis was alive, but . . . And Davis has been dead long enough that you'd think this hypothetical other lover would have seen the light of day. Maybe not out here, though."

I suggested maybe she'd bring him out of the closet at her

"not-a-party" that evening, and Willa laughed, turning toward me again, holding the bridle loosely with her sponge. You never knew, she said, but she already knew the lineup: the Murphys, the Wilsons, the Johnstons, the Oberlins, the Hayleys—the Hayleys were invited everywhere—and us. "And maybe Dac," she said.

"Emma's son?"

"But don't count on him. He's . . . well . . . not exactly reclusive, but extremely aloof." Michael, her ex, and Dac had been close growing up. Dac was Matt's godfather, she said, and at the mention of her son, we both glanced out the barn door to where the boys were piled up on the swing-set fort, Matthew looking about to push his brother down the slide against Craig's will. "Matt," Willa scolded, and Matt tried to look innocent.

Willa tossed the sponge into the bucket and began wiping the bridle with a cloth. "Now, where were we again?"

"Dac."

"Dac, right. So anyway, Michael says he used to be a regular guy, and he can seem pretty normal still, but he can also be pretty bizarre. Ever since Vietnam. Maybe it's understandable, what with Mai and—"

"He fought in Vietnam?"

"Has a Purple Heart to prove it."

"He couldn't duck the draft?"

"He volunteered, which was, if you ask me, pretty bizarre in itself. Who would sign up for that war, especially as late as he did?"

She began folding the saddle blankets and pads that had been laid out to dry on a saddle horse, declining my offer to help, leaving me to lean against the doorjamb and keep one eye on the boys. Her own personal theory about Dac, she said, was that he did it for Davis somehow. He adored Davis, you could tell that even now, she said. And his father had been "a major hero" in World War II.

"Anyway . . ." She put the last blanket on the shelf and mussed her hair again. "You wanted to know what to wear to Mrs. Crofton's?"

"I don't seem quite able to master the dress code in this place." I lifted my foot to show her my muddy loafers. "I wore them to the Hunter Trials today." I shrugged.

Willa smiled. "Well, Mrs. Crofton is pretty casual. I'm wearing corduroy slacks and a decent wool sweater, I think."

"Decent?" I asked, hoping for just a little more guidance.

"Clean, preferably without holes. Except where your neck and hands come out." She grinned.

3

I couldn't really see Emma's house from the road, just an impression of pale yellow and white buried in autumn leaves and smoke billowing out above the treetops. As we pulled farther up the drive, though, a simple wood clapboard structure with a porch wrapping around it like a lace collar came into view. The porch and the shutters and the wood framing the small-paned windows were painted a fresh bright white, the color of starched shirts, but richer, and below the porch, in front of the wood lattice that hid the crawl space, gnarly rosebushes and evergreens mingled in a dark black mulch.

Emma sat on the front porch steps, the sturdy brim of a chocolate brown felt hat shading her face. A yellow Labrador retriever sat at her feet, and puppies yipped and scurried around the yard and in the bushes and on the walk and on the porch, climbing on top of each other and on top of Emma. Ned and Charlie were out of the car, scooping up the puppies before we'd come to a stop, Ned saying, "Can we have one, *please,*" fluttering his dark eyelashes and smiling a goofy, wide-mouthed smile—my smile—even after I said I thought Boomer was more than enough dog for us.

"They've all been sold except the runt, which I am keeping for myself, anyway," Emma said. "Although if I were going to give him up to anyone, Ned, it would be you."

I sat on the top step with Emma, and we visited for a few minutes that way, with puppies and boys scrambling around us, the smell of burning wood in the air, and Emma's place stretching out before us. It was really something, Emma's place. Sitting on that front porch in the shadow of the woods, with the sound of the stream running through the sycamores and the long expanse of fields rolling out around, that farm was the entire world.

The sun was low when Emma said we ought to go around back and collect her son, Dac, who was out beyond the vegetable garden behind the house, looking through the viewfinder of a camera set on a tripod facing the woods. As we approached, he raised his index finger to his lips without turning to us, then wagged it toward a deer feeder at the edge of the grass. Beyond the feeder, through the multiflora at the edge of the woods, I could just make out the soft brown and marshmallow white of a fawn and its mother. Dac's moment came then, the fawn poking its black nose out tentatively, then stepping from the woods into the field. It perked its ears just as the shutter clicked, then started as Emma's mother dog lumbered around the corner of the stone garden wall and caught its scent. The dog raced off, barking up a storm, but the deer bounded easily away. Even in the best of shape, that dog did not stand a chance.

"That'll be some picture," I said.

Dac wore jeans and a plain white T-shirt under a heathery Harris tweed jacket, and he smelled of horses and peppermint. He looked to be a few years older than me, and he was attractive enough, though there was something brooding about him, something that darkened his eyes almost to black. He smiled briefly, a polite smile that made him look very like

Emma, though without quite so much cheekbone and with short-cropped, curly blond hair. "I'm Dac Crofton," he said in a voice oddly inconsistent with his eyes, a voice as creamy as a scoop of ice cream just begun to melt.

"And that's Dac's camera, which he is almost never without," Emma said. Then to Dac, "This is Nelly Grace, of course."

"Nelly," Dac said with a nod.

I admired his camera, a top-of-the-line Canon, and he spoke softly in response, toeing the ground as Ned and Charlie swarmed around us, begging him to let them click the cable release. He handed it to Charlie, asking if he knew how to use it, and Charlie nodded, his square, solemn face so like his father's, his eyes, too, Wesley's serious brown.

"You push here," he said. "Mom taught me how. She used to take pictures, too, before Daddy died."

I fingered Charlie's fine, dark hair, feeling naked, exposed, wanting to say something to soothe him, but what could I say? That I still took photographs even though I didn't? That I would soon, that our life would return to normal soon? That I would always be there for them, that nothing would ever happen to me, that they'd never be left alone, abandoned? That I'd never once imagined I might be happier without their dad?

Emma frowned—briefly, nonjudgmentally—before leaning down to Charlie's level. "I bet your mum takes wonderful pictures, doesn't she?" Then looking at Ned, "Now why don't you each have a practice with that gadget of Dac's. Pretend you're as good as your mum is. Then we'll go in for snacks."

The boys circled around Emma as we walked toward the house that afternoon, enthralled by her stories of country life. She'd once run over a five-foot-long black snake with the

mower deck on her tractor, she said, over there by the silo.
And when the barn caught fire one summer, the fire truck
pumped water from the pond to put out the flames. The boys
listened eagerly, nodding their heads and poking at each other,
pointing to things around the farm and asking questions. Ned
asked if she'd ever seen a snapping turtle, and Emma said just
last week she and Dac caught one as big around as the garbage
can into which they lured him with a piece of bacon. "He was
lucky," she said. "We wanted to see how big he was. You
know what we usually do with snapping turtles?"

The boys pranced around her, shouting, "What? What?"

"Dac sticks his fingers out at them, to bait them, and I
whop them on the head with an ax."

The boys exploded into a chorus of admiring *wow*s and *no
way*s and *cool*s.

"Your fingers?" I said to Dac.

Dac grinned, and with that grin the darkness gave way, a
window shade snapping up. "Mother is a bit prone to exaggeration," he said. "Actually, I use the handle from an old
broom. I train horses for a living, so I can't exactly afford to
lose my hands."

I wondered what that meant, training horses for a living.
You'd have to win a lot, I guessed, to make it work.

"Your horses must do pretty well," I said. "The ones I saw
did."

He shrugged his broad shoulders.

"Second place in that first race," I said. "And it was so close."

"But not first," he said, and in that moment he reminded
me of my father—my father who was never quite satisfied
even with his finest photographs.

We went through the back door, the floor—pale pine, so worn
at the threshold that it dipped—creaking beneath Ned's and

Charlie's antsy feet. Emma led us into the kitchen, a small room that might originally have been a butler's pantry, wedged as it was between the dining room and the mudroom. It was an old kitchen, with old-fashioned appliances: a roundish refrigerator with a single door; a freestanding oven that, if it worked (which seemed unlikely), could cook the biggest turkey you could find. A small, scarred pine table graced the middle of the room, and the cabinets had those window-type doors, old ones with thick, wavy glass through which you could see, among other things, precariously stacked china and several jars of Emma's Peach. I remember thinking that if it were my kitchen, I'd feel compelled to explain to visitors what I had in mind to modernize. Later—weeks? months?—I found myself wondering how I could ever have missed its charm.

Ned and Charlie made a beeline for the trays of hors d'oeuvres sitting on the pine table, simple things like cheese and crackers and nuts and chips and dips, while Dac took drink orders and I studied a set of framed photographs on the wall. They were vivid images, full of bright Kodachrome colors and yet perfectly natural, too, of all your favorite large zoo animals, taken in the wild either at close range or with a long lens. They were nice photos—perfect exposure, strong composition, sharp focus—but I was taken by something else, something more. It was almost as if some human emotion had been caught in those animal faces, some complex mixture of fear and desire.

"Very dramatic." I smiled at the curious face of a young giraffe who seemed inordinately interested in me. "Yours?"

I took a proffered glass of wine from Dac.

"I like to work in color," he said. "I like the way the same color looks different depending on the light, the time of day." He spoke modestly, as if all he contributed to the photographs was the mechanical pushing of a shutter release.

"So you take pictures too?" he said.

"Me? No, I—" I glanced at Charlie, happily downing cheese and Coke.

"I mean, yes. I— Not professionally or anything. But I—" I shrugged. "I used to take pictures, yes. But just, you know, the boys in front of the Christmas tree, that kind of thing. Nothing serious."

Almost nothing. And nothing at all since Wesley died, just as Charlie had said.

"And lately, I've had no time even for that," I said, "with the move and all."

We went into the family room, where a jumble of photographs, ribbons, and trophies were scattered about randomly with no apparent thought to spacing or overall visual effect. Not unlike the furniture: slipcovered sofas and chairs in rich prints and stripes, well worn—frumpy even—without being shoddy. Comfortable, like an old man's favorite hat. Ned and Charlie headed straight for the trophies, towing Dac along behind them, while I admired a young Emma's face in the pictures: Emma holding a baby; Emma disembarking from a boat, the hand of a toddler with Dac's curly hair in hers; a slightly older Emma on horseback, a nine- or ten-year-old Dac on a horse beside her; and then older Emmas and Dacs, sometimes alone, sometimes together, receiving trophies and awards. Emma, in answer to my questions, spoke matter-of-factly about these moments, but I had the feeling she was pleased to have been asked.

There were landscape photos on the walls too—not Ansel Adams or Sam Abell, but textured and rich. By comparison, the intermixed hunting scenes looked coarse, like the Findlay color images done in the 1930s, where the screen used to create the color could be seen in the print. When Emma and the boys went to answer the doorbell, I asked Dac if they were his.

"Not the hunters, but the rest," he said. "The ones without people are mine. The ones with people definitely are not."

"You don't photograph people?"

His face, like his voice, was sober and dark again, the window shade pulled back down.

"No," he said and then, without looking away but without pausing either, "The riding trophies are Mother's."

The subject had been changed.

The largest trophy sat on the traditional wood mantel, not in the center as you might have expected, but off to one side. I read the inscription: MARYLAND HUNT CUP WINNER. EMMA WHITFIELD CROFTON. 1963.

Across the room, Emma and the boys were returning with Willa and her gang and several others, everyone talking at once while the children spiraled around, and Emma was offering up Dac to take them to the barn, and they were exploding in a rush to accept the offer, flying off to the kitchen with Dac to get carrots for the horses.

In the peace that followed, I talked with a woman Emma had introduced as Sheila Wilson, but I was uncomfortable, disconcerted, as if I were talking to someone wearing mirrored sunglasses, and I was relieved when Willa came to my rescue, leaving several others chuckling over her last words. "Ben Wilson is definitely the better half of that couple," she whispered to me as she whisked me off toward the front door, where Emma was greeting another couple. "But Sheila inherited the money; she's one of those steel company families, U.S. Steel, I think. And these two?" She nodded toward the new couple. "George and Jan Murphy. They can't stand to touch each other, and they can't keep their hands off anyone else."

As Emma introduced me to the Murphys, a clock in the front hall struck five, and we all turned to look.

"What a beautiful grandfather clock," I said.

"It's a grand*mother* clock," Emma said. "I brought it with me from England when I came to the States."

The clock face was of ivory porcelain trimmed in a gold-colored metal—bronze maybe—and rich brown numbers, so dark they might be black. The thing you remembered about that clock, though, was not its beauty or even its delightful gong, but rather the sound of its perfectly circular pendulum swinging back and forth, back and forth, quietly clicking off each second as it did that day, making you almost glad time was passing away.

Once the party got rolling, the conversation seemed to me almost entirely about horses. I stood with Sheila Wilson and several other women, all holding their tidy bodies erect in their A-line skirts and neatly polished shoes. They talked about eventing, complimenting each other on how well they'd ridden that afternoon. "You really deserved a blue ribbon," one said to another. "No, you did." It appeared none of them had actually gotten a blue, though. They asked if I rode, but they didn't rechannel their conversation to include me when I said I didn't, nor did they think to explain anything to me. Perhaps having lived it their entire lives, it didn't occur to them that the language of dressage wasn't universally understood.

The men were less reserved but no less horsey. They stood in one circle in the middle of the room, kicking their legs and flailing their arms about, reenacting Thursday's ride for Willa, saying the ride wasn't the same without her. Emma leaned into the group, saying, "Now, you boys better be telling Nelly all the good things about hunting. Willa and I need some company out there chasing after the fox." And when Vic protested that he was perfectly good company, she laughed and said she meant at the front. The best riders ride at the front of the pack, she explained to me before disappearing into the kitchen, leaving me suddenly the center of attention, everyone vying to tell me amusing stories about the most un-amusing things: teeth they'd knocked out or limbs they'd bro-ken when their horses tripped over one another or refused a jump or simply bucked. They all seemed to know the stories. They completed each other's sentences and laughed even be-fore it was clear what they were talking about. The theatrics of the telling, though, the faces and the gyrations and the tones of voice, left me laughing, too. It was contagious. And when I said it sounded awfully dangerous, Mike Hayley said, "The danger—being able to laugh at the danger—is half the thrill."

Willa said she guessed everyone had heard about the jockey riding Shoot the Loop, and the group instantly quieted.

"The poor guy's first major race," Mike Hayley said quietly, "and he goes flying off his horse and breaks his neck."

"Dead?" Ben Wilson asked.

"Pronounced on arrival," someone said, but by then I was backing away from the group, excusing myself, picturing that red rider pitching forward from his horse and breaking his neck.

That's how Wesley had died; his car skidded off an icy road and in the roll down the embankment his neck snapped. It snapped and he was dead.

I found my way to the fireplace, feeling the sickness in my stomach I'd felt that day at the races, when the rider first fell. I'd watched him die, stood there at the fence and watched, and after they'd cleared away the body, after the ambulance drove off, I'd returned to the race, enjoyed the rest of it. En-joyed it recklessly, without once thinking of Wes.

I looked around for Ned and Charlie, wanting to gather them to me. They were just returning from the barn with Dac and a whole gaggle of children, one large gang you'd never guess my boys had for the most part just met.

"I've got one of these," someone beside me said—a tall, flush-faced man who fingered Emma's trophy, then leaned on the mantel and took another sip of his drink. "I do. I won the year after Emma did," he said. "I race. I'm a winner too."

I said that was nice, that was great.

"You're Emma's new friend Milly," he said. "Mac Oberlin." He held out his hand. When I gave him mine, saying, "Nelly," he didn't let go, but only leaned closer, his breath smelling of gin and potato chips.

"You know who she beat?" he whispered.

I stepped back away from him and disentangled my hand from his clammy grasp. "I'm going to guess you."

He laughed. "That she did, Milly. That she did. But I was third."

I nodded, looking around for a way out, catching Dac's eye.

"You know who was second?" Mac leaned so close to me now I thought he might topple over. "Her husband. And it was nose to nose."

Dac reached us just then, apologizing to Mac, saying he needed to borrow me for a minute, steering me to a corner where one of his photographs hung. "Sorry about Mac," he said. "He's not a bad guy, really, not when he's sober. He's from a good family—Oberlin Securities—but they aren't known for their ability to hold their drink."

I looked at the photo. "Nice," I said.

Dac looked surprised. "Mac?"

"The picture." I said I liked the composition, the focus on the broken fence line, and Dac, apparently flattered, said I sounded as if I knew what I was talking about.

"My dad's a photojournalist," I said.

"And you're following in his footsteps?"

"No."

He looked disappointed, just a little dulling of his eyes, and something in the look made his face seem familiar, as if I'd grown up next door to him or he were my brother's best friend.

"Not yet anyway," I said.

Dac introduced me to another guest, then, and disappeared, and it was much later—almost time to go—before I heard his voice again. I'd been talking with someone else when the sound of it startled me, something about the tone or the cadence or the pitch that, for the briefest moment, made me think it was Wes. The first time I heard Wes's voice, I was standing in the stacks of the medical library doing research for a biology paper, so lost in thought that he surprised me. He asked me something or excused himself to get by, I think, or maybe he just said hello, and I was captivated by the round, rich texture of his voice. He had just the trace of a Southern accent, a Tennessee accent, giving his speech a mellifluous rhythm, like the undulations of gently rolling hills in open countryside, rising and falling higher and lower and deeper and wider, surprising your senses—but not really—by the differences, and by the sameness, too, so that you might listen to him all day, being rocked and lulled, but never put to sleep.

But it wasn't Wes's voice this time. It was Dac's.

The view from the sofa where Dac sat was through French doors out onto the back porch, where the children ran around together, taking turns jumping from the raised porch to the ground below. The outside lights were on, and as I watched the mists of their breaths fog out into the cool evening air, it occurred to me that Wesley would have stayed on that sofa all evening had he been there, leaving only to go out and join the boys now and then. That image of Wesley tumbling around with our sons somehow turned into the image of his body lying dead on the stretcher in the morgue. I couldn't stop it from coming. I never could. The familiar feeling of being pressed in, suffocated, started in my chest. I forced myself to focus on the physical setting around me—a pink porcelain lamp with Chinese painting on it, a small black spider sprinting along the edge of the sofa table, Emma's animated face turned toward Dac. This was the thing I'd learned to do to cope: force new visual images in and the image of Wesley's body out.

I focused on Dac, on the image of his face, but then I heard his voice again and I couldn't push Wesley's out. I looked instead to Emma, took her in from head to toe: her back held straight and her shoulders square under a man-style white shirt, the tan of her slacks tapering down from her thin waist. She sat with her legs demurely crossed at the ankles, her feet tucked under the chair, knees turned to the side, the way my friends and I learned to sit in a junior high school ballroom dance class our parents made us attend. But we found it awkward and we sat that way only in that dance class, and I doubt any of us sit that way now. There was Emma, though, looking as if she'd been sitting that way forever. She was clearly comfortable—so comfortable that she'd removed her loafers. She sat there in her stocking feet.

She was surrounded by more people than there were seats. Women sat on the floor despite their skirts. Men leaned on the arms of the couch. People sat in kitchen chairs they'd pulled in, or simply stood. They seemed to be listening to Emma speak rather than conversing, as if Emma were a wise woman, though she was speaking only of the pits and pratfalls of a racecourse she'd walked that afternoon. Mike Hayley brought her a drink, saying, "Mrs. Crofton," to get her attention, and she paused to take a sip, then asked me to sit with them, saying she'd hardly seen me all evening and she was feeling deprived. "We were just talking about the hunt," she said. "The opening meet was last week."

Willa scooted over next to Dac to make room for me on the couch, and I sat and listened to Emma talk about the pleasure of riding through the woods at my great-grandparents' place—she called it my place—jumping the big log across the upper path and making it over the four-board fence. Mike Hayley was quick to explain that the point of foxhunting in America was not the kill, but only the chase, that they rarely caught the fox. "The hunt usually ends with the fox running to ground or the hounds losing its scent," he said, no doubt fearing I might side with the fox and forbid the hunters to ride through my farm.

"Watching the convoluted path the hounds take following the fox's scent, I sometimes think the fox is having more fun with us than we are with him," Willa said, looking steadily at Emma, leaving me the sense she didn't care for her. Though Emma had invited Willa to this party and to the races, and Willa had come.

"Foxhunting makes for the wildest ride—that's what it's all about," she said.

"It's a big part of the social life out here," Mike Hayley said. "Like belonging to a country club."

"But not nearly so civilized," Willa said. "Think less genteel. More like a middle-aged softball team after a case of beer."

The cubbing season, when young hounds were introduced into the pack, was nearly over, they said; it was almost time to trade in their "ratcatchers," hacking jackets and ties or turtlenecks, for their more formal hunting attire. And they started talking then about the Blessing of the Hunt held at St. James's Church every Thanksgiving, an event which, by all accounts, I shouldn't miss. It ranked right up there with the Greenfield

Hunt Club Christmas Ball, someone said. Emma suggested I might even like to hunt with them that day, and I had to admit I hadn't ridden since I was a girl, and even then I'd only ever ridden in a ring.

"I'd love to teach you to ride," Emma offered, leaving me wondering why she seemed to take such a fast liking to me. And then she was insisting, only apologizing that I would have to wait a bit for her to take up my "equestrian education." She was leaving town for a few days.

Willa discreetly poked my side, raising her eyebrows slightly. Was this the "disappearing" she'd spoken of?

On the other side of Willa, Dac leaned forward so I could see him and he me, and said if his mother wouldn't think he was poaching on her new student, he could take me riding once or twice while she was out of town.

Emma peered curiously at him and then nodded.

"You can trot and jump?" she said to me.

"Very little jumps."

"But you could manage a small tree trunk over the path?"

I said I thought I could.

Emma turned to Dac. "Take her through the woods and past Patterson's. And then the left path. Not past the old woodshed. The other one."

"The—"

"Yes. That's where. But don't tell. Let's let it be a surprise, shall we?"

"Yes." Dac smiled, looking from his mother, who wore a similar smile, to me. "There's that one coop, though."

"Nelly can use the gate," Emma said.

Dac nodded, then turned to me. "I've got an old school horse that rides as easy as a merry-go-round pony. How about Thursday? The boys will be in school?"

I glanced at Ned and Charlie, still happily running around outside with the other children.

"Say about ten o'clock?" Dac said.

I made a last polite pass at protesting, but was pleased to see Emma brush her hand through the air as if to dust away my words. "I'm due back the day before Thanksgiving," she said. "I'll take over from Dac then." She nodded her head twice as if to say "and that is that."

"The week after Thanksgiving, then," I said.

"But you must do me one favor." Emma smiled mischievously. "Come to the Blessing of the Hunt?"

"I wouldn't miss it."

"And do bring your camera this time? Would you do that for me?"

I looked at the faces around Emma's sitting room, all politely awaiting my response. Outside, Charlie jumped from the edge of the porch, his fine, dark hair flopping into his eyes as he landed solidly in the mulch a few feet below.

"Of course, Emma," I said, pushing away the echo of Charlie's voice: *My mom used to take pictures, too, before Daddy died.* "Of course I will."

4

Getting ready for bed that night after Emma's little "not-a-party," I imagined how Wesley and I might have reviewed the evening—the people we'd met and what we thought of each of them—had he still been alive. He'd have spent half the night with Ben Wilson, a fellow Civil War buff, talking Shiloh and Ambrose Burnside, Bloody Lane, the "battle of the boots." He'd have liked Emma, too—he liked strong women who weren't a threat to him—though he'd have wondered whether we ought to be calling her Mrs. Crofton; even I'd noticed that everyone did. He wouldn't have cared for Dac, though. He'd have stood in the bathroom in his boxer shorts, toothbrush poised to enter his mouth, asking, "What kind of guy won't take pictures of people, anyway?" And maybe I'd have been calmer this time, more conciliatory, not misunderstanding his jealousy or feeling suffocated by it—which had it been the night of that last argument?

I slept fitfully, dreaming of wandering through dark tunnels looking for babies I had somehow lost. Swimming up from the dream, I reached for Wes, awoke only to the pillow that had been his. In that brief, disoriented moment, I thought it still held the faintest trace of the smell of his skin.

It was not yet dawn, but I got up and pulled on blue jeans, a sweatshirt, and wool socks, feeling I'd never shake off the early morning chill. I looked in on the boys: Ned's body strewn sideways across the bed, Charlie tossing a little, mumbling something. I leaned close to make out Charlie's words, wanting to wake him, to wake them both, to have their company to break the loneliness of the morning. His lips stopped moving and his breathing slowed.

In the kitchen, I selected a knife from the block—a bigger, sharper one than I needed to open boxes—and I went down to the basement, bringing Boomer along for protection against the rats and snakes and hulking violent men I imagined in the darkness. His tail struck my leg as it wagged.

It was a cold, old basement, with a dank, musty smell, and the dark outlines of things around me could have been, or could have hidden, anything. I groped for the light string, found it, yanked it. The harsh fluorescent light poured over boxes in various stages of being unpacked, their contents strewn around, piles everywhere: chaotic but safe, like a bargain basement store dressing room in the middle of an advertised sale. The boxes I wanted were behind wardrobe boxes filled with drapes, too heavy to move. I climbed back into the corner and sliced the tape, tugged open the cardboard flaps, pulled the newspaper packing away.

My camera bag felt heavy in my hands as I lifted it from the box. I opened the bag and looked for a long moment at the black hulk of the camera: the shot counter, the silver slides where the flash attached, the 28–105 lens with its sunshield turned backward, covering the little white numbers of the focal range. I lifted the camera from the bag finally, feeling the cold hardness against my fingers, my palms. I brought it to my face, the coldness now on my brow, on the tip of my nose. I breathed in deeply and scanned the basement through the viewfinder, focusing on a packing box, a spiderweb, Boomer licking his paw on the cement floor.

There was no film in the camera.

I found a roll of medium-speed black-and-white in the packing paper strewn around the basement floor and loaded it, closing the camera and listening to the automatic winder move the film into place. The number 37 lit up on the display, then the shutter snapped automatically, once, the display changing to 36. In the silence that followed, the furnace clicked on and began to hum, pumping heat to warm my boys as they slept.

I set the camera back in the bag and dug through another box for my developing tank, my safelight fixture, my rubber gloves, my trays. I opened the tank, pulled out the steel spiral, and turned off the overhead light, no longer fearful of the darkness, as if the faint chemical smell might keep the monsters at bay. I sat on the cold cement floor and popped open an exposed roll of film with my can opener. I had no chemicals—they were on the list of things the movers wouldn't haul—but still I threaded the film into the cold steel of the spiral, thinking of my father as my fingers felt their way along in the dark.

I must have been quite young, three or four, when I discovered that Dad would let me keep him company in his darkroom. In my earliest memory, I am in the red darkness with him, the cold, damp cement floor against my bottom and my legs and the sharp chemical smell in my nose. Dad spent much of my growing-up on the road, leaving on, say, a Sunday evening, planning to be back in a week. A week often stretched into two or three, though, or sometimes to a month, and when he came home it was always briefly, three or four days, maybe a week at Christmas, and there were Christmases, too, when he appeared only by voice over a static-filled phone. Four of us competed for Dad's attention when he was home too: my mother, my two brothers, and me—or five, really, the fifth being his photographs. Even when he was home for only twenty-four hours, Dad would spend part of that time in his darkroom, developing his private photos, the ones he kept locked in his metal box.

Dad never spoke as he got organized in his darkroom, while the bright overhead bulb cast a shadow across his face. I would watch silently as he measured chemicals, checked temperatures, made sure everything was in its place. After he turned out the light, though, and began in total darkness to feed the film into the developing spiral with his oversized hands, the soft patter of his darkroom voice would surround me like a warm bath, and I'd relax into it, stretching out my legs and leaning against the wall.

First, Dad would talk about the film he was loading, his gentle bassoon of a voice taking me to the places he'd been when he'd taken the pictures, making me feel as if I, too, had met the people he'd met. He'd talk in low tones about the hope he had that his pictures—not the ones he was developing for himself, but the ones he'd already sent on to his editor—would help the people in them, improve their worlds, their lives. And then he'd talk about how lucky we were to live in a safe town, in a plentiful, peaceful country, to have the life we did. It was never a lecture, though—more like a prayer of thanks offered up to his Roman Catholic God. And later, when the film had dried and we returned to do the printing, Dad would flip on the safelight, and as my eyes adjusted to the dim red glow, he would come into focus and I'd see the dry riverbeds of thought across his forehead, the soft spray of lines from the corners of his eyes. He nearly wept sometimes as his pictures emerged on the bromide paper, as if the ghosts seep-ing up from the prints somehow haunted him. But he'd blink back the tears and grow quiet, turn his back to me, busy himself with putting caps on bottles or wiping off counters as if he weren't weeping, as if I couldn't tell.

Still, I felt that darkroom father who seemed to so love his strangers loved me more than anyone else.

On my eighth birthday, Dad gave me my first camera, a Leica that had been his. He'd arrived home from someplace in Africa late the night before, long past my bedtime, but I knew he'd be there because he'd promised to be home for my birthday. And there he was, sitting at the kitchen table still dressed in his traveling clothes when I came down for school.

I dropped my schoolbooks in the doorway and ran to him, and he scooped me up in his arms and tickled me and asked how his "favorite little subject" had been. I said, "Never better," in as deep a voice as I could manage, imitating him, and we laughed together while Mom flipped vanilla-smelling pancakes and yelled up the stairs for Danny to hurry or he'd miss the bus. I begged Dad then to tell a new story. Whenever he returned—especially from Africa but really from anywhere— he had some story about monkeys playing animal-skin drums, or parrots singing Elvis Presley songs in Spanish, or men who could read backward or carve statues out of ice or do some other fantastic thing. But this time, he only laughed and said, "Later, Nelly, later. We've got gifts to open now!"

I looked around the kitchen, expecting to see a wrapped package, but found only my mother in creased slacks, my unshaven father, my brother Jimmy in his high chair with his thumb in his mouth and his index finger in his nose—all with eyes fixed on me.

Dad pointed at the table, set with plates and unmatched glasses of milk, maple syrup and butter, and, nestled oddly in the middle where sometimes there were flowers from the yard or candlesticks, my father's camera in its worn leather case. The lenses, enclosed in their cylinders of cracked black leather, rested against the camera, and the straps of all the cases were tied together with a yellow ribbon looped into an awkward bow.

"It's your camera now," Dad said.

When the words sank in, I grabbed the straps at the ribbon and pulled the camera and lenses off the table, scattering plates and splattering milk and sending silverware clattering to the floor as I danced around.

Mom wiped the milk from the table with a dishrag, saying, "Nelly, please." Milk dribbled to the floor. "*See, Patrick,*" she said, turning to Dad, exhaling through her nose the way she did when she was annoyed with him. She wrung the milk from the rag into the sink. "When the children miss the bus," she said, "*you* can get them to school."

Dad only stifled his laughter and slipped up behind her at the sink. He wrapped his arms around her waist, nestled into her long, graceful neck, and whispered, "Lizzy, Lizzy. You're missing the birth of the next Dorothea Lange for the sake of a little spilt milk."

I'd ripped the case off the camera by then, and pressed the cold metal to my face. Through the viewfinder, I watched Mom move Dad's hands off her hips and turn to her pancakes, pretending to be irritated but smiling to herself at the stove. I clicked and clicked and clicked, the automatic flash popping, filling the kitchen with little lightning bolts of flash.

My father cleared his throat, and I framed him in the viewfinder. He was holding up a canister of film.

"Film, Squirt." He laughed. "You need film."

When I got home from school that afternoon, Dad was sleeping, as he often did the day he returned from overseas. I got

Danny to help me load the film and mount the camera on his tripod in my bedroom. "You can't shoot pictures in here," he said. I pushed him out the door, shut it, and turned the lock.

"You gotta have something interesting, Smelleroo," he continued from the hall.

I framed my first shot with the window in the center (I'd seen pictures Dad had done that way, with people framed in windows and doors), and I tried hard to do everything he'd said at breakfast. I focused precisely, so that nothing was fuzzy. What else had he said? To be aware of the light. Well, of course, since I was focused on the window there would be enough light, I thought. Dad had said something about stops too. "F-stops," which had something to do with those numbers on the lens. I turned the lens first one way, to the lowest number, then the other, to the highest, but I couldn't really tell any difference, just that little black pointer bobbing up and down at the edge. I set it at a middle number, where the pointer fell inside the box. And then I set the automatic timer just exactly as Dad had shown me—I loved the gentle buzzing sound it made—and I rushed to stand in front of the window. I smiled my broad smile at the camera, revealing my two missing teeth, and in that instant the timer clicked off and the shutter exploded open and shut.

I shot the remaining eleven frames of the roll that afternoon while my father slept off his jet lag. I caught my mother in her apron, frying potatoes; Danny stretched out on the couch, reading; Jimmy in his playpen, watching Danny from inside the mesh. After I'd used up the roll, I got Danny to come down to the darkroom with me, to help me develop it, and the next afternoon we slipped down together to make the prints. We worked in secret, whispering, hiding what we were doing from Dad, hurrying to finish before he left the next afternoon on another assignment. When the prints were dry, I took that first shot—my first self-portrait—and I wrapped it in blue paper and a white ribbon, and I marched up the stairs to my father's study.

Dad lowered his newspaper and smiled. "My, my. What's this? For me?"

He undid the wrapping, saw the photograph, and smiled again. I thought I'd bust with pride.

"It's a pretty nice picture," he said. "Pretty nice."

Already, I could feel my bubble pop.

"But see how you're backlit?" He pulled me close, into the heavy musk and cigarette smell of him. "The sunshine coming through the window? It screws up your light meter, so the subject—you—ends up a bit dark."

I stood next to his chair, conscious of the heat of his arm around me.

"There are several ways you can compensate for backlighting," he said. "You can take a close-up reading of your subject's face or change positions or, if your whole roll is going to be backlit, you can plan to shorten your development time a little. Did you remember to measure the temperature of your chemicals?"

Somehow I managed to nod.

"Well, so now the negative is what it is. But we can still improve the print. We can burn in the background or dodge the face or both. It's not hard. If we have time before I leave tomorrow, I'll show you how."

"Okay," I whispered, and, when it was clear he was done with me, I ran upstairs to my room, where I buried my face in my pillow and cried.

I stayed in bed the next morning, claiming I didn't feel well. But after Dad left that afternoon, I got Danny to show me how to burn in and how to dodge, and I made a new print. When it was dry, I took it up to my bedroom and made myself study it for the longest time before I ripped it up into tiny pieces, tearing and tearing until the shreds were so small that, when I flung them into the air, they fluttered in the lamplight like oversized specks of black and white and gray dust. I watched them settle onto the carpet, still and mocking. And then I burrowed under the covers, not stopping to take my shoes off, and I curled up into a tight ball and held myself together like that, suffocating in the fabric darkness.

When I awoke, I was in my bed and in my pajamas, and bright morning sunlight outlined the pulled windowshade. The pieces of photograph I'd scattered the night before formed a tidy pile on my desk. Beside the pile sat a new roll of film, thirty-six exposures, with a note taped to it in my mother's careful hand: "Just do your best and find joy in what you do."

I dropped the shredded pieces of photograph into my empty trash can, then wadded up the note and threw it on top, to bury my mistake. Mom's neat handwriting showed in the crumpled ball though, and I found myself flattening it out again, and reading it, and smoothing it and neatly folding it, tucking it into the bottom drawer of my desk, where, in the years that followed, I would hide my photographs.

When Dad returned from his next assignment, my darkroom sessions with him seemed changed. He still talked about his life as he loaded the spiral in the darkness, but after the lights came back on, our visit would evolve into a kind of lesson, Dad explaining what he'd done with a given photograph from a technical standpoint, how he'd framed the shot or dealt with the difficulty of the lighting, how he'd panned the camera to capture the action or what filter he'd used and why. He began to include Danny, too, and even the few minutes of darkness while he was loading the spiral became filled with information, with, "Let's talk about different ways to use motion in a still." I listened, knowing I was expected to learn, but afraid to appear too interested, afraid to need so badly to succeed where I had already failed.

Sometime later, I began to pretend indifference to photography, shrugging when asked if I took pictures and burying photography magazines under my mattress like an adolescent boy hides pictures of naked girls. I feigned reluctance to attend Dad's darkroom sessions and impatience at his instructions, acting as if I weren't even listening sometimes, as if I cared less than not at all. I was listening, though, focusing on every detail of what my father taught us, making myself remember it all and then, after he left again, practicing and practicing. I never missed a darkroom session.

I spent the next hours and days and years taking photographs, mostly of people—of other people, but also of myself. I'd sometimes show them to my mother, and I'm nearly certain she searched them out—the ones she hadn't seen—while I was at school. I'd show them to my grandmother, too, tucking my best shots into my pocket when we went to her house in hopes I'd find some time alone with her. But I kept those photographs as sequestered from my father as the photos he kept locked in his box. Still, each time I watched his hand reach for the chain that would turn off the overhead light and envelop us in blackness, I felt the hope rise up in me. And each time the light clicked back on, I knew I'd lost my darkroom father, that the birthday gift of his old camera had somehow replaced the gift of himself.

5

Monday morning dawned damp and misty, no day to take photographs, but still I went from the school carpool line directly to the nearest photo store. The parking lot was empty, the store not yet open, only a single low light glowing in the dark morning void, and the rain began as I sat waiting: single drops momentarily suspended on the windshield, then joining other drops, forming little rivulets before hitting something on the glass and splitting again into thinner lines. Inside the store, more lights came on, bright against the darkening sky, and a figure appeared, a young man, I saw, before he was obscured by the wash of heavier and heavier raindrops, and, finally, by a single sheet of water pouring down the glass.

Inside the shop, I bought thirteen rolls of black-and-white film, bucking luck and cost (next time I'd buy bulk load), and I paid cash. Back in the car, I took each roll out of its box and, in the rain and with no umbrella, I went back to the garbage can by the door and threw the boxes in the trash. I told myself it was a symbolic gesture, that there would be no turning back now. Myself as photographer, as photojournalist. It didn't really feel like that, though. It felt like some reaction to Wesley, to that sense that he was there watching what I did, saying, "Now's not the time; the boys need you now." Or to something even more deeply ingrained in me: myself as that eight-year-old girl.

I spent the next few days trying to reconcile myself with my camera. I took it out from the cabinet in the laundry room where I'd stored it only to put it back, unused, again and again. I carried it with me on walks with Boomer, hoping to find something irresistible to photograph, something to move me to act without thinking, or despite my thinking. I took it on drives—to the boys' school, to Fells Point, to the downtown waterfront—sure there would be something newsworthy to photograph somewhere, thinking maybe my problem was not that I couldn't photograph, but that there was nothing out in the country to catch my eye. Even in the city, though, nothing seemed to move me. I could not push the shutter release.

Nights, I stayed up far too late exploring every inch of the basement, looking for the best space for a darkroom, returning again just before dawn to sit in the dark of each enclosed space for a few minutes, to judge the blackness against the beginnings of morning light. In that predawn of Thursday morning, I settled on an area that must have been the laundry room at one time, before my great-grandparents built the one upstairs. It was small, windowless, with cabinets and a countertop, two light fixtures, an outlet, and a hose bib and floor drain I could use until I got sinks. With the dim morning light beginning to filter through the open door, I sliced open the last box of my equipment, carefully freed from paper wrapping my timer, my thermometer, funnels and graduates, photo sponges and clothespins, my trays. I was just at the bottom of the box, lifting out my printing easel, when I heard the light morning footsteps of barefooted boys.

When I arrived at Emma's barn at ten that morning for my ride with Dac, I found him in discussion with several people

about what they were to do with the horses that day, everyone joking together the way Wesley and his medical students
did the year he was chief resident. I hung back as I had then,
standing in the doorway, inhaling the fresh hay sweetness of
the barn and wondering where we would be riding, what
Emma had planned for me. After a minute, Dac saw me, and
he waved me in as he waved his troops out, saying, "Nelly,"
and looking suddenly almost shy.

"Nelly, this is Harry," he said, patting the neck of a horse
cross-tied beside him. If there was any hint of the shadow I'd
seen in his eyes the night I'd met him, I didn't see it. "Now,
Harry," he said, wagging a finger at the horse, "you be sweet
to Ms. Grace."

He pulled his riding cap on and asked if I was ready for this,
and I pulled my cap on, too, and he cupped his hands and gave
me a leg up, and I hoisted myself onto Harry, conscious of my
bottom practically brushing Dac's face.

Dac retrieved a second horse, the one Emma had ridden
the day I met her, saying, "This is Flashy."

"We've met," I said. "Old friends."

"All right, then," he said. "You know to keep your heels
down?"

I said I knew.

"The ground will be a bit bumpy. And if the horse decides
to bolt, there won't be any fence to keep him in."

I nodded. I understood I needed to stay in control of the
horse.

We set out across Emma's farm then, riding side by side, me
concentrating on keeping my heels down, my hands quiet.
After a moment, I asked where we were going, but Dac only
smiled mischievously and said, "You'll have to see for yourself,
Nelly Grace."

We made small talk after that, about the riding protocol: one never rode too close to a house, although the hounds might run right across a front porch, following the scent of the fox, and everyone respected the boundaries of the few farms, like the sheep farm next to the Hayleys' place, that didn't permit riders. The area was generally open, though, and people were committed to keeping it that way, putting their lands in an agricultural trust to ensure they wouldn't ever be developed, and even pooling resources to buy land that might otherwise fall to developers' hands. We talked about his mother, too, visiting friends in Montana, and then Dac confessed he had a favor to ask: he was interested in renting my barn and paddocks if I wasn't planning to use them anytime soon—for a fair price, of course. It would mean a little more traffic on my drive, he said, but he'd also keep my fence lines and hay my fields and buy the hay at market price, and he'd clear my drive when it snowed.

"Snow," I said. "And fence lines and fields." Soon enough it would snow and there would be that long drive to clear and I didn't own a shovel, much less a tractor and a blade. "Ned and Charlie would love to have horses on the farm," I said, and we agreed on a day several weeks later when he'd move his horses in.

We entered the woods behind Emma's place, settling into a surprisingly comfortable silence, the only sound the crunching of dry leaves on the path, the occasional snort of a horse. We rode single file, ducking now and then to avoid the bare, leafless branches, Dac jumping gracefully over logs fallen across the path while I moved into position, grasped a handful of mane, and tried to stay on the horse. I was warm despite the chill in the air, getting sweaty under my cap by the time we stopped at the bottom of a short uphill path ending in a small clearing at the far edge of the woods. Ahead, a coop not much lower than the board fence looked to be the only entrance into the field.

"You promised only little jumps," I said.

Dac broke into a healthy trot, shouting over his shoulder, "There's a gate to the left," as Flashy soared easily over the coop.

That day I had better sense than to try to jump a coop three times as high as any jump I'd ever taken—and solid, unyielding wood to boot. I walked Harry to the top of the hill, dismounted and guided him through a rusty metal gate, then used the bottom fence board as a mounting block. Dac watched without offering assistance, not laughing, but with an odd sort of amusement in his eyes that made me blush.

From the top of the hill we looked over cleared farmland, the remaining stubble of last summer's corn and the pale gold of mowed hay fields edged with board fencing weathered to a soft gray. Several horses galloped in a paddock below, running after each other like children playing tag. Beyond the paddock the faded green of a wintertime lawn rose up to a beautiful old stone home, its two stories small against the chinquapin oaks in the yard. Dac said he must have taken a million photographs from right there, from that very spot. "In the snow, this view looks like the perfect Christmas card, only better," he said.

I closed my eyes for a moment, imagining my father as a boy taking the shot, thinking that at that time of year you'd photograph it in the late afternoon, when the low sunlight would enhance the warm fall reds. But my father was at the farm only in the summers, and I couldn't see him photographing landscapes anyway. He shot nothing but the cold, hard news.

"When did you start taking pictures, Dac?" I asked.

He said his father and he built a darkroom when he was in the sixth grade and he'd had a camera for a year or two by then, and I told him my father had taught me to use a camera, too, when I was just a baby, almost. "Dad makes his living with the camera," I said. "News work. Anyway, that's how I got to know him, I guess, sitting with him in his darkroom."

"Pat Sullivan develops his own work?" Dac said.

"How did you—?"

My horse tugged at the reins, and when I tried to steady him, he stepped backward and to the side, drawing me almost into Dac.

"Know who your father is? No secrets out here, Nelly." He paused, leaving me looking out toward the soft gray chimney smoke, wondering if that could be true.

"Your dad used to play with my dad when they were kids," he said.

"When he came to visit his grandparents," I said.

"And he's famous. And from here, in a way. So we all know who he is. Or want to say we do. Not that we'd ever admit that, of course. And Sullivan's an old name out here. Your place? It's still called the Sullivan place, and always will be, too. Like the Oberlin place, Dogwood Hill. Old man Oberlin—" He tipped his head to one side, the angle emphasizing his chin: a strong, square chin, like Wesley's. "You remember meeting Mac Oberlin at Mother's?"

"The drinker."

He grinned and said Dogwood Hill, Mac's grandfather's house, was sold out of the family when he died thirty years ago, and had just changed hands again last summer. "You know how the new people are introduced?" he said. "As 'the people who bought the old Oberlin place.' "

"After thirty years?"

"Kind of scary, huh?" He laughed, a warm chuckle you

could climb into, though a shadow of the darkness was there too. "You're a part of that, whether you like it or not. Your name may be Nelly Grace, but you'll always be a Sullivan out here."

He licked his chapped lips, then asked if my father and I were close, as if it were a perfectly natural thing to ask someone you'd just met. I looked out to the horizon, the sky scattered with white wisps of clouds, and said I was an only daughter. "But my brother Danny is my father's pride and joy," I said.

Danny, now a photojournalist with the *Los Angeles Times*.

Dac glanced over his shoulder at the woods behind us. "My father and I spent a lot of time together, but we were . . . different. In a way that kind of sat there between us." He combed Flashy's mane with his fingers, watching his hand. "It took me almost until he died, I guess, to appreciate what he was all about."

Harry pulled on the reins again, then nickered lightly and stretched his neck down to nip at the pale grass. I let my hands drop to his withers, wondering if I'd even begun to know what my father was "all about."

"Your photos of this place must be beautiful," I said.

"I've never done it justice, but I'm sure you could," he said, his eyes squinting in amusement, teasing me.

I said I was better with people, mentally flipping through my favorite portraits, discarding several I didn't want to explain. "I have one of my grandma making pie, her fingers covered with crust dough, streaks of sunlight coming through the kitchen window and flour kind of generally all over the place. She had a really wonderful face, deeply lined, but round and soft, gentle. And these big triangle eyes that turn down at the corners. Green. You can't tell from the photo, but they were intensely green. Like—"

Like his eyes.

I focused on the farm below, the horses, the earthy smell of the forest behind us. "Like the forest," I said. "That color green." Much darker green than mine.

Dac's taste in photographers, I learned that afternoon, ran more toward what my father liked to call the mathematicians of the art: Paul Outerbridge and Lee Friedlander. I told him I preferred the photojournalists: Robert Capa, Gene Smith, Margaret Bourke-White. One of my favorite photos was Dorothea Lange's *Homeless Family, Oklahoma, 1938,* a picture of a migrant family walking down the road, the mother and two little girls in the foreground, the father and two other children farther up the road. You can't see any of the people's faces, I said, but she captures the emotion in people's bodies, in their gestures and the way they hold themselves. She delivers that mother's life, makes you want to change it.

"What Lange delivers in that photo," Dac said, "is the impossibility of ever effecting that change."

I tightened my chin strap, a little surprised he knew the photo, and puzzled by the change in his tone.

"Well, the difficulty of doing it, anyway," I said.

"Impossibility."

I looked at him, but he didn't look back.

"Things do change," I said.

"Like this in front of us?" He swept his arm out toward the farm below. "Imagine how lovely this will look when it's a sea of rooftops. Or a highway or a factory."

I sat there for a moment, taken aback. "A lot of things do change for the better," I said finally. "Small things and slowly sometimes. But they add up. Look at Frank's *Trolley,* for example." Robert Frank, whose photos often touched on racial inequality in 1950s America, shot *Trolley* looking in through the windows of a New Orleans trolley to black faces in the back, white in the front. "You don't see that anymore," I said.

"Talk about disturbing photographs. In that one everyone looks disturbed. The little girl in the middle. The boy in the suit. Mai used to say it was kind of universal, being disturbed."

"I—"

"Everyone is, most of the time. And why shouldn't we be, after all?"

I cleared my throat, wondering who Mai was, wondering what had happened to the easygoing, upbeat guy who'd introduced me to my horse.

"Frank is with me on this," he said. "I mean, his earlier stuff is almost all pretty disturbing. People in sad places in their lives. And his later stuff? Looks like he's pretty disturbed himself. Like *Sick of Goodby's*."

I knew the photo: two frames, the top one an arm—just an arm—holding a tiny baby doll by the head, dangling it over the water, with "Sick Of" written above it in dripping blood; then in the "Goodby's" frame at the bottom, no doll, just an empty mirror.

"I can never tell which are the mirrors in that photo and which are the real, unreflected thing," I said.

Dac shrugged. "That's life."

We rode along in an awkward silence after that, Dac riding stiffly, though he held the reins easily, steadily. I realized I was clenching mine. That was why Harry kept plunging his head. He was trying to shake the bit. He wasn't snorting, though. Even Harry wouldn't break the silence. It had seemed so nice at the beginning of the ride, just the crunching leaves and an occasional snort of a horse. But in the field now it was too quiet, not even a leaf to crunch.

When we entered the woods again, I made a foray into breaking the quiet, asking what Dac thought about Dois-neau's *Le Baiser de l'Hôtel de Ville*. The man and woman kissing in a street in Paris. Not, by my father's values, a moment to be published. Pain, you could publish. Terror, horror, embarrassment, fear, those were all okay. Birth, death, confusion, wonder. Even lust. But not the intimate moments of love and not grief.

Grief I understood. Most photojournalists thought grief was out of bounds. There'd been a big flap years ago when a photographer caught a mother just in the moment the drowned body of her son was found. But I'd never heard of anyone but my father refusing to publish love.

"You mean, does it bother me that Doisneau's kiss—this impulsive moment of random joy—might have been staged?" Dac said.

The actors—the people who claimed to be the actors— had sued for some of the profits from commercialization of the print.

"No," he said. "In every other form of art, artists use models."

I looked into the woods ahead of us. "I guess I've always thought of photography as capturing a real-life moment. I guess it doesn't seem right to me to represent something as real if it's not."

"Spoken like a true photojournalist," Dac said.

No, I thought. Only the daughter of one.

We'd come to a low place where the path widened, pine trees towering around us and the blue of the sky overhead rimmed with softly needled branches, the ground underneath us covered with a blanket of the same soft needles dried to a subtle brown. Dac turned and waited for me and I came up beside him, into a place where sunlight filtered unevenly through the trees. "This is beautiful," I said, and we rode side by side until the pine trees gave way to sycamores and the path turned alongside a stream. It narrowed and we followed it single file

again, traveling upstream, listening to the sound of the running water. The path ended at a small waterfall—just a burble
of stream over a low outcropping of stone, but the effect was
enchanting. I dismounted and pulled my cap and gloves off
and put my hand in the falling water, cold and fresh and clean.

"Whose is this, Dac?" I asked.

He dismounted and took his riding cap off, carried it in his
hand as he came toward me.

I stood between Dac and the stream, watching the water
but aware of his approach. "Whose is this?" I repeated.
"Whose property are we on?"

He came up to me, stood right next to me, the two of us at
the edge of the stream, in the sunshine, and I was watching
the water and Dac was watching me and I wondered suddenly if he was going to kiss me. I didn't want him to kiss me,
but still the feelings bubbled up. His face moved closer to
mine and I closed my eyes, smelled the peppermint of his
breath. And just when I thought his lips would touch my skin,
just as I held my breath for it, he whispered, "Yours, Nelly.
From the edge of the pine grove, these woods are yours."

6

The phone rang at noon the day before Thanksgiving, as I was sifting through photos I'd taken when I was twenty-five, twenty-one, ten. I went into the kitchen to answer it, regretting my promise to Emma to bring my camera to the Blessing of the Hunt the next day; after I'd dropped Ned and Charlie at school that morning, I'd told myself this was it, my last chance, time to take a photograph, any photograph, but instead I'd spent all morning staring at my old work—photos from another life—spread over the scarred cherry of Wesley's desk.

"What are you and the boys doing for Christmas?" my father's voice boomed in response to my phone-answering hello. He was in Los Angeles having Thanksgiving with my brother Danny, and he thought he might spend Christmas with us at the farm, he said. He might even stay for a while, a few weeks at least, and maybe as much as a month. I told him that would be wonderful, that it would be nice for the boys and nice for me too. It would be a difficult Christmas, our first without Wes.

After we hung up, I stood, telephone in hand, looking out the window, imagining my father traveling, just him and his camera and his box of photographs, a few clothes in a duffel bag. He still had the house in Chicago, but he'd rarely spent so much as a night there since Mom died. He threw himself into his work even more now than when we were young.

Given a choice between his camera and pretty much anything else, Dad had chosen his camera, except when Mom was sick. He'd always been that way and he knew it and he even admitted it in his own guilt-free way. Like the photos he kept in his metal file box, the way he spent some portion of the little time he was home when we were growing up developing those prints. He called those photos his "addiction." Not a hobby or a pastime or a passion, but an addiction. They were like an addiction too. He kept them locked in his box and shared them with no one, not even Mom when she was alive. I saw some of them when he developed them, and I used to slip down to the darkroom to study them more closely as they were drying, hung on a clothesline with wooden clothespins. But that was it. Once they were dry they were sequestered behind the lock, never to be seen again, except by him. I wasn't sure he even looked at them much himself. I'd seen him with those pictures only once, one morning the summer I was fifteen. I'd awakened early, maybe five o'clock, and padded down to the kitchen for a glass of juice, only to find Dad at the kitchen table, still wearing the jeans and khaki shirt he'd worn the night before. He was red-eyed and red-nosed and pulling on his hair absently, and the ice cubes were small in his big glass of scotch. His box sat open on the table in front of him, and he studied a photograph in his hand. I watched him for a moment before he saw me, and when he did look up, he smiled and said, "Good morning!" as if he sat at the table drinking scotch every morning at 5 A.M. He placed the photo in the box, closed the lid, and snapped the lock shut, pulling on it to confirm it had caught. That was the last time I'd seen that box open, the only time.

I blinked against the hard afternoon light, the farm stretching beyond the window, the memory of my father. My father. I set the phone back in its cradle and went straight to the cabinet where I kept my camera, imagining that I was Dad, that no matter what else was going on in my life, my photography came first. I took the camera out and threw on a jacket, whistled for Boomer and went outside, began looking for things to photograph. I selected subjects—a rusted horseshoe hanging above the entrance to the barn, the bridge arcing over the stream, a few brown leaves clinging to the gray-and-white bark of a sycamore tree—and I framed the shots carefully, focused precisely, set the f-stop and the shutter speed, adjusting for the light. But in the end, I found fault in each selection, and I moved on to something else without taking the shot.

At the crunch of tires on gravel, Boomer's ears perked and he barked, and I looked to see Dac's truck pulling in, already coming to a stop on the drive.

"I came to see if you wanted to ride," he said as he hopped out of the truck and greeted Boomer with a much appreciated head pat. "But I see you're putting your time to better use." He indicated the camera with a nod. "May I?"

"Sure," I said. "Sure. Of course."

He took the camera, focusing the lens on the barn, the paddock fence, the run-in shed. "Black-and-white?" he said. He lowered the camera, revealing those oddly dark green eyes.

Wes's eyes were brown. Had been brown.

"It captures every ounce of character in a person, if you catch them as themselves," I said.

"When they're not obsessing about the camera."

"Right."

"Which everyone does."

"Right. All the time."

He looked at the camera again, ran a finger over the expo-sure counter, looked down the drive to the bridge. "You haven't taken a shot yet, have you?"

He gave me a look and I knew he knew the truth, but I said, "Maybe I have."

Dac smiled slightly and shook his head. "Your exposure counter."

I looked down at my camera. My exposure counter was still set on thirty-six.

"Was what happened with your husband that bad?" he asked.

A few nights before Wesley died, he and I had gone to a party, a birthday celebration for Gabe Myers, one of the surgeons with whom Wesley worked and probably the closest thing he had to a friend. Gabe was recently divorced—not his choice—and turning forty, and the other surgeons had thrown a surprise party to cheer him up. I thought I was doing my part by dancing with him, but Wesley didn't see it that way, and maybe I had an idea of that at the party, but if I did, I dismissed it or rationalized why I was right or simply ig-nored Wes, forgot about him the way it seemed he forgot about me at the hospital every day. At home, though, before I'd even removed my shoes, Wes started in about it—I'd em-barrassed him, fawning all over Gabe in front of everyone, what could I possibly have been thinking about?—the ab-solute calmness in his voice belying his anger. "Are you hav-ing an affair with the guy," he said, "or do you just want everyone to think you are?"

In response, I raked up every unpleasant thing Wesley had done or said since we'd first met. I didn't even know why I did it, why his accusation so upset me, why our arguments so often came to this point. I just kept slinging words at him as he stripped down to his boxers, washed his face, wet his toothbrush, as he responded in single words or not at all, continuing the familiar motions, convincing himself the situation was still in control.

"What the hell do you care, anyway?" I said. "You don't care, really. You just want a perfect family to present to the world, to round out your perfect career."

He stood stock-still for a moment, bare feet on the tile floor and toothbrush in hand, the words hanging in the air between us, my accusation that he had become what his own father had been.

"How can you say that?" he said, the calm, in-control mask slipping from his face. "I'm always here for you. Every minute."

I swallowed against the words I didn't want to say, knew I shouldn't say. I swallowed again.

"You're here when you're tired of being at the hospital," I said. "You give us so little time that we feel we have to be convenient to you or you won't give us *any* time at all."

Wes crossed his arms over his bare stomach, his knuckles white around the toothbrush.

I stared silently, my feet beginning to ache in my high heels.

"Any time for *you,*" he said. "Any time for—"

"Any time for me, fine! Any time for me! But if we're going to move to Baltimore—"

"Oh, come off it, Nelly! Get a grip on yourself. You're out of control. Look at yourself. Look at your face."

I swallowed against the urge to turn to the mirror.

"If we're going to move," I said more calmly, "why can't we think about making more time for what I might do?"

"You *can't* be a photojournalist." His voice full of impatience, of having been over this ground, not wanting to go over it again. "Think about it, Nelly. Even if you really did want to do it, you're going to . . . what? Pick up on a moment's notice and jet off around the world like your father? Leaving the boys *where*?"

"But *you* can spend all your time on your career and still be a good father?"

"I spend plenty of time with the boys!" His neck reddening the way it did when he was furious and trying not to be. "Do I play golf? Do I hole up alone reading books?"

"Charlie will be in school full-time next fall, Wes. The boys don't need—"

"My mother was there every day when I came home from school. I could tell her what happened, good or bad. My boys are going to have that too."

I looked away, caught a glimpse of myself in the mirror: red, blotchy, awful face, ugly face, selfish face.

"Wes, I . . . I love Ned and Charlie more than anything, you know that, but I . . ."

Our eyes met in the mirror, his dark and unyielding.

"Fine," he said. "Just fine."

"If we both pitched in, Wes—"

He slammed the toothbrush down on the counter, clipping the soap dish, the white porcelain shattering in the sink. "What do you want me to do, Nelly! It's time to pick up the boys, so I just say, 'I'm sorry, patient on the table, but I've got to run. Can you sew yourself back up?' "

"Yes, of course, Wes!" Pushing against the fear that I didn't really even know what I wanted him to do, what I might do if I were free to do something, what I *could* do, whether I could do anything. "Yes, of course, I'm completely unreasonable!"

I left then, slamming every door on the way, my high heels clicking hard and loud against the wood floors. I walked out the door and climbed into the car and drove aimlessly for hours, speeding over empty roads until the first traffic began again, the newspaper delivery truck. When I got home, Wes was asleep in bed. I changed into blue jeans, made a pot of coffee, and tried to read the paper. It was the dark early morning of wintertime.

I was starting the same article over again for the third time when Wes came into the kitchen. He pulled a cup from the cabinet, poured the now-thick coffee. "You shouldn't drive when you're so upset," he said.

I looked at my hands on the newspaper, the tips of my fingers tinged gray from the newsprint. I still remember how they shook. "I want a divorce," I said.

He set the coffeepot back on the burner carefully, soundlessly. "No," he said. "No you don't. Think of the boys."

Ned and Charlie ate Cheerios that morning, fighting over who got which place mat and who was poaching on whose space. When they'd finished, they fed Boomer their leftover milk and ran off to play together, their world unchanged.

I sat alone in the empty kitchen, with spilt milk on the table and dirty bowls in the sink.

Wes and I didn't really talk in the days following that morning. I'd work up my resolve to talk to him when he got home from the hospital, no matter how late, but then he'd come in and I could see, even in the dim light, the sag of his shoulders, the slowness of his movements, the flat look in his eyes that told me he'd lost a child, a baby he'd been treating hadn't made it, had died in the OR or afterward.

In the mornings, I would listen to Wes moving around in the kitchen. When we first met, he ate only Shredded Wheat for breakfast. I used to find it comforting as I lay snuggled in bed, knowing exactly what he was doing in the kitchen, what he was pouring into his bowl, though I teased him about it, about the sameness of his morning meal. When had I stopped? I couldn't even remember now when he'd begun to eat other cereals. A month ago? A year ago? More?

Those mornings after that blowup, I'd pad into the kitchen to see Wesley's sunken, hollow face, the gray peppered throughout his once solidly dark hair. Some part of me wanted to reach out and touch him, to say never mind, let's forget all this and go back to where we were, but I never did. Then, coming home from work five days later, with all that space still between us, Wes drove his car off that icy road.

7

I read to the boys for a long time that evening, the night before Thanksgiving, before the Blessing of the Hunt. I sat in the center of the couch, Ned and Charlie tucked up at my sides and Boomer at our feet, a blanket spread over us as a chill wind howled through the gutters and rattled the windowpanes. I read three long Beatrix Potters: *The Tale of Mr. Jeremy Fisher* and *The Tailor of Gloucester* and all 123 pages of *The Tale of Little Pig Robinson*. I was procrastinating, I would see in retrospect, though not that night. That night, I just read on and on, until Ned had fallen asleep, leaving only Charlie to hear how Pig Robinson, visited by Stumpy and little dog Tipkins, was found to be contented and not much inclined to return to Stymouth again. I closed the book and fitted it back into the boxed set, tucked Charlie into bed and sang to him. After he was sleeping soundly, I carried Ned to his bed, singing to him, too, though he was already fast asleep. I picked up the playroom then, loading LEGOs back into their plastic tub, putting the Brio train back on its tidy wooden track, scolding Boomer for chewing up yet another block. I put away the dishes, washed the pans, cleaned the stove.

Even then, I didn't pull my camera out.

I poured myself a glass of wine and sat with a stack of old photographs. The top photo was my raindrop picture, a shot of the boys sitting on the steps of our covered porch in Cleveland, dressed only in their underwear, trying to catch raindrops on their curled-up tongues. I looked at that photo for the longest time without really looking at it at all, without so much as taking a sip of wine. Thinking I would just skip the Blessing of the Hunt the next morning. There was no reason I had to go. Thinking maybe the weather would be bad. Maybe it would rain. Thunder and lightning. Sleet.

I looked more closely at the photograph. I'd taken two pictures of the moment captured in that photo, the first at an $f/2$ aperture, the lens wide open so there'd be no depth of field and the subjects would pop out of a gauzy background, but as I shot I realized I'd lose the raindrops and I flipped the settings and shot again, pushing the film so that when I overdeveloped it my raindrops nearly glistened despite the flat light. I looked now not at the sharpness of the focus or the framing of the shot, though, but at my sons' laughing faces in the soft gray light of a rainy morning. When had we last laughed like that? When would we again, if not soon?

I stuffed the photos back into the drawer of Wesley's desk and slid it shut, hiding them away like my father hid his photographs in his metal box. I got up from Wesley's desk then, and went straight to the cabinet, pulled out my camera. I set my tripod up in the center of the kitchen where I could get the best light, and screwed the camera on tightly. I placed a chair against the far wall and focused on it.

I could just photograph the chair.

I adjusted the overhead lights, measured with my light meter, adjusted the aperture. I checked the focus again, double-checked it, double-checked the light with the light meter, tested the flash. I set the automatic timer, turning the knob, then held my breath as I pushed the button, released it.

I stared at the empty chair for what seemed a long moment. Then settled, chin up, shoulders back, onto the uncomfortable wooden seat.

The timer hummed as the seconds ticked away.

Smile, I told myself. Laugh.

I tried to bring to mind my boys' smiling faces catching raindrops, but what came instead were sounds: the click of the lock closing off my father's box of photographs; the spill of Wesley's Shredded Wheat into an empty bowl; my father's voice saying, "See how you're backlit?"; the ring of the doorbell, the turn of the doorknob, the voice of the policeman standing on my front porch, saying, "Mrs. Grace?" with his hat in his hands.

The shutter released then. One single, solid snap.

Just as it had that day I'd taken my first photograph, that one when I was eight. I'd bounced the flash off the ceiling this time. I'd adjusted the exposure to compensate for the brightness of the white wall behind me. The negative would be better, easier to print.

But like that first photograph, it was a self-portrait. Me, trying to picture who I was, who I could become.

8

The wind that blew the night before Thanksgiving moved out over the ocean before morning, leaving tending-toward-winter temperatures and a strikingly sharp blue sky. The slate-roofed spire of St. James's Church stood proud against that blue, its stone walls and arched, stained-glass windows brightened by the dramatic sunlight, its browning grounds brightened by the red-jacketed, black-capped hunters readying their horses for the Blessing of the Hunt as the boys and I arrived. The boys took off to join Matt and Craig, and I climbed from the car and pulled my camera from its case, felt the weight of it in my hands.

I scanned the hunters, saw Willa, and Kirby and Joan, and several others I recognized from Emma's not-a-party, but no Emma herself, and no Dac. And then I spotted her—not on a horse, but leaning on a pair of crutches behind the fence separating the spectators from the field, her left leg encased to the knee in a cast. She wore her hunting coat, but not her britches—they wouldn't have fit over the cast—and a bright red bowler. No horse already saddled beside her. No riding cap for her today.

I positioned myself so the sun was behind me, the stone

church beyond Emma, all the while pretending to be taking in the scene, keeping far enough away so she wouldn't notice me. I felt eyes watching me as I raised my camera and framed her in the viewfinder, but when I glanced at the boys, they were deep into a game of freeze tag. I focused tightly on Emma, on her red bowler, her hunting coat, her face looking out over the field of horses, her longing laid bare.

I adjusted my shutter speed and my aperture, rechecked the focus, took a deep breath.

And shot.

As the film forwarded in the camera, I felt the tension fall away.

I moved closer to Emma, focusing tightly on her face, trying to capture that look in her eyes. I shot once, but that wasn't quite it, wasn't quite what I was going for. I moved a few paces closer, a little to the right. And there it was. At this angle, I could get that look. I focused and pressed the shutter release, capturing that hint of sadness in Emma's face, that something more than a simple sorrow at not riding the hunt.

A look of surprise shot across Emma's face as she saw me. "You did bring your camera! Good for you! But you're wasting your film on an immobilized old woman."

"Did you get on the wrong bull while you were in Montana or something?" I said. "How in the world did you break your leg?"

Emma laughed, but didn't explain. She said instead, "Do you like it living out here in the country, Nelly? This . . ." She indicated the field on the other side of the fence, the hunters all in their reds and blacks—tall, short, thin, and fat in every combination, but all with straight, proud backs—sitting easily on their horses, holding the reins loosely and chatting with each other and with people along the fence as a pack of Jack Russell terriers encircled the huntsman at the far side of the field. "This is lovely, of course, and you could perhaps sell it to *The Baltimore Sun* or to some horse magazine, but . . ."

I swallowed against what Emma didn't say, that this was no place for an aspiring photojournalist to settle down, that there would never be work enough here to keep me busy, much less meaningful work. I raised my camera, took a shot of Charlie, one of Ned, one of all the children swarming around Reverend Prescott—Philip, he insisted we call him.

Emma frowned.

Philip stepped up onto a bale of hay, preparing to say the blessing, but the yapping of the hounds caused such a ruckus that it seemed his voice would be lost in the din. And then the huntsman must have done something those dogs understood because a hush fell over everyone, even the hounds.

I raised my camera again, conscious of Emma shaking her head, adjusting her crutches, slowly hobbling away.

Philip began speaking then, his deep voice talking of the land we lived on and the horses and the hounds and ourselves, blessing each in its turn. I took his picture again and again, his picture and pictures of the things he blessed, the horses and hounds and riders and the people around us, all the time listening to the lyrical blessing, trying to commit to memory his words.

Thinking, too, about Emma's question. What was I doing living out here?

Thinking surely there was a title for a photo spread somewhere in Philip's words. And it came, at the end of the blessing, the line I would use, the thing Philip blessed last and most enthusiastically: the long life of the fox.

"To the Long Life of the Fox," I said quietly, now imagining myself applying for a staff position with *The Baltimore Sun*, stretching that fantasy out into the future, to *Time* magazine spreads, *Newsweek* covers, an acceptance speech for the

Pulitzer in which I thanked Dad for teaching me everything I knew.

That's what I was doing—fantasizing about Dad's proud smile as he listened to that acceptance speech—when I caught sight of Dac out of the corner of my eye. He was close behind me; I could almost touch his red hunting coat, the nose of his roan horse, the riding cap held against his hip.

"You brought your camera," he said.

"I promised your mother."

"You should always have your camera," he said.

I smoothed the collar of my jacket—I wasn't naked, my clothes were still there—and ducked behind my camera, photographing Dac deliberately but quickly, capturing an odd expression: that mix of fear and desire I'd seen in the animal photographs in Emma's kitchen.

Was that him, or me?

"You don't have to convince me," he said. "I've been watching you take photographs since Philip began his little speech. The whole gang, everyone in their country best."

I reluctantly lowered the camera, idly twisted the lens. "Everyone here seems to know everyone else, so you get all that great interaction," I said.

"We do, don't we?" he said. "So how is it your father has owned that farm all these years and we never met?"

I looked to the boys, actually standing still, anticipating the hunters taking off. "My great-grandparents died before I was born," I said as if that explained it, as if it didn't strike me as odd, now that I thought about it, that I'd never been to the farm as a girl. "Dad was always busy," I said. "And the farm was always rented."

The hunting horn sounded loudly, a long, funny honk, and the hounds began yapping again. Dac put his cap on, but left the chin strap dangling by his neck.

"You couldn't keep me away from your place if I owned it," Dac said. "The pond. The woods. That little waterfall we rode to the other day." The hunting horn sounded again and he glanced over at the riders, then swung up onto his horse. "Maybe you'll come ride with me again sometime, since Mother is out of commission?"

I said I'd like that.

He fastened his chin strap. "I'll call you," he said, and he settled into a trot, headed off toward where the hounds were already scampering, still yapping, noses to the ground. The children around me began yapping and scampering, too, as the spectators applauded, and I stood watching the hunters make their way across the fields and disappear over a hill.

9

Emma stopped by "just to bring some apples" from her farm that Saturday, and we had coffee and visited, and it wasn't until I heard the hunting horn sounding in the distance that I realized this was the time she usually hunted: Tuesday, Thursday, and Saturday afternoons. After that, she began dropping by while the rest of our neighbors were out on their horses, at first bringing some excuse for coming—acorn squash from her fall garden, homemade bread, jars of jam—but soon just coming to visit, no longer feeling the need to bring a toll to gain admittance. We talked about what was in the newspaper those afternoons, the odd social customs of the country, and our neighbors' theories on Emma's broken leg—a source of some gossip. "A little secret can go a long way out here," she said.

The fourth of those afternoons, a Saturday, we were making apple pie together when Emma asked, "Why did you move out here, Nelly? Why did you leave Chicago after Wesley died? What is there here for you?"

I wiped my hands on my bright red apron and picked up the rolling pin.

"If you don't mind my asking," she said.

Laughter sounded from the playroom, where the boys (Willa's and mine; I was watching Matt and Craig while Willa hunted; she'd take them all out for pizza later) were making a LEGO world of some sort.

"I wasn't sure I could live out here alone with the boys," I said. "Before Wesley died, I'd never . . ."

Never done anything.

"I'd never lived by myself."

Emma looked at me curiously. "I lived alone in England, during the war," she said, returning her attention to the apple she was peeling. "When Davis was in the service."

I applied the rolling pin to a ball of the crust dough wedged between two pieces of waxed paper, thinking it wasn't the same, it wasn't like she was really alone then, Davis wasn't home but his shoes were still in the closet, she'd still have thought of his side of the bed as his.

"In some ways it was harder than when Davis died," she continued. "When he died, Dac was . . . He was grown-up but he was living with us still, or again, so I wasn't left completely alone. During the war, I didn't have Dac yet, and I didn't have anyone else."

Her parents had died, she said, and she had no siblings. Davis flew, so he made it home as much as anybody, more than the troops at the front by a long shot. But he went down, in September of 1942. She'd just seen him—he'd come home to London to be sworn in to the American army air corps; he'd been fighting with the RAF, but now the Americans were in the war. And then he was sent out on an escort mission over France and they hit unexpected winds. His squadron descended, thinking they were back over England, but they were only over Brest, in occupied France, without enough fuel to climb again. "He was 'Missing—Presumed Dead' for ten months," she said.

She cored her apple and sliced it on the wooden cutting board. The house was still except for the sound of Emma slicing, leaving me silently hoping the boys weren't feeding the goldfish to the dog.

"Every ring of the phone, every knock at the door, every time the post came . . ." Emma paused, then tossed the apple slices from the cutting board into the bowl.

"What did you do?" I asked softly.

She chose another apple from the bag. "Well, I drank, to be honest," she said. "Heavily and often and pretty much anything. I made a show of life, of course. I got on the tube every morning. I made the proper noises in response to sympathetic inquiries from my colleagues which, mercifully, came less and less often. But alone in my flat at night, I drank." She looked up, straight into my eyes.

"How's that pastry coming there?" she said.

I peeled off the top layer of waxed paper, put the pan upside down on the crust, and flipped the crust into the pan, a trick I'd learned from my grandma, who always said the secret to a great pie was a great crust.

The sound of boys shouting in the playroom flooded the kitchen, then died back again.

"I had a group of friends who'd meet at a pub most evenings," Emma said. "They were not light drinkers, that group, but even they began to be concerned. They drew straws, it seems, and the shortest straw, an American boy stationed in England"—she looked up at me—"an old friend of Davis's, actually, he got the chore of telling me I was drinking a bit much. Just the two of us at the pub that night. Everyone else gone home or somewhere else. And when I went home that night, I knew Davis was dead and I began to bury him. And I stopped drinking quite so much and I started back on with my life."

I stood looking at her, with the top crust still a ball in front of me and the rolling pin in my hand.

"Those were wonderful friends," she said. "Wartime friends, and we all went different ways not long after, but I've never forgotten." She was silent for a minute, briefly somewhere else, but then she smiled slightly and looked up at me.

"Enough?" she said.

I blinked against a swell of emotion, feeling closer to Emma than I'd felt to anyone since we'd moved East. "I like to hear," I said.

Emma tossed another handful of apple slices into the bowl, laughing lightly. "I meant of the apples."

I smiled. "Plenty," I said, and I tossed a cup of sugar (one half each of brown and white), a few dashes of cinnamon, a dash of nutmeg, and a handful of flour into the bowl. Emma stirred the mixture, coating the apple slices sugary sweet. I picked one out and ate it while I began to roll the top crust.

"But Davis didn't die," I prompted.

"No. Three months later a telegram came, and I knew it was the telegram, and I just closed the door. But the woman rang again and said it was good news, she was certain. I didn't open the door, but I was listening, wanting to believe her but afraid to. The message was short, she said through the closed door; she could see through the envelope. The dreadful news always came in longer telegrams. And I opened the door then and tore open the telegram."

"And it said?"

" 'Alive and Kicking. Stop. Love You Love You Love You.' " Emma laughed again, a sort of half-laugh, but there was no laughter in her face. "To him it was all so simple," she said. "Almost a joke."

I stopped rolling the crust for a moment. "Or that was the front he put up?"

She picked a slice of apple out of the bowl with her long fingers. "Yes . . . Davis was like that, somehow, in a way I couldn't be. He just took his whole life in stride." She nodded to herself. "Or appeared to, anyway."

She pondered the apple slice for a moment, then took a small bite.

"You'd have liked him, Nelly. Everyone did," she said. "He was fabulously handsome, too—I know I sound inexcusably vain to say so, but he was. Look." She pulled her wallet from her bag and opened it to reveal a photo inserted in a photo sleeve.

I dumped the apples from the bowl into the crust-lined pan, wiped my hands on my apron, and took the wallet from her extended hand.

"That's Davis, just before we were married."

A black-and-white portrait of a square-jawed, eager-eyed young man in a service uniform, a Royal Air Force uniform with an Eagle Squadron patch on the left shoulder. Beside it, a second photo: the same square jaw on a gray-haired, well-lined face. The pale eyes looked content, comfortable, like they might easily hold your gaze for a long time.

"The second one was taken five years or so before he died," Emma said.

I flipped to the next set of photo sleeves. "Dac?" I said, looking at a wan child of three or so on one side, and then a big, healthy boy of thirteen.

He'd had polio, Emma explained. He'd lost the use of his legs, but he'd recovered completely. They'd been blessed, just as they'd been blessed to get him back from Vietnam. He'd had a hard time of it there too. "But he's fine now," she said, nodding twice, sharply. "He's fine now."

I frowned, remembering Dac's words: *Mai used to say it was kind of universal, being disturbed, and why shouldn't we be?*

"He's your only child?" I said.

"We had a daughter, Hannah, but she was stillborn."

"Hannah," I repeated.

"After my mother. And Dac is named after Davis, and his father and his grandfather and so on, of course."

I looked again at the photograph. "Dac looks more like you than like Davis."

Emma tucked the wallet back into her bag, then smiled slightly, eyeing the walls, the kitchen desk top, the refrigerator. "And where, Nelly, are your photos?" she said.

I'd shot off rolls of film in the days after Thanksgiving, developed them, even begun to contemplate the possibility of doing something with them, putting together a portfolio. I'd imagined writing a query letter, struggled with how I might sign it: Nelly Grace didn't seem very professional, so I'd considered Eleanor Grace. But Eleanor Grace seemed an entirely different person than me somehow.

"My photos," I said, "are in the basement, waiting for the paint on the walls to dry."

The walls were not the least bit damp, she said with a note of disapproval, and when I explained that the paint was in a box by the photos, she laughed and asked what we were waiting for. And to my protest that she couldn't possibly paint with her broken leg, she simply said, "Nonsense, I get along pretty well on this old leg," and we smiled at each other, knowing we'd crossed some bridge together, that we were now friends.

Willa came to the door not much later, ringing the doorbell and, without waiting for any more answer than Boomer's bark, poking her head into the kitchen, her face flushed, happy, the tip of her nose red from the cold. "Oh, hello, Mrs. Crofton," she said, looking not so much surprised as suddenly on her guard.

"Hello, Willa," Emma said. "How was the hunt?"

Willa mussed her hair, the gesture lacking its usual energy, and said it was fine, the hunt was fine. It had been a small field because of the weather; they went out toward Blackrock and through the Five Star Farm woods, running on the same line for two hours before the fox went to ground. I felt myself frowning as I watched the interchange, wondering how I could feel so uneasy with the two of them together when I felt so comfortable with each of them.

Willa called to the boys then, shouting, "Pizza time!" as I finished crimping the crust and slid the pie into the oven, the heat baking my face and my chest.

Emma and I spent some time settling into painting that after-noon after Willa and the boys left, deciding who should do what and what should be done first, pushing the table and chairs out of the way and spreading the drop cloth out on the floor. I left the can of Spackle in the basement, thinking the paint would cover the flaws well enough, but Emma insisted the paint wouldn't stick unless the walls were cleaned first—all that kitchen grease—and the cracks and dings would soon start breaking through even if not visible at first. So I retrieved the Spackle after all, thinking as I mounted the basement stairs again that I should introduce Emma to my father, thinking, yes, I'd have a tree-trimming party when Dad arrived for Christmas, to introduce them. They were both such perfec-tionists.

Upstairs again, I put on some music and we settled into an easy rhythm with our steel wool and our putty knives, and after a moment Emma said that I still hadn't answered her question. "Why *did* you move out here, Nelly?" she said.

I sighed, and then I gave her the short version of the story: how the first time I turned the corner into the drive and caught a glimpse of the farm through bare tree branches, my breath caught in my throat and my eyes watered and I wanted, even before I saw the house, to call it home. I said if I'd had any doubts after that, they were put to rest the next weekend, when I flew out from Chicago with the boys, to show them the place. We were blessed with the miracle of a late April snowstorm, and the three of us sat on the bank of the stream on a borrowed toboggan, talking about why the snow was frozen but the stream wasn't, why the fish didn't need clothes, where the water went in such an awful hurry. It wasn't just that we were enjoying ourselves for the first time since Wesley had died either. It was more than that. I found myself wondering about things I'd ceased to notice, things I'd not begun to explore.

Emma frowned as if she knew that explanation was incomplete, that I was lying just a little, holding back. So I started over, beginning this time with us living in Chicago, in the suburbs, where we'd been less than a year. We'd come from Cleveland, where Wesley had been the young darling of pediatric heart surgery, and before that St. Louis, where he did his internship, but we'd started in Chicago where my father was, and where I, at least, expected we might stay. I'd begun to settle into the kind of life that was always expected of me and that, in some way, I suppose I'd come to expect of myself. I was knee-deep in motherhood, overwhelmed by the task, and if I had time to think of moving at all, it was only to assume we would someday trade our old picket fence for a newer, fancier one. It caught me off guard when Wes mentioned the possibility of trading picket fences for paddock fences, of moving to my great-grandfather's place. Why this sudden need for change? But Wesley had been offered a great opportunity at Johns Hopkins, and Dad had mentioned the farm, saying he'd inherited it from his grandparents—a surprise to me—and that the current lease expired in August. We could move in after that if we'd like, he said.

"Don't go taking on more land than you can use," Wesley's grandfather, himself raised on a farm, had said when we first mentioned the idea, and I was secretly inclined to agree. It was fine for Wes. He would go off every morning—not just Monday through Friday, but truly every morning, or so it seemed, and sometimes in the middle of the night, if he even came home at night—to a climate-controlled environment where he and a cast of characters in blue-green scrubs and matching booties would carry on life as he knew it for most of his waking hours, in the same white-walled stainless-steel rooms in which he felt most at ease. And what could I say? If he'd been off playing poker or playing basketball or even playing at some business in the city, well then, yes. But what could I say? "So, Wes, what is it now? Do you really need to go in and save another baby's life?"

So I was a bit skeptical of this farm thing, but I went along with the idea for a while, thinking surely this would all pass before anything irrevocable was done. Instead, even before we'd come to look at Baltimore, Wesley drove off that icy road and rolled his car and broke his neck and my life as I knew it—that white-picket-fence world—didn't seem to matter anymore. And it wasn't until I turned the corner into the drive at the farm months after his death that I began to feel I could look beyond the end of each single day. A whole life of new possibilities opened up for me then, with no white picket fences to keep me in.

Emma smiled a sort of sad smile. "You can't be happy trying to fit into someone else's life," she said. "But what I wonder is this . . ." She met my gaze. "Are you running toward something here, Nelly, or are you running away?"

Outside the window, the faded brown of the fields

stretched to the faded brown of the woods, broken only by the white of the paddock fences, the murky blue green of the pond. No flicks of deer jumping fences today, no rider coming up my drive.

"Emma," I said, "why does everyone call you Mrs. Crofton?"

She frowned at me as if trying to decide whether to answer my question or insist I answer hers.

"Almost everyone," I said. "Everyone but Kirby and Joan."

She rubbed at the end of one crutch as if to wipe away some flaw. "I suppose they mean it to be respectful," she said. "Though it does make a person feel rather ancient. As if they all took literature from me in upper school, and have never recovered from it."

I smiled slightly.

"I can't tell you how much it pleased me that first day we met, to hear you call me Emma," she said.

"I can't tell you how much it pleased me to have you bring me jam," I said.

The oven timer buzzed then—insistent, demanding—calling us back to the bare kitchen walls, the pie, the paint. We set our painting things aside, and I served up big slices of pie while Emma heaped on scoops of ice cream.

"The perfect dinner," she said. "You're going to have to share your secret recipe with me."

"Only if you'll share your secret with me," I said. "How you broke your leg."

Emma laughed, then leaned across the table, caught me up with her eyes. "I tripped putting on my drawers, Nelly. Now don't you dare tell anyone!"

Emma and I painted during our afternoon visits after that—that Tuesday and Thursday, and she came Friday, too, to help me paint the living room and entry hall before our tree-trimming party Sunday, after my father would arrive. I'd wanted to take her picture again ever since the Blessing of the Hunt, so Tuesday before we got started I asked if I might photograph her. I posed her in the oversized yellow wing chair in my living room, with her back to the fireplace, and I set up my tripod in front of her and, almost as an afterthought, leaned her crutches against one arm of the chair, pointing toward her face; it would help focus the viewer's attention, and it would add an interesting counterpoint to Emma's strength.

"Look toward me," I said. If she faced toward the camera from where she sat, the light from the window fell nicely on her face, reflecting in her eyes between one and three o'clock, creating no uneven shadowing. "And try to pretend the camera isn't here. Just do or say whatever comes to mind."

I measured with my light meter and adjusted the aperture, remembering my father teaching me to do so, thinking Dad would like Emma, that it would be fun to introduce them. He'd like all my new friends, I thought; that's why a tree-trimming party was such a good idea, so he could meet them. But I wasn't quite sure.

Emma reached up with her right hand to pat her hair. "Distract me," she said. "Ask me something."

I smiled. How could anyone not like Emma? The question was, Would Emma like Dad?

"Okay," I said. "What's your favorite color?"

"For what?"

I snapped a close-up of her face, with her eyebrows just slightly raised. "You have different favorite colors for different things?"

"Don't you?" she said, her eyes challenging me.

I laughed as I snapped a second shot. "Okay, for eyes then."

"Blue," she said, the expression in her own eyes defining her face.

"Blue like Davis's?"

"No, like my other lover's!"

Maybe she was lying, teasing. I didn't care. Whatever she was doing, it was going to make great photographs. Exactly Emma, I thought.

"Not a chance," I said. "You're the faithful type!"

"But I've been a widow for years now!"

"Now? As in currently?"

She laughed, first with her head thrown back, then facing me with her mouth in an irrepressible smile, deep lines running from eyes to jaw. Two great, great shots.

"You think I'm too old to have a lover? Sex doesn't have to end at sixty-five!"

"I just thought I would have heard," I said, feigning deep apology. "Though now that I think of it, I have heard some muttering about you disappearing—"

"Disappearing!" Emma looked genuinely surprised.

I clicked the shutter release, caught the expression at its fullest. "Just a little talk, you know," I said.

"Disappearing! How delightful!" Emma laughed and laughed. "I'll take you someday to one of the places I 'disappear' to, if you'll promise to bring your camera. And color film, too, so you can catch the color of my other lover's eyes!" Still laughing, she said, "There are a lot of things about me you don't know, Nelly Grace."

I asked her to name one, and she told me to ask her something I wanted to know.

"Okay," I said, thinking, the shutter still clicking. "Okay. Why did you want to leave England?"

Through the lens of the camera I saw the lines in her forehead deepen. She flicked her wrist in the air.

I put the lens cap on the camera and sat on the coffee table in front of her chair.

"Tell me," I said. "Why?"

"Why did you leave Chicago?" she countered.

"I already told you. No white picket fences."

"There's more to it than that, Nelly."

"You're changing the subject, Emma."

She drew her lips together, her lower lip slightly out. "All right, then. You want to know why I left England? Fine." She closed her eyes for a moment, and though she didn't move, her shoulders seemed to sink just a bit, her cotillion posture slipping away. When she opened her eyes, though, they were the eyes of the Emma I'd come to know. "When I was fourteen," she said, "my father shot my mother, then put the gun in his mouth and killed himself."

The solid look in her eyes warned she would not be pitied.

She wasn't allowed to see the bodies, she said. She supposed they thought it would be too traumatic. But for years afterward she fantasized that her mother wasn't really dead. Her father had been in government service, and she'd imagined they'd had to go underground, disappear. "I spent hours and hours thinking up reasons they'd had to leave me behind, alone in that dreary village," she said. "I spent years imagining the moment Mum would come back for me."

She looked out the window, across the stretch of pale grass and on to the cold surface of the pond. "I was the girl whose father shot her mother after that. The girl who lived with her aunt." She wrapped her arms around herself as if to ward off a chill, but her back remained straight, her chin level. "What I wouldn't have given back then to have just one single friend," she said. "I left the town when I was seventeen and I will tell you I set out to get as far away as I could get. And this is pretty far—rather farther than even I had imagined."

"This is a long way," I said.

"I suppose I thought I'd just blend in here. Who knew everyone here would be from here, would have a known and more or less respectable past?" She ran a hand through her hair. "It's rather a pedigreed society, isn't it?"

I nodded. "It's a pretty small place in some ways."

"And I came with no papers at all. Lord knows no one here would have had me if they'd known where I was from." She sighed.

"I never even told Davis about my parents," she said. "I always thought I'd tell him someday, but then the days piled up into years, and then we'd lived a whole life together and I'd never told him."

"Why couldn't you tell him in the beginning?" I asked quietly.

And why had she chosen to tell me?

"Davis was a remarkable person in many ways," she said finally. "But in some ways, he was just like everyone else."

I nodded slowly. "But he loved you, Emma."

In the distance, a train whistle sounded, the long, low tone echoing somehow, vibrating in the empty air so that it seemed not a single note repeated, but a series of notes, the beginning of some haunting melody.

"No," Emma said after a moment. "No, it wasn't me Davis loved, not really. It was the me I wanted him to know. The me I knew he wanted me to be."

10

Before that conversation with Emma, I'm not sure I was aware that I, too, had spent my life trying to be the person others wanted me to be. Even my earliest interest in photography was driven in part by my need to catch Dad's attention. And after my eighth birthday, when my photography became a thing I tried to hide from him, I imagined a day when I would emerge from my veil of secrecy to present an irrefutably stunning photograph to him. I became my harshest critic, and it was two years later, when I was ten, before I took another photograph that I thought might rise even to the level of good: the picture of Grandma in our kitchen making pie, the one I'd described to Dac.

Grandma lived not far from us when we were in Chicago, and when Dad was home we'd go over to her house for Sunday supper: old-fashioned meals served on lace tablecloths and china, mounds of ham or roast beef or turkey with gravy, always served with mashed potatoes, vegetables in cream sauce, and homemade bread—potato bread or monkey bread or cheese rolls, all tasting of yeast. We'd eat a whole pie and the beginnings of a second, and about an hour after the dishes had been washed and put away, we'd slip off one at a time to the kitchen, where we'd slice another sliver and eat it from the pan.

What I loved about visiting Grandma was not the dinners, though, but our time in her kitchen while she cooked, her special time for me. Dad would be watching football or baseball or basketball with Grandpa and Uncle Bob and my brothers and cousins, and my mother would be chatting with Aunt Sally on the patio or in the living room, all having been banished from the kitchen by Grandma, who declared she needed no help but mine. And while everyone else was occupied, she'd ask what I'd brought for her this time, and I'd pull out my best photos. She'd wipe her hands on her apron before taking them, and she'd use one of her colorful expressions to praise them, odd phrases I never heard anywhere else—not "You can't judge a book by its cover," but "You can't tell how far a frog will jump by the way he looks." My pictures were not just lovely, they were "prettier than a perfect pie crust" or "as perfect as a newly plowed field."

I was fifteen when she died, and I was frantic with the loss. When my mother told me, I shut myself in my room and sat by my window, wanting to put my hand through it. And after the funeral, after all her friends and neighbors had left her house with their empty casserole dishes and we'd driven home, I finally did smash through that window, creating a scar on my right wrist that is still a fine white line, her death marked indelibly on my skin.

Oddly, that picture of Grandma—the one I thought might be good—was taken not in her kitchen, but in my mother's, a few days after my mother took an overdose of pills that nearly killed her. We'd all come home from school one afternoon, calling to let Mom know we were home, and she hadn't answered. A few minutes later, I found her sleeping in her bed and I couldn't wake her. It was Danny who figured out what had happened, who listened to her breathing and felt the weakness of her pulse. He was calm, his voice almost adult as he called for an ambulance. I followed his orders, doing everything he said until he climbed into the ambulance next to my mother's stretcher, leaving me to take care of Jimmy with the help of a strange policeman. As I stood in the driveway, watching the ambulance disappear down the street, I thought of every little meanness I'd done to Mom, all the ways this must be my fault. I remember that. And I remember my sense of relief at the sight of Grandma's face, at the soft patter of her voice making me feel that somehow it would all be okay. It was Grandma who tracked down Dad that afternoon. It was Grandma who fed us and bathed us and tucked us in that night and allowed us to stay home from school the next day, a Friday. And I've always believed it was Grandma, with her old-fashioned sense of decency, who developed the official story: my mother had suffered a miscarriage for which she had to be hospitalized.

My father, for his part, arrived home the next morning to find that Mom, despite her attempt, was not going to die. He confirmed that Grandma could care for us until Mom was again able to do so, then flew back to his life, by himself. In my memory, he was with us for only hours, though Danny says he stayed more than a week.

I do remember Dad being home, though, when Grandma was making that pie—the one in the picture. He had been in his bedroom, getting ready to leave, and though I didn't hear him come into the kitchen, Grandma must have known he was there. She turned, and that's when I snapped the picture. I caught the warmth of the sunlight coming through the window beside her and the dry feel of the flour on her face. But what makes that picture is something I caught in her expression, some transition from the feel of dough in her fingers to some more complex reaction to my father's leaving—perhaps anger, perhaps concern, perhaps both.

I remember, too, eating the pie late that afternoon—Danny, Jimmy, Grandma, Dad, and me. Dad said, as he always did after the first bite, "Makes you want to hit your mamma," an expression of Grandma's which meant something tasted great. That particular day, though, with Mom still in the hospital and Dad about to leave, I did want to hit my mother, to make her hurt the way I was hurting, to crawl up into her arms and feel the touch of her lips on my hair. And I began to mash my pie with my fork, mashing and mashing, splattering lemon cream and meringue off my plate onto the table.

Grandma looked to my father, who did not know what to say. And it was Grandma who reached out and touched my arm, the gentlest touch. "That's a feeling you're entitled to have," she said.

Her words were not enough for me, though; I picked up my plate and smashed it down on top of my father's, sending pie spewing onto his shirtfront, the table, the floor. Dad didn't say a word, didn't move except to look down at the plates and then back up at me before I fled from the room.

That evening when Dad pulled his locked file box of photographs from the closet shelf and put it by the front door, next to his suitcase, I was sure he was leaving for good. So as he was putting on his overcoat—running late for his flight— I plunked myself down atop his box and refused to move. That would make him stay, or if not stay then bring him back. What it seemed to me he loved most of all: his photographs.

But he only laughed, and he said softly, "Those are my best pictures, Nelly. I need to take them with me." And when I didn't move, he kept talking to me in that same quiet voice, and though I didn't exactly understand what he was saying, something about his tone, the slope of his shoulders, the soft, sad look on his face, made me shift in my seat atop the box. "You won't come back," I whispered.

"Oh, Squirt." He sat down in front of me so we were on the same level, and he took my small hands and enfolded them in his. "I'll always come back for you. I promise." He wrapped his arms around me and lifted me up, and I wrapped my arms and legs around him and held him as tightly as I could.

"Look," he said, reaching into his pocket, still holding me. "Take this." He opened my palm and placed in it the key to his box.

I rolled the old brass skeleton key between my fingers, watching it twirl against my skin.

"You keep it for me," Dad said. "And whenever you think I might not come back, you can pull it out and look at it, and you'll know I will."

My father did come back, and my sense of dread at his leaving faded as he kept coming back again and again. And each time he did come home, I waited for him to ask for the key so he could open his box. He never did, though. He never once did. But by the time I realized he had a duplicate, that he didn't need the key he'd given me, I no longer feared he would leave for good.

PART TWO

11

Dad's old Jeep crossed the bridge that Saturday evening two weeks before Christmas almost to the minute when he'd said he'd arrive. Ned and Charlie, who'd been waiting impatiently all day, bolted out the door shrieking, "Grandpa Pat! Grandpa Pat!" as Boomer raced alongside the Jeep up the drive. I, too, had been waiting with the same nervous energy that had marked Dad's arrival when I was a child, but I didn't run out to greet him. I stood in the doorway as he pulled the Jeep to a stop, climbed out, and lifted first Charlie, then Ned, high in the air, swinging them around, teasing them with the promise of exotic foreign surprises in his suitcase, announcing he'd come only to help them explore the wonders of the farm.

He winked in my direction. I smiled, and he grinned.

He'd put back on most of the weight he'd lost when Mom died, and his body felt strong as he wrapped me up in a hug.

"You look good," I said, feeling awkward, almost shy.

"You too. Country life must agree with you."

I nodded. "How was the drive?"

Dad settled into the guest room, unpacking his suitcase and delivering his surprises for the boys, carved wooden masks he'd picked up in Peru, colorful, comic things meant to ward off evil spirits. At dinner, he told stories of the strange places he'd been, wonderful tales told at a child's level; he still had that instinct for what would capture a young imagination. For all their strangeness, the gifts and the stories were familiar, much like the gifts and stories had been when he was the father and I the child, though they were now differently received. From a grandfather, they were gems of thoughtfulness and wonder. From a father who was seldom home, they'd been dismal reminders that he would always leave again.

When I locked up before bed that night, I paused in the entryway to look at the photos I'd hung there just that morning, family pictures taken by my father and by Wesley's parents and by our grandparents. They were old favorites, photographs that had hung in our entry hall in every house Wes and I had lived in, but as I headed on to bed, I couldn't shake the feeling something was wrong with them.

The moon glowed brightly that night, and a frost lay thick on the ground, reflecting the light so it seemed forever to be almost dawn. Long before the sun rose, though, I climbed from the warmth of my covers and made my way through the dark house, the bluestone cold against my bare feet. In the entryway, I turned on the lights, blinking against the brightness. The photographs hanging there were lovely: my mother and father, my grandparents, my brothers, my boys. But they were not mine.

I thought of Emma then, imagined her as a young woman marrying a man she'd barely met, moving across the ocean and into a world she knew nothing about.

And my walls were painted now.

I pulled down an entire row of pictures, stacked them in my arms and carried them down to my darkroom, to where

I'd moved all my photos, even the ones I'd kept in Wesley's desk before Dad arrived. There, I opened the frames, pulled out the photographs, replaced them with ones I'd taken. Not my most serious photos; not those I'd taken trying to be someone, but my best family photos: the raindrop picture, Ned and Charlie trying to catch those raindrops on their tongues; one of them with Boomer as a tiny puppy; one of Mom putting on lipstick; one of my brothers when we were all young. I paused for a moment over a photo of my younger brother, Jimmy, sitting silly-faced under a fishing hat much too big for him, his skinny legs stretched across the front porch stairs. He was a sickly child—bronchitis, pneumonia, and asthma—and Mom was always taking him to some doctor, leaving Danny and me alone. If Danny ever resented Jimmy, though, I never saw it; he was better than I was at that kind of thing. He was better than I was at most things.

I frowned to myself, but I put the photo of Jimmy in one of the frames, then dug out one of Danny and framed it too. And when only one frame remained empty, I started digging through the remainder of the box, searching for a single picture: Grandma making that pie.

By the time the doorbell rang Sunday afternoon, we'd managed to find the boxes with the ornaments, replace burnt-out lightbulbs on the strings, and put the lights on the tree. A buffet of sandwich meats, cheeses, rolls, and cut vegetables sat on the table, together with bakery-bought Christmas cookies the boys and I agreed to pretend we made. Eggnog filled the punch bowl. Bing Crosby sang "White Christmas" from a tape. Still, I was feeling apprehensive. Wes and I had had an awkward sort of tradition about trimming the Christmas tree, one born of necessity the year Charlie was first old enough to fight with Ned over who would put on the star. That year,

Wesley balanced them both on his shoulders so that each could hold a point of the star. He'd managed to pull this off even last year, when Ned alone had weighed sixty-some pounds. But I was not Wesley, and I didn't have a prayer of lifting over a hundred pounds of wriggling boys, and even if I did, it would not have been the same.

Willa, Matthew, and Craig were the first to arrive that afternoon, together with Boomer, who was reminded that his place for this party was outside. The four boys trotted off immediately to the cookie tray and the tree, leaving Dad and Willa and me with our introductions. We'd barely closed the front door when the bell rang again: Kirby and Joan.

"Joan!" Dad said the moment he saw her. He took both of her hands in his and they kissed each other's cheeks.

"Pat Sullivan," Joan said. "I haven't seen you in fifty years!"

They jumped immediately into old memories—remember when? . . . remember when?—and soon we were hearing about the summer Joan was sixteen, the summer Dad had his first camera. Joan said my father left the summer before still just a boy, small for his age, but he came back a handsome young man. "We girls spent that whole summer angling to get him to take our pictures," she said. "He broke all our hearts, though, leaving at the end of the summer without a word about keeping in touch!"

"Only because I couldn't have you," Dad said. "You and Davis were a hot item by the time I got here. I didn't stand a chance."

"That's just how much you don't know," Joan said, her eyes lit with the memory of being the belle of the ball. "I made Davis dance with the other girls so your father would have to dance with me," she said to me. "But he was all wrapped up in being the Davis Crofton fan club. I'm trying to flirt with him and he's talking about what a swell guy Davis is, how much fun they had that day doing whatever it was they did."

My father laughed. "Well, I could hardly steal my best friend's girl."

Their obvious delight at seeing each other after so many years infected us. The party was off to a terrific start. But as we settled into the living room—the boys careening back and forth from tree to ornaments to tree—I watched my father, wondering why, if he'd so enjoyed this place as a child, he'd never brought us here when we were young. Why had he never come back?

The next time the doorbell rang, it was Emma, her face gleeful under a fuzzy Santa hat, a more sober Dac standing beside her with several more hats in his hand. Emma hobbled in and hugged me as best she could given her crutches, ex-claiming almost immediately, "You've put up your photos! Now I can see just how gangly a child you were!"

Dac leaned toward me and I had a second of not knowing what he was doing before he lightly kissed my cheek. He moved to help his mother out of her coat then, but she was already intent on the black-and-whites on the wall.

Dac, giving up on the coat for the moment, moved up be-hind me for a closer look at the photographs, his breath warm on my neck. The two of them studied the pictures, comment-ing, questioning, complimenting the ones I'd taken myself. I explained each picture: my mother as a young girl, eight or nine, in a uniform-like dress with a T-shirt peeking out from underneath; me as a baby, my mouth wide even then; an en-gagement picture of Wesley's parents, looking stoic and cold. Both Dac and Emma lingered over the photo of Grandma— my photo—and I wondered what it was they thought they saw. Then Emma bent down a little from the perch of her crutches to see a lower picture, jingling the bell at the tip of her Santa hat.

Dac, leaning forward, touched his hand to my shoulder but drew it back immediately, as if he'd felt the same shock of the touch I had. He stuck the hand in his pocket, and when I stole a glance at his face he was still staring at the picture of Grandma. He nodded to himself and said, "Hmmm."

Emma was looking at a picture of Dad with his brothers and sisters, the five Sullivan children outside in the dead of winter, snow covering the ground. The older four, in shirt-sleeves, obviously having rushed outside solely for the picture, are smiling, looking at the camera, probably wondering if their ears will look big, which they do. But it's Dad's face, with his head slightly cocked and a pout on his lips, that draws everyone's attention, and not just because he's the youngest, an adorable four-year-old. It's as if he knew, even then and even from the other side of the lens, what the camera wanted, what it could make appear interesting, attractive, charming.

"That," I said to Emma, "is my father."

"Yes . . . ," Emma said. She studied each of the faces care-fully, as if trying to get to know them, lingering last and longest on Dad. She pointed at him in the picture. "This one," she said. She looked up at me.

"Right."

Emma looked again at the picture of Dad.

Dac moved over, away from me, and leaned down to see the picture, too. His one hand remained in his pocket, the other still holding the Santa hats.

Emma moved on to a wedding photo of my parents. "Your mother and father?" She looked up at me, jingling the bell on her hat again.

An explosion of boy voices—laughing or fighting?—sounded from the living room, but quickly subsided.

"Leaving the church after they were married," I said.

She pulled the red cap off her head and handed it to Dac as she studied the photo.

"She was lovely, your mother, wasn't she? You look so much like her."

I looked at the photo: Mom as beautiful as I remembered her, but different. Stronger, less fragile, more sure of herself. "I always thought she was beautiful and I was all mouth."

Dac continued to study the photograph, but there was a flash of something—amusement?—in his eyes.

"Please, let's go into the living room," I said. "I'd like you both to meet my dad."

"Your father?" Emma straightened up on her crutches, her voice registering surprise and something else too. A little nervous? Almost giddy, but not quite. Not the way I'd have thought Emma would respond to being introduced to anyone.

"He's here for Christmas. I'm sure I told you—"

"I don't—Yes, yes, you must have." Emma's gaze darted to the picture again, then back to me. "How delightful. Your father!" She reached up to pat her hair, liberating one of her crutches, which clattered to the floor.

Dac and I both stooped to retrieve it, almost bumping heads. "I'll get it," we said at the same time. I laughed self-consciously and Dac laughed, too, as he picked up the crutch and handed it to Emma.

Dad looked up from two ornaments he was untangling for Ned and Charlie as Dac and Emma and I entered the living room. "Emma," he said, standing up and taking Emma's hand even before I could introduce them. Her hand looked child-like in his despite her long fingers. Dad handed me the still-tangled ornaments and put his left hand over their joined right hands so hers was enveloped entirely in his. For a moment, I thought he might kiss her.

"What a pleasure to meet you," Emma said.

Dad let go of her hand, looking a bit disoriented. "Lord, it's good to see you again, Emma."

Again? I looked at Emma. She appeared to be studying the tree, the tree skirt, the ornaments. But of course Dad had known Davis, Joan had said so, said Davis was Dad's childhood friend. Funny that Emma had never mentioned having met him.

"It's Patrick," Dad said to Emma, though he never called himself Patrick. No one called him Patrick. Others called him Pat or Sully, and he always introduced himself as Pat.

"You don't recognize me?" A flash of embarrassment, maybe even hurt, crossed his face.

"Mo-om," Charlie said, and I quickly untangled the ornaments, ignoring their bickering over who got which one.

"Of course, Patrick Sullivan," Emma said. "Davis's friend. I'm Emma Crof— But of course you know that."

"Emma," Dad said, still looking a bit put out by Emma's failure to remember him. "I always thought it was such a beautiful name."

"It's very common in England," Emma said dismissively. "A very common English name."

She looked far from common, though, standing perfectly straight, her eyes jumping with something I'd have sworn was excitement, like a well-bred hostess greeting guests at her first dinner party, anxious and thrilled.

"Well, it's certainly nice to see you again," Dad said.

"Yes, Patrick," Emma said. "It certainly is."

I sat on the couch, and Dac sat beside me, his arm stretched comfortably across the back so that each time I leaned into the cushion, my hair or my neck brushed the sleeve of his shirt. Though we all talked together, the conversation centered around Dad and Emma, who were asking each other question after question, raising their voices over the music and the clamor of the boys. I glanced at Joan, wondering if she felt upstaged. She leaned back against Kirby, and he fingered her hair.

"Davis and I spent every waking minute together during the summers, when I came to visit my grandparents," Dad said, apparently for my benefit. "Even some nonwaking ones. He and I used to sleep out under the stars together, in an open-air fort we built in the woods." And then to Emma, "Is he—?"

Emma said Davis had passed away three years ago.

"I see," Dad said. "That long ago?" As if the years somehow made a difference to him. Perhaps he was surprised he hadn't heard of his childhood buddy's death, or maybe he was wondering how long it would take him to adjust to being without Mom. His reaction to Mom's illness had surprised me. I'd assumed he'd stopped loving her years before, sometime before she'd tried to kill herself, I'd thought in retrospect. But when we found out she was dying, he dropped everything to be with her.

Emma asked Dad about himself, and he talked about his work—how much he enjoyed taking pictures and how retirement wouldn't be his cup of tea—all the while full of his old energy, laughing and telling stories, jumping up to refill our glasses or our plates, or to help the boys put ornaments on the higher branches of the tree.

"Nelly told me you retired when Elizabeth took ill," Emma said.

Dad pulled absently at his gray hair, nodding slightly. "I've been back at it for a couple years now, though. Getting along with my life."

"Getting along," Emma said. "Yes. That's what we do, isn't it? I know when Davis died, I—" She looked at the rest of us suddenly, as if we'd just arrived. She smiled kindly at me, meaning to include me, include my loss of Wes.

"I suppose I threw myself into my riding," she said.

It wasn't what she'd started to say, but no one seemed to notice. No one but me and perhaps Willa, though Willa looked not so much puzzled or curious as simply blank. And then already the subject had changed: Dac was offering to re-fill eggnog glasses and Dad stood to help him while Emma asked to have a closer look at an ornament Ned had chosen. Willa's eyes, a little melancholy now, almost sad, flickered be-tween Emma and her boys.

We all admired the boys' tree, heavily decorated on the bot-tom and with fewer and fewer ornaments higher up. Kirby said it reminded him of those their children had decorated in their early years, and that led to a story about the year they'd replaced the candles on their tree with electric lights. It seemed everyone had a story to tell from some past Christmas then, and they were all laughing, relaxed. I laughed, too, con-scious of Dac's arm behind me. Not around me. Just there, resting on the back of the couch.

I got up on the excuse of getting more eggnog from the kitchen. My camera sat on the kitchen counter, where I'd put it earlier, thinking I might take a shot or two this afternoon. I took the eggnog, left the camera behind.

When I came back, Dac was lifting the boys one by one so they could trim the higher branches of the tree, the jingling of their new Santa hats adding to the music from the stereo. I got up several more times, for more eggnog or sandwiches or to change the music, each time thinking I should bring out the camera, each time failing to do so. Finally, I moved the cookie plate over to the coffee table in front of us and we ate cookies and drank eggnog until there was nothing left but the dregs in our glasses and the crumbs on the plates. And then the boys had finished with the ornaments and Charlie was pulling the star from its box.

He stared at it for a long moment, at the clear plastic, at the dull, unlit bulbs, his face clouding over as Matt and Craig evaporated into silent shadows beside Willa, the tension so suddenly thick even they sensed it.

Charlie looked up at Ned and handed the star out to him. "You can do the star, Neddy," he said quietly. "You're taller."

Ned shrank back from Charlie as if the star in his hand were made of something far more noxious or repulsive than mere plastic. His face screwed up not in sorrow, like Charlie's, but in anger, and he raised his hand and, before I could stop him, whacked the star out of Charlie's hands with a single closed-fist blow. The plastic hit the edge of the table with a crack, then tumbled onto the rug.

I was already there, beside them, picking up the star and cooing to them, cooing especially to Charlie, whose eyes were flooding with tears. "We can do the star together," I said. "We'll all do the star together."

I tried to straighten the cracked tip, where the star had hit the table. The plastic broke through entirely, leaving the tip dangling by a wire running to its light.

"You broke it, Mommy!" Ned said, tears welling up in his eyes now too. "You broke it!"

It was all I could do to keep hold of my own emotions as I carefully set the plastic tip back into place.

"It's fine, Neddy," I said. "It's fine, see. I'll glue it back later, but let's put it on the tree now, okay?"

I wiped Charlie's face with my sleeve, then had him sit on my left shoulder. I thought I could stand under his weight, but looking at Ned, I knew there was no way to pull this off.

And then Dac was there, standing behind me. "You look like you could use some help," he said, his voice not quite even. "I see how this works." He lifted Charlie from my shoulder and resettled him with his legs straddling the back of my neck. "That's better, isn't it?" he said to Charlie.

He gave me a hand so I could stand up under Charlie's weight, then hoisted Ned onto his own shoulders. "Now where's that beautiful star?" he said.

I handed the star with its broken tip up to Ned with a gentle, "Here you go, Neddy," keeping his eye as he wiped his nose on his sleeve, then held the star out to Charlie. Together, they set it in place.

Dad plugged in the lights and we all looked silently at the tree.

We were saved by Willa, who began to applaud wildly. Dad and Emma joined in, Dad standing, Willa standing, Dad helping Emma to her feet as Kirby and Joan, too, stood. Dac and I lowered the boys back to the ground, and then everyone was clapping and the boys were lining up in front of the tree as if for a stage call, even Ned and Charlie smiling reluctantly at the applause. And as they took their bows, sweeping toward the floor, I started clapping, too. I clapped and clapped, smacking my palms together so hard they began to hurt, but afraid to let the ovation come to an end, afraid to let go of the pain, the balm for my grief, my guilt.

We said our good-byes in the dim light of the front porch that evening, the boys wrestling together with Boomer on the winter-brown lawn. I stood with Dac, who was thanking me overly politely for inviting him, the uncertain look on his face leaving me thinking he wanted to say more. But everyone was there, outside in the cold winter air with us: Dad, Kirby and Joan, Willa and Emma. Emma was looking our way too—had she been watching us?—though when I looked up she turned and said something to Dad.

I offered my hand to Dac, thanking him for coming in as overly polite a tone as he had thanked me for inviting him. He looked at my extended hand, his expression a little bewildered, uncertain, disturbed. Disturbed like he'd said he thought everyone was. Mai had said that, he'd said. But who was Mai?

"I'll see you in the morning?" he said, taking my hand finally, shaking it awkwardly. "When I move my horses into your barn?"

I looked down to Ned and Charlie, Ned wrestling a little too aggressively, Charlie looking ready to retreat to his bed. Their Santa hats lay abandoned on the ground and, like me, they hadn't put on their coats.

"We'll probably be out Christmas shopping," I said.

"I'll be here early. Hours before the stores open."

I tried to extract my hand from his, but he tightened his grip and pulled me closer.

"Come with me to the Hunt Ball?" he said.

"The Hunt Ball?" I'd received my own invitation, the gold ink on the heavy ecru envelope reading "Mrs. Wesley Grace," as if nothing were left of the Nelly Sullivan I had been.

"The Saturday before Christmas," Dac said. "It'll be—"

"I can't," I blurted, not loudly I didn't think, but still everyone turned in our direction, even the boys. They looked up from the lawn and there I was, standing with my hand in Dac's. They stared at us, at Dac and me standing too close together, and their young, vulnerable faces looked so like their father's.

"I can't, Dac," I whispered, pulling my hand from his and wrapping my arms around myself, shivering in the cold night air.

Dac stared at me for a moment. "I—"

"I can't." I shook my head. "No."

He turned away from me then. He turned away from me without another word and headed down the steps.

At the walkway, he looked back up to the porch, to Emma, realizing she might need help. Dad was already beside her, though, guiding her crutches and holding her arm, ready in case she stumbled. At the bottom, he put his hands on her shoulders. "I'd like to see you again," he said.

"Yes," Emma said.

But they didn't set a date. They just left it at that, we'll get together, as if it would just happen, magically, by itself.

12

I was already up, showered and dressed the next morning, standing at the kitchen window watching the bridge for Dac when his truck and the first trailer of horses pulled into the drive. Dad and the boys were still sleeping, as I'd hoped they would be. I set my coffee on the counter, shrugged on my coat and headed out the door, down toward the barn, rehearsing what I'd worked out to say the night before. I appreciated his invitation, I'd tell him. And I hadn't meant to be rude last night. He'd just caught me by surprise. But the truth was I didn't want a relationship. Not right now. I needed to be on my own for a while. He could understand that, couldn't he? And besides, I couldn't possibly go to the Hunt Ball with him or with anyone. Not yet. Not with the boys. They weren't ready for that; they weren't ready for anyone to replace their dad.

Or maybe I could just say that, about the boys. I could just say I couldn't go with him because of the boys. They weren't ready to see me dating yet, not even a casual date. Dac probably wasn't even thinking about a relationship, anyway. It wasn't like he'd given me any hint that he was interested in me—he'd never even tried to kiss me, not more than a friendly kiss. He was nice to me and he took me riding as a kind of quid pro quo for renting him my barn. That's probably why he'd invited me to the ball. There hadn't, after all, been any hint of his wanting to be anything more than friends.

I paused outside the barn. Inside, a stall door slammed, a horse snorted, a door slammed again. Dac was already inside.

I needed to be on my own, I reminded myself again. I had enough to worry about already: taking care of the boys and working on my photography, for starters, figuring out whether I could do anything with my photographs. And Wesley, like Dac, had been supportive of my photography; he'd wanted a career for me, too, before we'd had Ned and Charlie and they'd needed a full-time parent, or Wes had thought they did, and maybe I had too.

But I didn't have to get into any of that. I'd just tell Dac that of course I couldn't go to the Hunt Ball with him, not so soon after Wesley's death, not with the boys.

A second truck and trailer pulled onto the road and headed toward the bridge—they'd be here in a minute.

I opened the barn door. "Dac?"

"Nelly!" A woman's voice, Emma's voice.

She hobbled out from one of the stalls on her crutches, wiping her hands on her heavy barn jacket, mud thick on her one paddock boot. "I didn't think you'd be up this early. Did the noise wake you?"

"No, no, Emma, I—I thought you were Dac."

She reached up and adjusted her hat, the leather one that had been Davis's. "Dac is supervising the loading of the horses at our barn—he knows which ones he's moving. I'm settling them in over here. Let me get the others started—we've got everyone working today; it's a big job, moving horses like this—and we can have a cup of coffee together. You have coffee made?"

"Sure," I said. "I mean . . . Sure. But I'll make some fresh."

Two men were lowering the ramp of the second trailer when Emma and I, deciding against the stale coffee in my kitchen after all, settled onto the porch steps a few minutes later. The men talked together for a minute and then one headed for the barn and the other grabbed a lead line from the back of the pickup and climbed the ramp.

"I'm glad to be able to talk with you this morning," Emma said. "I wanted to apologize for Dac, for his behavior last night, inviting you to the Hunt Ball."

I shifted uncomfortably, the cement porch cold through my jeans.

"He was only trying to be kind, of course, trying to include you," she continued. "Plenty of people go to the Hunt Ball without dates, but you wouldn't know that, would you? So Dac thought you might be more comfortable going with him. As friends, of course."

"As friends," I said. "Of course."

"He wouldn't dream of anything more than that, I assure you. Not with you so recently widowed. I'm afraid he didn't consider how impossible it would be for you to go with any date, even just as a friend. But of course you couldn't, could you? Not with your little sons still so close to their daddy's death."

At the trailer, the man with the lead line attached it to a chestnut horse, then tried to coax the horse down the ramp. The horse balked, snorting, and the man stopped, patted its neck, and cooed to it.

"No," I said. "I couldn't, of course not. It would be too soon."

"Yes, of course it would," Emma said. "Of course it's too soon."

I wrapped my arms across my front, tucked in my hands, the chill morning air cutting through my gloves.

"I didn't mean to be rude to him," I said.

"You weren't rude, Nelly." Emma smiled sympathetically. "You weren't rude at all. And you needn't worry about Dac, about his feelings. His invitation was only a gesture of friendship." She nodded twice, sharply, the oversized hat slipping slightly with the gesture. "You needn't worry about him. You needn't say another word."

"It was nice of him to offer," I said. "Nice of him to include me."

"It gets him into trouble sometimes, his kindness. You can see how a young woman might think he means more than he does, might read something into his kindness that isn't there."

I hunched forward against the cold. "I could see that," I said. "Though I'd never thought of it until you—"

"No, of course you didn't, Nelly. Of course you didn't. You're much more sensible than that."

Down at the trailer, the horse backed all the way up the ramp, into the trailer. The man holding the lead line tossed it down, exasperated, slammed the trailer door shut, and stomped off toward the barn.

13

When Willa brought the boys home from school the next Wednesday—her day for carpool—she brought something with her, an envelope. "From Emma," she said. "Your tickets."

I handed her the cup of coffee I'd brought out to greet her. "Tickets?" I said, taking the envelope and looking at it curiously as we made our way to the back patio to find the boys already kicking a soccer ball around on the lawn.

"I thought it was your idea, yours and your dad's," she said. "The play, I mean."

"Tickets to a *play*?"

Dad was downtown, visiting an old newspaper friend that afternoon, but I was quite sure it would never have been his idea to go see even a movie, much less a play. Willa was explaining without hesitation, though, that "Mrs. Crofton" had called her the day before, saying Dad and I and she and Dac and Kirby and Joan were going to see some Wendy Wasserstein play that next Tuesday, and would she like to come?

I started to protest that I didn't even have a baby-sitter, but Willa, holding her coffee in front of herself as she rested her forearms against the fence, had already moved on, was already telling me about "girls' night in" the following Wednesday, naming a dozen women who got together once a month, taking turns hosting, including Joan.

"Not Emma?" I said.

Willa raised an eyebrow. "That would be 'Mrs. Crofton' to the rest of us? No, she's not here Wednesdays, anyway."

"Not here?" I said, doubting somehow whether Willa would have included her in girls' night in even if she were. "Where does Emma go on Wednesdays?"

Willa shrugged. "She's never offered details."

I took a sip of my coffee, wrapped my hands around the warm cup. We stood watching, listening, as Ned trash-talked Matt from the goal. Matt shot, and scored.

"Hey, Willa," I said, "you have any idea who Mai is?"

Willa's eyebrow arched sharply. "Dac's Mai? Emma told you about her?"

Her.

I said Dac had mentioned her when he took me riding.

"Did he?" She frowned curiously. "Now that *is* interesting. What did he say? Has he heard from her?"

I took another sip of my coffee, watched Charlie fetch the soccer ball from inside the paddock fence, tried to seem nonchalant, as if this were no more than gossip to me. Dac had just mentioned her in passing, I said, nothing specific. "So who is she?" I said.

"Why don't you ask your buddy *Emma*?" Willa's voice thick with sarcasm now—not uncharacteristic for her, but it caught me off guard. "Maybe she'll give *you* the details," she said.

"Emma?" I said. "I should ask Emma?"

Willa looked out at the boys playing soccer, Ned shooting at the goal, missing widely.

"No. I'm sorry." She peered into her coffee cup, then took

a big swallow. "I'm sorry. Don't ask her. Really. I was just being flip. Mean-spirited."

When she looked up, there was an apologetic sadness in her face.

"So who is she, Willa?"

She ran her fingers through her hair, not mussing it as she usually did, but in a wearier gesture. "Take a wild guess."

"His Vietnamese lover?"

"You're a smart one, Nelly Grace. Not just any lover, though. He—"

I waited for Willa to continue, but she shook her head. "I'm sorry, I shouldn't have said anything."

"Willa!"

She pushed back from the fence and turned and went inside. I found her standing at my kitchen sink, pouring the rest of her coffee down the drain. She did not turn when I came in.

"Willa?"

"I can't tell you, Nelly," she said. "Really I can't. It's one thing to gossip a little bit. You know I'll give you the gossip. But I can't talk about this. Really, I can't."

14

Eight of us went to the play together that Tuesday before the Hunt Ball: Emma, Dac, Kirby and Joan, Willa and her date, whose name was Paul, and my father and me. We met at Pastori's, an Italian restaurant in a charming little brownstone-laden neighborhood that had retained its residential roots. Inside the tiny restaurant, red-checked tablecloths covered small square tables, red carnations stood in white porcelain bud vases, and the smell of garlic and butter wafted through the air. Mr. Pastori, a stout, cabbage-headed man, greeted us with Italian enthusiasm, hugging first Willa, then Paul, Kirby, Joan, Dac, and, though I'd never met him before, me. He shook my father's hand, saying, "You are the photographer, yes?" then took both of Emma's hands in his own, still speaking to my father, saying, "Mrs. Crofton, she tells me you are the special guest."

At the table—a grouping of three tables pushed together in the center of the room—Dac pulled out a chair for me. "How about another ride some morning this week?" he said. "Quid pro quo, since your dad is taking my mother."

"Taking her riding?"

Dac laughed. "Christmas shopping. I'm not much of a shopper."

I glanced at my father, already laughing at something Emma was saying. He wasn't much of a shopper himself.

"Of course," I said. "Christmas shopping."

Mr. Pastori handed us our menus and Dac began to rave about the zuppa pavese, a sort of fried-egg breakfast in a soup, and the osso bucco, a veal dish that Kirby ordered. And then somehow we were all quiet, focused on Kirby. He'd caught our attention. He leaned forward, toward the table, his bushy eyebrows squirreling together and his dark eyes bearing down on Paul. "So, Paul," he said to Willa's date, "Willa tells us you're a political consultant of some sort."

The interrogation had begun.

Kirby dominated the conversation, asking question after question of Paul, clearly trying to hoe up character flaws Willa might have missed. "Exactly what is a Libertarian, anyway?" "Your marriage lasted how long? Just two years?" "And your family, they are . . . ?" Kirby and Joan had been neighbors of Willa's for a long time, and they could still be seen shaking their heads over Willa and Michael's separation, clinging to the belief that Willa should "come to her senses, if not for herself, then for the sake of those sweet boys." Now Kirby was bordering on being rude to Paul, though not quite crossing the line. You could imagine Paul sitting at a bare metal table, bright light in his eyes, a tape recorder rolling and a cop with his sleeves rolled up hovering over him.

For everyone else, though, the conversation was rather amusing. Dad and Emma kept exchanging looks, and Joan's eyes glimmered, and even Willa kept suppressing a smile that tried to creep across her lips. Dac, who'd barely touched his meal—a black pasta dish—seemed to be taking a particularly keen interest, and I found myself wondering if he had some greater interest in Willa than I'd fathomed before.

Kirby continued to grill Paul as he scooped up the marrow from his veal bone with a little marrow spoon. He sat back only as the entrée was being cleared, and began to speak of world politics, a topic with which Paul would be comfortable, given his job.

Willa patted Paul's hand.

When the dessert menus came, no one else opened theirs, and I was resigned to skipping when the waiter came and Kirby ordered a casatta cake for the table, saying, "You must have the casatta here, Nelly." I closed my menu and handed it to the waiter, and as Mr. Pastori poured coffee, Kirby turned the conversation to whether the president would send more troops to Eastern Europe. The discussion became spirited, perhaps louder than appropriate in the small dining room, but we were enjoying ourselves. He wouldn't do it, Kirby said. It was like Vietnam. We didn't really understand what was going on but, like Vietnam, their problems couldn't be solved by U.S. troops.

Paul agreed that we didn't belong in Vietnam, it wasn't a war worth fighting, but he insisted it *was* winnable. "All this nonsense about it being different from other wars? All war is hell and Vietnam was no exception. The only difference was that the patriotic folks at home had to face Vietnam on the evening news. That and the general level of incompetence our troops displayed, killing civilians left and right."

Emma, startled, looked to Dac, who shifted forward beside me, his cake untouched.

"We're not talking about Vietnam—" Emma began, but Paul didn't hear her.

"If we were going to be there at all, we should have moved in early, with a real presence," he said, his voice filling with the passion of someone enjoying a healthy debate. "We should

have bombed the Ho Chi Minh Trail to smithereens. Cut off
the supplies running through Laos to the VC fighting in the
south. Isolated the guerrillas. If we'd had some courage, some
guts, we could have controlled the situation. We just wouldn't
step up to the plate."

By the time he'd finished, we were all focused on Dac. His
spoon, still full of sugar, hung suspended over his cup.

"Were you there?" he asked, his face moving almost imper-
ceptibly closer to Paul.

My father set a hand on Emma's arm, the gesture—the
broad hand on the bony forearm—sending an odd ache up
my neck.

"In Vietnam?" Paul moved his chair back slightly, leaned
away from the table, crossed his arms and his legs. He looked
around at the rest of us.

"Were—you—in—Vietnam?" Dac said each word slowly
and distinctly, as if he were talking to someone who spoke little English. "Did you fight there?"

Our entire table fell silent, and the conversation throughout the small restaurant died away as well, leaving only the
sound of something sizzling in the kitchen. My father sat
looking from Dac to Emma, who looked flustered, upset,
while Willa sat uncharacteristically mute, glaring not at Dac
or Paul but at Emma, as if this were somehow all Emma's
fault.

Paul coughed. His back straightened. "No." He returned
Dac's stare. "No, I wasn't in Vietnam."

"Then you don't know what the fuck you're talking
about," Dac said in a low voice.

Paul sat perfectly still, looking frozen and rather horrible,
like the casts of those people preserved by the lava flow in
Pompeii.

Behind me, a lady whispered, "What did he say?"

Mr. Pastori blundered boldly into the silence, holding up a small bottle of wine. "My dear Mrs. Crofton. I must have your excellent opinion, Mrs. Crofton." He pulled the cork smoothly from the bottle as conversation exploded at the tables around us, champagne bubbles flowing over the top. "You are ready for dessert wine, no? You must taste this for me." He set a glass in front of her and poured while our waiter distributed glasses. "It is from the town of my family. The winegrower, he is the son of my father's good friend, I played with the daughter when I was in diapers. I should have stayed and played when my family moved to this country; the daughter is now a beautiful woman, *bella, bella.*" He kissed his lips to his fingers. "And wealthy too!" He finished pouring as he prattled on. "Drink now! You like? Yes? *Presto! Presto!* It is time for your theater."

At the theater, we did our best until the lights dimmed, reading interesting tidbits from the actors' biographies in the program and talking about the reviews we'd read. Fortunately, the play was unbearably funny, and by intermission even Dac and Paul were laughing. Still, everyone claimed a need to use the restroom or a killing thirst. Only Emma and I remained seated, Emma straight-backed, saying she and her crutches were staying comfortably where they were.

"Emma," I said after everyone else had scattered. "Is Dac—?"

Sounds of the audience drifted around us: light conversation, a lady's high-pitched titter, a purse snapping shut.

"Dac had a bit of a hard time overseas," she said, her posture stiff, her gaze fixed on the stage. "Killing people doesn't suit everyone, after all."

The next afternoon, Willa sat at my kitchen table bemoaning the perils of being on the organizing committee for the Hunt

Ball, a thankless task. The photographer she'd hired had come down with the chicken pox. "Where am I going to find a photographer on no notice?" she said. "And at Christmastime, no less."

The ball was Saturday night, just three days away. I still had the invitation, an artfully printed green-and-gold thing that opened from the center outward, like double doors, and was sealed with a pretty gold sticker embossed with the words GREENFIELD HUNT. Inside: "The pleasure of your company is requested . . ." and, discreetly at the bottom, "White Tie or Scarlet and Ballgowns" and the price. It reminded me of the first formal invitation Wes and I had received after we were married, when I'd been thrilled to be Mrs. Wesley Grace, when my biggest concern had been how to fill out the response card, whether to conform to the dangling capital *m* before the space for our names, to give Wesley the title of Mr. rather than Dr., or to put myself first to employ the *m:* Mrs. and Dr. Wesley Grace—or better: Mrs. and Dr. Nelly Grace. I'd finally crossed out the *m* and inked in *Dr. and Mrs. Wesley Grace,* relieving myself, at least, of the need to conform my own upright, rounded penmanship to the sleek, perfect slant of the *m*.

"I could help photograph, Willa," I offered impulsively. And then thought again of the invitation, *Mrs. Wesley Grace,* thought of Dac asking me to go with him, Ned and Charlie looking up at me standing on the porch with him, holding hands.

Before I could retract the offer, though, Willa was saying, "Would you, Nelly? That's not why I came down here, I swear. Okay, well, maybe the thought had crossed my mind. But would you? Jenny—she works for Joan, you've met her— she can baby-sit for you, I've already checked. And I've got a gown that would be perfect for you."

I laughed. "Looks like you've thought of everything. Well, maybe my father would chip in too."

I stood, picked up two empty glasses left over from breakfast, took them to the sink, immediately regretting my words, the possibility that my own photographs might end up in an album with his, side by side for the world to compare.

"I heard Mrs. Crofton was bringing your father!" Willa said.

I turned to look at her, felt myself gawking. "To the Hunt Ball?"

"They're becoming an item, it seems. Lips are flapping, flapping, flapping! I think it's great. The romance, I mean. Not the gossip. Who'd think you'd find true love in your seventies?"

I turned back to the sink, carefully rinsed the glasses, opened the dishwasher, set them in, closed it again.

"I'm sure they're just friends," I said.

Though they'd obviously planned the theater outing together—a play?—and he was taking her shopping the next morning. Shopping! Expecting not to return until evening, he'd said, so we shouldn't wait dinner for him.

"I'm sure Dad's just enjoying the company of someone his own age," I said, returning to the table now, facing Willa with a steady gaze.

Willa tried to suppress a grin.

"And Emma too," I said. "That's all it is."

Willa nodded seriously, still working her lips for a moment before she gave up the battle and grinned broadly.

"Look closer," she said.

15

I slipped into Emma's barn quietly that Thursday to find Dac alone, brushing Harry's back in long, smooth strokes. I'd considered calling to cancel our ride in the wake of the pretheater dinner, but it was a more than perfect day, the air full of spring though it was not yet Christmas, and a part of me did want to go anyway, a part of me was intrigued. I said good morning, and he looked up and smiled and said, "Hey there!" in a voice that belonged to the Dac who knew how to handle snapping turtles, the Dac who raced horses for a living, the Dac who could use a star-effect filter to create shooting rays from a setting sun.

"Want me to help?" I asked, silently hoping he'd say no lest I leave the girth too loose and slide off the horse midride.

He grinned. "Just enjoy the luxury of a valet ride one more time. Next time, I'll put you to work."

I smiled. "I can't wait to ride."

He swung the saddle and blanket onto Harry's back in one easy motion. "It's therapeutic, isn't it? A long peaceful trail ride, when you need a little serenity, or a full-out, fence-jumping romp. Either way."

I said I didn't know about fence-jumping romps, but it

seemed to me that riding the hunt would be about as exciting as anything—any everyday type of thing, anyway.

"Just about," he said.

"You have some more exciting hobby?" I teased.

He studied me for a minute in a friendly, curious way, then
reached under Harry's belly and caught the girth, slid the
leather ends through the buckles of the saddle. "Flying," he
said. "Flying is more exciting."

"Airplanes, you mean?"

"No, like Peter Pan." He laughed. "Let me dust you with
pixie dust and off we'll go!"

"Hang gliders," I said, just to make the point. "Helicopters.
Rockets."

"Okay, right," he conceded.

"You fly the space shuttle, I guess!"

He grinned. "Okay. Uncle. I give."

"Seriously," I said. "You fly airplanes?"

He pulled the girth tighter. "I don't anymore, actually." He
readjusted the buckle, not looking at me. "I flew jets in the
service."

There it was.

"Hmm . . . ," I said.

He smiled sadly. "You should have been a psychiatrist," he
said. "You've got the 'hmm' down pat."

"Hmm . . ." No idea where this was going. No idea how to
derail it.

Dac shook his head. "It's like being an alcoholic—you're
recovering the rest of your life, but you never really recover,
you just learn to take each day as it comes." A long pause, the
silence filled only with the smell of hay and manure, the swish
of a horse's tail, a dog barking in the distance, not Boomer's
bark. "Yes, I flew in Vietnam, while I was there."

The psychiatrist would have said, "Tell me about it." I

might have said it, too, if I'd had any idea whether he would laugh or get mad.

"The planes were a dream—fast and tight," he said, his voice lacking the enthusiasm suggested by the words.

"But? . . ."

"But it was not real life up there. You were totally out of touch." He flattened the saddle flap over the buckles, ran the stirrups down.

"Let's see your arm." He adjusted the stirrups to the length of my arm, then disappeared into the tack room.

I stood there, holding Harry's reins, remembering a picture my father had taken—dead soldiers, American boys, entwined in trampled elephant grass—until Dac returned, carrying the tack for Flashy. He set the saddle down on the ground and, bridle in hand, approached the horse.

"How long were you in Vietnam?" I asked.

He turned his back to me and slipped the bit into Flashy's mouth. "Too long for me, it turns out," he said. "But I didn't realize it until I came back." He checked the tightness of the bridle with his fingers, then brought the reins over Flashy's head. He patted the horse's neck.

"My father spent time there, taking pictures," I said.

Dad, now out shopping with Emma. I couldn't imagine Dad at a mall.

"He said it was as bad as life gets, only worse," I said.

Dac reached down to pick up the saddle. "For the grunts— the ground troops—I think it must have been." He swung the saddle, blanket, and pad onto Flashy. The pad flew loose and he stooped to pick it up. "Flying was a pretty cushy job, as those jobs went. We were scared shitless in the air, sure. Every cell in your body on full alert. But the rest of the time wasn't so bad if you could forget the fear in the air."

He tucked the pad under the saddle, straightening the blanket first. "That's not even right, really." His fingers worried over the braid of the reins. "There was a thrill in it too. A sick sort of thing in retrospect, but not then." His fingers stopped moving, though his boot scuffed lightly at the dirt floor of the barn. "Then, you thought you were the best there was, you were the world's greatest guys doing the world's most noble thing. In a way the fear just sharpened the thrill."

He reached underneath the horse's belly for the girth, fastened it to the saddle. He moved slowly, deliberately, watching his hands as he worked. He tightened the girth, pulling up hard, adjusting the buckle.

"Then why were you there too long?" I said.

He slid two fingers under the girth and left them there, standing stock-still now, the set of his shoulders like that of the 1930s farmer in Lange's *Back,* a dead-broke man pretending an interest in buying his neighbor's land. "I was coming home," he said. "I'd beat the odds and I was done. I'd thought about staying for another tour of duty, but Nixon was moving us out pretty quickly. June 1972."

Flashy's tail swished at a black fly. Dac brushed it away with a flip of his hand.

"In the airport in Seattle, I picked up this copy of *Life* magazine and started paging through it and . . . and there was this big photo spread, this little girl running naked and . . ."

In the distance, a train whistle sounded.

"I know the shot," I said quietly. Nick Ut. It won him the Pulitzer.

"And this mother in the photo beside it, her little boy, he's got . . . burnt fragments of his clothes are . . ." He took a deep, steadying breath. "The mother is running to save him, and the kid is already dead. Napalm." He ran his fingers through his hair and rubbed the back of his neck, his fingers sliding underneath his collar, pressing on the pale, vulnerable skin. "And me, I'm just up there in the air, having the fucking time of my life."

He sighed. "The drop was a mistake, of course. 'Collateral damage.' A big fucking mistake."

He pulled the stirrup down, the metal scraping against the leather, smacking at the end.

"You were at war," I said. "You did what you were supposed to do."

He fingered the cold metal of the stirrup. "I get to Baltimore, and I'm sobbing like a baby, right there at the gate, and Mother is holding me and Dad's just standing there like he wants to be anywhere else." He began to stroke Flashy's neck again. "No one ever even asked me what had happened, not even later. I wrote Mai about it once, but . . ."

He reached down again to check the tightness of the girth, as if he hadn't already done it.

"Mai," I repeated.

He turned and looked at me then, smiling a sad-eyed, close-lipped smile. "Let me give you a leg up," he said.

He cupped his hands, and I stepped into them, swung up onto the horse. "You didn't make the decisions," I said gently. "You just did your job."

"That's what my psychiatrist said: 'The human mind's ability to deal with what it's dealt is remarkable.' She said she had a patient who shot a gook—his word—then slept within spitting distance of the body, thinking about his girlfriend back home and masturbating, not giving the dead guy a second thought. It didn't trouble him at all at the time. That was normal, she said. But later, when this guy gets home, he can't even get it—" He pulled on his jacket and gloves. "He can't do anything with his girlfriend, and he ends up putting a gun to his head."

I sank my heels deep into the stirrups. "What did your psychiatrist think of that?" I said softly.

He swung up onto Flashy. "Not good," he said. "No fucking good."

We rode slowly at first, listening to the clip-clop of the horses' walk. As we neared the path into the woods, Dac moved into an easy trot and I followed, concentrating on squeezing and releasing my legs as I posted, keeping my heels down in the stirrups so I wouldn't lose my balance. When Dac abruptly launched into a full-speed gallop, I didn't hesitate. I tapped Harry lightly with my left heel, and he moved easily into the more fluid motion of the canter. I was beginning to get cocky, feeling the wind on my face and the horse underneath me, when the sole of my boot began to slip.

I looked down, my second mistake.

When I looked up again, I panicked. A solid coop loomed at the entrance to the woods, only yards away. I flailed the reins wildly, caught between trying to stop Harry before we got to the coop—too late—and trying to get into jumping position for a far higher jump than I'd ever tried.

Harry stopped right at the coop, refusing the jump.

I pitched forward, feeling as if I were moving in slow motion, trying to regain my balance even as I was hitting the wood.

I was still lying where I'd landed, among the thorny twigs of a multiflora bush growing over the coop, when Dac got back to me.

"Oh shit, oh shit. I'm sorry," he said as, in an instant, he was off Flashy and putting his hands on my cheeks. "Are you okay? Oh shit, I am so sorry." Speaking so quickly I couldn't get in an answer.

"Oh shit," he said again.

"I think I'm okay," I managed, though the leg that struck the coop first hurt like hell. "Really, I think I'm fine." Feeling the tears well up, blinking them back. "A little bruised, maybe, but then I bruise just watching other people fall."

"Stand carefully," he said, offering me a hand. "I shouldn't have taken off like that. I could have gotten you killed."

"I didn't have to follow you."

He had me put weight carefully on the leg that had hit the coop first, feeling the ankle, the knee. I said I thought I just bruised the hip. "Maybe this will teach me to keep my heels down," I said.

"You're not light-headed? You've got a nasty scrape on your forehead, just above your eye." He wiped a tear from my cheek as if I were a child with a scratch.

Gently, he undid my chin strap and removed my riding cap, then moved my hair, sweaty wet from riding, away from my forehead. His eyes were soft and full of concern and I could see, this closely, that their green color was subtly flecked with gold. He touched my forehead, then looked at his fingers, rubbed them together, showed me the little bit of blood on his hand.

"You're hurt."

"I'm okay. It's just a scrape from the thorns."

He lifted my chin to turn my face up to his, the way Wesley used to, and I knew he was going to kiss me this time. I closed my eyes as his lips moved closer to mine, and we kissed, gently at first, and then harder, unrestrained. I'd forgotten how good it felt to kiss.

The next morning, after I'd dropped the boys at school—the last day before winter break and they got out at noon, so I didn't have much time—I drove downtown to the Enoch Pratt Library, only to find the doors locked; it didn't open until ten o'clock. But it was a good morning for taking pictures—a soft haze muted the slanting morning light—and I had my camera with me, and there was a homeless woman sleeping in an entryway, one arm crooked loosely around the wheel of a shopping cart full of such a sad collection of things that I knew I ought to photograph her. By the time I got my camera from the car, though, the woman was awake, or something like awake. She hadn't moved under her rough, army-green blanket, but her eyes fluttered open, looking not so much at me as into me. I hesitated even after her lids had settled back together again. I'd never photographed a stranger, not one who wasn't a politician or a costumed character on a parade float, someone expecting to be photographed or too wrapped up in what he or she was doing to care.

I walked on past her, stopping up the sidewalk a ways and focusing on the library building, seeing suddenly how invasive a photographer could be. How did Lange and Frank and others like them—my father—make careers out of taking such photographs? Were they aware of how intrusive their lenses were? Did they just not care? Did they justify themselves as promoting a greater good, or were they simply in cold pursuit of memorable shots?

I walked by the woman two more times, screwing up my courage at each pass. She was sleeping again, I told myself. She wouldn't even know.

Still, when I did finally take her picture, I didn't choose the best angle, frame the shot well, adjust the f-stop or even focus, not really. I pushed the shutter release and hurried on.

Inside the library, I went directly to the reference room and asked for the back issues of *Life* for June 1972. I knew the photographs Dac had spoken of, but still I wanted to see them again.

The librarian ordered the magazine from storage, and when a thick hardbound volume came up, she set it on a table and nodded at me. "Yours," she said, and I took the book and sat with my back to the room and its two other occupants, flipping through the pages until I found the June issue, the two-page photo spread, "The Beat of Life."

The larger photo, the Nick Ut, never failed to stop my breath. There are other people on the road—adults, soldiers, even other Vietnamese children—but all anyone sees is that girl. I studied her, thinking I'd never be able to take that shot; if I wasn't too overwhelmed to move, I wouldn't give a thought to the camera before I tried to help her. It's supposed to become reflex, though, taking the photograph. A professional has to believe the best way he can help that child or other children like her is to take the picture.

Maybe someday, I thought, I'll be able to take a shot like that.

To the left of the Nick Ut was a smaller photo, by David Burnett: a mother running with a child, the child's clothes fused to his skin, the child dead. I shaded my face with my hands though no one could see me where I sat. I shaded my face and I blinked back the tears, wondering if the photo was so powerful because it was less familiar, or because the one thing I couldn't bear would be the loss of one of my sons. I closed my eyes to the photograph, wondering if I really wanted to be a photojournalist, to fill my life with those kinds of pictures, to harden myself to them. You'd have to harden yourself to them, I saw as the shadow of that photo echoed against my closed eyelids. You'd have to harden yourself to survive.

16

When I arrived at the hotel Saturday evening for the Hunt Ball, a doorman in uniform and white gloves scurried around from the passenger side to open my door. Feeling the cold winter evening on my bare arms and back, I looked with some envy at the fur-coated ladies making their way across the lobby inside; I'd done my hair and put on a little makeup and donned my borrowed gown—dressing in the closet for reasons I'm sure I didn't understand myself—but I had no appropriate coat.

"Excuse me, ma'am." The young valet's voice caught my attention. He held up my camera bag. "Did you mean to leave this on the seat? Might be safer in the trunk."

I took it from him and slung it over my shoulder, then opened the bag and pulled out my camera.

Just behind me, Emma and Dad pulled up in her truck—Emma driving, much to my surprise. A second valet, caught on the passenger side as had been the one who took my car, could not get around fast enough to open her door. Emma opened it herself, then hiked up the skirt of her gown—black satin with rows of simple gold piping run horizontally—to reveal one strong but graceful, blue-veined calf, and one white cast. She hopped out of that rusty old truck onto her stocking-clad foot, holding a single black satin pump in her hand. Her wide-brimmed black-and-gold hat—probably the only flowerless, bowless hat arriving at the ball—remained in place on her head, framing her gleeful face.

I didn't hesitate before snapping the shot, and then another as Emma, holding the door handle for balance, reached down to slip the shoe on her good foot. I wasn't self-conscious, wasn't thinking about anything but the shots, until Dad appeared in the viewfinder.

He seemed to be peering into the lens as if uncertain it was really me on the other side of the camera. His gaze dropped then, to my bare shoulders, my dress.

He gave a low whistle, looking up to the lens again. "That's quite red," he said.

"It's Willa's," I said, lowering the camera as if it might somehow hide the fitted bodice, the full skirt, my bare arms, bare shoulders. "She talked me into borrowing it," I said. Talked me into it despite the redness of it, despite the deep V of its back, despite my protests that I wasn't going to the dance, I was just the photographer. "Stunning," she'd said. "Unforgettable."

"You don't like it?" I said.

"No, it's . . . it's striking, really. It's just more attention-getting than I'd have expected."

He made a circular motion with his hand, and I turned one full turn. He made a half-turn motion, and I turned so that my back was to him. He whistled again.

"I guess widows don't stay in mourning as long as they used to," he said.

And I was glad then that my back was to him; his voice had no edge to it, but still I felt as if I'd been slapped.

"Patrick," Emma said in a scolding tone. "Nelly looks lovely, Patrick," she said.

When I turned back to him, finally, she was placing her hand lightly on the arm he offered her, tucking her crutch under her other arm, smiling at him. They had that kind of gawky look of teenagers just beginning to date.

It seemed no time at all since Mom had died.

The lilt of a waltz spilling out into the lobby drew us to the ballroom, where men and women of all ages swirled around the dance floor, the full skirts of the women's dresses swishing in rhythm to the dip of the waltz, light reflecting from their sequins and rhinestones, and from the jewels on their fingers and wrists, ears and throats. The men, dressed in the same white tie and tails my father wore or in unfamiliar red formal jackets, seemed almost an afterthought.

Willa and Paul stood in receiving-line formation with the other members of the planning committee just inside the entrance to the room, Willa in a strapless green satin sheath that showed her slim figure, with an emerald pendant just above the rise of her breasts—not a real emerald, I knew, but only because she'd told me. Her black kid gloves extended above her elbows, highlighting the smooth skin and well-toned muscles of her upper arms and shoulders, a side benefit of her riding. She'd tried to convince me to wear gloves, too, but I'd thought the dress alone was as much style as I could pull off in one night. Around the room, though, half the women were elbow-length or deeper in satin or leather gloves.

The band finished the waltz and moved badly into a rock-and-roll number.

"Versatility," Willa said, taking my hand, "is the most important quality of a band for this crowd. They have to play music to accommodate the tastes of Molly Jackson"—she indicated a teenager beginning to bop to the music in her traditional debutante's white gown (it was an unwritten rule that women wore white gowns only in the year they came out and on their wedding days)—"as well as that of her great-grandmother." Willa nodded to an elegant elderly woman being escorted from the floor. "They don't have to play anything well!"

She kissed me on the cheek, saying in mock Southern drawl, "I'm so glad you came."

At the end of the receiving line I scanned the room for Dac, a wash of some emotion flowing through me as I determined he wasn't there. I didn't want to see him, really. I'd told him I couldn't go and I'd meant I couldn't go *with him* and even Emma had said he understood. Still, I crossed the room, half looking for the anchor of my table and half looking for a buoy to hold on to, as confident as a solo at the senior prom.

I lifted my camera to my face and looked through the viewfinder, breaking the mass of people into two or three faces at a time. The lights were a bit too bright in the room, the band a little too loud.

I spotted my table: Number Seven, a card atop it announced in a fancy script matching the card I'd been given when I arrived, the same script as the invitation, the *Mrs. Wesley Grace*. Joan was just leaving the table—in a bright pink sheath with oversized black polka dots, a 1970s type of thing that should have been awful—escorted by a man I didn't know. The two settled into a fox-trot, Joan's gloved left hand resting on the man's shoulder, his bare right hand on a polka dot at the small of her back.

Dac, I realized with a start, was standing across the table from me, tapping his foot to the music and watching the band. I fell back a step, but the motion caught his eye, and the recognition there flickered into some other expression.

"Nelly," he said.

"Dac."

He looked different in his red jacket, not uncomfortable but vaguely inharmonic, his turbulent blond curls at odds with the stiff white of his wing collar, the perfect knot of his bow tie.

"So you're the photographer tonight," he said.

I nodded. "I guess so."

Across the dance floor, Dad leaned toward Emma, saying something, and she nodded, responding, pointing toward Joan and her partner with the hand that didn't hold her crutch.

I made my way around the table, looking at the neatly arranged place cards: Mrs. Jenkins, et cetera for our usual crowd, Willa and Paul, Kirby and Joan, Dac and me, Mr. Sullivan—my dad—and Emma.

"I'm sorry your mother can't dance tonight," I said to Dac.

He smiled. "Don't count Mother out," he said, nodding to Dad and Emma, now stepping out onto the dance floor, leaving Emma's crutch, abandoned, leaning against a chair. Joan and her partner laughed beside them as Emma began to dance gingerly on her cast.

And it seemed, then, that everyone was dancing but Dac and me, and I wished for a moment that I hadn't come. Remembering my camera, though, I lifted it and focused on one of the couples, a woman in black dancing with a red-jacketed man.

"The red jackets, Dac." I clicked a shot. "What are they?"

"Our pinks?" He pulled on the sleeve of his jacket, which looked older than he did.

I cleared my throat. "Not your *reds*?"

Dac laughed. "They're called 'pinks' after some long-dead tailor. *P-i-n-q-u-e,* I believe, or maybe *P-i-n-k-e.* But they are also called 'scarlets.' They're a hunting tradition."

I looked through the viewfinder out onto the dance floor, to my father's black coat, his shoulder, Emma's head resting there. I couldn't see her face, but his eyes were closed as they danced a simple two-step, all Emma could manage with her cast. I imagined my father humming to the music as they danced. I didn't take the shot.

"Why are the jackets so—?" I groped for a polite way to say *worn-out.*

"Old? Ratty looking?" Dac raised an eyebrow. "Downright frowsy, wouldn't you say?"

"Frowsy!" I laughed despite myself. "Yes, frowsy. That's the word I was looking for."

Dac, too, laughed. "Traditionally, pinks are passed down from one hunter to another. It's a big deal—an honor, really— to receive someone's pinks, tattered as they may be. Some say it's just a way for the old money to identify itself, and maybe it is, but if you look around, you'll see some of the jackets have far outlived the family money."

I looked around, found my father again. He leaned over and whispered·something in Emma's ear. She turned her head up to him.

"Your coat was your father's?" I said, the words catching in my throat.

"My mother gave it to me after he died."

I turned to him, surprised. "Not your father?"

He smiled flatly. "Would you like to dance?" he said.

He took my camera and set it on my chair and gave me his arm despite my protest that I wasn't much of a dancer. I set my left hand on his shoulder, on the seam of his red jacket. He put his right hand firmly on the small of my back and slid his left hand into my right, his skin rough on my ungloved hand.

"This is all right?" Dac asked. "Since you're here, anyway?"

I told myself none of the dancers was paying us any attention, we were just dancing—two friends dancing, no different than Joan and the man I hadn't met—as Dac guided me smoothly, easily, around the floor. With Wesley, I'd always thought consciously of the one-two-three of the beat, but with Dac, I whirled and lilted. We danced properly, plenty of space between us, and he spoke lightly, charmingly, and I smiled involuntarily, Cinderella unexpectedly dancing at the ball.

The band moved into a fox-trot, and other couples snuggled together, heads settling onto shoulders, eyes closing. Dac and I remained with that space between us though—he didn't pull me closer, didn't lean into me or whisper in my ear—and I danced open-eyed, watching Dad and Emma still in their slow two-step. They looked like they might kiss, but then Dad said something and Emma's face lit up. You could hear a trace of her laughter over the music if you listened hard enough.

Between the salad and the entrée—the proverbial rubber chicken, except that here it was rubber prime rib—Emma leaned across Kirby's momentarily empty seat and said quietly that I had a nice way with the people I photographed, that they seemed not even to be aware of me much of the time and even when they were, I put them at ease. She leaned closer and said in a lower voice, "I've some friends, a different sort than this crowd, but I need some photographs of them for . . ." She looked across the table at Dad, whose attention was turned to Willa. "It's quite a long story, but could I possibly persuade you, do you think, to take their photographs for me someday?"

"Of course, Emma. I'd be happy to, but—"

"Yes," Emma said to herself, nodding sharply. "Yes, that will be perfect."

Kirby pulled out his chair then and settled back in between us. "What will be perfect, Emma?" he said.

"Why, to have the next dance with you, Kirby," Emma said

without missing a beat, and the two of them hobbled off to the dance floor, leaving me to wonder alone about Emma's mysterious friends.

The chocolate mousse was served not much later, and the obligatory people made the obligatory speeches, everyone else remaining politely confined to their seats. I moved freely with my camera, glad that my father seemed oblivious of it, glad not to have to take even these pitiful pictures meant only for a hunt club scrapbook under his watchful eye. Just as it seemed the speeches would never end, Emma, master of the hounds, hobbled to the podium on her crutches, gave a perfunctory thanks to the ball organizers, and concluded with a quick "I could go on and on about the fine job the committee has done, but you can see it for yourself after all, and I'm liable to topple over on these crutches if I stand here too long." She did not sit down afterward, though. She hobbled back to the edge of the dance floor, leaned her crutches against a chair, and began again to dance with Dad.

I didn't dance after dinner; Dac had slipped away somewhere and even my father, who'd danced with me at every opportunity I could recall when I was growing up, didn't ask me to dance. I kept taking pictures, kept watching Dad and Emma: Dad whispering to Emma when he pulled out her chair, or maybe kissing her ear; the two of them dancing, Emma practically nuzzling his chest; Dad stroking her hair. And then Dac was behind me, speaking directly into my ear, loud enough to be heard over the music: "With the way things are going, we could be related pretty soon."

I nearly dropped my camera.

When I turned, he was close to me, closer than we'd been when we danced.

"I don't think my father's ready for anything like that," I said.

The dance ended and a pop tune began, and still Dac stood close to me, looking at me. I took a step back, capped my lens. "I need to get some air," I said.

He studied me for a long moment, then offered his arm. I'd meant I needed to be by myself, but I loaded my camera back in its case, threw it over my shoulder, and set my hand on his sleeve.

We took a stiff, silent turn around the lobby, then stopped beside the fountain, multitiered white stone with water spilling from tier to tier. Dac dipped a cupped hand into the bottom pool, lifted a handful of water. It trickled through his fingers drop by drop, plinking quietly back into the pool.

Music and laughter spilled gently from the ballroom. A young couple emerged and pushed out through the main hotel doors, laughing. He lit her cigarette and she said something and they kissed, an intimate, embarrassing kiss.

Dac looked at me, a long, searching look. "It's hard to be without someone for a long time," he said.

At the front desk, a white-gloved bellman loaded matching bags onto a brass cart and headed off for one of the rooms. I imagined Ned and Charlie snuggled under their blankets in their own room back at the farm.

Dac had only invited me to the ball to be friendly, I reminded myself. Even Emma had said so.

"I think it's probably especially hard when you've had someone all your life," Dac said, "like my mother has, and your father, too."

I felt myself sinking into the tiny tips of my pointy high heels. He wasn't talking about himself, about us; he was talking about Dad and Emma.

He frowned slightly. "I know you—"

"You don't even *know* my father!" I said, my words echoing off the marble of the lobby. Startled, I lowered my voice. "He lived his whole life by himself, Dac, with just his camera for company. He wasn't lonely then, without Mom and me. He doesn't get lonely." I focused on the water overflowing the top of the fountain, falling through the air, landing with a gentle gurgle in the pool below it, in the pool below that, in the bottom pool.

"He's not lonely now," I said.

I felt Dac's concerned gaze, but I couldn't turn to face him. I wrapped my arms around my camera case and remained focused on the fountain, staring into that bottom pool, where so many coins had settled, each in the wake of someone's silent wish.

17

Dad came into the kitchen the next morning humming some old song I didn't recognize, greeting Boomer with an enthusiastic two-handed neck rub, saying to me, "Good morning, sweet daughter of mine!" He poured a cup of coffee and sat across from me. "That sure was fun last night. I saw you with your camera. Any chance you got a decent shot of Emma and me?"

As if it were so improbable, as if I'd be lucky not to have cut off the tops of everyone's heads.

"You looked like you were having a wonderful time for a man who—"

Who what?

Whose wife was barely dead.

"I see," Dad said softly. He set his coffee cup down and pulled on his hair. "Would you like to talk about this?"

I stood to refill my cup, to have a reason to turn away from him. The coffee slopped over the edge of the spout, a few drops hitting the burner, sizzling, the rest splattering across the countertop. "So there is something to talk about?" I said.

Though how could there be?

He watched me for a long moment; I could feel his gaze.

"I think I'm in love with your friend Emma," he said finally, his voice with the same soft quality it'd had when he'd given me the key to his box. "I think that's a wonderful thing to be able to talk about."

Emma and Dad continued to spend time together after the Hunt Ball, and it became pretty clear who was wooing whom. Dad dressed carefully before he went to see her, appearing each time before he left with damp, combed hair. He shaved twice a day, humming old love songs, or what I took to be love songs, although I didn't know the words. Sometimes he would suddenly stop humming, as if he'd cut himself, but each time he would hum on again. And then I'd watch as he drove off in his old Jeep, which he now—uncharacteristically—kept washed and waxed. He'd slow at the end of the driveway and turn the rearview mirror toward himself, comb his hair with his fingers, straighten the collar of his shirt. I imagined him smiling at his reflection before repositioning the mirror and pulling onto the road.

He often took flowers to Emma—not red roses like he'd sometimes brought my mother, but springtime flowers like tulips and daffodils, flowers I hadn't thought you could get in the wintertime. He got them in quantities, took them by the dozens, setting them gently on the passenger seat of the Jeep. Emma would put them out not in carved crystal vases, but in an old tin watering can that was transformed by the addition of those flowers into a more charming thing than you'd ever have thought it could be.

Dad didn't call Emma sweetheart either—the only pet name I'd ever heard him use with Mom. He called her silly names like Sugar Lump and Silver Bell and Pumpkin Pie, names that seemed more personal, more intimate, than sweetheart was ever meant to be. I told myself he must have had more personal names for my mother, names spoken only in her presence or at least outside that of my brothers and me. I had no explanation, though, for why he'd never used Mom's pet names publicly, yet was now so free with his affection for Emma. Maybe he'd been like this with Mom when they first met. Maybe he'd been for years and I'd just been too young, too oblivious, too much their child, to see. Maybe it was my father—older, wiser, more self-assured. It seemed to me a greater change than that, though: not a reincarnation, but a birth of a romantic man I'd never seen.

I was having trouble taking pictures in those days before Christmas. I'd wake up in the morning and say to myself, okay, this is the day, Dad is taking the boys sledding and I'm going to get some photos done. But then he'd pad into the kitchen to pour his black coffee, and within minutes I'd have thought of eighteen chores I had to do first, ridiculous things like organizing closets or polishing silver or sweeping ashes from the fireplace. And then Emma would call and I'd drop everything to spend time with her; she spent a lot of time with my father, but she seemed also to make more time than ever for me. She came over not just Tuesday and Thursday afternoons, hunting time, but other days, as well, and while Dad entertained the boys we painted my bedroom, then started on my bath. The time was not the same with Dad in the mix, though. As I was talking to Emma, I'd be aware of the sound of his footsteps, a door opening, his whistle floating through the house.

18

One time in the frozen food aisle of the grocery store back in Chicago, I passed the brand of pizza Wes liked to fix for himself when he came home from the hospital in the middle of the night or for himself and the boys on Sunday afternoons, and it was all I could do just to get to the checkout. Afterward I sat in the car for over an hour, melted ice cream soaking through the paper sack and onto the backseat. Christmas was like that, only worse: I'd be fine one minute, but then something would remind me that Wes had always done this or that with the boys and now he'd never do it again. Sitting with Ned and Charlie at Christmas Eve services at St. James's, I focused on Emma's hat, three rows in front of me—a blue trilby with a white ribbon band in a sea of red and green—and tried not to think of the seat Wes didn't occupy. Later, after Dad and the boys had gone to bed, I put out the Santa gifts by myself. Wes had always been the one to eat the milk and cookies the boys put out for Santa; I scraped this year's cookies—homemade Santas and trees and wreaths cut and decorated by the boys—into Boomer's bowl on the back porch, careful to leave a few crumbs on the plate. I stood watching as Boomer wolfed them down, then wiped the few sugar sprinkles from the edge of his dish. Inside, I poured the milk down the drain, set the empty glass and plate back on the fireplace mantel, and unplugged the tree lights. I stood there a long time, staring at the shadow of the broken star.

Christmas morning, while the boys were pulling presents from under the tree, reading the tags and flipping the gifts to the intended receivers, I couldn't stop thinking that none of those gifts said *Daddy*. The boys were doing okay, though. In the excitement of opening gifts, they seemed not to focus on the absence of their father, and even after the gifts were opened, when Wesley would have helped them play with their new things, Dad jumped in pretty quickly to fill the gap. Watching them, I felt suddenly exhausted, and fled to the kitchen to slide the turkey into the oven. An excuse, yes. An escape.

When I got back to the living room, Ned and Charlie were playing on the floor in the glow of the colored Christmas lights, lost in imaginary worlds. Around them, empty boxes and torn wrapping paper cluttered the space. Neither of them noticed, except to step on the paper or kick an empty box out of the way. I watched them, feeling as confused as the jumble of toys and boxes and wrap littered there.

Even the dog, contentedly gnawing his Christmas bone, failed to notice me.

"I thought I might run over to Emma's for a few minutes, to take her a gift," I said.

Ned and Charlie looked up from what they were doing, but didn't protest.

"Grandpa will be here if you need anything," I said.

When Emma opened her door, her grandmother clock was striking ten.

"Merry Christmas," I said.

She took my hand, squeezing it, looking past me. "You left Ned and Charlie with your father?"

I nodded, and I handed her a package wrapped in paper the color of the hat she'd worn the night before, trimmed with white ribbon, as the hat had been. "You don't have to open it now," I said.

Emma again squeezed my hand. "Of course I will. Come into the library. I've something for you too. It's under the tree."

As we passed the door to the kitchen, I heard Dac wondering aloud whether he ought to undo the wire that held the turkey's legs together to get the stuffing in.

"I've been ordered out of the kitchen, and I've taken the order to heart," Emma said. "I'm giving odds that he doesn't know to remove the innards from the cavity of the bird, though. And I took the precaution of making the trifle myself before he came, so at least we'll have dessert."

I tucked my flannel shirt more firmly into my jeans, ran my fingers through my hair. "Merry Christmas!" I shouted above the clatter of pans.

Dac appeared in the open doorway, wiping his hands with a dishrag, the sleeves of a rich red oxford shirt rolled up for his work. "Are you opening your present?"

"I'm opening mine first," Emma said, her long fingers already working the white ribbon off the package, peeling back the thin blue paper wrap to reveal three framed photographs. She smiled at the top one, Dac and his horse that Thanksgiving, at the Blessing of the Hunt. "We'll call this *Portrait of a Son in His Element,* shall we?" she said, handing Dac the photo. "I don't believe I've a picture that captures Dac so well."

"Nice focus," he said. "Nice light. But I don't know about this subject."

Emma laughed that warm laugh that had become so familiar to me, and I laughed, too. They liked the photograph. They
thought it was good.

Emma pulled the tissue away from the next photo, the one
I'd taken of her leaning against the paddock fence with her
crutches, watching the hunters prepare to ride away without
her. I had another, better photograph of her, the last one I'd
taken that day, but I wasn't sure she'd like it. There was something in it—a sadness to it I hadn't seen before or since. I had
the sense she didn't want it to be seen.

"We'll call this one *Portrait of a Rider on the Wrong Side of the
Fence*," I said.

"I'll be out there before you know it, you wait and see,"
Emma said.

I said nothing she did would surprise me.

Dac set the first two photos on the sofa table, a long, narrow marble-topped thing, old and French, while his mother
pulled the tissue paper from the third, the photograph I'd
taken of myself the night before the Blessing of the Hunt.

"*Portrait of the Artist as a Young Woman, Finding Herself*,"
Emma said, and she smiled, an expression that on anyone else
would be called a grin but was, on Emma, more sophisticated
than that. "I like the spot on the wall behind you," she said. "It
will remind me of painting, of why we painted."

"The spot on the wall?" I took the photo from her: sure
enough, there was a brighter circle on the wall above my
head, where the old paint hadn't faded under the wall clock.
What was it about having the camera focused on myself that
made it so impossible for me to get the shot right, that made
me so blind to the flaws around me even when they showed
up in the print?

"May I see it?" Dac asked.

I pulled the photograph close to me. "I don't——" But in response to the vulnerable look in his eyes, I handed him the picture, saying, "Of course, sure."

He laughed when he saw it. "*I* think we should call it *Saint Nelly*. The bright spot looks like a halo over your head—the way your halo would be, of course. Understated. Subtle. You're not a gaudy wings-and-halo type of angel."

As if the flaw in the photo pleased him, made the photo unique, interesting, good.

"So it's your turn now, Nelly," Emma said. "You must open your gift."

Dac echoed her, saying that was what he'd come out for, to see me open it, and he did have a turkey to cook.

"The gift was Dac's idea, actually," Emma said.

"The outside part was," Dac said. "I hope you like it. I think you will."

He pulled a large rectangular package out from under the tree, and I knew instantly that it was an artist's portfolio for carrying my prints. When I unwrapped it, I smelled the sweet, oily smell of new leather, touched its buttery smoothness. I let my fingers linger on the discreetly embossed initials: ESG, Eleanor Sullivan Grace. Of course they would be my initials, but the fact that they were made my eyes well up.

"We thought it would come in handy for showing your photographs," Emma said. "And you need to look inside."

"Inside?"

"There's something inside it," Dac said. "Mom's idea. Open it up."

I opened the portfolio all the way, the long zipper moving noiselessly over the teeth, to find a plain white envelope taped inside. I slipped it open, pulled out two light blue tickets.

"Train tickets. Two round-trips," Dac said.

"To New York," Emma said. "To show your work. That's the best way to go about making a career of it, isn't it? Dac said he thought it would be."

"Mother is going with you," Dac said. "I believe she means to make sure you go through with it."

"If you don't mind, Nelly," Emma said. "You tell me when you're ready." She smiled. "Anytime is fine, but no time like the present. Perhaps right after the first? I've something I want to share with you while we're up that way too. Something I know you'll— Something I should very much like for you to see. Some people I'd like you to know."

"You're going to be great someday," Dac said. "Famous. We'll all claim to be your best friend."

And I knew they had no idea what they were talking about, what it took to be a photojournalist, but I wanted to agree with them, to say, yes, isn't it going to be wonderful, I'm going to be famous, my photographs will change the world.

"That is what you want, isn't it?" Emma said. She nodded twice, sharply. "Yes. Of course it is."

And there was Wesley's voice, saying the boys needed me, that I couldn't be a photojournalist and a good mother, too, and my father, with his arm pulling me close, asking if I'd measured the temperature of my chemicals, asking if there was any chance I'd gotten a decent shot of Emma and him. But I looked at Dac, at Emma, and I nodded slowly. "Yes," I said. "Yes, that's what I want."

19

When I left Emma's, I gave Dac a lift back to his place; he'd forgotten the cranberry sauce and had to fetch it before his mother discovered the omission. We drove the long way around, out to the road and around to Dark Hollow, where his driveway was. In better weather, we might have cut across the field—the way he'd come on foot—but only a narrow dirt road connected his place to his mother's, and the snow we'd had the night before made it impassable by car.

Dac sat quietly in the passenger seat, his silence consuming the space in the car, and I had the impression again that Wesley was watching me, or not so much watching as seeing, aware of all I did. I rolled down the window, took a gulp of cold air into my lungs.

At his place, Dac asked me to come in for a minute, he had something for me, "just a little something, not much." I hesitated, but I did go in, following him through the mud porch (past bowls of dog food, coats hung from pegs on the wall, mud-caked riding boots), and into a tiny living space, where an old wooden table marked with water rings was all that separated the kitchen from the sitting room and its unmatched couch and chair, its wood-burning stove, its photograph-covered walls and riding-trophy-covered shelves. There, he picked up one of the photos—a small, framed photo from a bookshelf by the front window—and handed it to me. It looked almost familiar: a stream and the farmland bordering it, with two people sitting on the bank.

"It's lovely," I said, looking not at the landscape but at the two people. "You took this?"

"It's the view from your bridge, looking downstream, before the new barn was built. I thought you might like to have it."

I studied him. He waited for me to speak.

"But you don't photograph people."

"They're your great-grandparents," he said, fingering the rim of the cup on one of the trophies.

My father's grandparents. They'd built the house in which I now lived.

"When did you stop photographing people, Dac?" I said gently.

His fingers on the trophy stopped moving, but he didn't seem surprised by the question.

"Your father taught me a little about photography, did you know that?" he said. "He came here once when I was a kid. He showed me— Mom was schooling a new horse in the ring and I was taking pictures when he got here, and he showed me how to pan."

His green eyes blinked, but he didn't look away.

"When did you stop photographing people, Dac?" I repeated.

He studied the floor for a moment, then looked back up at me. "In Vietnam," he said.

"I see," I whispered. And I did see. I saw what he saw when he looked through a viewfinder at a person. He saw that little girl running down the road, the little boy dead in his mother's arms.

I went to give him a kiss on the cheek to thank him, feeling awkward, not knowing how I felt, not wanting to know.
He took my face in his hands and he looked at me forever and
then he kissed me, a long, full kiss, the way he'd kissed me
after I'd fallen that day we rode. I felt the color rise in me, but
I held his steady gaze, sinking into the green, the subtle flecks
of gold. I reached up and touched a finger to the coarse hair
of his eyebrow, traced the line of his temple, his jaw. At the
base of his neck, I felt the shift of muscle as he swallowed.

His hand brushed over my breast, lightly, but even through
the flannel of my shirt, the satin of my bra, I felt it like the
moan of an animal, the hoot of an owl, the throaty caution of
a dog. And then he was touching the base of my throat, his
fingers working loose the top button of my flannel shirt,
touching my skin underneath.

I fingered the small white button of his red oxford shirt,
unbuttoned it.

He pulled me to him, holding me still against him, pressing
my head to his chest. His breath, warm on the top of my head,
smelled not of peppermint, but of sage.

"Is this okay?" he whispered.

I tilted my head up to him, unbuttoned the next button of
his shirt, then the next, slid my hands around his sides to the
small of his back. I nestled my face against his neck, entangled
my fingers in the curly blond hair of his chest, and we stood
there, in the middle of his sitting room, with the bright light
of the winter morning streaming through the side window,
landing at our feet.

He kissed my neck, my shoulders, my breasts, brushing his
lips over my skin. "Are you sure?" he said, but he was already
kneeling down, unbuttoning the top button of my jeans, kissing the winter white skin of my belly. And when he pulled
me down to the floor, into that splash of sunshine, the warmth

of it merged with the heat of his body and flowed into my skin.

Afterward, I lay there on the worn carpet, nestled up against Dac's body, in that state of immobility a step beyond relaxed. Outside, the wind blew snow off the roof. It floated down past the window, a small snow cloud above us in the otherwise clear Christmas sky.

20

When I returned home from Dac's, the house was overly quiet, the smell of cooking turkey hanging heavy in the air. It was nearly noon. I closed the door noiselessly behind me, certain that something had gone wrong. Wasn't anybody home? Maybe someone had gotten hurt. Maybe the boys had gotten wild with their new toys and one of them had stumbled, fallen against the fireplace mantel. They'd gone to the hospital, Dad had tried to reach me and I wasn't at Emma's and they'd had to go on without me, Ned holding a clean cloth to Charlie's elbow or his eyebrow while my father drove. It couldn't be worse than that, could it? If it had been, Dad would have called from the hospital and when there was no answer he would have called Emma again and she would have told him I'd dropped Dac off on the way and so maybe I was still at his place or we'd had a flat or something, and Emma would have called Dac and we'd have answered, or we'd have heard the answering machine, Emma's voice saying she was looking for me, that one of the boys was hurt.

I picked up a faint murmur coming from the family room. It was deep, adult. My father's voice. They'd just fallen asleep,

then. Napping. They'd gotten up so early to see what Santa
had brought them. Maybe Charlie was napping and Ned was
being quiet, letting him sleep on the couch where he'd
dropped off or where Dad had moved him after he'd fallen
asleep on the floor.

I slipped off my coat and hung it on the closet doorknob. I
smelled like Dac, like sex. But I needed to see my boys.

I followed the sound of Dad's voice, found the three of
them snuggled together on the couch, Boomer the only one
napping. Ned and Charlie had been crying, their eyes were
red and their noses were running and they were tucked up
right next to Dad on the couch. He sat with his arms around
them, murmuring softly as he had at Wesley's funeral, when
he'd told them it was all right to cry. I couldn't make out his
words.

"Mom!" Charlie was up off the couch and hugging his
arms around my waist, and so was Ned, with Boomer's tail
battering our legs as he circled us.

"We're having a bit of a bad spell," Dad said. "They've been
missing their daddy."

"Oh no," I said, and I knelt down and pulled them all
toward me, pulled us all together into a big group hug. "I'm
so sorry. I'm so sorry I wasn't here."

I felt guilty all day, guilty as we ate Christmas dinner, the smell
of the sage in the dressing reminding me of Dac, of his breath.
I couldn't eat a bite. I felt guilty as I helped Ned build his new
model, guilty as I played "real" Monopoly—not Monopoly
Junior—and ran the boys' baths and made sure they brushed
their teeth. I even felt guilty as I read *The Tale of Mrs. Tittle-
mouse* for the second time that night, though the boys had recovered long before then, were lost in laughing at the story,
saying to each other in silly voices, "I will not have Mr. Jack-

son; he never wipes his feet" and "No teeth, no teeth." And I sat in their room for the longest time after they'd fallen asleep, watching them breathe.

I was going to bed myself—I was exhausted and Dad was gone anyway, he'd headed over to Emma's not long after dinner—when I went in to check on the boys one last time and found Charlie lying awake, his eyes sleepy but open. I sat on the edge of his bed, stroked his forehead. "What woke you up?"

He turned onto his side, facing me. "Do you miss Daddy?" he asked.

"Oh, sweetheart." I wanted to cry for not having been there, for having been with Dac.

"Sometimes already I can't even remember what he looks like," he said.

The tears bubbled over in my eyes then, and I wrapped him up in a hug. "I know, sweetie. I know. But you won't forget him. We can talk about him and remember him together. You won't forget him. Just think about things you did with him. Remember the time you fell off your bicycle—remember you were just learning to ride it and you fell, you've still got the scar on your chin, if you look real closely you can see it. And you said you didn't want to go to the hospital and couldn't Daddy just fix it, so Daddy said okay?"

"But then he didn't," Charlie said.

"He washed out the cut and then he got ready to stitch you up but he couldn't."

"He almost passed out," Charlie said.

"You know why?"

Charlie shrugged.

"Your daddy used to sew up people a lot littler than you—little babies—every day. He used to see lots and lots of blood and he never passed out with them."

"Never?"

"Not once. He couldn't sew you up, honey, because he loved you. Because he loved you and the sight of your blood—your blood—scared him. That's why he almost passed out. Because he loved you."

"He held my hand at the hospital."

"That's right. He did. See, you remember."

"And he got Dr. Gabe to do my stitches because Dr. Gabe was the best, 'cept for Daddy."

Dr. Gabe, with whom I'd danced at the party that night Wes and I fought.

"That's right."

"And you know what Dr. Gabe said, Mommy?"

"What, sweetheart?"

"He told me I could keep my eyes open but Daddy had to close his so he wouldn't faint."

I laughed. "That's right," I said. "That's right. I'd forgotten that."

"I like Dr. Gabe," Charlie said.

"Me too. Dr. Gabe was pretty nice."

I stroked his forehead. He closed his eyes and I thought he would go back to sleep, but then his eyes fluttered open again.

"Mommy?"

"What, honey?"

"Can I have a picture of Daddy? I could keep it by my bed."

"Of course, sweetheart. Of course you can. We'll get you one in the morning. First thing in the morning."

"Can I get it now?"

"Of course. I'll run down and get you one now."

"Can I come too?"

"Well, the pictures are down in the basement, honey. Why don't I just get one and bring it up. It'll only take me a minute. I'll bring up a bunch and you can choose."

"Mommy?"

"What is it, sweetheart?"

He looked up at me, his pupils huge in the dim light, his eyes Wesley's eyes.

"Mommy, why do you keep Daddy in the basement?"

I blinked against the dim light, the sharp words. "That's where the pictures are, sweetie," I said gently. "All the pictures are there. Not just Daddy."

Charlie considered this for a minute. "Do you still love Daddy?" he asked.

As I looked at him, a thousand thoughts flashed through my mind. I remembered the day he was born, the way Wesley had held Charlie in his arms and brought him to me, kissing his little head and looking so proud. I remembered the day Wesley graduated from medical school, a hot day and he was sweating under his cap and gown and I called him Dr. Grace and he laughed and picked me up and spun me around. I remembered, even before that, the day I'd had a photo in the college paper—the governor had come to speak and he'd been surprised by a belligerent question from the crowd and he'd flashed angry, only for the briefest moment but I'd caught it, I'd caught that anger on film. And the picture was picked up by the city paper, not the *Tribune* but the *Sun-Times*. Wesley came home that night with thirty copies of that paper—we were struggling students at the time, but still he bought thirty copies and a bottle of champagne.

What had happened to us?

"Of course I still love Daddy," I said to Charlie. "I'll always love Daddy, honey. Now you close your eyes and go on to sleep and I'll bring up some pictures for you and you can choose which one you want in the morning, okay?"

"Will you get one right now? I'll stay awake until you get back."

"Okay, honey. I'll be right back. You stay awake if you want to. That's fine. You stay awake."

I went down to the basement then, and as I went through my box of old photographs, I kept trying to push Charlie's words out of my mind. "Mommy, why do you keep Daddy in the basement?" I tried to shake the question but the words clung tightly, there together with the image of Wesley holding Charlie's hand while Dr. Gabe sewed up his chin, Wesley with his eyes closed, the way Dac's eyes had been closed that morning as we made love.

I hurriedly pulled pictures of Wesley from the box, not wanting to leave Charlie alone for too long, not wanting to be alone in that basement myself. But by the time I got back upstairs, Charlie was fast asleep.

21

As Dad and the boys bundled up to go out the next morning, the phone rang: Dac offering to take me out for a ride. I wanted to say I couldn't go with him, I couldn't see him anymore, but the boys were swarming around me, Ned asking where his mittens were, Charlie wanting his shoes tied, wanting to know why I wasn't getting ready to go.

"Your mother isn't invited," Dad said to Charlie. "Just you and Ned and me, three boys on the loose."

"Really, Dad, I'd like to go," I repeated for the third time that morning, against his protests that he didn't get any time alone with his grandsons, that I needed a rest anyway, that, he was very sorry to inform me, boys sometimes had more fun without girls along.

"Pardon?" Dac said.

"Dad's taking the boys to the aquarium," I said. "We're in the midst of the chaos that marks Ned and Charlie getting ready to leave the house."

"So you can ride, then?"

I sighed, knowing I should tell him in person that the day before had been a mistake, that I couldn't see him anymore, that the boys weren't ready and probably I wasn't ready myself.

"Okay, sure," I said. "What time?"

And when we rode together that morning, just Dac and me, I kept thinking I had to work my way around to telling him I couldn't see him, that the day before had been a mistake and I was sorry but I couldn't do that. But Dac was talking about his horses, about how they'd done in their races that fall and where they'd be racing next, how one's leg was healing and another was refusing to eat, and I was talking about Charlie's watercolor that was going to be displayed at the airport, Neddy's perfect score on his math test, the song they'd made up. And then we were talking about ourselves, Dac hoping someday to have a Derby contender, as his father once had, me wanting to have a major magazine cover, as Dad had repeatedly had. We laughed at ourselves for still wanting to be like our fathers. It felt good to laugh.

And then the ride was over and there'd been no discussion of us, no talk of relationship, no mention of Wesley or Mai or Dad and Emma or anyone else. Dac gave the horses to a young man in the barn, asking him to take care of them, then walked me up to my car. He was saying he had to get going, there was a lot to do with the horses that day and he had to get to it, and I was thinking maybe this was his way of saying that he thought yesterday was a mistake, too, that he just wanted to be friends, when he kissed me. He kissed me with his full-lipped peppermint mouth and then he opened my car door and said he'd call me later. And I climbed in and he closed the door and waved as I drove off.

On the way home, I stopped by Willa's, found her in the tack room still in her riding cap, its chin strap dangling. "Nell," she said. "Hey, you're getting to be quite a rider!" She'd seen me take the little coop out of Patterson's woods, she said; she'd almost joined us but she thought she might be interrupting. I shrugged—she might have been—and she promised if I heard any gossip, she wouldn't be the source. "Scout's honor," she said, lifting her hand in the air as if to take an oath. "Can I pry a little?" she said. "Is it serious?"

I admitted I didn't know.

"Well, one thing's for sure: Emma will be ecstatic." She pulled her cap off and mussed her hair, damp from the riding. "She'll find you a big improvement over Mai."

I moved into the opening, asking her who Mai was, pleading, when she hesitated, that I couldn't ask him myself.

She hung her cap from a hook by the door and pulled a body brush and currycomb from the shelf, never taking her gaze off my face. A black barn cat jumped up to the space where the comb and brush had been.

"You're falling in love with him, aren't you?" Willa sighed. "Dac married her, Nell. They were married in Vietnam. As far as I know, they've never actually divorced."

"Married? Dac isn't married!" I slumped back against the saddle Willa had ridden, her favorite because it was broken in perfectly to the contours of her back end. Dac had never said anything about being married. "So where is she, then?" I said flatly.

"Good question." Willa began to clean the brush with the currycomb. "Still in Vietnam, I guess. All I know is he came back from Vietnam and he was talking about her, about arranging for her to come here, but then we never saw her. And he was weirding out at the time, I mean really weirding out. And then he disappears for maybe a month and no one talks about it but it's pretty clear he's taken a detour to Sheppard Pratt, at least it is to us."

"Sheppard Pratt?"

"It's a . . . a loony bin. You know. A psychiatric hospital. One of the best."

"Oh."

I fingered the leather of the saddle. A psychiatric hospital. Emma had never told me that.

I asked Willa what she thought happened, trying to regain my balance, to sound light, curious, while some knot in my chest slowly made its way to my heart. "To Mai, I mean," I said.

"Honestly?" Willa scooted the cat off the shelf and set the brush and comb back on it. "If you repeat this, Nell, you won't make me any friends." She picked up a saddle blanket and folded it, then held it to herself. "I think Emma let Mai know she wouldn't be welcome here, that a Vietnamese girl would never fit into Dac's life," she said. "I think Emma paid her a lot of money to go away, and didn't really leave her any choice."

"Not Emma," I said. "Maybe Davis—"

"Not Davis." Willa's voice was firm. "You had to know Davis. He wasn't . . ." Willa set the saddle blanket down, smoothing it with her hands. She paused then, every inch of her body still. "Davis was awkward at expressing his emotions," she said, "but there was no doubt he would have done anything, accepted anything, for Dac."

"And you just know this?"

Willa stiffened at the edge in my voice. She smoothed the saddle blanket again, watching her hands. "He told me," she said.

"Who?"

"I was in love with him."

"With Dac?"

"No."

I stared at her, trying to sort out what she was saying. She stared back at me, her arms crossed over her chest.

"You were in love with Dac?"

She looked as if she would cry, but then her face hardened. "No, Nell. I just said no, didn't you hear me? No."

And then it struck me. "Not with— With Davis?"

Willa mussed her hair like she did, but mechanically this time. She looked at the barn floor for a minute, then met my gaze. She shook her head. "Yes," she said.

"You and Davis were—?"

"Yes."

"Did Emma—?"

"Yes, Nelly. Yes. Yes to it all. Yes I loved him. Yes I slept with him. Yes I would have left Michael for him if I didn't have the boys. Yes, yes, yes. All of it. All right?" She leaned back against the tack table and stared up at the ceiling. "All right?" she whispered.

"God, I'm sorry, Willa. I just . . . I didn't . . ."

She ran her fingers slowly through her hair, pulling at the ends. "No, no one does. Emma made sure of that."

"Emma?"

"She said she didn't want to be unreasonable about it, but of course I could see she couldn't have me sleeping with her husband, couldn't I? So what she thought we ought to do was just put it behind us, pretend it never happened and move ahead. She'd invite me to parties and I'd come. 'You'll be sure to come when I invite you, Willa,' she said. And if Davis and I ever saw each other again, if she ever even suspected it, or suspected I'd even so much as told anyone about it . . ."

"She—?"

"She said she had pictures."

"Pictures?" I nearly laughed. "Like private-eye stuff?"

Willa shrugged. "I don't really believe it either, but I don't know."

"And you were afraid she'd show them to Michael."

Willa shook her head. "I could have—"

She turned her back to me, began putting things up in a determined way, putting saddle pads with saddles, straightening bridles that were already straight. "Don't let her know I told you about it, Nell," she said after a moment. "I shouldn't have told you. It— Don't let her know you know, all right?" She turned and met my gaze. "Promise me that."

Dac called later that afternoon, as he'd said he would after our ride, after he'd kissed me good-bye. I heard his voice on the answering machine and I stood listening, wondering if it was really true. Was he really married? I didn't answer the phone. I listened and when he hung up I erased the message and I didn't call him back until the next morning, when I knew he would be out working with the horses. When he called later that next afternoon to see if I was free for New Year's Eve, I said Dad would be going out with Emma and I couldn't get a baby-sitter at this late date, and when he offered to come over after Ned and Charlie were asleep, I said I'd promised them they could stay up to watch the ball drop over Times Square, though I knew that no matter how hard they tried, they'd fall asleep long before that.

He called several other times that week, and stopped by when he was checking on the horses he kept at my barn, but I always had some excuse not to see him: I was taking the boys somewhere or doing something with Dad while he was in town, or I had only an hour to myself and I needed to get out to take some photographs. He even offered to take pictures with me—he'd bring his camera and I could teach him a few things, he said—but I told him I didn't think I could take photos as well with anyone around, which was true, or might have been true if I'd been taking any. I hadn't taken a photograph since the Hunt Ball. I was paralyzed again, as I had been before Thanksgiving. Because my father was there? Because I had those tickets to New York? Because some part of me was afraid Wesley was right, that I couldn't be both a photojournalist and a good mom?

All the time I kept telling myself I had to tell Dac I couldn't see him, and I kept going over in my mind how I would tell him, what I would say. But each time he called, I wouldn't know where to start and each time we hung up, I wouldn't have said anything. And when he called the last time, early one morning that first week in January, getting the machine, leaving a message that he'd just got a line on a horse in California and he was flying out the next morning, I didn't pick up. I lay in bed listening to his invitation to ride anytime that day, to his hope we could see each other before he left. It wasn't even eight yet, but I'd promised to take the boys down to D.C. for the day, to the Air and Space Museum and the Smithsonian and some of the monuments. Dad was doing something with Emma; it was going to be just the boys and me, and we were staying for dinner. It would be after eleven when we got back, far too late to see Dac before he left.

22

Emma and I were painting again, putting the second coat on my bathroom walls one Tuesday afternoon in January, two weeks before Dad was to leave, when he came in on the pretext of offering us coffee. He returned a few minutes later with three cups, settling himself comfortably on the edge of the tub, and starting to talk about a new photography exhibit at the National Gallery in Washington. "Strictly women photographers," he said. "I understand a lot of Maggie Bourke-White's photos will be exhibited. I had the privilege of meeting her during the war. She was the first woman to be accredited as a war photographer, you know. The first to fly a combat mission."

I did know. I'd admired her work for as long as I could remember. She had a way of making the people she photographed seem familiar, almost like you'd known them, so that your compassion for them was heightened, made more immediate and real.

"The exhibit opens Thursday, and I've been asked to attend the opening. I thought you might like to come."

I fixed on my paintbrush for a moment, the creamy white

smoothed over the dark strands. Maybe this invitation from my dad was just an invitation, but it seemed more than that to me.

When I looked up from my brush to say I'd love to go, Dad was looking at Emma. His face was like a schoolboy's: smitten, a little uncertain, anxious to please.

He'd been addressing Emma. Only Emma.

I looked at Emma. She would say she'd love to go but she already had plans. She'd suggest he take me instead.

"I'd love to," Emma said. "I'd love to go." No buts.

I jumped up, tipping the paint can I'd been working with, barely catching it before it spilled. I felt myself spilling out too. Ridiculous. Childish.

"I almost forgot, I have an errand I've got to get done before I pick up the boys," I said.

Behind me, as I fled out the door, Emma said, "But Nelly—"

I didn't stop to put on my boots.

I finished painting the bathroom myself that Thursday of the National Gallery opening, spattering paint on the floor and leaving the brushes to grow hard and brittle when I was done. There was no reason Emma shouldn't see my father, I told myself as I painted. Mom was dead. I couldn't change that. Dad was still living. Before Dad and Emma met, I'd even begun to hope for something like this to happen. Dad had gone back to work after Mom died, but he'd seemed to be drifting aimlessly, unhappily, looking sadly for something he couldn't find. Each time I talked to him, he had that hollow sound in his voice—not his words, but the lack of energy, the absence of enthusiasm—that was not like Dad at all. I'd even contemplated getting him a dog, maybe breeding Boomer and taking a puppy for him, though that was ridiculous, of course. What would Dad do with a dog, as much as he traveled? But I'd read in a magazine that people who had pets lived longer than those who didn't.

So why shouldn't Emma be the one to help him get on with his life? She was like part of my family already, and she was a strong enough woman to be good for him.

But when he took her off on his travels, where would I be? It was petty, I knew, unbelievably selfish, adolescent. And maybe he wouldn't take her with him. Why would he? He'd never taken Mom and he'd certainly never taken me. But it seemed, somehow, that he would take Emma. It seemed Emma would not be left behind.

That Saturday, my father announced Emma was coming to pick him up for lunch and she'd love to see me when she came by. She'd phoned several times, he said, but I hadn't returned the calls. Had I gotten the messages? I said I was sorry I'd miss her, but I'd promised the boys I'd take them to Patterson's to go sledding, and we were on our way out the door. And when I passed Emma's truck on our road, I didn't stop or roll down my window to say hello, as she did. I did wave, though, and I did think about the last thing Dad had said to me, as, keys jingling in my hand, I'd headed out the door: "I don't know what's eating at you, and if you don't want to talk about it, I guess that's your business. But remember that saying of your grandma's: 'Anger is like acid—it destroys the vessel that holds it.' "

I'd brought my camera with me that Saturday afternoon, thinking I might take some pictures of the boys sledding, that I had to take some pictures because I hadn't taken a picture since the Hunt Ball and it was only getting more difficult. And that day, driven, I see now, looking back on it, by that anger my father had talked about, I took rolls of pictures, choosing my shots carefully, setting them up perfectly. I kept taking pictures until my film was used up, and then I told the boys it was time to go.

Dad was home when I got there, but I made dinner, fed Boomer, put the boys to bed, and turned in myself, saying little to him. Before I went to sleep, though, I set my alarm for four in the morning, and when it went off I quietly slipped down to my darkroom, where I worked until the boys started waking up at six.

In the days that followed I took more and more photos, dragging my camera everywhere my father didn't go. They were not news photos, I knew that, but it seemed the only news in Baltimore that winter involved car crashes and drug wars, and I could imagine myself hurrying to a crash site in hopes there would be injuries, even fatalities, almost less than I could imagine myself pointing my camera at a drug dealer's gun. They were photographs—good photographs, I told myself as I set my alarm each night for four the next morning, as I worked quietly in the darkroom at dawn. And then I began to slip the photos up to my room, and I would pull them out at night and I would look at them critically before returning them to the basement, sorting them into two piles: ones that were rejects, and ones I might place in my new portfolio, to take to New York.

23

The boys and I parked by the small cemetery at St. James's a little late that next Sunday, my birthday, and slipped through the heavy brown doors just as the service began. The small church was crowded, the plain, dark pews on either side of the single aisle filled with a proper Episcopal crowd— including Emma, sitting eight rows back, wearing a yellow trilby with a navy blue-and-white striped ribbon into which a white feather was tucked. There were several seats available in her pew, but we took seats farther forward and across the aisle.

After the service, I tried to get out quickly, but Emma—her cast removed now—was between us and the doors. When she reached me, she took me by the elbow and moved to take my hand, which I left limply in her enthusiastic grasp.

"Happy birthday!" she said. "Happy birthday!"

I said, "Hello." I might have said nothing, just turned and walked away. I might have wrapped my arms around her and hugged her and never let go.

"You've been avoiding me," she said with that same warmly scolding look I'd seen the day we made apple pie together, when I'd said my photos were waiting for the paint to dry.

I said I hadn't meant to avoid her, really.

"You have." Said kindly, though, as if she understood.

Ned and Charlie had escaped my control and were zigzag-ging in and out of the pews, their heads and shoulders bob-bing up and down as they went from kneeler to floor to kneeler again. I shot them a stern look, which Ned caught. After he stopped, frozen in the act, Charlie noticed him, then me, and stopped dead in his tracks. It amazed me how well they fell into line sometimes since their father was gone.

Behind me, Emma spoke again, saying she'd really missed me, and when I turned to look at her, her eyes were moist.

"I've a birthday gift for you," she said, her back perfectly straight, the conservative set of her simple navy blue wool dress offset by the flamboyant yellow hat, the feather. "May I bring it by?"

"I'm not sure if we'll be around," I said.

She crossed her arms and we stood silently, looking at each other for a moment, two almost angry faces in a church. I wanted to go back and unwind what I'd started then, retract the invitations for the tree-trimming at which I'd introduced Emma and my father, decorate the damned tree myself.

"It's not a choice," Emma said. "I'm not choosing your fa-ther over you."

The church around us was almost empty, the remaining stragglers exchanging farewells.

"Nor am I going to replace your mother. But she's gone, Nelly. And if she loved your father, she'd want him to be happy in the time he has left, which—you must realize—isn't likely to be that many years."

When I didn't respond, Emma shook her head, then turned and walked away, the yellow of her hat, the blue-and-white ribbon finished in a straight seam disappearing down the aisle and out into the cold.

I rounded up Ned and Charlie, took them home, went into the kitchen. My father, reading the paper at the kitchen table, looked up and offered to help me fix brunch, which should have set off alarm bells in my mind; he wasn't the helping-in-the-kitchen type.

"You saw Emma at church?" he said.

I cut him a look, and turned to the stove.

"I'm here," he said quietly. "If you want, we can talk."

I took a cast-iron frying pan from the cabinet, banged it on the stove.

He tugged absently at his hair. "Or not," he said.

I pulled a carton of eggs from the refrigerator, a package of bacon from the meat drawer.

"Well, I guess talking doesn't always help," he said.

I cracked an egg on the edge of the sink. The shell shattered, the yolk breaking, everything running together and onto my fingers. I smashed the mess into the sink. "I can't talk to you," I said.

"You always could, before."

"Oh, fuck, I could not!"

He looked wounded, pathetic. "When could you not talk to me? You could. You always could. We used to sit in my darkroom—"

"Right. Until the whopping old age of eight."

I picked up the frying pan. The weight of it felt good, steadying.

Dad looked confused. "I don't understand."

"How about after Mom tried to kill herself? You weren't even there to talk to!"

He looked as shocked as I felt, as surprised by the words as I was.

I wanted to want to take them back, wanted to believe what Danny believed, that he'd stayed with us a long time then, that my memory was wrong and he'd stayed with us until we were okay, stayed as long as he could without losing his job. But I didn't feel that, didn't feel that understanding, didn't feel anything but abandoned, lost. "You just blew in and out of town and you were gone," I said, and I slammed the frying pan onto the counter and walked out.

The doorbell rang just as I yanked open the front door, and Dac's face appeared from behind a tall wooden crate, about as tall as I was, with a huge red velvet bow tied around the pine wood. At his words—it was his mother's clock and he wasn't ever to set foot in her house again if I didn't accept it—the angry energy drained from me. I felt suddenly limp, exhausted, sad, as Emma's voice echoed through my mind: "A grandmother clock. I brought it with me from England when I came to the States."

I thought of Grandma, and I missed her, and I missed Emma.

"I've got something for you too," Dac said. "Any chance you could get away later, maybe after the boys are in bed?"

I sighed, rubbed my hand over my forehead, tugged at my hair in a way that, I realized as I was doing it, was like my father. "I don't think so, Dac," I said. "I just don't think I can tonight."

Dac looked away then, concentrating on the clock. He asked where I wanted it and I suggested he just set it in the front hall, out of the weather. "Don't uncrate, it though. I can't accept it," I said, avoiding his eyes, his touch.

When Emma opened her door, we simply hugged for a long moment, and Emma said, "Can you believe that in Hollywood women don't hug or kiss anymore? They just pucker their lips in the air beside each other's hair and say, 'Kiss, kiss.' "

I wiped my eyes, pulled myself together. "Come on," I said.

"No, it's true," she said. "I heard Paul Harvey talk about it the other day. So they won't mess up their lips."

We're over the hump, I thought, sliding back into the friendship I almost threw out.

I told her I couldn't keep the clock, that it was too much, but she cut me off midsentence. It was not, as everyone supposed, the only inheritance she had, she said. It wasn't even from her family. "It was given to me by a friend, a very dear friend, during the time that Davis was missing, after I'd thrown out the bottle, so to speak," she said. "When he gave it to me, he said it was to remind me not to use time carelessly."

I traced the thin white scar on my hand, remembering one of Grandma's sayings: "Don't use time or words carelessly. Neither can be retrieved."

"He was the last best friend I had before you, Nelly," Emma said. "I want you to have the clock he gave me. I don't want you to forget that we, too, will run out of time someday."

Emma and I sat in wicker rocking chairs in her sunroom that afternoon, warm sunshine streaming in through the glass walls around us, falling on the table and on the tray of scones and clotted cream and the little silver butter knives and jam, and on the yellow daffodils in Emma's old tin watering can. We rocked in the chairs, drinking sweet, creamy tea from china cups, looking out at the brown of the winter farm, and talking. No paintbrushes this time. No Dad whistling in the background. Just Emma and me talking. She told me about when she'd first come to the farm with Davis; it had been about this time of year, she said, not long after Christmas, and the farm hadn't looked much different than it did now. At the mention of Davis's name, I thought of what Willa had told me, wondered whether she and Davis had really had an affair; Willa was attractive, self-confident, sexy, and considerably younger than Emma, but Emma seemed to me a woman with whom a man would not fall out of love.

Not long after they moved here, Emma said—that next summer—Dac had gotten polio, and she was glad they were here, near Johns Hopkins Hospital. She'd never forget that time: spending nights alone in bed while Davis slept at the hospital; Kirby and Joan bringing them dinners and helping with the farm and just being there to listen, to tell her Dac would get better. She'd never forget the sight of the iron lung machine, the weight of Dac's body when she held him in the hospital, the fear, as his legs moved awkwardly in the braces, that he'd never again walk by himself. It was the worst time of their lives, she said. "Worse than when Davis was missing in action, worse even than when Dac came back from Vietnam."

As she took up her teacup, I thought of Dac, of the photo of the little boy dead in his mother's arms, and I asked Emma what had happened to him in Vietnam. She was a long time answering, and when she spoke, it was to confirm what he'd told me, that Dac had come home in such a state they didn't know what to do. "We took him to a doctor we knew—quietly, of course," she said, "and she talked to him and she thought . . . Well, she thought he ought to benefit from a rest. And we all agreed. Dac himself agreed. So we did that. We sent him to a hospital where he could recompose himself."

She couldn't say "a psychiatric hospital"; she had that old-fashioned embarrassment about needing that kind of help.

I asked if she thought it might have had anything to do with Mai, and Emma abruptly stopped rocking. "Dac just mentioned her once," I said. "I thought . . ." I shifted uncomfortably in my chair.

She plucked a daffodil from the watering can. "Dac hasn't spoken of that girl in years," she said. "I'd rather hoped he'd put her out of his mind."

I nodded, trying to look merely curious.

"The troubles with Mai came afterward, while Dac was hospitalized," she said. "I suppose that was my fault.

"I don't know why I'm telling you this, Nelly," she said. "You're like my confessor. I tell you everything, and when I die you'll look after my soul."

I said I was afraid she was overestimating my powers, and she laughed softly.

"Perhaps," she said. "But even so, I believe you'll find I'm closer to the truth."

She studied the flower in her hand the way I might study a photograph, tracing the lines of it with her fingers, yet not touching it, not wanting to spoil its beauty. I'd like to have caught the moment, the gesture, in the lens.

"You know who Mai was, then?" she said.

I nodded.

"Yes. Well, Dac had been talking about this girl before he went into the hospital. Talking about bringing her to the States, even. I thought it a bad idea, to be honest, a dreadful idea, and Davis did, too, I'm sure. But it seemed so important to Dac. So I told him I would look into it while he was in the hospital, I told him not to worry, that I'd see about it, that all he needed to worry about was getting well. And I did look into it. I found the girl. But by the time I found her, she was pregnant." Emma sat back in her chair, still holding the daffodil. "She seemed to think the child was Dac's, but Dac knew nothing about it, and I couldn't tell him then, not with him so sick. It would have been another stress and he certainly didn't need another stress."

"That's what the doctors thought?"

"Well, they certainly would have, wouldn't they?" she said. There seemed no point in discussing it, she said. They didn't even know if the child was Dac's. Perhaps Mai knew Dac had money; perhaps he was the richest of her boyfriends. Not that the money was an issue for Davis and her. They were just worried about Dac, about his health, his future. "And of course he couldn't make any decision in the state he was in," she said. "So I brought the girl to the States myself, almost immediately. I set her up in an apartment and I arranged doctors for her."

"You arranged for her to come here?"

"Of course."

"To Baltimore?"

"Not to Baltimore. I didn't know what Dac would want to do, and it seemed it would be easier to . . . to keep things quiet if there was some distance."

She set Mai up in New York, she said. She thought when the child was born they could do a blood test.

"Frankly, I rather hoped that even if the child was his, he wouldn't feel more than a financial responsibility of sorts. I suppose I even tried to scare Mai off. I . . ." She sat silently for a moment, absently twirling the stem of the flower between her fingers. "I sent her a letter saying how much we were looking forward to meeting her, and I said I hoped she wouldn't feel awkward living here, in our part of the country, even though there were no Vietnamese among our friends. No nonwhites. I hinted she might never be welcomed by our neighbors, perhaps not for the rest of her life. I'd like to say I believed that then, that I believed there'd be a big flap about a Vietnamese wife, but . . ." Emma stripped one of the petals off the daffodil, apparently unaware that she was doing so. She sat looking out through the window to the stretch of brown farm, her shoulders sunken, the lopsided daffodil looking pathetic.

"You've said yourself, Emma, that . . . well, that you feared there'd be a scandal if your past came to light. So maybe you did believe it?"

Emma began to rock back and forth in her chair again, unconsciously stripping a second petal, dropping it to her lap. Her past was a long time ago, she said, and she'd kept her secret for fifty years, so who she was or where she'd come from . . . Yes, there'd have been a flap about that. But with Mai?

"The world had changed a bit by then, hadn't it?" she said. "They might have lived elsewhere, too, of course, but . . . but he was so fragile then."

I sat back in my rocking chair, imagining how protective I'd feel if Ned or Charlie were sick, or worried, or sad, thinking I never wanted them to move away.

It turned out not to matter, Emma said, stripping the last petal from the daffodil. By the time Dac was well enough to make decisions, Mai had disappeared. She'd taken the money Emma had given her and gone elsewhere.

"So you see, I'd been right not to tell him," she said.

"You didn't tell him anything?"

"I told him I hadn't been able to find her. I couldn't tell him I'd found her and brought her over and she'd taken our money and disappeared. He was so weak even after he got out of the hospital, Nelly. Knowing Mai had disappeared with a child would only have added to the stress he was under, and there was nothing he could have done about it. If I could have found Mai, if I could have found her then, of course I'd have told him. But she disappeared. *She* disappeared. And why would she have disappeared if the child were his?"

"It's not like you—" I looked to the scones and clotted cream, already beginning to spoil in the hot sun. "Mai made her own choice, right?" I said.

"It's not like I paid her, is it?" Emma laughed sadly. "That is what people think, isn't it? That I paid her to disappear."

"Well, I—"

"It's all right, Nelly. I've always known there was gossip, though not too much, I don't imagine. Michael is not much of a talker, and Willa can be discreet when she sets her mind to it. And I don't believe Dac ever spoke of that girl to anyone else."

Emma looked at the daffodil, the bare stem in her hand, the petals in her lap. Surprised, she picked up the petals and set them on the table. I wished again that I had my camera, that I could have caught that expression.

"Of course, I did give her that money," she said. "Maybe what I did was wrong. The little girl . . . I don't know. Maybe I should have told Dac more than I did." She looked straight at me then, as if making her mind up about it. "But Dac needed to put that nonsense behind him, all that Vietnam nonsense," she said. "It was best for him, and he couldn't do it himself." She leaned forward in her rocking chair and stuck the bare flower stem into the watering can, knocking drops of water to the table. "It was best for him and I did it and I don't regret it," she said. "Not for a moment. Not one bit."

24

Despite my admonition to Dac not to uncrate the clock, the first thing I heard when I arrived home that afternoon was the clicking away of seconds in my front hall. I heard the clock ticking as I played Monopoly with the boys in the playroom. I heard it as I read the paper while Dad and the boys fixed a birthday dinner for me. I heard it as Dad lit the candles on my cake, then lost the sound of it as Dad and the boys sang "Happy Birthday to You." But the ticking returned as I searched my mind for a worthy wish, and then the clock began to toll the hour. By the sixth gong, I'd made my wish: that I would not run out of time.

Before Wesley died, time was something I took largely for granted. In some ways I understood the importance of time—even a fraction of a second—better than most: it could be the difference between a blurred photograph and a clear one in a fast action shot; the difference between having good light and bad as the sun moved behind a cloud; even the difference between getting a great photo and getting no picture at all. On a larger scale, too, I was sensitive to the passing of time. I marked the days and years by the changes in Ned's and Charlie's bodies, in their vocabularies, in the things they could and couldn't do for themselves as stuffed bears were thrown over for blocks, which were thrown over for bicycles and bats and balls. So I knew that time was passing. Still, when the boys asked me to do something and I was too tired, I'd suggest we do it another day, never doubting another day would come. After Wesley died, though, the fear that any moment could be my last would sometimes overcome me. I'd be helping Ned with his spelling or teaching Charlie how to tie his shoes, showing them how to make paper airplanes or how to draw a star, and I'd find myself wanting to cry for the fear that I might die any minute, never getting to do these little things with them again.

Dad left not long after we'd finished the cake and ice cream that night, to have late drinks with some old buddy who was in town. The boys went to bed early and Boomer fell asleep by the back door and I was left in the quiet of the house, all by myself. I pulled out my photos and sat in the kitchen to work on my portfolio, the ticking of Emma's clock in my hallway making me more aware of time's passing than I'd ever been. I began to be confused by the marking of those seconds, how to spend them. If I had only a second left, that was easy. I'd wrap my arms around my sons and give them all the love a second can embrace. If I had only a minute or an hour or a day or a week, then I'd give every precious tick of that clock to them—to us. But what if I had a long lifetime ahead of me? What if I had years of empty days while they were in school, empty evenings while they played basketball or chess or delivered newspapers or went on dates? What if I had decades left, years that would bring only occasional visits from my sons and their spouses, who would inevitably fill their time with lives of their own?

Emma's tickets to New York now haunted me from their place on my dresser. Though a part of me wanted to catch the next train, a part of me wanted to throw the tickets out.

The clock did serve its purpose, though, reminding me that my time with Emma would someday end. And it reminded me that Dac, too, did not have endless amounts of time, and I wasn't being fair to him. So I got up from the table, called Emma and invited her to breakfast the next morning, and after I finished talking with her, I dialed Dac's number. When he answered I asked him if he could come over after all. Ned and Charlie were sleeping, I said, and Dad had gone into the city, and I wanted to talk to him, I thought we needed to talk.

Dac knocked lightly at my front door that night, but I was already there, opening it. He had a present in one hand—the size and thickness of it suggesting something framed—and a bottle of Dom Pérignon in the other, and he was wearing his standard jeans and white T-shirt with his jacket on over it, not zipped, and he looked great.

"Happy birthday!" he whispered, stepping into the entryway, holding out the present but not kissing me, not making any move to kiss me.

"I can't accept it, Dac," I said softly.

He closed the door behind him. "Okay," he said cautiously, smiling awkwardly. "But wouldn't you maybe like to see what it is first, before you turn it down?"

I might have lost my nerve, but there was that clock ticking the seconds away behind me. I glanced at it and then at Dac, I made myself look at him, at his soft curls and his green eyes and his kind, questioning smile.

"I can't see you, Dac. I came to tell you that the day after Christmas and I don't know why I didn't, but I didn't and I'm sorry. I can't see you. I'm not ready for a relationship and even if I were, the boys aren't ready for it and I don't want to hurt you, I really don't want to hurt you but I just think I'll . . . I'll end up hurting you worse, or hurting myself, I don't know, and I've got the boys to think about and my photography and I just don't think—"

"Slow down, Nelly," Dac said. "Slow down. It's okay. It's okay." And then he took me in his arms and I was bawling, I didn't even know why, but I was bawling and Dac was holding me in his arms, holding the champagne and the present in one hand and patting my back with the other, saying, "It's okay, it's okay," while I was telling him everything, it was all spilling out—my fight with Wesley before he died and my still wanting to be a photojournalist, even after that, and Charlie asking why I kept Wesley in the basement and me saying I didn't, they were only pictures, but of course I did, I kept Wesley hidden away where I wouldn't have to think about him. And all the while Dac kept patting me, saying it was okay, it was okay, he understood. And when I finally caught my breath, when I finally managed to stop crying, he wiped the tears from my eyes with a handkerchief, and he took my hand and sat me down at the kitchen table, where I had my photographs spread out.

"How 'bout a glass of champagne?" he said. "It can't possibly make you feel worse."

He worked the wire off the bottle, covered the cork with a dish towel, and eased it off. A little mist of champagne followed the cork from the bottle, but the pop was subdued and not a drop spilled.

In the cabinet to the right of the sink, he found two jelly glasses, one with a picture of Dino the Dinosaur on it—the one Ned and Charlie always fought over—and one with Bamm-Bamm, the boy with the bat.

"I've got champagne glasses," I said, sniffling, wiping my eyes again and thinking how awful I must look.

"I always liked Bamm-Bamm," Dac said, and he filled the Dino glass with champagne and handed it to me.

"So I get Dino," I said.

"You sort of look like Dino now, with your red eyes and red nose." He grinned and I couldn't help laughing.

"Well, that sure makes me feel better," I said.

He filled the Bamm-Bamm glass and sat in the chair next to me and clicked his glass to mine. "Happy birthday," he said, and we sipped the champagne and he slid the present in front of me. "I want you to have it," he said. "Open it, at least. Open it and if you still don't want it, well, it's not exactly returnable so I guess if you don't want it, I'll have to donate it to a museum or something."

"A museum?" I said, too intrigued now not to open it.

I peeled off the wrapping carefully, uncovering a framed Dorothea Lange photograph, a middle-aged woman outside a farmhouse, hanging laundry while, in the background, a man sat on the back porch in his T-shirt, reading a newspaper and smoking a cigarette. It might have been in her *American Country Woman* collection, though it wasn't included in the book that had been published after her death, I didn't think.

"Dac, I— This is lovely, but I can't accept it."

"It's one of her late photos," Dac said, looking at the photograph. "After she'd stopped focusing so much on 'event pictures' and started photographing people in relation to other people rather than to events. It's not as valuable as the earlier prints, but it made me think of you." He met my eye then. "You could do that, you know," he said. "I know you can't just fly off to cover every war or earthquake, at least not while the boys are young, but you have a way of getting inside people, like you have with Mother. In all my life, I've never seen

Mother . . ." He looked away, pursed his lips, then looked back directly into my eyes. "She's never let anyone close to her like she's let you. You can do that with people. You can get close to them." He nodded twice, like his mother might have. "You can get those photographs."

I looked at the picture, ran my finger around the frame, not knowing what to say. "Really, I can't accept it."

"I want you to have it."

"But it must have cost a fortune."

Dac laughed halfheartedly. "You forget I'm a Crofton," he said. "What am I going to spend my money on if not my friends? I don't even have an heir to leave it to, and try as I might, I can't seem to lose it on my horses.

"Take it, Nelly," he said softly. "I want you to have it. I want you to hang it on the mirror in your bathroom—"

"In my bathroom!"

"—so when you wash your face every morning you can look at it and think, I can do that, I can be the next Dorothea Lange."

The next Dorothea Lange. The words brought back my eighth birthday, the camera on the table, the straps tied together with ribbon, my mother wiping up the milk.

"I can't accept it, Dac," I repeated. "It's too much."

"It wasn't that expensive. Her earlier photos, those are, but this one—"

"I can't."

Dac looked exasperated. "Okay, how 'bout this? How 'bout I exchange this for one of yours? Call it prudent buying, since I expect your photographs to be worth more than Ms. Lange's someday."

I laughed.

"Let's have them, lady. Let's see your photographs."

I hesitated, taking a long sip of champagne, then scooted

my maybe-good-enough-to-go-to-New-York pile across the table to him. "Okay, fine," I said. "Pick any one you want."

He looked through the photos and we talked about them, Dac asking which ones I was thinking of putting in my portfolio and me telling him and the two of us talking for a while about the choices I'd made. "What about this one?" he asked, holding up a picture of a homeless woman, the one I'd photographed in front of the library the day I'd gone in search of the photographs he'd seen in Vietnam.

"I don't think so," I said. "Technically, it's pretty pathetic."

I wasn't thinking about the photo, though. I was thinking about Dac and Vietnam and Mai and the child Dac didn't even know about.

"It captures something, though," Dac said.

"What it captures is the way a photo blurs when you move the camera."

Dac laughed. "Still, it does capture something. You should take it to New York."

"You take it if you like it," I said. Somehow, I liked the choice, liked that he'd chosen a picture that, though he didn't know it, had something to do with him. "I can make another print if I decide you're right."

Dac studied the photo for a moment. "You *are* going to be successful, Nelly. You're going to be successful and then I'm going to say, Oh yeah, I know Nelly Grace, I used to date her. Or sort of like dated her. Or at least I can say I rented your barn."

I laughed, and he kissed me lightly on the cheek then, a friendly peck, and said he ought to get going. If I needed any help hanging the photograph from my mirror, he said, I should call him tomorrow. He shrugged on his coat and a moment later he was gone and I was left standing alone in the entryway, listening to the steady ticking of the clock.

25

Bright winter sunlight slanted through my kitchen window the next morning as I sorted through my cabinets for my jar of Emma's Peach, which was nowhere to be found. Dad was brimming with energy even before Emma arrived for breakfast, so exuberant I should have known something was up, but I was lost in my own thoughts. I'd had in mind to talk to Emma over breakfast about our trek up to New York—I did want to go and I was nearly ready to go now, I'd even spent my early morning hours drafting a query letter, considering where I might send it as I sat in bed, pencil and pad in hand, staring at the Dorothea Lange propped up on my dresser. But I didn't want to talk about going to New York in front of Dad.

"I'm going to Eastern Europe, to cover the fighting," Dad said to Emma as I fried the bacon. "There's nothing like a war pic for the cover."

He'd have a break in three weeks, he said, a long weekend. "I thought we could meet in London," he said to Emma. "I'll have the travel agent arrange your flights."

Emma had an uneasy look on her face, which made me uneasy too. "Which weekend?" she said.

"Which weekend?"

Emma nodded. "Which weekend, Patrick?"

Dad pulled a small calendar from his pocket and flipped through it. "March third."

"I can't go then," Emma said, not unkindly.

"Can't—"

"It's the weekend of the Hunt Cup. I can't go."

Dad looked as crushed as I'd felt the afternoon he invited Emma to the photography exhibit at the National Gallery.

I set the bacon, eggs, toast, and butter on the table, along with a jar of strawberry jam, then refilled our coffee cups and poured juice. As I sat and poked at the bright yellow center of my egg, Emma said she, too, had good news to report: her doctor had given her the go-ahead to start riding again. "Timely authorization," she said. "I was about to ride, anyway." She almost single-handedly carried on the conversation after that, talking about riding the hunt again. Never mind that she hadn't ridden in months. And then she began to talk of riding in the Hunt Cup, and I could see the lightbulb go on in Dad's mind: that's why.

"You're going to *ride* in the Hunt Cup?" he said.

The Hunt Cup was one of the most prestigious races around, and one of the toughest. Emma had ridden in it, won it—she had that trophy on her mantel—but she'd been a young woman then, and she'd be seventy that July. Never mind her leg.

"This year?" I said.

"Foolish Heart is the favorite," she said. "And why shouldn't I ride him? He *is* my horse."

She didn't appear to be joking.

I poured myself another cup of coffee, using the minute it took to give Dad a chance to jump in here, and when he didn't, to think through my reply. "Well, there is this little business of your leg," I said finally. "What does your doctor say? Have you talked to him about it?"

The question brought the conversation to a halt.

Dad moved to fill the silence. "Once you're riding again, you can see how you feel."

"I thought I'd ride this afternoon," Emma said. Then, turning her attention back to me, "I hoped I could persuade you to join me, Nelly. It'll be the easiest ride you've ever taken. I'm only to walk the horse. No trots, no canters, no jumps. No fun at all. But won't you come with me?"

Dad eagerly offered to go. "I haven't ridden in years," he said, "but I'm sure I could manage to stay in the saddle through a walk."

"Not this time, Patrick." Emma's smile left no opening for changing her mind. "I've been thinking for a long time I'd like my first ride to be with Nelly. After all, without her these last few months, I'd have gone to the grave with boredom." She turned to me. "Won't you come with me, Nelly?"

I nodded. "Yes, Emma. Of course I will."

Emma's voice sounded a strident "I'm riding him" from inside her barn as I arrived for our hack that afternoon. I peeked inside to see her standing, brush in hand, next to a cross-tied horse. Her back was to me, and she appeared to be speaking to the hayloft opening. I didn't see anyone else.

"You may be the trainer," she said, "but I'm still the owner."

A square bale of hay dropped from the opening, and then another, and a pair of men's boots appeared at the top of the ladder, followed by legs, hips, shoulders, head. Dac.

I'd done the right thing, telling him I couldn't see him, I reminded myself. And he wasn't ready for a relationship either. If he were, he'd have told me about Mai himself.

He reached the bottom of the ladder, brushed golden sticks

of hay from his jeans. "Over my dead body," he said, "because I want to keep your stubborn old body alive, Mother. You're not riding in the Hunt Cup."

He saw me then, just a glance in my direction, a flicker of his eyes.

"Forget your age for a minute, Mother," he said. "The race is only a few weeks away and you haven't even ridden since you broke your leg."

"Forget my leg a minute," Emma shot back. "Let's talk about my age. I could be dead by next year's race."

"Nelly, help me out." Dac's face open, vulnerable. "Tell your friend here she can't ride in the Hunt Cup."

Emma turned to see me, her eyes not as hard as I'd expected given the tone of her voice.

"She'll fall and kill herself," Dac said.

Emma frowned, narrowing her eyes at me. "You're against me too?"

I nodded, though I hated to; she was always so supportive of me. But my opposition would have no impact on her decision; when Emma set her mind to something, she did not let go.

She fell silent. Dac held firm.

"The Old-Fashioned, then," Emma said as if the thought had just occurred to her. "Surely you won't object to the Old-Fashioned."

The Old-Fashioned was a race of sorts, a club event, with only club riders. The participants were spirited, some would say they went about it with reckless abandon, even craziness. But it was not the caliber of the Hunt Cup, not even close.

Dac straightened himself up. He considered her proposal for a moment, then nodded. "If you're riding well by then."

"Only because of the leg," Emma said. "I'm not ruling out next year . . ."

"We'll talk about next year when it comes." Dac began to stack the bales against the stalls, the discussion over.

Emma sulked a bit, seeming quite disappointed. She turned her back to Dac, applied herself to the brushing of her horse. When she told me which horse I'd be riding, though, her voice did not sound defeated, and, while she did not smile, I thought I saw a satisfied, even delighted, look in her eyes. It struck me then: it was the Old-Fashioned she'd been after all along.

Emma and I walked the horses out past Five Star Farm in a comfortable silence. I was thinking about Dad leaving, thinking I would miss him but also that I might, once he was gone, do something finally with my photographs, when Emma pointed out the place where the Old-Fashioned race would start.

"In the Old-Fashioned, you pick your own course," she said. "You start and end here, and there are several points you have to pass in between, but how a rider gets about the course is up to him or her. The fastest rider is not necessarily the winner. You have to be smart about the course you pick. Be smart and have guts."

As we crested Patterson's hill and turned to head back in, I looked out across the valley to my place and, beyond it, Willa's, and I thought about Willa, about Davis and her. She would have been so much younger than Davis, young enough to be his daughter. I tried to imagine being in love like that.

Emma rode ahead of me down the hill and alongside the stream at the bottom, a quiet stream now, frozen at the edges, but she was talking about how high it often ran by the time of the Old-Fashioned. "A lot of rain or a lot of snowmelt can change your course dramatically," she said. She pointed to a narrowing in the water, where the stream cut between two steep banks. "If the weather stays dry, I'll cross there, but so will everyone else. I need a little rain, just enough to put everyone else off jumping the stream here. Not too much, though. Too much and it's too risky, it gets too slick to scramble up the far bank."

"But if you make it, no one can beat you?" I said.

"Not unless they've crossed here ahead of me."

"And if you miss?"

"You're out of the race. And probably short your best horse."

She ducked under a low branch overhanging the path and I ducked, too, and when I sat back up, Emma was moving away from me in an easy trot, her shoulders square and proud. We trotted for a few minutes, my mind now concentrating on keeping my heels down, not slowing until we came out of the woods.

"I thought you were supposed to take it easy," I said as I settled in beside Emma again.

"Those doctors!" Emma laughed. "They just don't want to be sued. But I'm not wasting my time, not like your father wastes his. Did you know he's already decided not to start that assignment for another month? And not like you either, Nelly."

"Me? I don't waste time."

Emma shot me a sidelong glance. "Those tickets to New York? They don't need aging."

"My portfolio isn't quite ready."

"Next week," Emma said.

"I want to make sure I'm ready. I don't want to blow my chance, like you could blow yours trying to do too much too early on that leg."

Emma laughed. "I'll let you in on a little secret, Nelly," she said, leaning over from her horse. "I've been riding since the very day my cast came off."

With that, she moved into a canter, shouting back over her shoulder, "Line up your interviews, Nelly Grace. It's time to go to New York!"

26

I was twelve the first time I went to New York. Mom drove us in the station wagon to meet Dad there, and we were so excited, we asked how long it would take about once every five minutes from Youngstown, Ohio, where we'd stopped for the night. My brothers groaned as, rather than crossing the Hudson River at the George Washington Bridge and heading into the city, we went south and came up around the other side of Manhattan, to cross over on the Brooklyn Bridge as Mom had promised me we could.

"Who cares about a stupid ol' bridge?" Danny complained from the way-back, where he was stretched out, reading. But I had my camera by my feet, and as we came to the bridge, I rolled down my window and began snapping pictures: views of the bridge with the skyline in the background, the Empire State Building. When Danny realized what I was up to, his complaining changed into a whine that he should have a turn in my seat.

"You've got a window," Mom said, trying to keep the peace.

"It doesn't roll down, Mom," Danny said. "And it's covered with road dirt. It's not fair. Smelly's getting all the shots."

As we crossed the bridge, I hung out the window and shot upward, capturing the cables and the stone arches all converging to the American flag standing straight in the breeze. Mom screamed at me to get my head back in the car before I was decapitated. "All right, you move over this instant, young lady. Danny, move your sister over to the middle. Nelly, if you're going to behave like that, I want you in the middle seat."

"Yeah. Move over, Smell," Danny said.

I did move over, but I took my time about it, making a long process of putting my lens cap on my camera and tucking it back into my bag. And by the time Danny took over my seat, the bridge was disappearing behind us. He was able to get only one poor shot.

The next morning, Dad woke Danny and me early, telling us to get dressed and get our cameras, we had places to go and things to photograph. I balked, saying I wanted to stay at the hotel with Mom, that I was too tired to get up, though I was already wide awake. Dad pulled the covers up over my head, burying me in darkness. "Suit yourself," he said. "It's a nice camera. A *really* nice camera. You wouldn't think it would hurt you to use it now and then. But suit yourself."

I waited until Dad had gone back into his and Mom's room, then got up and dressed quickly. When he came back in, Danny was tying his shoes and I was ready, my camera slung over my shoulder.

"You decided to come?" Dad asked.

I shrugged.

We took the subway, the E train, I remember, because it made me think of an E ticket ride, the best in Disneyland. We got off in Greenwich Village, then walked a few blocks to a place called Balducci's, where Dad bought us sweet rolls and juice for breakfast. As we sat on a bench outside, Dad asked Danny and me to look around for a minute. He took a sip of his coffee and we bit into our pastries.

"What's the first thing you photograph here?" he asked. "Look carefully. This is a test."

I chewed slowly and swallowed, the dry, bready bite a cotton ball choking down my throat. What caught my eye was a squat old lady who seemed likely to topple over from the weight of the suitcase she carried, a square hard suitcase of beaten leather, nearly as worn as the heels of her shoes. What in the world was such an old woman doing carrying a suitcase as she walked alone down the street? Where she was going? What, if anything, did she have packed inside?

I avoided Dad's eyes, not wanting to be called upon first. I looked from the intriguing old woman to Dad's pastry, which sat untouched in its bag between us on the bench.

His fingers tapped idly on his camera, the wide-angle lens.

"Ladies first," he said.

I looked up at him and, certain my voice would betray me, pointed to the woman.

Dad looked.

The woman stopped at the street corner, set the suitcase down on the pavement and looked around oddly, as if she'd just realized she was in New York City, as if she'd just awakened from a trance. Dad continued to watch her for a moment, then lifted his camera, focused on her and pushed the shutter release. He lowered his camera and watched as she lifted her suitcase again and made her way across the street. He focused again, this time not on her face but lower, on the suitcase, on her hand where it gripped the handle as if holding on for life.

He'd changed his lens sometime after we'd sat down, I saw as he took the shot. He was using his telephoto.

When I looked to the street again, the woman with the suitcase had disappeared.

Dad nodded to himself, still focused on the street where the woman had been, an odd smile on his face.

"And what about you, Danny?" he said.

"That there," Danny announced confidently, pointing across the street to the Gothic red brick of the Jefferson Market Courthouse and its high clock tower. Even I, no connoisseur of buildings, could see it was spectacular. And I'd been so caught up by that woman.

"How would you photograph the courthouse?" Dad asked Danny, proving by his follow-up that Danny had chosen correctly.

You'd use the wide-angle, get the building and the contrast to its surroundings. That's why Dad had had the wide-angle on. I stole a glance at his camera. He was unscrewing the telephoto. The wide-angle rested in his lap, waiting to be put back on. He continued to look at Danny while his fingers easily made the switch.

"The clock tower," Danny said.

"I see." Dad studied the clock tower for a moment, his gaze traveling from the steep pitch of its roof down to the arch over the clock face—the time was 8:45—and on down to where the roof and the arch were echoed in stone at the turret base. He looked at Danny and me again, smiling, almost laughing. "I'm afraid you've both failed." He nodded at our cameras, still with the lens caps on. "If you're waiting for the light to get better, Danny, it doesn't get any better than this. And you, Nelly, while you were eating breakfast, your shot just walked away. That lady is gone, and she's taken her mysterious suitcase with her. You see a great shot, you've got to take it. You can't wait till after you eat."

27

The Thursday Emma and I were to leave for New York, I awoke at five in the morning, having barely slept. I dressed in slacks, a cotton shirt, and flats—good traveling clothes—all the while looking at the Dorothea Lange propped up on my dresser. I took the photo downstairs, where I started a pot of coffee and stuck a cup under the stream of hot liquid until it was full. The sun was not yet up when I sat on the living room couch with my coffee, looking at the photograph, the outline of the woman barely distinguishable in the dim light.

I was ready. I'd selected my best work for my portfolio. I'd carefully crafted the letters I'd sent, carefully selected the sample work to send with them, and by some miracle a few people had actually responded, actually agreed to see me. Some miracle, or the fact that I'd signed my query letters "Eleanor *Sullivan* Grace"? But the combination sounded more professional than Nelly Grace or even Eleanor Grace, and it felt more comfortable somehow, more me, and Sullivan was a common name and it was my name and no one would likely have made the connection to my father, and even if they had, these were busy professionals; they'd seen my work and surely they wouldn't have agreed to see me just because I was my father's child.

When I heard the shower in Dad's room, I turned on the light, returned the Lange photograph to my bedroom, put on boots and a winter coat, and walked with Boomer to get the paper from the box. When we'd first moved to the country, I'd thought this would be a good way to get a little daily exercise, walking the half-mile up our little road to the corner, where the paper was left in a white plastic *Baltimore Sun* box, but this was the first time I'd walked instead of taking the car.

It was snowing lightly outside, beginning to accumulate. A dusting of snow on the sycamores reflected the last bit of moon. Over the hill to the east, the sky glowed faintly where the sun would soon come up behind the clouds. I wished I'd brought my camera.

The sun was up by the time I got back to the house with the newspaper. I left the dog to dry off in the mudroom, and sat at the kitchen table with a second cup of coffee, reading the headlines without really reading. Dad came in and took a coffee cup from the cabinet.

"You're up awfully early," he said.

I looked up.

"Umm," I said, and I turned back to the newspaper, making a serious attempt to read this time, fearing that if I kept thinking about New York, Dad would somehow be able to read my mind, to see how anxious I was.

"Well," he said, as if he might make some comment, but he didn't. He poured coffee into his cup, spooned in sugar, and stirred. I felt him watching me. I wasn't watching him, but I was aware of his movement around the room: the click of a cabinet door opening, a bowl set on the counter, another cabinet door, a cereal box opening and flakes spilling out.

"I hope you have a nice time in New York," he said.

Not so much as a nod of encouragement. Not even a "good luck."

"Take good care of my boys," I said.

Emma and I sat on the hard wooden benches of the station until our train was announced, then carried our bags down the stairs to the platform just as it whooshed in. Emma said something as I braced myself against the draft of the rushing train, but I couldn't hear her over the noise. We boarded and settled into our seats, big seats that looked comfortable, thickly padded and covered with soft cloth, but sitting on them was like sitting on the crusty top of a snowdrift: there was softness underneath, but the surface was brittle and un-yielding, some comfort engineer's failure.

The conductor announced this was a Metroliner bound for Wilmington, Philadelphia, Newark, and New York.

"We're off," Emma said. "This train is bound for glory. No turning back."

Emma and I passed the time looking at the newspaper, sharing tidbits we read to each other like an old married cou-ple at the breakfast table. We fell silent somewhere outside Philadelphia, judging from the freeway overpass signs. Emma closed her eyes, napping, and I settled into the view out the window—a world so unlike mine, it was hard to believe it ex-isted so close to my own. Rust blanketed everything. It cov-ered big, abandoned old machinery. It lined the roof of a sad old warehouse, the blue and green glass windows of which were shattered, not even boarded up. It rotted even sadder old homes that were attached, one after another after another, by shared walls, as far as I could see.

In a nicer neighborhood these houses would have been called town houses, but these were no town houses, not with their boarded-up windows, the end house opening out almost onto the tracks, separated from them only by broken cement walls, old tires, and piles of abandoned beer cans, again with the rust, always the rust. Even the slum children in Jacob Riis's photographs had better homes. Surely these places could house only ghosts of an unfortunate past. But laundry hung on the line, socks in bleached white pairs dotting the filth.

They'd have made an emotional photograph, those white white socks. It was one of the few shots I'd like to have had in color, the world itself so gray that, properly composed, the photo would be punctuated only by the whiteness of the socks and the single color of the rust.

Farther down the tracks, the houses—always attached houses—backed up to a cliff right over the tracks. You could just jump right out there, into the path of a train, if you were of a mind to. And why wouldn't you be tempted to, if you lived here? Only a photographer could see opportunity here; it was what was left to us after the world turned to television and film. The opportunity to expose, and through exposure, to change. The opportunity to personalize extreme despair. To show the rust.

The scene whizzed by as the train sped on, was gone before I could have unpacked my gear. The quality, taking the shot through the train window, would have been poor, anyway. My confidence flagged, though. There were pictures like that to be had, and they weren't in my portfolio.

As we arrived at Penn Station an hour or so later, I could feel we were in New York. The movement of the passengers around us became quicker, more excited, almost frantic. Even the train conductor, whose flat voice had called out each stop in the same disinterested tone, said, "New York, New York! Ladies and gentlemen, this is our last stop," with some emotion that could be taken for joy.

As I stepped off the train, I felt pressed, enclosed.

Emma inhaled deeply, her eyes like a child's on Christmas morning. "Don't you love this!" she said.

"Ugh." I made a face.

"And those, I suppose," said Emma, "are the two most widely held opinions of New York."

Outside the train station, a young man with ratty hair and torn clothes sat on the ground, holding a cup with his only hand, his only arm. "Spare some change for a Vietnam vet?" he asked.

I looked away. With my camera, maybe I could take his picture. Without it, I found it hard even to look.

Emma, though, looked directly at the man as she handed him a twenty-dollar bill. "I hope you find your way out of wherever you are," she said.

My first interview that afternoon was both easier and harder than I'd expected. I arrived a little early, so I sat on a park bench across the street and watched an old man scatter seeds for the pigeons, his chin and mouth and nose tucked into a wool scarf, a crumpled hat pulled over his eyes. A few minutes before the interview, I went into the building, up the elevator, and into a monochromatic waiting room where I sat on a white couch, warming in the artificial heat, listening to a receptionist politely answer the phone. I tried to look relaxed, professional, indifferent, but my hands yearned to twist in my lap, my feet itched to tap at the floor.

After twenty minutes or so, a man in his fifties, probably, came out to greet me and showed me into his office. He was cordial, polite. He offered me coffee, which I declined, afraid I'd spill it on myself, and he asked me if I'd mind if he smoked. We made polite conversation for a minute—about how long I'd been in New York, where I was staying—and then he asked to see my portfolio and I handed it to him and he opened it, began flipping through the prints.

He looked up after a few minutes, after he'd been through the Hunt Ball shots, and stubbed out his cigarette. "You *are* Pat Sullivan's daughter then," he said.

I swallowed against the sudden knowledge that this was why he'd agreed to see me, that he was doing my father a favor. Because who was Nelly Grace if she wasn't Pat Sullivan's daughter? Just a woman with no résumé, no experience—only a few long-gone years on a college newspaper and one fluke of a shot that had landed in the *Chicago Sun-Times.*

"Yes," I said.

He smiled. "I thought so, the minute I saw the material you sent. I know your father. We worked together in Vietnam. You're the one in the photo, then, the daughter. And you're in Chicago? A great news town—"

"Baltimore," I said, and to his questioning gaze, "We moved to Baltimore this fall, my sons and I did."

He glanced to his own family photo on the bookshelf, an old photo of four young boys and an attractive woman, the mother who no doubt had been home for his children when they returned from school. "I see," he said.

He looked down at my portfolio again. "Well, if talent is hereditary," he said, "then you're in luck." And after he'd finished looking at my portfolio, he asked me what I wanted to do, where I wanted to work. But he didn't offer me a job. "I've really enjoyed meeting you, Ms. Sullivan," he said.

Not Ms. Grace, but Ms. Sullivan.

"We'll be in touch," he said. "And give my regards to your father," his final words.

That was the way it went all afternoon, too: "We'll be in touch" offered noncommittally, politely, from men who as often as not asked me to give their regards to my father. The only thing close to a job offer I got was, "How would you feel about being in Budapest by tomorrow night?"

After the last door closed behind me, I fled back to the hotel in search of Emma like a child seeking out her mother after a bad day at school. But the only response to my calls of "Emma! Emma!" in our suite was silence. Silence and a note propped up on the coffee table, where it couldn't be missed:

> I've rung up an old friend on an impulse, and we've gone downstairs for a drink. Come find us when you return and tell us all about how it went.

The only thing less appealing at this point than sharing my debut interview performance with a woman I'd never met was doing it all over again. But the next day's interviews were already scheduled.

I ran water in the tub, adding the entire contents of the complimentary bubble bath, thinking I should pilfer all the little bottles to take home for Ned and Charlie—the shampoo, the cream rinse, the hand lotion, the bubble bath—but too tired even to do that. Clean, if not refreshed, I slipped into wool slacks and a sweater, ran a comb through my hair, and rode the elevator down to meet Emma and her friend.

When I saw Emma with a tall, white-haired man at the door of the bar, obviously saying their farewells, I breathed a sigh of relief. A brief introduction, and I'd be off the hook. Emma and I would have dinner alone.

"Nelly! There you are!" Emma said. "You're later than I thought you'd be. It must have gone well."

"It went," I said. "I won't bore your friend with the details." I turned to Emma's friend. "Nelly Grace," I said.

"Of course," the man answered in a smooth English accent, much heavier than Emma's. "You're Pat's daughter. Emma's told me all about you. I'm Carl Peters." Then to Emma, "You wouldn't think Sully would have such a lovely daughter, would you? Her looks must come from her mum." He winked at me. "I knew your father when we were all much younger, before you were born, no doubt."

He took Emma's hands in his. "Next time, do give me some notice and I'll treat you girls to a night on the town. I need to run now, though." He turned to me and, without dropping Emma's hands, explained he had a business dinner to attend, that he'd cancel but he was to speak. "And I leave for London in the morning. But I'm glad to have met you, Nelly."

He kissed Emma on the cheek and said good-bye to her, the look in his eyes leaving me the impression he'd once been in love with her, and might still be.

"Imagine that: Carl Peters looking stuffy," Emma said after he'd left. "I suppose we all do now, though. The price of getting older."

"You're not old, Emma," I protested.

Emma looked me up and down, mock disappointment in her eyes. "I simply said getting old*er*," she said. "Not *old*."

The muted street sounds interrupted my sleep that night in a way that the tree frogs and crickets, or the gentle snoring of my sons, never did, and I was tired and a little discouraged the next morning, and even more so by the end of the second day of sitting and waiting, rising when my name was called, declining coffee, professing not to mind smoking just as I had the day before, the differences in each interview unremarkable: one interviewer was a woman, one didn't smoke, one offered me a Coke instead of coffee, and one didn't offer me anything at all. Still, I tried to keep my spirits up as I hurried to my last appointment, not wanting to be late. I pushed through a door into yet another austere reception area, this one shabbier than the others, leaving me with a vague sense I'd been rolling downhill ever since I'd arrived in New York. I took a seat in a bland chair, flipped through the same newspapers and magazines, watched the minutes tick away on the clock behind the receptionist: five o'clock; five thirty; five forty-eight; five fifty-one, fifty-two, fifty-three. When I was finally shepherded into an office, a white-haired, heavyset man sat writing at a cluttered desk, puffing vexedly on a fat cigar. I stood at the edge of the office for a moment, then shifted my weight, making just the slightest noise of my portfolio rubbing against my suit. Still nothing. I watched him write.

"Have a seat," he said after another minute, still writing, still not looking up.

I walked to the desk, sat in one of the hard leather chairs across from him.

"You got two minutes," he said, still writing.

I hesitated, then opened my portfolio and set it facing him on his desk, careful not to disturb the clutter. He looked up then, not at me but at my photographs, silently flipping through them. After the first half-dozen, he took a puff on his cigar.

"You got anything other than cute kids, honey?"

"Well, I've got—"

"And these rich old guys in these red tuxedos"—he flipped rapidly through my Hunt Ball pictures—"hanging on to their jeweled broads?"

I looked down at my portfolio, mentally paging through it, hoping to find something to point him to, something to change his mind. But there were no white socks among my photos. Not even a little rust.

"Not much," I said.

He looked at me for the first time.

"You wanna be a photojournalist?" he asked. "Or you wanna job in the portrait department at Sears? You need to tell a story, honey. You got a story to tell me? I gotta see it in the prints."

As I let myself out, he was already writing again.

Outside his office building, I sank down onto a cement bench. It was late, the sun long down, and the evening was cold and windy, the concrete damp against my bottom and legs even through my coat. I tucked my chin into my scarf, turned my back to the wind, and in the glare of electric lights, opened my portfolio, intending to rip up my photographs. I was no photographer. I was only fooling myself. Despite their words, no one would ever "be in touch."

The wind caught several of the photos, carried them skittering across the wet pavement as I instinctively grabbed for the rest. Ned and Charlie smiled up at me from the top of the remaining pictures, their faces laughing as they nearly fell off the porch, trying to catch raindrops with their tongues—those raindrops I'd been so pleased to have caught.

I looked out to the city, filled with people tucked deeply into overcoats, hurrying to the subway or trying to flag down cabs. Across the street, a man stopped at a sidewalk newsstand, a stand filled with newspapers and magazines—newspapers and magazines in turn filled with photographs, thousands of photographs, millions of them. Photographs taken by thousands of photographers who had jobs, who were talented enough to sell their work.

The photograph under my hand rippled against the wind. I looked down at it, at those smiling faces. They'd be missing me now, wondering why I wasn't home to feed them dinner, to tuck them into bed, kiss them good night.

The picture wasn't photojournalism. It was just "cute kids." Maybe it wasn't even good. Maybe it was the best picture I would ever take and I would never get better, I'd never be a photojournalist, the only place my photos would be seen would be on my own walls. Still, my boys' faces smiled up at me from that photograph. It wasn't one I could destroy.

28

Emma had made us a dinner reservation at a little Thai-French place in TriBeCa that night—very low-key, she said. I had no idea what Thai-French was, but the thought of getting out of Midtown was appealing. TriBeCa was south of Greenwich Village, south of SoHo even, about as far from Midtown as you could go in New York at night without worrying about your life. And it was trendy, interesting, the galleries full of avant-garde photography, avant-garde art.

The restaurant smelled of ginger and cilantro and other, stranger spices I couldn't name, and the decor was as striking: spare black and white—even the cement floor and the pipes on the unfinished ceiling were painted black—punctuated by single red tulips in black vases on white tablecloths, a contrast that would make a nice color shot. The opera music playing in the background, too, was as unfamiliar, as oddly soothing: a sad something the words of which I couldn't understand.

A waitress in a black midriff top, revealing a rattlesnake tattoo around her waist, took our order. Emma and I talked about that snake in low tones after she left. She was back, delivering our appetizers, by the time Emma asked how my interviews had gone.

Emma was a good listener, asking questions meant to make me feel better as my story of the day spilled out. What was I thinking about, I said, bringing photos of my children, bringing nothing that looked anything like news? I'd blown my one good shot; they'd made time to see me only because they knew my father, and they wouldn't do it again.

Emma set her hand gently on my arm. "The best things start slowly and rise gently," she said, sounding as like Grandma as anyone ever had. "By the time you're at the top, people will think of you as always having been there. This is just the start."

Saturday morning, Emma was up early, bustling around the sitting room in a way I suspected was intended to wake me up. She had something planned for the day, she said. Two things, actually, and would I indulge her?

She took me to the International Center of Photography, where they were having a multiartist exhibit, which they rarely do: "A Century of Shadow Catchers: Photojournalism in the Twentieth Century." On the ground floor, we admired the photographs of Henri Cartier-Bresson, Dmitri Baltermants, and Bruce Davidson.

"Not very many women represented here," Emma said.

Mary Ellen Mark. Margaret Bourke-White. Dorothea Lange. Emma was right, though. They were the only women shown. They'd been my favorites growing up, maybe because they were female and I thought if they could do it, I could too. But I'd never really considered the sacrifices they'd made to get there: Margaret Bourke-White dedicated one of her books to Patricia, the child she longed for but never had. Dorothea Lange left her children in boarding schools and with friends while she went on the road to take photos and, later, during the Depression, in foster homes.

"They're showing one of your father's photos upstairs," Emma said.

"My father's?" He'd never had a photo shown here. "How do you know?"

Emma fixed unblinking eyes on me. "I know many things, Nelly Grace."

Upstairs, we found Dad's photograph of a Birmingham, Alabama, protest against school integration in 1963. When he'd taken the picture, he wasn't so many years older than I was now, but he'd already had thousands of pictures published, already begun to win awards, to be a recognized name.

We stood looking at the photograph—a central angry face in a sea of angry faces and ugly protest signs. We didn't speak. We just stood there side by side, thinking how good the photo was. That's what I was thinking, anyway, I was thinking about how good it was and wondering what it was he did that I didn't do, what made his photographs so much better than mine. I was looking at the face in the photo, the angle of the light shadowing the eyes slightly, darkening the anger so it wasn't just that one person's anger, but the anger of everyone else in the photo, the anger of anyone who looked at that photo, my father's own anger—not anger shared with the protesters but anger against them—laid out to the world.

"It reminds me of that first photograph of yours I ever saw," Emma said. "That day I came to meet you."

I frowned, trying to remember. I'd held a photo in my hand that day; I'd been embarrassed for Emma to see it. A protester, that teacher on the picket line. That was the parallel Emma was seeing.

"Someday, you and your father will be the first father-daughter exhibit here," Emma said, her gaze still on the picture.

I, too, kept my gaze fixed on the shadowed eyes in the

photo, the anger. "I think the road from the Sears portrait department to the ICP is a long one." I made myself face Emma and grin as if I were kidding.

She trained scolding blue eyes on me.

I cleared my throat, again forcing the smile. "Though I suppose if it comes to that—"

"*When* it comes to that."

"—I'll have to insist they include my brother." Wondering through the forced smile what Danny had to do with anything, why the thought of my brother joining my father and me in an exhibit that would never happen anyway made my chest ache.

Emma looked at me still, her eyes now those of a spirited woman a third her age. "You certainly will *not,*" she said, leaving me thinking of the trophy sitting on her mantel, Emma riding her heart out to beat her husband in that race some long time before I met her, Emma admonishing me about "that nonsense about how you play."

But there was my mother's admonition, too, her neat handwriting: "Just do your best and find joy in what you do."

And riding to win didn't assure victory, not if you didn't have talent, not if you couldn't even stay on the horse. Not that I could hop the next plane to Budapest, anyway. Not that I could ever consider putting my boys in boarding schools, much less foster homes.

29

As we boarded the train back to Maryland, I remembered that Emma had said she had two things planned for me that day, and I asked her about the second. "It's coming," she said. "Be patient." And when the train stopped in Newark, she said, "We get off here."

"Newark?"

Emma ignored my surprise.

"I'm taking you to a very special place, Nelly," she said. "But you're sworn to secrecy. It's kind of a home away from home for me."

"In Newark?"

"You'll just have to see."

When the cab pulled up to an old but large and nicely kept house, a two-story with dormers in the roof, Emma paid our fare, then marched up the walk without explanation. I followed. As we climbed the stairs of the front porch, I noticed a discreet brass plaque above the doorbell: THE HANNAH CLARK HOME, FOUNDED 1978.

"It's a home for children," Emma said. "For girls who haven't any parents, or who have run away from those they have." She was already opening the front door without knocking, and a plump fiftyish woman was wiping her hands on a purple apron, saying, "Emma! What are you doing here today? It's Saturday. But it's so good to see you." And Emma was introducing her, saying, "Nelly, this is Brenda. Brenda, this is Nelly Grace, the photographer friend of mine I was telling you about."

We were ushered into a large family room, where a group of women and children lounged comfortably together, reading books and playing games. The girls ranged in age from toddlers to teenagers and spanned a rainbow of races. The youngest ones ran to Emma, pleading to be picked up, and the older ones flocked in her direction too. Emma seemed to lose herself to them, listening to their proud exclamations of their little triumphs: a perfect score on a biology test or making the basketball team, a new haircut, a new song to sing.

I stood at the sidelines, watching, wanting to join in but not sure how.

After a moment, Emma turned to me and brought me forward, her arm on mine. She introduced me as her "very dear friend Nelly," and told them I was a photographer, well on my way to being famous.

I opened my mouth to protest this billing.

"And she's come to take pictures of you all," Emma said.

"But—"

"She promised me she would, didn't you, Nelly?"

I had, at the Hunt Ball. I'd promised to take photographs of her friends.

"Now get your camera out and let's get started. You do have film, don't you? If not, I've brought some."

The girls swarmed around me, asking questions about my work and myself, begging me to open my portfolio, to show them how my camera worked, to let them have a turn focusing or maybe even taking just one picture, just one, please, just one.

"Are you really famous?" a Hispanic girl named Lily asked. She was about Charlie's age, and when I stooped to her level to answer her, to disclaim Emma's exaggeration, I thought of him.

"Emma says when you take our pictures, we can be in the newspaper," she bubbled on, "and then more girls like us will come here. They won't have to sleep in the subway stations."

I swallowed against the thought of Ned or Charlie sleeping in a subway station.

"It's cold in the subway, even when you have a blanket," Lily said. "You want to see my coat? It's red and it's brand-new, Santa brought it, and I haven't spilled anything on it and I always hang it up."

I nodded, blinking back the wash of emotion, the rush of embarrassment. I had everything in the world, really—two healthy sons and my father still alive and brothers I could visit and a beautiful farm I called home—but all the light in the room came from Lily's face, the light of a full moon large on the horizon, casting off the dark.

"I'd love to see your coat, Lily," I said.

She took my hand and led me up to the second floor, past rooms with bunk beds that slept six or eight. Emma stayed downstairs, but all the girls followed us, calling for my attention: "This is my room, see, that's my new soccer ball. Me and Melissa play every day. Vonnie taught us how." "That's Maybel, the doll Santa brought me. She really drinks a bottle." "I got Cinderella underpants, see. Pam did, too." They pulled me into their rooms to show me new clothes, toys, games, and books, even a telescope for seeing to the stars, all exactly what they'd asked Santa for when they went to see him at the mall.

"I don't really believe in Santa anymore," the girl with the telescope confided in me.

"Nor did I used to," whispered Brenda, still in her purple apron. "But someone is Santa for these girls every year. Emma organizes it, but I haven't a clue how she does it, how she arranges for each girl to get exactly what she wants. Brand-new too."

I smiled, remembering Emma's arrival at our tree-trimming party in her jingling Santa hat, and my portfolio and the tickets to New York. Yes, there was a Santa, or at least a Ms. Emma Claus.

I pulled my camera out then, and I wrote the date on my pad of paper, the one I used to keep track of my shots: the when and where and who. As I photographed the girls, singly and in groups, in poses and as they were playing, cooking dinner, doing homework, I asked them about themselves, about who they were and where they came from and about the dreams they had, who they wanted to be, where they wanted to go. I tried to capture that on film, tried to capture who they were and what could possibly be the source of the light that, despite all odds, still shone in their hopeful eyes.

Several of the youngest girls said they wanted to be Vonnie when they grew up. That's how they said it, not that they wanted to be like Vonnie, but that they wanted to *be* her. I wondered who she was and when I asked Brenda, she showed me a photograph of a striking young Asian woman she called Yvonne. She was at Columbia University now, Brenda said, but she grew up at Hannah Clark.

Looking at the photograph, I wondered how difficult it must be to find homes for these girls if even those as bright and beautiful as this Yvonne could not be placed.

I thought of my father then, of that photo of his hanging in the ICP. He couldn't change the fact of the scene—he was a photojournalist; he was there to capture reality. But still he could shade the canvas. In straight light, using a fill-in flash to eliminate the shadows, his protesters might have appeared righteous, worthy, standing up for what they believed in, justified in the anger they felt. But he hadn't photographed them in straight light, hadn't used a fill-in flash. He'd left the shadow dark across the eyes, using the angle of the light to express his own rage, to make the photo say what he wanted to be heard.

It was, I realized, something he did that I didn't much do.

As I photographed that day, I remained conscious of the light, the shadow—not just a technicality to be managed, backlighting to deal with as I hadn't dealt with it in that first self-portrait, but also a tool. Something I could use to sculpt the mood, the emotion of the shots I took. A way to pour myself out into my work.

And when Emma said we would miss the last reasonable train if we didn't move along, it seemed I'd only just arrived, just pulled out my camera, though I'd shot four rolls already, or almost four rolls. I had one shot left, and I lifted my camera to shoot a picture of Emma.

She raised her hand toward the camera just as I was pressing the shutter release.

"Emma!"

"Just the girls, Nelly," she said. "Not me."

As we climbed into the cab to head back to the Newark station, the girls waved from the front porch, untouched by the cold in their warm winter coats.

"I don't understand," I said.

"I work there," Emma said. "Every Wednesday. I volunteer. I help make dinner sometimes, clean house, read to the girls. And I spend a lot of time trying to find homes for them, places where they can have normal lives, where they'll be loved."

She'd begun to come up after Davis died, she said. "These girls helped me through that time. The least I can do is give something back.

"Now, you're sworn to secrecy, Nelly. Don't forget."

"Why don't you want people to know?" I asked as the cab pulled up to the train station. "It's so generous, what you do."

Emma did not answer. She paid the driver, opened the door, and got out.

We sat quietly on the train back to Baltimore. Emma flipped through a magazine that had been left on the seat she'd taken, and I looked out the window to the rust I knew lurked there somewhere in the darkness, puzzling over Emma's "home away from home." It made sense that, since Emma was orphaned as a child, she would want to help children who'd been left without parents. There had to be a reason, though, why she kept it secret. More than just modesty.

"They call you Emma," I said, realizing it was true only as I said it. "No one there calls you Mrs. Crofton. They all call you Emma. Even the youngest girls."

Emma smiled. "My friends here in Newark don't have a clue who I am. They don't think of me as rich and unreachable, untouchable. But they know more about me—about *me*—than anyone I know in Baltimore."

I nodded, as much to myself as to Emma.

"Anyone except you." Emma took my hand in hers. "Anyone except you."

We sat hand in hand like that for a moment, not looking at each other or talking, but only touching, being rocked together by the sway of the train moving swiftly on the tracks. I might have fallen asleep were it not for the sudden rush of a northbound train outside my window. I turned toward it, startled, then relaxed. Only another train.

Emma's face reflected faintly in the window. It reminded

me of my mother's face. The shape? The lay of the hair? The neck? Mom had had that same long, graceful neck.

"Who was Hannah Clark?" I asked, still looking at Emma's reflection in the window.

"Hannah Clark?" Emma echoed, but her voice was flat, distant, as if she were somewhere else.

I turned and looked at her, but she looked past me, out the window to the silent darkness where the train had just been. I was afraid for a moment that she'd taken ill.

"Emma?" I said.

"Hannah Clark," she said, her voice melancholy. She looked at me then, and she smiled slightly. "Did I tell you we've built two other Hannah Clark Homes? One in Los Angeles and another in El Paso. And we've a fourth under construction in Mexico."

But there was still a shadow of that lost look in her eyes, a shadow of the expression that had been on her face when she told me how her parents had died. And I wondered, then, about Emma's father, wondered what would drive a man to kill his own wife.

30

It was well past dinnertime Saturday night when we got back from New York, and we hadn't eaten on the train, but when I dropped Emma off at her place and she invited me in for a little supper, I almost said no. I wanted to see Ned and Charlie. But they would be in bed, and I wouldn't be able to sleep for hours.

"Just a quick bowl of soup—homemade split pea," she said, and I agreed finally, and in her kitchen she pulled out a bottle of champagne too—champagne she'd put in to chill before we set off for New York.

"It *was* a successful trip, Nelly," Emma said to my skeptical eyeing of the champagne. "You *were* offered a job."

"Not anything I could take."

"Not anything you wanted to take. Still, you were offered that job in Budapest."

She picked up the champagne bottle and two glasses in one hand, her bowl of soup in the other, and headed for the wing chairs by the fireplace. She built a fire and poured the champagne. I felt unworthy, but I drank anyway, and we sat quietly eating our soup for a few minutes, lulled by the crackling of the burning wood. It seemed so quiet in the house without the ticking of Emma's clock. It would be striking midnight in my front entry hall.

After a few minutes, Emma set her soup bowl down on the side table and eyed me over her champagne glass. "Are you sure being a photographer is what you want?" she asked.

I concentrated on the champagne in the bottom of my glass, considering the question, considering my surprise at it. Emma had always seemed so supportive, more certain than *I* was.

"What makes you ask?" I said.

"What makes you not answer yes?"

I tipped my champagne glass to my lips, drained it.

"You *are* talented, Nelly."

I shrugged. "People who would know don't say I am."

She sighed. "You don't think your father—?" She got up, walked to the window, and stood looking out for several minutes, her fingers trailing over the sash. "Your father is an interesting man," she said, her back still to me. "Do you know what he carries with his gear? Ask him sometime. He doesn't . . . It's hard to understand him, Nelly. You can't tell what he's feeling if he doesn't want you to. That I know. That I have learned."

She walked to the wing chair in which she'd been sitting, and stood with her hands resting on its back. I breathed the smoky smell of the fire, watched its blue and yellow licks against the blackened brick. A spark popped out of the fireplace, and Emma swept it off the rug.

"You are so clearly his daughter," she said. "You're just like him—all the good parts of him, anyway."

She poured herself another glass of champagne, then set the bottle on the table, set her glass beside it. "I think I'd like a glass of scotch instead," she said. "How about you?"

I said I didn't drink scotch, that I'd never acquired a taste for it.

"You've never had good scotch," she said. "It isn't a taste you have to work to acquire."

She disappeared into the kitchen, came back with two highball glasses and a liquor bottle. "Glenrothes," she said, and as she tipped the bottle I read the raised letters on it: GLEN-ROTHES SINGLE SPEYSIDE MALT, and the date it was barreled and the date it was bottled inked in on the label, which was signed by the people responsible and stamped 1969.

Emma splashed some of the amber liquid into the second glass and handed it to me. I guessed I wasn't going to be given a choice.

I tipped my glass and took the smallest sip imaginable. Not even a hint of sharpness; this scotch had a soft, round flavor that made me want to hold the sip, roll it around in my mouth, let it linger on my tongue.

"You may not know it yet, Nelly Grace," Emma said, "but you're the scotch-drinking type."

I woke the next morning with a pillow under my head and a blanket covering my body. I smelled coffee and heard whistling from the kitchen. A pot banged. Bacon sizzled. I felt disoriented. "Stormy Weather" was not in Dad's whistling repertoire.

I sat up, took in the ash-filled fireplace, the wing chairs opposite the couch I was sitting on, my shoes on the floor in front of me. I was otherwise fully dressed. My head hurt, a dull champagne-and-scotch ache, and the room smelled of stale liquor and burnt wood, and my mouth had that morning-after-a-late-night taste.

Damn. The boys would wonder what had happened to me.

I threw on my shoes and hurried into the kitchen to say good-bye to Emma. It was Dac, though, moving pans around on the old white stove. Dac in jeans and a plaid flannel shirt rolled at the sleeves, his hair tousled. He hadn't shaved.

"Nelly." He smiled the way he'd smiled after we'd made love Christmas Day. "You'll want coffee, no doubt," he said, pouring a cup and handing it to me. "What were you and Mother up to last night? When I came in, you were both asleep on the couches. An empty champagne bottle and this"—he lifted the scotch bottle by the neck—"on the coffee table."

"You checking up on your mother?" I said.

"Well, the lights were on all night." He returned to the stove, began turning pieces of bacon over with a fork, grease spattering from the pan. "This morning they were still on, so I thought I'd better make sure Mother was okay." He flipped the last piece of bacon. "So?"

"So?"

"So what were you two up to?"

"Where's your mother?" I asked.

"Taking a shower. Trying to wash the scotch out of her head, I should think."

"What did she say?"

He paused, fork in hand, grease still spattering, and grinned. "She said you were talking about how to put on makeup and different ways to fix your hair."

I laughed. "That sounds about right, from what I remember. Though I can't say my memory is that reliable, given the champagne and the scotch."

"Well, I know you're both lying, but I'm fixing a celebratory breakfast anyway." Dac opened the refrigerator door, pulled out the butter, then poured me a glass of juice.

"What are you celebrating?"

"Mother says you left all of New York City breathless in your wake. Or in the wake of your photographs. Something like that."

"Mm . . ." I took a sip of the juice, wonderfully fresh in my cottony mouth. I tried not to think about the interviews, the Sears portrait department. "Your mother must have been talking about someone else," I said.

Dac looked at me, a long searching look, I thought. How often had he looked at Mai like that?

"What do you want, Nelly?" he asked.

I leaned against the old white refrigerator. "I don't know, Dac. I guess . . ."

I guess that whole last fight with Wesley had been over nothing, I'd said I wanted a divorce over absolutely nothing.

"I guess I'm just worried about the boys, about how they'd take us being . . ."

Though Ned and Charlie both liked Dac. Whenever he was at the barn, they went to visit him, they put on their boots and ran down to "help" him, and he was sweet enough to let them help.

I shrugged.

"Oh." Dac looked confused for a minute, a little puzzled, taken aback. And then a smile crept across his lips. "Umm . . . actually, I meant for breakfast."

"Oh, I— I can't stay. The boys . . ."

"Scrambled eggs? Bacon? Toast?"

I cleared my throat. "Really, I . . ."

He put his spatula down and looked at me, an even longer look than before. "So there is hope for me yet, maybe?"

I crossed my arms, feeling the hangover tightness in my head.

Dac laughed warmly. "I'll take that as a maybe, but you can't be held to anything with your head in the shape it's in right now. Or maybe you're waiting for me to commit to letting you have the Bamm-Bamm glass whenever we drink champagne?"

I smiled weakly.

"Drink your coffee—it'll help. Then I'll let you go."

I followed orders.

"Here, I want you to try something else too." He took my hand and moved me a few steps. I didn't know what to expect but I moved to where he guided me, a few steps away from the refrigerator door. "Close your eyes," he said.

I closed them. It made my head feel a little better, but my stomach a little worse.

The refrigerator sucked open. Cool air spilled out. The lid of a jar turned. And when Dac asked me to open my mouth, I did.

He slid a spoonful of cool semiliquid onto my tongue.

"Peach jam," I said, my eyes still closed. "That's delicious."

"Not just any peach jam," Dac whispered. "This is Emma's Peach."

I felt his breath close to me, felt a bit of jam at the corner of my mouth, felt Dac's finger wiping it away. I opened my eyes. His eyes, green speckled with gold, looked back at me.

And then a quiet shuffle, a movement.

I took a step back, startled. Emma stood, frozen in the doorway, watching us.

"Nelly." She pulled her sweater closer about her, did not otherwise move. "Good morning, Nelly," she said. "I didn't know you were up."

31

When I returned from taking the boys to school the next morning, Emma and Dad were sitting in the kitchen. As I entered, he rose from his chair and kissed Emma on the cheek, saying he'd better get a move on or he'd be having dinner at the Plaza rather than lunch, and he'd be eating alone. He told me he'd likely spend the night in New York, catch a train back in the morning. "Tell the boys I'm up for a hot Monopoly game tomorrow afternoon, after school," he said.

"If there *is* school tomorrow," I said. "They're saying eight to twelve inches of snow, starting late this morning."

After Dad left, Emma suggested we start the stenciling in the boys' bathroom, a row of rockets and spaceships in primary colors across the wall. I found a level in the basement and I was the stencil taper—I measured with the level to continue the line, then taped the stencil in place—while Emma was the painter, dabbing at the rockets and spaceships with a paintbrush. The painting went easily, but our conversation was uncharacteristically awkward; my open-ended questions met with curt answers: "How's your riding coming?" . . . "Bet-

ter" . . . "You ready for the Old-Fashioned?" . . . "Maybe." . . .
"But you're still set on riding in it?" . . . "I've got twelve days
yet." We worked silently through the taping and painting of
two more panels, and it was not until Emma finished painting
the stencil for the fifth time—we were almost halfway across
the wall—that I found out what this visit was about.

"You and Dac are getting to be quite good friends, it
seems," she said, and something about her tone made me cau-
tious. I busied myself pulling the stencil off the wall, position-
ing it farther along the faintly penciled line, trying to imagine
how she could be angry about my seeing Dac—even if I were
seeing him, which I wasn't.

"I like Dac," I said carefully. "Of course I like him. Very
much."

Emma held her paintbrush in the air and studied me. "I
see."

I applied myself to taping the stencil in place, embarrassed
by the specter of Dac and me naked in the sunlight on his sitting room floor, by the thought of Emma imagining us like
that.

She looked at the stencil for a long moment. "I . . ." She
hesitated, studying her paintbrush. "I don't think a relationship between you and Dac would work, Nelly."

I pulled a long piece of masking tape off the roll. "Why is
that, Emma?" Calmly, almost conversationally, even my an-
noyance at the tape bunching up on itself reined in.

"I don't think you're right for each other, Nelly. I don't
think it will last in the long run."

I peeled the tape from my skin, formed it carefully into a
ball, and placed it into the garbage, pulled another strip of
tape. It bunched up worse than the last one.

"This is a small place," she said. "I don't want you—either

of you—to end up uncomfortable. I don't want it to be awkward for any of us."

I tried to straighten the tape, but it stuck together even worse, catching strands of my hair up in it now, pulling them out when I tried to disentangle them.

"But you're seeing Dad, Emma," I said.

"It's different."

"Different how, Emma?" Different like Mai had been different?

"It just is."

"Different *how,* Emma?" I tore my hair from the tape, wadded the damned tape into a sticky ball. "You think I'm wild about your seeing Dad? In case you have any doubt, I hate it. And it's no different at all."

Emma squinted her eyes shut and shook her head. "I can't . . ." She set her paintbrush in the sink and walked out of the bathroom, down the stairs, and out the front door. She didn't even stop to get her coat.

I sat on the bathroom floor and listened for the sound of her truck.

Surely she didn't think I would hurt Dac.

After a few moments, when I'd heard nothing but a train whistle in the distance, I went down the stairs myself and looked out the window. Emma stood by the front paddock. The predicted snow had begun to fall.

I grabbed our coats and set out after her. When I reached the paddock, I draped her coat over her shoulders, and we stood watching the horses frolic in snow that came down harder and harder, in huge, soft flakes that settled on Emma's hair.

"Nelly," she said finally. She knocked some snow off the top rail of the fence, frowning, then reached out and brushed the snow off my shoulders. She didn't seem angry, but the silence was disconcerting.

"Nelly, Dac is . . ."

I ran a hand through my hair, the cold snow melting against my fingers.

Emma hugged her bare arms to herself under the drape of her coat and took a deep breath. "I knew your father," she said, "during the war. We used to run around together, Davis and I and your father and several others. Remember Carl? I introduced you to him in New York, at the hotel."

Carl Peters. He'd known my father, said I didn't look like him.

"We all used to go out dancing together. We used to meet at one another's flats to play cards and drink scotch. Your father was—I don't know—he and Davis had known each other since childhood. And when Davis was missing and we thought he was dead, your father was . . ." She stood looking at me, the dusting of white thickening on her hair, her shoulders, melting only on her uncovered arms. "Your father was a . . . a friend to me too. A wonderful friend. He helped me back on my feet. Helped me stop drinking. I told you— remember?—that day we made apple pie."

My father? The friend was my father?

"I guess I fell in love with him then, he was . . ." She looked across the empty paddock. "He was so kind to me. When they couldn't find Davis. When I thought he was dead." She shifted her weight, her arms still crossed in front of her. A bit of snow fell from her coat. "I might have left Davis for him, I think, but your father wouldn't have done that to Davis. Or your mother."

"But what does that—?" I looked at her, then laughed uncomfortably. "Are you trying to tell me Dac is—?"

"Dac's had a hard time, a lot of hard times, ever since he was a child," she said, the snowflakes landing on her arms no longer melting. "And Davis was a good father. He slept at the hospital, and when Dac would wake crying, he was there. I think that's what got Dac through, having Davis as his father got Dac through a lot, thinking he could grow up to be like Davis."

"Dac . . . But you can't mean—" I leaned into the paddock fence, bile rising in my throat, leaving a bitter taste. I watched her breath mist into the air and mingle with the falling flakes, waiting silently for her to continue, to laugh, to say it was all a sick joke or she was mistaken or I was misunderstanding her—anything.

"He still does that." She pulled on her hat and slid her arms into the sleeves of her jacket, the snow continuing to land on her sweater front, melting as it touched. "He still thinks about what Davis would have done."

I looked away, stared at the ground, at the thin veneer of white covering the gray-white lawn, melting at the point where the ground met my feet. My God, she was serious.

I felt her eyes on me, wanting me to meet them, but I couldn't, I simply couldn't. After a moment, she turned and walked to her truck. I looked up then, to see her back, her square, proud shoulders, as she opened the door. She paused, holding on to the handle but not getting in.

"I should have told you that I knew your father," she said. "I always thought I would, but the time never seemed quite right."

She swung up into the snow-covered truck, and a moment later the rattle of the engine broke the hushed winter quiet. The wiper blades moved across the windshield, pushing the snow aside, revealing her face staring blankly ahead through the window as she shifted into gear and drove off. The truck made its way up the road, past Willa's, past Kirby and Joan's. She slowed at the stop sign, her brake lights flashing red, but she didn't stop. The truck rolled forward, disappearing over the crest of the hill, and only the snow was left, falling heavily now, even Emma's tire tracks disappearing, the ruts filling as the snow continued to fall.

32

The radio announcers were increasingly warning that the storm would be severe, that before the next morning more than a foot would fall. Two or three inches accumulated by early afternoon. I paced around the house, watching the flakes drift through the air outside the windows, watching them pile up on the ground. I went over and over Emma's words, the stiffness in her posture, the emptiness in her voice. I considered the moments I'd seen Dad and her together, the flicker in her eyes the first time she met him, the eagerness in his voice when he spoke to her, their laughter as they danced around Emma's cast. And I thought about Dac, too, the feel of his fingers on my bare skin. It could not be a brother's touch; it was not my brother's touch. Emma was . . . was what? Mistaken? Confused? Lying to me?

It turned surprisingly warm that afternoon. By the time I picked the boys up from school, the snow had started to melt, and I began to hope the weather report was wrong, a false alarm. It turned bitterly cold again that evening, though, before the melted snow even had time to fall from the trees; ice covered the grove of sycamores outside my kitchen window, transforming it into a crystal forest, and with each breath of wind a crystal storm broke free from the trees and tinkled to the ground. That night it began to snow again, and by Tuesday morning there were drifts two feet high over the bottom layer of ice. We couldn't get anywhere that we couldn't walk.

Dad called to say he would wait out the storm in New York.

Dac called to ask if I could feed the horses. "Don't turn them out," he said. "They could slip on the ice, or get out and not be able to get back." He asked me to give them food and water. He'd be over to check on them and to muck the stalls as soon as the roads were clear.

I listened, telling myself he was not my brother, he simply was not.

"Dac," I said. "Your mother . . . Is she okay?"

He said before she broke her leg, she could manage fine, but he worried about her now, in this kind of storm; he was going over on his skis, to check on her.

But it wasn't the snow I'd been thinking about.

School was canceled, of course, and the boys and I made the most of it, first trying to build a snowman and, when the snow wouldn't stick, making angels instead, lying on the ground and flapping our arms and legs. Willa and her boys trudged down to our place with their toboggan in tow, and we all went sledding on the hill behind our house, Boomer chasing along beside us, his tail wagging so enthusiastically that it hurt when it hit our legs. It was all great fun, or it should have been, anyway.

Tuesday night turned bitterly cold and windy. Some combination of wind and ice and snow knocked out our power and phone lines, and we were still without power when we went to sleep that night. The boys and I slept on the floor in the den, huddled together close to the wood-burning stove.

Three across in the cockpit, Wesley flying the plane, me trying to pin-point our target in the confusion of the ground below while Dad takes

reconnaissance pictures, using his old camera, the one he gave me
when I was eight. Each time he clicks the shutter release, the flash
turns into flak exploding in the air.

"We're hit!" Wesley screams. "I can't control her! We need to bail
out."

"No ejection seats." Dad's voice eerily calm. "We'll climb out on
the wings and jump."

He pulls me onto the wing and we jump together. He tugs on his
rip cord and his parachute pops up, balloons out into the air. He re-
sumes his picture-taking.

Again, the flak.

He drifts away from me.

I pull my rip cord, shouting, "Dad! Wait! What do I do?"

My own parachute catches me, much to my astonishment.

Wesley jumps after us, pulling on his cord. His chute doesn't release.

"Wesley!"

He reaches out to me, but won't let go of his stethoscope to grab my
hand. I grasp for it, catch the end that transmits the heartbeat, clench
the cold metal in my fist.

He says something, his voice muffled by his surgical mask, then re-
leases the stethoscope to reach for his scalpel.

"NO!" I cry. But he's already plunging away from me.

Flak rifles through my parachute and I rip toward the ground,
toward Wes, shouting, "Dad!" Reaching for my father.

"Nelly!" But it's not Dad's voice. It's Dac's. He swings my father's
camera toward me, clutching the end of the strap with his massive, cal-
lused hand. I grab for it, catch it.

Thank God, the boys won't have to sleep in the subway.

The strap snaps and I plummet toward the ground, hugging Dad's
old camera to my chest.

Flak explodes around me. Dac has become my father again. He fo-
cuses the lens on me as I drop away.

I look at my hands, confused. Dac threw me the camera. I have the camera.

But my hands hold only the empty camera bag, crushed against my chest, the leather twisted from the force of my grasp.

Emma's voice whispers in my ear, "You must hold on more tightly, Nelly. More tightly."

I flail my arms toward the voice, but the air is as empty as the camera bag.

I scream again, scream as loud as I can, but no one hears me, not even my children; I have made no sound at all. The scream echoes over and over inside me as I plummet silently toward the ground, away from the flash and the flak.

The lights in the room flickered as I woke, then popped on and stayed lit. The pump in the basement began its rattle, moving water through the radiant-heat pipes. I shivered with chill and lingering fear.

On the floor beside me, Ned and Charlie slept, undisturbed. I looked at my watch. Five o'clock.

I lifted the telephone receiver to call Dac, but the line was still dead.

Unable to return to sleep, I went down to the basement, carrying my flashlight and bringing Boomer, no longer having an excuse for the butcher knife; the boxes were all unpacked. I went slowly, shining the flashlight around until I found the string for the overhead light.

In the bottom of the moving box into which I'd moved my photographs, I found some old negatives, contact sheets, and prints I'd done when I was young. I flipped through the prints, remembering the times I'd taken them. There were a few of my mother, a few of friends I'd had in high school, but most were of my brothers, Danny and Jimmy. I laid pictures of them both side by side on the cement floor. They looked nothing alike, and yet they were clearly brothers; anyone who looked at the pictures could tell. There was enough in the wideness of their mouths, the arch of their eyebrows. I touched my own mouth, my own eyebrows. I belonged with them.

I forced myself to think about Dac: He was bigger—not taller but broader, bigger shouldered, and more muscular. His face was squarer. His hair was curly where theirs was straight. They both had oval eyes, as I did, eyes like our mother's. Dac had triangular eyes.

And I thought about Danny then, about how, though I'd sometimes hated him when we were younger, I'd looked up to him and, really, thought he was attractive. The thought of a sister about her brother though, nothing sexual about it. Still, I tried to imagine what it might be like to sleep with him, or with Jimmy. The thought was preposterous, bizarre. I could conjure up nothing but the ridiculous image of repenting that sin in the confessional of my childhood Catholic church. There weren't enough Hail Marys and Our Fathers in the world.

But I remembered, then, dancing with Dad at my cousin's wedding when I was in the fifth grade, pretending we were in love.

For days, the roads remained impassable, the outside unbearably cold as ice- and snowstorms alternated through. Ice hung in suspended drips from everything outside: from the bare branches of the trees, from the fences, from the roof, from the swing set. The icicles hung thin and straight, closely spaced, like fringe on a serape.

The only sign of life was a single bird, fawn-colored, with a spotted chest, a bright red crown, and a single, pure white mark on his back. He came to eat berries from the dogwood outside the living room, chipping away at the red fruit with his beak, freeing it from the icy hold of the tree.

I kept Ned and Charlie inside, letting them watch far too many Disney videos in the intermittent spells when the power wasn't down. They ate peanut butter sandwiches and Kraft macaroni and cheese and Campbell's chicken soup. The only fresh air they got was that which found its way through the gaps in the weatherproofing around our doors and windows, and the gusts that blew in twice a day when Boomer and I went to check on the horses; I turned the heat on as high as it would go in the tack room, the only heated part of the barn, then left the tack room door open, hoping some of the warmth would spill out to the stalls.

Each night, I'd stumble into bed exhausted. Unable to sleep, though, I'd climb out and slip down the basement stairs to my darkroom. I developed all the rolls I had, including the pictures I'd taken at the Hannah Clark Home. I ran contact sheets and printed everything worth printing and some not worth printing, like the shot with Emma's palm blocking her face. When I was done, I began to go through old contact sheets, searching for something other than "cute kid" pictures. I moved mechanically, not thinking but just doing until I found myself yawning, finally ready to sleep.

As the boys and I watched *Bambi* Friday night, I cried at the death of Bambi's mother, the crack of the hunter's shot. Too tired even to stumble into the bathroom for a tissue, I sat there sniveling and wiping my cheeks with the back of my hands. Real, salty tears. The boys snuggled in closer to me on the couch, and I wrapped my arms around them. "I'm okay," I told them. "Really, I'm okay. I just feel a little sad for Bambi."

"Mom, it's only a cartoon," Charlie said.

"She knows that," Ned said. "She's not stupid."

I patted them both on the knees, and went into the kitchen to make us popcorn. After that, I was careful to hold myself together at least until they were asleep.

By Sunday morning, the fresh hay-and-oats smell of the barn had turned fetid, overwhelmed by the smell of manure. I'd seen Willa mucking out her stalls with a pitchfork several times, scooping up the old hay and throwing it into a wheel-barrow, then dumping it on a pile behind the barn. I'd never done it, but I found a pitchfork and cleaned the stalls. Who knew when Dac would be able to get there?

That afternoon, though, the sun peeked through the gray sky and, in no time, the clouds disappeared. A bright sun began to melt the snow. I should have been happy that I could finally bundle up the boys and send them outside to burn off some of their pent-up energy. Instead I worried that the roads would become even slicker when it turned cold again after the sun set, and we'd never be able to get out. But the snow-plow came to dig us out that evening, and late that night, while I was in my darkroom, I heard the salt truck grinding its way down the road.

33

Under normal circumstances, I would have cheered at the television when, Monday morning, it was announced that school would be open, starting two hours late. But that morning, I was sure I'd go crazy facing the day's mundane chores alone after being trapped in the house so long. I couldn't call Emma, though, and Dad was still in New York and I couldn't imagine calling Dac, and when I did finally call him he didn't answer his phone. So after Willa picked the boys up for school, I took my camera from its hiding place in the laundry room cabinet and pulled on my coat.

As I was heading out the door, the phone rang and I grabbed it: Emma's voice, alarmed, asking me to come help her. No, she was fine, she wasn't hurt. "But Dac has just left, I just heard his truck pulling out and I need to speak with him. And my truck is stuck in a snowdrift."

Dac.

"You must come right away, Nelly. Right away!"

I set the phone back in its cradle and stood looking at it, unsettled. When it rang again, I picked up my camera, whistled for Boomer, and went out the door.

I wasn't much of a nature photographer, really, but I photographed all sorts of things that morning anyway: snow sitting on the sycamore trees, frozen in place, suspended in the
air above the branches like intricate strips of starched lace; the
creamy trunk of a young pear tree stripped bare of its bark by
deer foraging for something to eat; the one-way tracks of my
sons in the top layer of snow, little boot prints walking side by
side away from the house, their symmetry broken occasionally
by jagged holes where a foot had broken through the ice un-
derlayer and sunk into the deeper snow. I shook off my rest-
less gloom and lost myself to the intimate view through the
lens, working with the light now, using the light, the shadow.
I wouldn't even have realized how cold my feet were getting
had Dac not pulled up the drive, honking an enthusiastic
hello. At the fork, he turned right and pulled to a stop in front
of the barn. He swung down from the truck, moving not at all
like my father moved, his body bigger and yet more graceful,
not nearly as stiff.

I stuffed my camera back in the bag and ran down toward
the barn, following Boomer, slipping and sliding, losing my
balance and falling twice as I broke through the icy crust,
brushing the snow off my camera each time I stood back up.

Dac's laugh echoed through the farm.

When I reached him, I asked if his mother had caught up
with him. "Is she okay? She didn't quite seem herself when I
last saw her, and when she called this morning—"

"Not quite herself?"

I said she was . . . well, saying queer things, things that
didn't quite seem to make sense, and when he asked what
kind of things, I said I couldn't remember exactly, that it had
been a week ago, a long week. At the note of frustration in his
voice, I suggested maybe it was my fault, maybe I was hearing
queerly, and he frowned and gave Boomer the obligatory pat,

then said no, his mother had had a slight fever earlier that week.

"It's ridiculous, this long after the fact, I know," he said as we watched Boomer take off toward something down by the pond, "but ever since the doctor told me how unsterile the average Mexican medical clinic is, I've worried she'll get some—"

"Mexican clinic?"

"Where they treated her leg."

"But she was in Montana when she broke her leg."

Dac toed the snow with the tip of his boot, saying I must have gotten that from him, he didn't know how he got that wrong, but she was at some resort in Mexico.

"But she—" She'd told me she was in Montana, hadn't she? That was where she'd tripped putting on her drawers.

A gust of wind brushed my neck, sent a shiver through me. Mexico?

Did I tell you we've built two other Hannah Clark Homes? And we've a fourth under construction in Mexico.

"She's been talking strangely to me too," Dac said. "I figured it was just because we were cooped up together for so many days, with no relief from each other."

"Strangely?"

"Asking about things in the past, things that don't matter anymore." Dac paused, looking away from me, out across the snow-covered farm. "About Mai," he said. "She— You don't know who Mai is, do you? Let's just say she was a Vietnamese woman I was involved with." He shrugged. "I was in love with her." He began to kick at the snow with his boot. "I . . . Anyway, Mother asked me if I would have been happier if Mai had come home with me after the war."

I shifted my feet, flexed my fingers against the chill setting in. "Would you have?"

He stopped digging in the snow and frowned up at me. "It wasn't possible."

He looked back down at the hole he'd kicked, smoothed snow back into it with his foot.

"I'm sorry," I said.

He shrugged again, as if to say it was all in the past, and he said he'd better check on the horses, and he headed toward the barn. I hurried to his side and, grasping for something to say, told him I'd mucked the stalls.

He unlatched the barn door and held it open for me. "Above and beyond. What a nice landlady you are."

I flipped on the light. He pulled the door closed, led me to the tack room. It was like a dry sauna, the heater still running full blast and sunlight filtering through the dirty window. I unzipped my jacket and leaned against the tack table, where a saddle blanket had been left out to dry.

I took out my camera, focused it on Dac as he collected grooming equipment—brushes and hoof-picks—and threw them into a bucket. He seemed cute to me in the way teenage boys are cute. I remembered Joan talking about Dad at the tree-trimming party, about how all the girls had wanted him to take their pictures. What had she said after that? That Dad had ignored her flirtations with him. And he'd said of course he couldn't take Davis's girl.

Outside, the sun passed behind a cloud and its light dimmed.

Dac looked at me. I clicked a shot. He took a step toward me. I clicked again. He stepped right in front of me, pinning me up against the tack table, smelling of coffee and peppermint. I could hear only his breathing and the sound of horses in the stalls outside the door.

He simply wasn't my father's son. It was impossible, ridiculous, absurd.

He took my camera from me, his strong fingers firm on my skin.

I backed up onto the tack table, putting a little more space between us.

The sun reappeared, spilling bright light into the barn.

"You're bringing light back into my life, Nelly Grace," he said.

"Through a dirt-speckled window."

Dac put his eye to the viewfinder of the camera and focused it on me. "I've been in the dark a pretty long time," he said. "Too bright a light would hurt my eyes, anyway."

I looked into the lens as if I might see through it and on into him. "Why don't you take my picture, Dac?" I said softly.

He continued to look at me through the viewfinder.

"Just press, Dac. Your finger is already there." I nodded toward where the tip of his finger covered the shutter release. The broad triangular hands, the palms wide at the knuckles and so much narrower through the thumb pad and to the wrist, wrapped well under the bottom of the camera so that it seemed to nestle up into his hand like a bird in a nest.

It was the way my father held a camera, the way a camera sat in Dad's hands.

I watched, transfixed, as the knotty joint of Dac's index finger, my father's finger, pressed the shutter release just as I'd seen so many times in my life. The sound of the shutter sliding open and twisting closed echoed like a gunshot in my ears.

Dac lowered the camera, exhaled deeply. His mouth turned up at the edges.

"I forgot the flash." He grinned. "You should've told me I was forgetting the flash. To offset the sunlight through the window." He lifted the camera again, this time with the flash turned on. He pushed the shutter release, but nothing happened. He lowered the camera and looked at it, then shrugged and held it out to me. "The last shot."

I stared at the camera, not wanting to touch it.

He continued to hold it out to me, his mouth puckering into a frown and his green eyes—green like my grandma's eyes, like my father's—lost their grin. He looked puzzled, concerned.

"Nelly?" His voice soft. "You okay?"

I reached slowly for the camera, until my fingers touched it, and I grabbed at it, pulled it to me.

Dac did not let go, but pulled the camera toward himself, and me with it.

I turned away, yanking at the camera, bringing it with me, feeling the horrible warmth of his touch. The dam of emotion broke and the anger rushed through me: anger at Emma and my father; anger at Wes for dying, leaving me alone and feeling guilty, unloved; anger at Dac for letting me love him; anger at myself for it all.

I lifted the camera up above my head and smashed it down toward the bridle hook, missing widely, hitting the wall, the wood, the braided leather strap of the bridle, and I felt Dac's hands on my arms, touching me gently, his voice saying softly, "Nelly, what is it?" And then his grip firmer, his voice louder, "Nelly, let me help. I love you, Nelly. Please let me help." And my voice, "You can't love me, you can't love me," as I swung the camera again, hitting the bridle hook this time. The lens shattered, and in the void where the anger had been, a flood of grief came crashing in.

I pushed past Dac, bolted out of the tack room, fled past the stalls and the feed bins, wanting to get away, just get away from Dac, from Emma, from my own confusion, my anger, my hurt, everything.

Behind me, Dac shouted, "Nelly! Nelly! Wait!"

I flung the barn door open, the fresh cold air hitting my lungs.

Emma stood there, so close to me I had to step back.

"Emma." More an exhale than a word.

She looked at me, eyes hard, unyielding, as if I'd meddled in some important concern of hers that had nothing to do with me.

I stumbled past her and through the deep snow, to the house. Inside, I slammed the door shut and turned the lock, put on the chain. I dropped my camera and clambered up the stairs still in my boots, clumps of dirty snow littering the stairs behind me. I stripped my clothes off in the bathroom, tripping myself in my haste to be out of my jeans. Someone pounded on the door downstairs, pounded again. Then the ring of the doorbell. It rang and rang and rang. I turned the shower on steaming hot, but I could still hear the ringing, faintly, over the rush of the water as I climbed in.

I stood in the stream of hot water, let it fall over me, over my body, my shoulders, my hair. I let the water fall on me until it was cold, till my nipples were hard and my body was covered with goose bumps. I let the cold water flow over my body until I was shivering, so cold I could barely move. And then I wrapped myself in an oversized towel and climbed, towel and all, into bed. I climbed in on Wesley's side, my wet hair soaking his pillow. I tucked the covers—the sheet, the blanket, the quilt, the comforter—under my chin, and I curled up, pulling my body tightly together, pressing my knees into each other and into the skin of my chest.

34

I woke to the sound of the doorbell. Dac? The light through the window was fading. Late afternoon. Then the knocking, the pounding on the door again. A voice calling my name, a woman's voice, calling, "Nell. Ne-ell." Willa's voice.

And then my children shouting, "Mom! Mo-om!"

There were stories of the day's school adventures to listen to, artwork or projects to admire, snacks and dinner to prepare.

I called out that I was coming, repeated the words more loudly as I pulled on clean jeans and a sweatshirt, ran a brush through my matted hair, stumbled down the stairs. I slid off the chain slowly, hoping Willa wouldn't hear it, then unlocked and opened the door.

"Sorry," I said to Willa as Ned and Charlie tumbled into the house. "I didn't realize it was locked."

Willa looked unconvinced, concerned even, but she set a smile on her lips. "No problem. I sometimes lock my boys out, too, and it's not always unintentional!"

I wanted to close the door, but Willa was right there, asking if I was okay.

"Okay?" I repeated.

She said Dac was coming up the hill as she was coming back that morning. He'd told her about Mai.

"About Mai?"

"About Emma having found her."

"Found her?"

"You didn't—" Willa glanced back at her car, where her boys were waiting. "I just assumed—You look so— I thought he'd come down to tell you. God, I'm sorry, Nell. God, I can't believe you didn't know."

From the kitchen, sounds of cabinets opening and closing, then the refrigerator door. I was freezing, standing with the door open and a light dusting of snow blowing in around my bare feet.

"Go sit down, Nell," Willa said. "I'll get my boys and give them all a snack. Then I'll fix us some tea or something. You want some tea?"

I nodded, and went into the living room and sat on the couch, looking out the big window toward the pond. I listened to Willa finding her way around the kitchen, Ned and Charlie unusually quiet, Charlie asking if I was okay.

The teapot whistled, and Willa pulled it off the burner, and I heard her murmuring to the boys that I was feeling a little punk, a little sad, maybe. "Everyone gets sad once in a while, even us moms," she said. "Now how about you guys all eat your snacks and then you can play in the playroom for a little bit—not too loudly, okay? If you boys will play quietly till I come get you, I'll take you all out sledding. Until dinnertime. Is that a deal?"

Willa's boys cheered, but mine said only, "All right," "I guess."

Willa handed me a steaming cup of tea, creamy white with milk and smelling of orange spice and honey. I wrapped my hands around the cup, happy for the warmth of it, and took a sip. Willa settled into the yellow chair across from me, the one Emma sat in the afternoon I took her photograph, when she'd told me about her parents' deaths.

"What did Dac say, exactly?" I asked. "How did he seem?"

Willa took a sip of her tea, watched the steam rise from the cup for a moment, said Dac had been sort of anxious and at the same time—not exactly happy, she didn't think, but stirred up. "He didn't stop—I mean, we both stopped, we rolled down our windows and talked like that, but it's not like he came up to my place for a cup of coffee or anything. He was in a hurry." She set down her tea, sank back into her seat, and mussed her hair. "He said his mother had found Mai. I thought at first I'd misunderstood what he was saying. He wasn't making sense. But I'm sure he said his mother had found Mai. She was living in some orphanage or used to live there or something."

"An orphanage in Newark?"

Willa raised an eyebrow. "Right. That's where Dac said he was going when I saw him. He was leaving from your place. At least I thought he was coming from here."

I got up and went to the window.

"That's why I thought you knew," Willa said. "Anyway, he said he was driving up to Newark, leaving right then."

"To see Mai."

Willa came and stood beside me. "It doesn't mean he still loves her, you know, just because he's going to see her."

"Do you think that, Willa?" I stared through the window glass, past the dogwood tree and its bright red berries, to the frozen indentation of the snow-covered pond. "Do you think he might still love her?"

Willa didn't answer.

"You do, don't you?" I looked at her. But I didn't need her

to answer. I knew the answer myself. It wouldn't be just Mai he found. It would be Mai and his child, a whole family to love.

Willa sighed. "He hasn't seen her in—what?—about a million years, right? I don't know, Nell. I guess I kind of assumed maybe he'd come down to tell you . . . I don't know . . . that he needed to go see her or something, like to see how he felt."

I nodded.

"I came down here then—this morning—to see if you were okay. But Mrs. Crofton was here, at your front door, so I figured . . ."

"Emma."

"So I turned around at the bridge and went home."

"It was Emma at the door."

"I thought she would know more about it and, well, you two are so close."

I shook my head.

"I guess I misjudged Mrs. Crofton on this one," Willa said. "All these years I've thought she was responsible for Mai's disappearance, but she must have been looking for Mai all this time."

But Mai must have been in Newark—for how long? Working at the Hannah Clark Home. A nice Vietnamese girl who would never have fit into Dac's life.

"I think Emma has always known where Mai was," I said.

"Always known?" Lines formed between Willa's nose and mouth as she frowned. "Nell? Is that you talking? Has the cock crowed? Why would she find Mai now, or say she had? She thinks you're the greatest thing to hit this part of the country since the mushroom farmers started paying for horse manure. Why would she announce she'd found Mai now and risk messing up whatever is going on between you and Dac?"

Outside, a bird—the speckle-breasted one—settled on a branch of the dogwood.

"To keep him from me?" I said quietly.

"Don't be ridiculous, she—" She rubbed at her hair, her eyes puzzled. "She doesn't want you to see Dac?"

"No."

"You're sure of that."

"Yes."

"Certain?"

"Yes."

"I don't know, Nell. That makes no sense to me, but I'll tell you one thing. If Emma— If you—"

"If I what, Willa?"

Outside, the bird on the tree began to peck at a dogwood berry.

"What did Emma do, Willa, when she found out about you and Davis? I mean, it's not like she can hurt you now, is it? You and Michael have already split."

She sighed, ran her hand over her face. "You won't believe me."

I shrugged.

She picked up her teacup, peered into it, shaking her head. "It wasn't Michael. It wasn't Michael I was afraid she'd show those pictures to. Probably there *aren't* any pictures, I don't know, but I was afraid she'd—" She took a deep breath. "I was afraid she'd show them to the boys."

"To Matt and Craig?" I sat there watching her, disbelieving. "She said she'd show the pictures to *the boys*?"

"She didn't *say* it, no, but—"

"But Emma wouldn't—" My voice so loud that it startled the little bird on the dogwood, and he flew off.

But Emma wouldn't ever have done that to Matt and Craig.

But she wouldn't have had to; Willa would never have called the bluff.

"Willa," I said. "Willa, what was Mai's last name?"

"Mai's last name? Nell? I'm not sure I . . . Why do you care?"

I stared at the abandoned dogwood berry, its insides spilling out but its thin skin still clinging to the leafless branch.

I was watching Willa and the boys tromp out into the snow, Boomer joining them from wherever he'd been, when Willa turned back and shouted to me, "Pheng. That was it. Mai Pheng. With a *p-h,* I think. Hey, and I forgot to tell you, I found your camera on the floor in the hallway. A roll of film too. A spent one. I put them back in your bag and left it in the kitchen, okay? The camera's broken, though, I'm pretty sure."

I thanked her and closed the door, went to the phone, dialed Newark information and asked for the number for the Hannah Clark Home. I dialed the number and when a woman's voice answered, "Hannah Clark," I asked to speak to Mai Pheng.

"Mai Pheng?"

"Yes. Is she in?"

"I'm sorry, there's no one here by that name."

"No one?"

"I'm sorry," she said. "You must have the wrong number."

"You're sure?" I said.

"We used to have an Yvonne Pheng, but she's away at college now. Could you be looking for her?"

I said no, no, it was Mai Pheng I was looking for, I was sure of that, and I thanked her, and apologized for bothering her. She said it was no bother, and she hung up, and after a moment the angry phone-off-the-hook buzz sounded in my ear: Hang up. Hang up. Hang up.

35

In the darkroom that night, I began to develop the rolls of film I'd shot earlier, the pictures of the beautiful wreckage left behind by the storm. I'd tucked the boys into bed early—they were tired from their day at school and the afternoon sledding—and though I, too, was exhausted when I'd climbed in bed, I'd been unable to sleep. So I worked in the darkness of the darkroom, soothed by the mechanics of developing. I popped off the top of the first film canister with my can opener, cut the leader, clipped the end of the film to the center post, and turned the reel counterclockwise to pick up the film. I set the reel in the tank. Closed the lid. Reluctantly flipped on the light. I measured the temperature of the developer, poured it in and set the timer, tapped the tank gently to dislodge air bubbles, agitated it, and when the timer dinged, slowly poured the developer out. I poured in the stop bath, then the fixer. I used a fixer remover, not wanting to sit on the basement floor for twenty minutes washing my film with my hose at my floor drain. I'd hung the film to dry, clipped it to my line, and was wiping it with a photo sponge when I realized what I'd just developed. I'd forgotten, or perhaps blotted the memory of, the last three exposures on the roll: the two frames I'd taken of Dac and the one he'd shot of me.

My first impulse was to cut the negatives into pieces. My second, to burn the whole roll. My third, to cling more tightly to the mechanics, the process, as if letting go of that would leave me in a free fall. I pulled open cabinet doors, searching for the small hair dryer I use to speed the drying of a roll of film. When I'd dried the film and worked up the courage to look at it, found my magnifying loupe, I started with the photograph Dac took of me. No surprise there. I looked as stunned as I still felt.

I made myself put my eye back to the loupe to look at the pictures I'd taken of Dac.

God, I'd slept with him.

I moved mechanically, sliding the negative strip with the photos of Dac and me into the negative carrier of my enlarger, not thinking, not feeling, only moving myself numbly through the familiar task. I used my blower to remove dust, snapped the carrier closed and fitted it into the enlarger housing, concentrating on the feel of it, the smell, the touch. I set the printing easel to seven and a half by nine and a half inches, to create an eight-by-ten. I should have run a test strip first, but I couldn't do this twice.

After I placed the easel on the base of the enlarger, I turned on the safelight and flipped the overhead off, concentrating on the mechanics, trying not to think about anything else. With the aperture wide open, I adjusted the enlarger housing and the easel, then locked the housing in place on the post. I slid in the focusing paper, then peered through the blue of my grain focuser. Don't think about the picture, I told myself as I made the adjustments, made guesses as to f-stop and exposure time and set the lens, listening carefully to the click of the stops. I pulled the focusing paper and replaced it with a sheet of number 3 grade from my paper safe, shiny side up. I set the enlarger timer, turned it on.

After that, there was nothing to do as I developed the print except watch the image arise through the chemicals in the tray, the ghost of the print appear, the shades deepen and darken until I was faced with a photograph of Dac.

I should have made a negative print, I thought as I lifted the print from the tray. Everything light would be dark and everything dark would be light, the opposite of what you expected. That would be the true story of this photograph.

I sat on the floor then, exhausted, alone. I sat there with the cold cement underneath me, remembering the way Dac and I had lain together that one afternoon: the warmth of that splash of winter sunshine, the chill of the wind outside blowing the snow from the roof.

I'm not sure how long I sat there in the darkroom before I became aware of footsteps overhead, heavy steps.

"Boomer?" I whispered. But I had not brought him with me this time. He was upstairs somewhere. Why wasn't he barking?

The boys! I leapt up, bolted out of the darkroom and up the stairs. I was halfway up, taking steps two at a time, when the door at the top opened, spilling light and one long, male shadow down the steps. I gasped.

"Nelly?"

I thought I would collapse with relief.

"Dad?"

"What are you doing down here?"

"You scared the— I didn't— God, I didn't expect you."

"What are you doing down here in the basement?"

"I . . ." I looked up at him, his body framed in the doorway as Dac's had been framed when I took the first shot that afternoon.

"I . . ." I pointed back over my shoulder. "My darkroom . . ."

His voice lightened. "You have a darkroom down here? I didn't know." He came down a couple of steps.

I stood, frozen in place, listening to the sound of his voice. Dac's voice was deeper, wasn't it?

"May I see it?" he asked. "May I see your darkroom?"

"My darkroom?" I said stupidly.

"Nelly?" He pulled absently on his hair. "If you don't want me to see it, just say so."

"No, no," I said, blinking, remembering now the print of Dac hanging in the darkroom, thinking of all the pictures I'd never intended for my father to see. "I thought you . . . It's just a little . . ." I turned and looked down the stairs. "Watch your head," I said. "There's a low beam at the turn in the stairs."

I stood just inside the door, watching Dad move through the darkroom. His fingers touched things as he came to them, running lightly across my enlarger, picking up a tray and setting it back down, opening cabinets. He was almost to the clothesline where the picture of Dac hung when he turned to me.

"No sinks?"

I breathed out, pointing to the rubber hose that lay by the floor drain.

He looked, laughed. "Primitive, but it'll do." He stooped to examine it, then turned the spigot and watched the water run into the drain. As I watched him, the photograph of Dac hanging behind him, I remembered Dac talking once about not understanding what his father "was about" until after he died.

I looked at my father, trying to imagine him letting his son be raised as another man's child.

He couldn't have known. I wanted him not to. If he had a son he'd completely abandoned, then he was a different man from the father I thought I knew.

I couldn't imagine it was really true, but I couldn't ask him about it either. What would I say?

I looked across at the print of Dac. It was just a photograph. It wasn't captioned *Pat Sullivan's Son*. And Dad's fingers were already reaching toward it, touching the edge.

"Dad, did you know Emma when you were young?" The words blurted out to my father's back before I lost my nerve.

He turned toward me, seeming almost to have expected the question. His face showed no surprise.

He nodded cautiously. "I met her during the war. We talked about it—remember?—the day we decorated the Christmas tree. Davis and I were boyhood friends. I knew he'd gone to school in England, that he was flying with the British even before we were in the war. I looked him up after I was shipped overseas."

I chose my next words carefully. "Did you know her well?"

He studied me for a long moment. I held his gaze. His hand reached up and pulled on his hair.

I stood still, trying to keep myself from trembling.

"I was in England when Davis's plane went down," he said.

"You were the one who helped her stop drinking."

His hand went to the photo of Dac again, but he didn't seem to be seeing it. "I only held her hand," he said. "She did the hard work herself."

"You gave her the clock, the one she gave me for my birthday." My voice a whisper.

He nodded.

I traced the thin white scar on my hand with my finger. "And Grandma's saying about not spending time carelessly."

Dad smiled slightly. "I'd forgotten that."

"Did you love her then?"

He sighed, rested his palms on the countertop for a second, then crossed them in front of himself. "We all could have died any day. It's not an excuse, I know, but we were at war."

I said nothing, not knowing what to say.

"I used to wonder sometimes who would comfort your mother if I was killed."

"When you were with Emma."

He nodded slowly. "Yes."

He turned his back to me, and looked at the print of Dac. I held my breath, remembering the coffee and peppermint taste of Dac's kiss, the way the camera nestled in his hands.

"It's late," Dad said. "We ought to have been in bed hours ago."

He turned and headed up the basement stairs, his footsteps heavy on the painted wood. He paused briefly at the top of the stair before moving across the kitchen, through the front hall where my photos hung, on up the stairs to the second floor. A door squeaked on its hinges, and the footsteps ceased. There was a long moment of silence, only an owl hooting in low tones somewhere outside, and then the water pump thumped on and water began to hum through the pipes over my head.

36

The snow and ice melted quickly, moving us in just a few days from deep winter into the muddiest of springs. To compound the mess, it began to rain later that week, and it was still drizzling the Friday before the Old-Fashioned race. I hadn't wanted to go to the supper fund-raiser at the hunt club that evening—I didn't want to see Emma and I didn't want to see Dac either, and he'd left me a message that he'd be back from New Jersey and he needed to talk to me and would I meet him there. But Willa talked me into going, saying I couldn't avoid Dac forever. "Just come and get it over with," she said. "Come with me. I'll stick to you like glue, hold your hand, whisk you home the moment you begin to turn a gourdy orange."

Everyone was drinking warmer-uppers when we arrived—it was a cash bar, a big moneymaker, with quality liquors, Chivas and Crown Royal, though the wine was served from jugs and the beer was Bud. By dinnertime the bartender's cash box overflowed and the crowd was lively, even bawdy. We served ourselves lasagna and salad from big pans and bowls, then sat in chairs or on couches or on the carpets or the stairs, balancing china plates in our laps. The talk ran mostly to horses, to the contenders in the Hunt Cup, and to the race the next morning, the Old-Fashioned that many of the partygoers would ride. I wondered whether some of them could sober up in time for the start.

I didn't eat much; I had no appetite. I set my plate aside and excused myself, then walked through all the rooms of the hunt club, scanning the groups of people eating. Dad was there with Emma; they were sitting together on a sofa, speaking intently in tones not meant to be heard. But Dac was still nowhere to be seen.

After dinner, an auctioneer took to a microphone and began auctioning off pairs of contenders for the races, one rider for the Old-Fashioned and one for the Hunt Cup the following weekend. All proceeds from the bidding would be pooled, to be distributed one-third to the person who bought the winning Old-Fashioned rider, one-third to the person who bought the Hunt Cup winner, and one-third to the club.

"You have to watch this," Willa said, pulling me to a space on the floor at the side of the room. "You have to watch the bidding. But don't just watch the bidders and the auctioneer. Watch some of the spouses, the ones who don't hunt. Watch Sheila Wilson." She nodded toward a woman I'd met at Emma's, the one with the mirrored-sunglasses eyes.

"See if you can't tell it's her money Ben is betting," Willa said. "No sense of humor. You'd think she had a limited supply of funds, instead of about a billion bucks. And watch Elizabeth Gordon." Willa pointed discreetly across the room. "In the pink shirt. Her husband, Mark, on her right? He'll try to keep pace with Ben, and she'll hemorrhage. It's Mark's money—not inherited. But they don't have quite as much as the Wilsons."

I understood the understatement in her voice.

I expected the bidding to be lively, but still I was surprised to see the numbers go up into the high hundreds, the winning bids at seven-fifty, eight, even nine. And that was before the auctioneer announced the pair that included Willa in the Old-Fashioned, when the bidding really got serious.

"Five hundred," Ben Wilson opened. Opened!

"I have five hundred," the auctioneer chanted. "Five hundred, I have five hundred, do I hear six?"

"Seven-fifty," Mark Gordon countered.

"Seven-fifty, do I hear—?"

"One thousand."

Sheila Wilson frowned.

"Eleven hundred."

"Fifteen." Ben Wilson again, his voice easy, amused. He winked at Willa.

Willa rolled her eyes.

"Sixteen."

"Two thousand."

Mark Gordon sat upright and stiff, nervous. "Two thousand and fifty." His expression saying he knew he was in way over his head.

"Two thousand and fifty," the auctioneer sang out after a brief silence. "Two thousand and fifty, I have two thousand and fifty, do I hear twenty-one hundred, twenty-one hundred . . ."

Elizabeth Gordon tried to tell her husband something, but he paid her no attention.

Willa grinned beside me. "She's telling Mark he'll have to sell his horse. Same words every year."

"I have two thousand and fifty, do I hear twenty-one hundred, twenty-one hundred? Do I hear twenty seventy-five? Twenty seventy-five?" The auctioneer raised his gavel.

Mark's face went pale. He stared at Ben.

Ben looked over at Willa.

Willa shook her head as if to say she wanted no part of this, she wasn't the least bit flattered by this wrangling over her.

"Two thousand fifty-one," Ben Wilson said.

You could hear Elizabeth Gordon exhale before the room broke into raucous banter. The auctioneer, seeing the bidding was over, banged his gavel.

Sheila Wilson flashed a cold look at Willa.

Willa shrugged and mouthed, "Don't look at me."

The last pair to be announced included Emma in the Old-Fashioned and Foolish Heart in the Hunt Cup. My father opened with a hundred, and then a voice from the hallway said, "Five."

Dac's voice.

He stood, still in his overcoat, by the door.

I looked away, trying to push down the emptiness expanding in the pit of my stomach, swelling into my chest. Looked to the woman who stood next to Dac, a striking Asian woman nearly as tall as he was. Carrying every inch of her height upright.

But young. Eighteen at most. A girl-woman, too young to be Mai.

She looked familiar, too; I could have sworn I'd seen her before.

Beside me, Willa gave a low whistle. "Who is that?"

The entire room was looking at the woman who wasn't Mai, but she remained unflustered. She looked out over the crowd, her gaze fixing on Emma. Emma looked at her and smiled, though there was something not quite right about it, about Emma's smile.

Emma rose and made her way toward the door, to where Dac and the woman stood.

Kirby's voice broke the silence—"Six hundred"—and the auctioneer took up his call again.

"Who is she? Do you know who she is?" Willa said, oblivious of the bidding, though Dac had countered with a thousand and Kirby had answered with two.

And I was still watching the woman, realizing why she looked so familiar.

It was her resemblance to Dac.

But more than that too: I'd seen her picture.

I hadn't met her, but I *had* seen her picture.

Funny, I'd always imagined the child Emma had spoken of to be young, eight or ten, not much older than my boys. But Dac had left Vietnam almost twenty years ago. So of course she would be nearly grown.

"Her name is Yvonne," I whispered.

Vonnie, the girls at the Hannah Clark Home had called her, the ones who wanted to be like her, wanted to *be* her.

"Three thousand," Dac bid, and the auctioneer started in again.

Across the room, Yvonne stood proudly, as if she knew exactly who she was despite her youth, despite the fact that she'd just met her father. I wondered if her mother was at all like her. Mai could not be as strong, though, if she'd been scared off by Emma. Yvonne was a young woman determined to get what she wanted. She was like her grandmother, like Emma, in that way. You could see that, with the two of them standing together now. You could see a similar strength in their faces, in their determined smiles.

"Four thousand," Kirby said, and Dac responded with forty-two fifty.

Emma was saying something to Yvonne now, speaking softly as Kirby and Dac continued bidding. Yvonne was smiling, looking over the crowd, nodding her head. They'd already met.

"Forty-six hundred," Dac bid, grinning at Kirby.

"But what about Mai?" Willa said. "Dac told me he was going to see Mai."

"I don't know," I said, but I didn't know if Willa heard me. The thwack of the auctioneer's gavel sounded as I spoke.

"Sold to the man in the doorway for forty-six hundred dollars."

All eyes were fixed on Dac and Yvonne.

"This could be a double winner," Dac said to Kirby, who was shaking his head. "You just gave up a good bet."

Emma laughed. "Only if it *is* a double winner. Add it up. You just contributed more than a third of the pot. If you hit one but not the other, you're still behind."

The room erupted in laughter. Dac looked at the chalkboard, where the auctioneer was writing in the total: thirteen thousand nine hundred and seventy-five dollars.

Dac grinned sheepishly. "I guess the pressure's on for you to win tomorrow, Mother."

Emma laughed. "This leg . . ." She reached down and rubbed her calf. "I just don't know."

Only Willa and I weren't laughing. She was staring at Yvonne, trying to determine who she was, and I was staring at Emma, trying to figure it all out. Because Yvonne must have known Emma at the Hannah Clark Home—everyone there knew Emma and everyone knew Yvonne—and the coincidence wasn't possible, was it? That had to be the way Emma was playing it, though, because Emma had only to see Yvonne to know she was Dac's child.

But then, where was Mai?

Everyone began to rise, collecting belongings and saying farewells, Dac already surrounded by a crowd of curious neighbors.

I reached for Willa, wanting to tell her.

Beside her stood my father, with Emma again at his side.

"Nelly, I have to talk to you," Dad said.

"Won't you come over to my place for a drink?" Emma asked.

"I . . ." I looked at Emma, then across the room to Dac. Willa had taken a step back from us, was waiting for me without wanting to be interfering. "I've got to take Willa home," I said. "She rode with me."

"I need to tell you something," Dad said. "Something important."

"Can't you tell me here?"

Dad pulled on his hair, looked at Emma, shrugged.

"I don't—" Emma started.

It struck me then that if Dac was Dad's son—could that really be?—then Yvonne was his granddaughter. I looked across the room to where Dac and Yvonne were still surrounded.

"Emma and I are going to be married," Dad said.

"Married!" I blurted out. "Married?"

"Next weekend," my father said.

"But— But you don't know about Dac!"

"Dac?" Dad looked completely confused. "What does Dac have to do with it?"

"But—"

Dad laughed. "You want me to adopt him?"

I looked at Emma. I couldn't just blurt out, Dac is your son. But how could I keep it from him?

"He's your son," I said, my voice a whisper. "You don't have to adopt him, Dad. He's your biological son."

"My—?" Dad, confused, looked to Emma. "Nelly, what in the world—?"

Willa, still standing back, looked as confused as Dad. And then Dad's laughter boomed so loudly that the people still left in the room, including Dac and Yvonne, turned to see him.

He took my arm, shaking his head and saying, "An active imagination," apparently to himself, though I thought it was for Willa's benefit, and maybe Emma's too. "Will you two ladies excuse us for a second?" he said to them. He led me to the coatroom, pulled our coats off the hooks, and pushed me out the door as we shrugged them on.

"What in the world are you thinking, Nelly?" he said the moment the door closed behind us.

"I—"

"I'll say this just once." His breath making little puffs of white in the air. "Just once. Are you listening? Dac could not possibly be my son."

"But—"

"He was born more than a year after Emma and I were together, Nelly. Now that is enough."

He turned and walked back inside, leaving me to look out into the moonless night alone, my coat no protection from the chill wind that whipped across my face.

37

The weather report the next day called for early morning clouds clearing into a bright sunny afternoon, but when the boys and I arrived for the Old-Fashioned, the race course was still an awful mess of mud-streaked grass, pure mud patches, and mud-spattered fences dulled by a turbid sky. The riders were in high spirits, though, calling to the sun to come out and dry the world. I clung to my camera—it was still working; by some miracle only the one lens had been damaged—as I made my way through the mud, picking my path carefully at first, then giving up, glad that I knew to wear Wellingtons now, to leave my shiny loafers at home. I snapped a medium telephoto onto my camera, keeping one eye on Ned and Charlie sitting with Matt and Craig on the fence, looking through toy binoculars at who knows what. I took a few shots of them, then began taking double portraits of the red-hunting-coated riders and their horses: Joan and her horse, Edgar; Mike Hayley and Gentle Giant; Ben Wilson—who looked a bit green at the gills but no poorer for his bidding escapades last night—and his horse, Nasty Sam.

I spotted Emma almost immediately. She wore a red-and-white cap cover, the racing colors her horses had worn that first day at the races. Dad stood beside her.

I kept them at a distance as I worked.

Willa, the one person I did feel like talking to, was drawing her horse out of her trailer when I spotted her, at the same time keeping an eye on her sons. I took her picture. "I'll watch Matt and Craig," I said. "It's as easy to watch four as to watch two when they stick together like ours do."

She looked at the camera, obviously surprised it still worked.

"Only the lens was broken," I said.

"You okay?" she asked.

I nodded, not wanting to talk about Dac or Dad or Emma with so many people around.

"Kirby's got the boys—yours and mine," she said. "So you can take your pictures."

I asked her how she planned to ride the course, and she followed my lead, gabbing for a few minutes about the firmness of the ground (or the lack of it after all the snowmelt and the rain), the effect of the hills on the horses' stamina, the likelihood of getting caught up on two particularly nasty jumps. I pretended to listen as she saddled her horse, then wished her good luck as she headed off to make sure everything was ready at the start.

"Nelly?" The voice came from behind me as I stood watching Willa, and when I turned, there was Emma, standing uncomfortably close to me, her unfastened chin strap dangling at her neck as she held the reins of her horse.

"Your father isn't angry with you," she said. "He knows that was just some misunderstanding last night."

"I— Misunderstanding? Emma, you—"

"I apologize if you misunderstood something I said, Nelly."

"But you—" I took a step backward, my foot landing squarely in a puddle, the cold through the rubber of my boots chilling me to the bone.

Emma wrapped her arm underneath Flashy's neck and, with her other hand, patted his nose. She looked completely untroubled, as if she were just riding up to say hello, to tie Flashy to my tree again like she had when we'd first met. The sun had come out as she crossed our bridge that day, and here it was now, coming out again.

"You— You knew who I was from that first afternoon?" I said, the realization jelling only as I spoke. "From that first day you came to meet me?"

Emma frowned. "Yes, of course."

"But why did you—?"

"I was curious, Nelly." As if she'd only opened a box she wasn't supposed to open before Christmas. "I wanted to see what Patrick's daughter was like."

That was why she'd taken me under her wing, because of Dad?

"You'd have done the same if you were me," she said. "You'd have come to meet you too."

And though I wanted to deny it, to say that I wouldn't, that I was not at all like her, I could see myself dialing the number to the Hannah Clark Home as soon as I knew about Mai.

"And then I liked you, of course," Emma said, squinting into the sun now. "I liked you from the first and I wanted to be friends, and we are, Nelly, aren't we? We've been such good friends."

"Emma!"

People were glancing in our direction. I stepped out of the mud puddle, tried to calm myself.

I lowered my voice. "You told me Dac—"

"Dac belongs *here,* Nelly." She shifted her weight, falling back a little so that the shadow of Flashy's face fell across hers. "And you won't stay. You're too like your father. Haven't I always said you were? You'll take your camera and head off to conquer the world just as he did. And Dac can't go with you, Nelly. You don't even know him. You don't understand him. You can't take care of him like I can."

"But I . . ." I looked out across the landscape, at the cloud-shadows darkening the earth below where the sky had yet to clear. "Jesus. Is this what you did with Mai, Emma?"

She raised her chin. "For all I knew, Mai died in childbirth or sooner," she said. "Or had a child that wasn't Dac's."

I looked down at my mud-caked boots, felt the heaviness of my camera in my hands. "You've always known where Mai was, Emma," I said quietly. "She's been working at Hannah Clark all this time."

Emma fell back a step, nearly kicking her horse, who shied back too. But she held the rein.

"Mai was never at Hannah Clark," she said.

But I'd seen Yvonne's photograph there and Brenda—Brenda with her purple apron—told me the girl grew up there. So Emma expected me to believe what? That Mai wasn't there but Yvonne, for some reason, was? That Emma, who must have known Yvonne all these years, had only just discovered she was her grandchild? That Emma never noticed how much Yvonne looked like Dac?

"Yvonne was raised at Hannah Clark," I said. "Brenda—"

"Yvonne and I met for the first time yesterday afternoon," Emma said solidly. "When Dac brought her to the farm."

"For the first time?"

"She must have been off to college by the time I began to volunteer at Hannah Clark. Or perhaps just at school, in class, when I was there."

I stared at her, my camera limp in my hands, my boots

heavy with mud. This was more than an extraordinary coincidence. She had to have arranged the job for Mai—she'd founded Hannah Clark, for God's sake.

Hadn't she?

Did I tell you we've built two other Hannah Clark Homes? And we've a fourth under construction in Mexico.

Not "there are two other Hannah Clark Homes," but *we've* built them. And she was so damned secretive about working there.

Emma mounted her horse, swinging her right leg easily over the saddle. She pulled the reins in the direction of the start, where the other riders were beginning to gather, and she began to move away from me in a slow, steady walk, the blinding sunlight reflecting off the metal of her stirrups. I could see her expression no more clearly than when I'd studied her hazy reflection in the train window on the way back from New York, her neck so like my mother's long, graceful neck.

"Emma!" I called after her.

Hannah, that had been her daughter's name, the daughter who'd been stillborn. The daughter named after Emma's mother.

"Hannah Clark was your mother," I called.

Emma turned and stared at me then, the calm she had shown now replaced with a look of surprise, and then of sadness, the shadow of that lost look moving into her eyes as it had when she'd told me of her parents' deaths.

"You didn't just volunteer there," I said. "You founded the home. Years ago. You named it after your mom."

Emma didn't deny it, didn't insist again that she'd had nothing to do with the home until a few years ago. She just looked at me for a long moment, as if in speaking these words I'd betrayed her, said something unforgivable. When she turned away again, she kicked her horse hard with her heel. The horse jolted forward, moving roughly into a canter, carrying Emma off to the start of the race.

My fingers fumbled in my case for a new roll of film. Just think about the photographs, I said over and over to myself as I slid the film into place, closed the camera, listened to the mechanical hum of the film winding into place. Medium-speed film, the grain would be good and I didn't need the speed before the race began. I slipped on a wide-angle lens and moved to get a few shots of the entire field of riders, not wanting to focus on anyone too closely anymore. I spent the roll, trying to lose myself in the motions.

Still, in the back of my mind was my father's voice telling me he was marrying Emma, and Emma's voice, too, Emma telling me I didn't understand Dac, saying Dac belonged with her.

I pulled the spent roll from the camera and loaded some faster film as the riders jockeyed for position at the start. I popped the wide-angle off and attached my longest telephoto, and the starting gun sounded and the riders surged forward. I kept clicking the shutter release, keeping the riders in view until they topped the hill out back of the hunt club.

Emma's red-and-white cap was ahead of all the others as they disappeared.

After the riders were out of sight, I fiddled with the lens cap and made busy with my camera, not wanting to mingle for the few minutes before the riders reappeared. Out of the corner of my eye, I caught Dac approaching.

I walked away from him, pretending not to notice his call.

"Nelly!" He caught up with me, took hold of my upper arm.

"Dac. I can't talk." I lifted my camera. "I've got to take photos."

He looked at the camera, suppressing a smile. "Still works?"

I looked away, to the gap in the trees lining the stream, where Emma had told me she'd hoped to cross.

"You disappeared last night," Dac said.

I fingered the camera strap. "There were so many people around you. And I couldn't stay. The sitter . . ."

"I wanted to introduce you to—"

"Your daughter."

I looked to him, met his gaze, his face registering surprise.

"Your mother told me," I said.

"I've been given a second chance."

I smiled—smiled and held my camera tightly.

"I wish you'd told me about Mai, Dac."

He nodded. "I should have told you, Nelly. But it was all in the past."

I looked at him, wanting him to be giving me a leg up for a ride together, to be drinking expensive champagne from Dino and Bamm-Bamm glasses, to hear him say my photos would be worth more than Dorothea Lange's someday.

"You married her, Dac. She had your daughter."

"That was a long time ago, Nelly. A long, long time ago. A time when I was pretty messed up."

"You didn't love her?"

"It's not that simple."

"Didn't you ever love her, Dac?"

"I thought she was dead, Nelly. I thought she was dead when she was living two hours away, living with my daughter—*my daughter*, Nelly. She told my daughter I was dead!"

I looked away, to the tulips, red and yellow, lining the hunt club drive, the dogwoods blooming their lacy white against the muddy earth. "What if she thought you were, Dac?"

Across the field, the crowd began to collect again, focusing in the direction the riders were expected to come.

Dac exhaled, exasperated. He put his hands on my arms and looked at me with those eyes, green like Dad's and Grandma's, but flecked with gold. "What does it matter anyway, Nelly?"

"What does it matter?" I looked to the hill over which the riders had disappeared.

"You're married, Dac."

"Married? Nelly, Mai is dead."

Dead?

"Mai isn't dead, Dac," I said quietly. "Mai isn't dead." That was just the lie Emma had told him.

"She's been dead since Yvonne was six, Nelly."

"She's in Newark. She's—" Even as I said it, though, I realized I was wrong. Mai was dead. Yvonne was orphaned. That was why Emma had founded Hannah Clark. Not to give Mai a place to work. To give Yvonne a place to live.

The plaque beside the door at Hannah Clark: FOUNDED 1978. When Yvonne would have been about six.

"Mai is dead, Nelly," Dac said firmly. "She's dead and even if she weren't, it wouldn't matter. Not since I met you. Since I saw you at the Blessing of the Hunt with your camera, taking pictures. Maybe I loved Mai when I was in Vietnam or maybe I only thought I did, I don't even know anymore, but it's you I—"

"Don't, Dac!"

He looked at me, those green–gold eyes not understanding.

"I can't, Dac. I can't."

I jogged away from him, took a position along the fence. Across the way, Dad and Yvonne stood together, talking easily with Kirby, whose Dudley Do-Right chin was nodding up and down while the boys sat beside them on the fence. I trained my camera on the spot where Emma had talked about crossing the stream, where the banks were so steep. It would be far too wet to cross there, but I'd be able to see the riders pass through the break in the tree line. I might even glimpse who the leader was.

I felt Dac step up to the fence beside me. He was eating a peppermint now; I smelled it on his breath.

I looked through the viewfinder. Flashes of color appeared through the veil of budding tree limbs lining the stream, but it was impossible to tell who had the lead.

"Nelly, I have to tell you something."

I did not look at him.

"I couldn't have gone back to Mai," he said.

Still, I kept looking through the lens.

"Remember those pictures I told you about? The ones in *Life*? I wasn't in the airport when I saw them." He took a deep breath, and in my peripheral vision I saw him tilt his head back, then look down at the ground. "I was still in Vietnam, Nelly. I was still in Vietnam."

I kept looking through the viewfinder, half wanting to turn to him, half wanting to run away. A horse and rider appeared in the clearing, swinging wide and turning to cross the stream. I didn't have to see the face to know it was Emma. I didn't even have to see her square shoulders in her red jacket or the red and white of her cap.

"It was the morning of my last mission," Dac said. "I looked at those pictures, at those children, and then I climbed into my airplane and I flew my final run. I knew what I was doing, I just wanted to be finished, to go home, to get away from it. Never to think of it again."

An enthusiastic whoop that sounded victory shot across the long expanse of field. Emma's voice.

"Are you listening to me, Nelly?" Dac's voice soft beside me. "Do you understand what I'm saying?"

I watched Emma's horse approach the stream, wanting to

scream at Dac to shut up, to just shut up, I understood he was saying he had not wanted his own wife, not wanted the reminder of her Vietnamese face, not wanted to live with what he'd done. Was that supposed to make me feel better, that his guilt was stronger than his love, that he didn't feel the loss so much as the sense of relief?

I clicked the shutter release, Emma storming toward the stream, toward the steep, muddy embankment, but even as I photographed her I felt myself sinking away from my surroundings. Wasn't that how I felt, after all? Among all the mixed-up emotions of Wesley's death, wasn't that how I felt? Pain, loss, sorrow, loneliness, yes. But also . . . what?

A dreadful sense of freedom. An unbearable kind of relief.

Through the lens, Emma was taking off for her jump, bright sunlight breaking through the clouds above her, highlighting her triumph. I kept clicking as her horse's front feet landed just barely this side of the stream. The horse's hind feet would land forward of where the forefeet landed and the horse and rider would have cleared the stream. I exhaled—was it for Dac or Emma that I had held my breath? Or for myself?—and I kept focusing, squeezing the shutter release again and again, knowing I should respond to Dac but unable to speak.

As if the force of my breath had reached her, Emma teetered on the horse. I clicked a shot of her trying to regain her balance, never doubting that she would. But then I felt myself go even emptier than I already felt as, through the lens, I saw that she would not. She seemed to look to me as the reins slipped from her hands. I watched, paralyzed, as she pitched over the neck of her horse.

I sprang forward, almost dropping my camera in the mud. I scrambled over the fence beside Dac, who vaulted it as Emma tumbled. I ran and ran and ran toward where she lay, completely still on the ground. As I sprinted across the field, the second horse, already in the air over the stream, landed on that muddy bank and veered away from Emma, barely missing her. I gasped as I watched the third rider round the turn, then pull the horse back as it launched into the air above the stream. They missed Emma, but they missed the jump, too, the horse and rider spilling back down the muddy bank to the stream, disappearing from my sight. A cry rang out, and even in my panic I recognized Willa's voice.

A fourth rider, far enough behind the third to pull up, dismounted and plunged down the far bank into the stream. Behind him, others also halted, dismounted, and scrambled down through the mud.

When I reached Emma, Dac was on the ground, leaning over his mother's face, and one of the riders, soaked to the chest, was climbing up the bank from the stream, shouting, "Don't touch her!" He was a surgeon I'd met at the auction. His surgeon's hands were covered with mud.

He fell down to Emma, pushing Dac away from her and, in doing so, revealing her face to me. Her eyes were closed.

Someone breathed hard behind me. My father. He put a hand on my shoulder. I put my hand on his. Yvonne came up beside him.

I thought of Ned and Charlie then. They were standing with Willa's boys beside the fence they'd been sitting on, and Kirby was there, keeping them out of harm's way.

The surgeon reached under the sleeve of Emma's jacket, feeling her wrist. He kept moving his fingers; he couldn't find her pulse.

I touched my own wrist, my scar.

He leaned his ear to her lips, listening for her breath, then reached behind her neck and gently fingered her spine. He sat back on his heels and stared at Emma silently for a moment, wiping his forehead with his hands. When he looked up at Dac, there was a muddy streak across his brow.

"I'm sorry, Dac," he said.

By the stream, Willa was being helped up the bank by another rider, mud soaking her clothes and her wet hair plastered to her head. Tears streamed down her cheeks, washing away the dirt where they ran. When she saw Emma, she crumpled to the ground, saying, "Oh, God." Behind me, Dad began to weep.

An ambulance appeared moments later, lights flashing and siren blaring, but when they put Emma on the stretcher, they covered her face. Dac, Yvonne, and Dad climbed in beside her. When they drove away, it was without hurry, without sirens, without lights. Only one sound pierced the air: the gunshot that put Willa's horse out of its pain.

38

The bell tolled at St. James's Church, calling us to Emma's funeral, though the little stone church was already overflowing. People were crowded into the plain wooden pews, the small choir loft. They filled the folding chairs in the aisle, and spilled out into the entryway and onto the stone steps and beyond. Everyone sat or stood quietly, those in the church studying the flowers at the altar, simple arrangements of tulips from Emma's yard—Joan's suggestion and such a perfect one, so exactly what Emma would have wanted.

Philip entered from the back, leaving the doors open behind him so that the outsiders could hear. He took the pulpit and, in his eloquent but simple way, shared with us his own personal memories of Emma, little anecdotes from the thirty-five years he'd known her. Afterward, a short ceremony was held in the graveyard next to the church, among marble and granite markers bearing the names of families who'd lived in the valley since the church was built more than a century ago: the Worthings, for whom the valley was named; the Fairbanks; the Pattersons. We collected around Davis's grave, where Dac had had Emma's name carved beside his father's on the simple white marble tombstone. The stark whiteness of

EMMA WHITFIELD CROFTON reminded me that only a few days had passed since her death.

The sun shone harshly, creating sharp shadows on the faces around the grave as Kirby read Walt Whitman's "O Captain! My Captain!" a favorite of Emma's. Dac, too, read a poem, one about a foxhunter who wished when he died to be buried on a certain hill that he might, even in his death, feel the pounding of the foxhunters' hooves and hear the bellow of the hunting horn, the call of the hounds. As he read, I leaned against the trunk of a big old oak, its branches still bare of buds. I closed my eyes and listened to his voice, picturing the glow of perspiration on Emma's face as she rode, her upright carriage, the way her eyes shone with childlike glee in her lined face that first day we met. I could see her smile when I opened the portfolio Christmas Day and found the tickets to New York. I could feel the hope she'd wanted me to feel when she told me my father's and my photographs would someday hang side by side. I could almost touch the Emma who was so loved by the girls at the Hannah Clark Home, the Emma I, too, had loved.

That evening, while my father tucked Ned and Charlie in one last time, then packed his suitcase, I spread a few of my photographs on the kitchen table: Emma at the Blessing of the Hunt, Thanksgiving morning; Emma at the Hunt Ball, hopping from her truck onto one stockinged foot; Dac in his red jacket, his father's "pinks." I moved the photos around the table listlessly, telling myself that my father's leaving had no more to do with me now than it had that day he gave me the key to his box. He was just doing what he'd always done, trying to lose himself in his work.

He came down finally, and he set his suitcase beside the kitchen table, then sat across from me. He picked up one of the photographs: Emma in the yellow chair in my living room, teasing me about her blue-eyed lover.

"The boys are asleep," he said.

I nodded. "They've sure been glad to have you here."

He picked up another photograph, one of Dac.

Dac in the barn.

Just a photograph, after all. One of a million I'd taken in the hopes I'd finally have one good enough.

Just a photograph. Dac's face, the light of his eyes springing out from the print.

"What do you think?" I asked.

Dad looked at me, his green eyes questioning.

"Of the photo," I said.

He studied it for a moment, then looked up at me, studied me. "What do you think?" he said.

In the front hall, the clock struck once, the half hour.

"I think it's good," I said quietly.

I thought I read surprise in his face.

"Do you?" he asked. "Why?"

It wasn't good. He didn't like it.

Did it matter?

"It's nicely framed," I said. "He's nearly centered in the doorway behind him. That helps focus attention on him." The objectivity in my voice surprised me. I felt as if I were someone else speaking, or I were speaking about some other shot.

"I bounced the flash off the ceiling," I said. "He was close enough for me to do it. So the lighting is more natural, no bad shadows and no harsh highlights." The words spilling out. "I had pretty fast film in the camera, so I got enough light even though I lost some to the ceiling. Still, it's not too grainy. It blew up well." I took a deep breath. "And the subject is—

He's captured well. He's in motion, so his expression is more natural. I didn't have any time either. I took it in an instant. If I'd hesitated, if I'd had to stop to figure out what to do, I wouldn't have gotten it." I nodded, had a flash of Emma's nod, twice sharply. "Yes. It's a good shot," I said.

Dad peered at the shot, moving it close to his face. "It's about love," he said. He did not look up.

I shifted in the hard kitchen chair, looked at the photo again, the light in Dac's eyes. "I don't know," I said. "Even if it is, if you're saying I shouldn't have taken it because it's about love . . . ? I don't know. I guess I think it's okay to photograph love. I agree with you about not photographing grief, but I think love is okay. I think maybe it can bring people hope sometimes. I don't mean you should intrude clumsily into people's private lives, but there are people who are happy to share their love with the world."

Like Emma's children, those at her Hannah Clark Home. Lily, who'd been so happy just to show me her coat. So unlike my father, who showed his love to no one. Until he'd met Emma, met her again. Emma, whom he'd so openly admired and loved.

Did it matter?

"Is that the way Dac is?" Dad asked. "Is he demonstrative like that? He got that from his father, then. Davis was goofy in love with Emma."

He looked up at me, his eyes moist.

"Is that why you let her go?" I said.

Dad considered the question. "I didn't let her go, exactly. I didn't ever have her then. She loved Davis and he loved her. And I loved your mother, and I'd made commitments to her." He studied the picture of Dac for another moment. "Anyway, my unit was transferred from Gilford, just outside of London, to Ely. And then Davis was found, and the next time I saw Emma she was pregnant. So there just wasn't any doubt, really, who belonged with Emma. It wasn't my place."

Dad seemed vulnerable as he spoke those words. Unsure of himself, even, in a way I'd never imagined him to be.

He set the photo on the table and moved on to one of Emma, carefully holding it by the edges. "You've started taking pictures again?" he said. "I mean—"

Serious pictures, he meant. Photographs. Shots meant for more than to be pasted in scrapbooks, left to gather dust on a closet shelf.

"I've always taken pictures, Dad," I said.

"Have you? I always thought so, but . . ." He paused. "Just some or—? Just family pictures? And things like the dance?"

"Other stuff too."

He studied the photos on the table, nodding to himself. He was choosing his words carefully. "May I see them sometime? Some of the rest of them?"

I looked from his face to the photos.

"You have them here, at the house?" he said.

I nodded. "In a box in the basement. In my darkroom."

He frowned. "Why do you keep them in a box?"

I shrugged. "Why do you?"

"Me? Oh. The ones in my file box."

To my surprise, he headed down the basement stairs. I followed him, and when he asked I pointed out the box of my photographs.

He hoisted the box up onto the counter. "I haven't had any dinner," he said.

I looked at my watch: 9:41 P.M.

He picked up my last prints from the counter, then pulled the strips of negatives from the drying line—the shots from the Old-Fashioned—and set them all on top of the box. "If I

fix myself something, will you keep me company while I eat?"
He headed up the stairs, carrying my box of photographs, not
waiting for my answer.

"Sure," I muttered as I followed him up the stairs.

In the kitchen, Dad set the box on the table, made himself
a turkey sandwich, and poured a glass of milk. He set his plate
and glass on the table across from me, but did not sit. Instead,
he pulled open the box and pulled out a stack of photographs,
spread them out on the table. He took a listless bite of his
sandwich, then set it down and wiped his hands on his napkin before sitting and reaching out to pick up one of the photographs, one of Lily.

I thought about what her life must be like, what the lives of
children even worse off than Lily must be like. What about
that woman I'd seen outside the library downtown? Had she
had children? Where were they? And the veteran outside the
train station in New York, the one Emma had given twenty
dollars? I thought of those white socks hanging on that
clothesline by the train tracks in Philadelphia, of all that rust.
I didn't have to go to Budapest to find a need I might benefit
through my camera. Not getting war pics for the cover, just
making a dent in what needed to be dented. I could use the
Hannah Clark pictures to tell that story, to help those girls.
And if I couldn't get them published, they could still be used
in the adoption folders. Wouldn't that make a little dent?

Dad laid the photograph back on the table and picked up
another one, a print of the negative I'd printed over and over
throughout my life, myself as an eight-year-old child, with
those missing teeth. I'd made it as good a print as I could, finally, but the negative wasn't great, and the negative is everything. You can do things to make the print better, but you
can't make a great print from a negative that is flawed.

Dad set that picture down and moved the other prints around

on the table, his hands—wide across the knuckles, narrow through the thumb pad and to the wrist—so unlike mine. Mine were longer, more slender, almost insubstantial by comparison.

My mother's hands?

No, Grandma's hands.

I watched Dad's fingers move across the photographs, wondering what he thought of them, whether he'd be proud to say I was his daughter when my work appeared in print. I'd always wanted to know, but I'd only wanted a positive answer.

I picked up the photograph he'd just set down, the eight-year-old girl craving her father's attention, his love. I still wanted to know that each time he'd said good-bye to me it had torn at him, each time he'd taken a picture of a child or climbed into his bed in some foreign hotel or sipped coffee as he read the *Herald Tribune* or looked out an airplane window or listened to the strange buzz of an English telephone, he'd thought of me, wished I were with him. I wanted to know he regretted all those days he hadn't gotten to see me. Not that he'd do it differently, but that he'd realized the cost of it as much as I had, that he had shared the cost.

Dad ate the last of his sandwich, drained his milk, then pushed the plate and glass aside. He picked up one of the strips of negatives, fished a magnifying loupe from the pocket of his vest and peered through it at the strip. He looked up, his expression absorbed. He peered through the loupe again, then picked up the negative strip by the edges. He reached across the table and set it in front of me.

"What's this one?" he asked.

I set down the picture I was holding and took the loupe from him. "Snow sitting on the branches of the sycamore tree," I said, orienting myself. "I opened the aperture an extra stop and a half. So the snow is white, not gray. Despite the brightness of the sunlight reflecting off the snow, the shot isn't underexposed."

I watched him, thinking I was a grown woman now, not the eight-year-old girl in the picture. I had an eight-year-old of my own. What did I want from him anyway? Didn't I just want to know what he thought, good or bad? What was it about my father that made it so hard for me to ask?

Dad picked up a print of Ned inside the barn, bright light coming from the open door to his left. Something about it—the way the light fell, maybe?—made me think of the Dorothea Lange on my dresser. I could do that. I could get close to people like she did. I could take those photos, like I had at Hannah Clark.

"And this?" Dad asked, holding up the picture.

I took it from him, studied it. "The way the light's coming from the side makes the shadows work," I said. "They add texture to the picture, make it more three-dimensional. And they create a mood."

Dad nodded to himself. "Hmmm . . ."

I took a deep breath, exhaled, looked at the photos on the table. "So what do you think, Dad?"

He looked up from the picture in his hands. "What do I think?"

I tried to make my voice strong, but it came out quietly. "The photographs. You've never told me what you thought of my work."

He looked surprised. "I've always told you exactly what I thought," he protested. "Remember the first time you ever brought me a photograph?" He picked up my eight-year-old self-portrait from the table in front of me. "This one. A less sophisticated print of this." He slid it back across the table. "Even then, I told you exactly what I thought."

I picked up the print and sat back in my chair, studying it. "You told me it was backlit."

"Right."

"You told me how to make it better."

"Right." His voice slightly higher at the end of the word, as if it were almost a question.

"You never said this photograph is good, this one isn't, you've captured something here, this is terrific, this is just not moving me, it's missing."

He was looking at me, frowning, his lips pressed together.

"You never said, 'Yes, you have talent, Nelly.' "

Dad set down the photo he was holding and leaned back in his chair, crossing his arms. "You were hardheaded as a child, and I see that hasn't changed." He shook his head. "We'd be there in the darkroom, and I'd be trying to help you and your brother, and you would just be itching to be left alone so you could do it yourself. You wouldn't even show me your photographs, you were so stubborn. You didn't want my criticism."

"I—"

"You wanted to figure it all out for yourself. The hard way. Did you learn a lot from those magazines you kept hidden? And then I'd overhear you bragging to your grandma, babbling on about where you'd been when you took a photo you were showing her, how you'd gotten the shot, how clever you were to get it."

"But I—"

I looked at my self-portrait again, trying to remember the moment I'd given it to him, to remember the moment differently. Had he said anything positive about it? What exactly had he said?

I couldn't remember. All I remembered was the criticism, the backlighting.

Dad picked up another photo—Emma reaching out to block the camera at Hannah Clark.

Was Emma really gone, just like that? Just like Wesley was?

My mind flashed to the boys. Were they sleeping well? Were they warm enough?

Dad held the picture of Emma to him, touching it to his chest.

"It's not an easy way to make a living, you know," he said. "You have to come to it believing in yourself. Some really talented people give up before they even get started."

He smiled almost apologetically, and something in that smile reminded me of Emma—of Emma standing in the International Center of Photography in New York, saying someday my photos would hang beside his.

"I know," I said. "Remember, I'm the one who just got roundly rejected in New York."

"In New York?" He fingered the picture of Emma, looking puzzled. Had he not known why I was going to New York?

"I didn't—" we both said at once.

"I didn't know that's why you went," he said.

I nodded. "I didn't know you didn't know."

"So it was bloody?"

"One guy asked me if I was looking for a job in the Sears portrait department."

Dad laughed, trying not to.

"Personally, I didn't find it that amusing." But it was sort of funny now, somehow.

Dad sighed. "What would you do, Nelly, if I said you didn't have any talent, that your pictures weren't good?"

I sat back in my chair, folded my hands, rested them on the edge of the table. The light overhead cast a shadow, my clasped hands spreading out over the photograph of me without my front teeth, enveloping it.

I looked directly at my father. "I'd say you were wrong," I said.

Dad nodded, leaned back in his chair, pulling at his hair. He might have been smiling; I couldn't tell.

"So what are you going to do?" he said.

What was I going to do.

I pulled several of the prints I'd taken at Hannah Clark from the stack. I picked out a shot of the discreet nameplate at the front door, THE HANNAH CLARK HOME, and slid it across the table to Dad. I pulled several others, too, choosing them carefully, sliding them to him in the order I wanted him to see them. At last, I picked up a shot of Lily, that little girl who'd slept in the subway station, wrapped warmly in her very own coat, her eyes looking straight into the camera, the bright light of possibilities smiling up from them.

I handed the photo to my father.

"The guy who referred me to the Sears portrait department?" I said. "He was right. I have some technically good shots in my portfolio, but they don't tell a story. There's a story here, though, in these photographs."

Lily's story. The story of every motherless, fatherless child. Not my story. Nothing at all about me, and all about me too. Captured shadow. Captured light.

"I'm going to send these photos to that guy, laid out just like this, with a proposal for a story," I said.

Dad laughed. "To the guy who referred you to the Sears portrait department?"

"At least he's honest. At least he'll say what he thinks."

Dad shook his head. "You're going to be frustrated out there, Nelly. You're going to feel like the foreign guys are beating the pants off you because they get so many more covers. Nothing like a nice war pic for the front. You'll see. You'll start hoping for a nice little civil war."

In the silence as I considered this, the furnace clicked on and began to hum.

"Not with two boys," I said.

Dad lowered the photo of Emma, studied it. "Well, remember that," he said. "And remember how high a price the foreign guys pay. While you're tucking in your little boys, those poor schmucks are eating low-grade meat in some fleabag hotel at best, lucky if they've got hot water to shower in, wondering how big their kids have gotten since the last time they were home."

He studied the picture more closely, then looked at me.

I nodded. "Was it worth it?"

Dad set the photo aside and stood and began to stack the other photographs into neat little piles, not looking at them but only tidying up, organizing my life. I watched his hands move across my photographs. He kept stacking them, and when they were all collected he began to straighten the piles.

"Was it worth it, Dad?" I repeated.

Dad looked up from the pile he was straightening as if he were surprised I was there, surprised he was there himself.

"Does it matter anymore?" he asked. "You and your brothers are grown and your mom is gone."

He picked his dishes up from the table, took them to the sink. When I looked up, he was standing with his back to me, rinsing his plate. He set it on the counter by the sink and dried his hands on the dish towel. "I'd better get going," he said.

He walked to the table and picked up a photo of Emma— not one of the better shots, but the one at Hannah Clark, her trying to block the camera. "May I keep this one?" he said. Without waiting for an answer, he slipped it into his jacket pocket, and lifted his suitcase.

"Already it'll be after midnight before I get to New York," he said.

We walked out of the kitchen together, past my photographs hanging in the dim light of the hallway. I opened the door, kissed him good-bye, stood watching as he climbed into the Jeep, set the suitcase on the passenger seat, started the engine, and turned on the lights. He pulled down the drive and turned up the hill, past Willa's house, past Kirby and Joan's. His brake lights flashed once at the top, briefly lighting the darkness red before he turned left onto Dover Road and disappeared into the night.

Epilogue

The flames pop in the fireplace in Dad's study, and I look again at the photograph of Emma, not the one I gave him, but the picture of her as a young woman that I've found in his locked metal box. The photo is old, frayed at the edges, creased across the top left corner, torn along the fold. It has been handled a lot.

I touch the dog-eared corner of the photograph to the fire and it catches slowly. I hold it over the hearth, watching the flames grow. They creep down the photograph, toward the face of my father's Emma. The face becomes only ashes before I lean forward and place the photo into the fire.

Dad's camera is still on his desktop. I open the bag, meaning to see if any exposures remain. What I see taped to the inside of the camera case, though, makes me smile and makes me cry. It's that first photograph I took, me with my front teeth missing. Not one of the later prints I made, the better ones, but that first awful job.

It's more worn even than the picture of Emma. It has been in this place a long time.

Standing there looking at that picture, I think I can see, finally, what Dad saw when he looked at it.

With Dad's camera, I return to the fireplace to burn the photographs he kept for himself. I dig the negatives out of the box and place them with the prints. And I hear his voice now, hear him telling me these photos were his best. "But they're pictures I had no right to take, Nelly, moments that deserve more dignity than to be splashed across a magazine cover, or captioned *Anonymous Soldier Feeling Pain,* things the guys back in New York just trying to sell print would never understand." And I can see him now too—not just his hands clasping my sons' hands, not just his lips speaking to them. I see him as I saw him when I was a girl: my father standing tall, his eyes moist as his ghosts seep up from the bromide paper in the tray. I see him busying himself putting caps on bottles, wiping off counters, as if he weren't weeping, as if I couldn't tell.

I breathe deeply, exhale.

And then I place the whole stack of Dad's photographs onto the burning logs.

For a moment, it seems the weight of the pictures will extinguish the fire altogether. The licks of flame disappear. But then an edge catches, and then another and another, and multicolored flames rise into the air, casting a warm red glow across the room.

Acknowledgments

So many people have helped me in the tortured progress of bringing this novel from conception to print: Madeleine Mysko's enthusiasm for the first fragile pages will not soon be forgotten, nor will Alice McDermott's gentle critique of fifty very raw first draft pages, and her patience with later pages as well. Cord Clayton's advice in matters photographic was indispensable (as in all matters, all mistakes are mine), as was the friendship and support of Sonia Aguilar and Jennifer Du-Chene. Friends who were kind enough to critique later drafts for me include Mary Strandlund, Leslie Lytle, Dianne Klein, Grant Clayton, Margaret Traurig, and Anna Tyler Waite (thanks, Mom!). And it was certainly the warm welcome of my Baltimore friends, especially Humpy and Louise Stump, Amanda Wharton, Mike and Ann Hankin, Barbie and Peter Horneffer, and the late Sheila Jackson, that inspired me to want to re-create this lovely world on the page.

My children, Chris and Nick Clayton, have supported me in so many ways and with such youthful wisdom and patience that it breaks my heart. My father, Don Waite, and my brothers, Pat, Mike, Mark, and David, have been similarly supportive, as have Ashley Clayton, Page Clayton, and the late Philip

Davidson; thanks especially to Mark, for encouraging me to write.

As for Mac Clayton and Brenda Vantrease, their willingness to wade through draft after draft after draft of this book should certainly qualify them for knighthood or sainthood or some more remarkable hood that I will have to invent to do them justice. Their unwavering belief in this book and in me, and the humor and the care they have always brought to the process of critiquing our work—and to our friendship as well—leave me, after so many hours spent struggling together to get the best words onto our pages, at a profound loss to find those even adequate to express my gratitude. In truth, their names ought to appear on the cover beside mine.

Author's Note

The reader who sets this copy of *The Language of Light* side by side with the hardcover version will notice some slight differences. I don't think it will reveal too much to anyone peeking ahead at this note to say the only substantive change is in the is-he-or-isn't-he aspect of Nelly's relationship with Dac. The ending that appeared in hardcover left that question open, the result of a compromise early in the process of bringing the book out. The fault is my own; I proposed the open ending as a solution that saved me from having to argue against one I didn't think worked at a time when I so wanted to see this first novel—which was ten years in the making— find its way onto bookstore shelves. I rationalized the compromise on the theory that Nelly's relationship with Dac was not the most important aspect of the story in any event, so I ought to be comfortable letting the reader decide. The end result, though—if the number of times I've been asked "Is he or isn't he?" is any indication—has been that the open question became a main focus, drawing attention away from the place I'd meant to leave the reader: focused on Nelly's own choices. The restored ending included here is the original, and was the ending of the novel at the time it was chosen as a finalist for the Bellwether Prize.

I tried to leave the remainder of the novel intact, but in rereading it to restore the ending, I found an overabundance of the word "and" as well as several inadvertent repetitions of words within easy sight of one another that the compulsive writer in me could not let stand. I'm forever grateful to my lovely editor, Caitlin Alexander, for being sympathetic to this need to tidy just a bit, as well as for her support in restoring the ending. When I suggested that possibility, she asked only one question: "Which way would you end it?" When I told her, she responded that she and the whole gang at Ballantine agreed. "If you wanted to go the other way," she said, "I'd have had to talk you out of it." It is a real blessing to be in her hands.

THE
LANGUAGE
OF
LIGHT

Meg Waite Clayton

A Reader's Guide

On Photography and *The Language of Light*

by Meg Waite Clayton

"The Language of Light" comes from the title of a 1952 photograph by Clarence John Laughlin, which John Szarkowski, in *Looking at Photographs,* describes as one in which "the ghosts have fled, and only the pattern of their spell remains." It's a magical black-and-white photograph of the space between a window shade and a casement that for me evokes the moonlight through the window in the opening scene of my novel, and something of the longing and loss I try to deliver in that scene. The title seemed just right given the way light—in the context of trying to capture it through photography—is used as a metaphor throughout the book.

The novel was steeped in photography long before I chose that title, though—one of the final changes I made to the book. Like my fictional Nelly, I received the gift of a wonderful camera at a young age, from a father who was not a photojournalist like Nelly's father is, but rather an executive at a company that made cameras. It may, actually, have been meant for my older brother, who is the one who set up the darkroom in our basement and taught me to develop film, but it remains in my possession and has for as long as I can remember. In any event, that gift has left me ever fascinated with the medium of photographs. Despite my efforts to learn more about how to use a camera in order to deliver a believable photographer-protagonist—reading photography books, visiting stores, and exploring the world through my own viewfinder—I remain sadly untalented in the art of film. But one of the things I love about writing is that it allows me to imagine having talents I lack.

Some of the photos described in the novel are family photos: the photo of young Pat and his siblings in Chapter 11, for example, is actually a description of a photo of my father and his siblings. Most of the personal photos, though, are figments of my imagination, including the photo of Emma that is first seen in the prologue. The photos by real-life photographers are all photos I've seen and admire, and the descriptions come largely from journaling as I sat in front of them.

I went to a number of photo exhibits in the course of writing *The Language of Light,* the most memorable of which I saw during a few days I spent immersing myself in the collections of the great New York museums in the fall of 1994, including my first trip to the International Center of Photography. I followed that up with a trip to the National Gallery later that fall and visits in June 1997 to a Dorothea Lange exhibit at the Cheekwood museum in Nashville, Tennessee. These visits were the first time I saw most of the actual photographs, some of which I knew of from books, and others of which were completely new to me. At MoMA, I saw Walker Evans's disturbingly angled *Spectator Sport*. At the Met, August Sander's unemployed man stood hat in hand in a photograph, shadowed by a building while light at the road's end drew my eye away from him. At the ICP, Cornell Capa's devastating photos of Latin American children left me grateful for the safety of my own sons, and with a deeper appreciation for an El Salvadoran friend. Another photo there, Paul Calvert's shot of a

mother's reaction to seeing the drowned bodies of her children left me wondering if that was a moment anyone should photograph, a question I ultimately explored in the novel. At the National Gallery, Robert Frank's *Trolley* first haunted me, as did a quote of his that has stayed with me ever since: "When people look at my pictures, I want them to feel the way they do when they want to read a line of a poem twice."

At Cheekwood, I spent the better part of a day just sitting by myself in front of Dorothea Lange's photographs, and I returned to see several again. She was and remains my favorite photographer. Her ability to deliver whole heartbreaking stories in tiny gestures is truly extraordinary: the woman's hand to her mouth in *Migrant Mother, Nipomo, California,* with her children's faces turned away; the earnest hands over hearts and enthusiastically opened mouths of the Japanese

© Adrienne Defendi

American schoolgirls in her 1942 *Salute of Innocence*. And it's a quote by Lange from *The Making of a Documentary Photographer* that perhaps best expresses the way I try to approach writing: " 'I draw from the secrets of my heart,' " she says, quoting Albrecht Dürer, then adds, "And that's what I have, in the end. That's what it comes to and that's best. Provided, of course, you've got an educated heart and a sense of some kind of general responsibility. The secret places of the heart are the real mainsprings of one's action."

I keep a number of photos, personal and not, in my office for inspiration. The personal ones tend toward family: my husband and me in Florence on our honeymoon, at a bar his father once took him to; my children at ages eight and ten, in wetsuits on the beach at Carmel; my father and me sitting together on a throne at a dinner party in Beijing. But the ones I turn to most often as I'm writing are two less personal shots. One is a photograph by my friend Adrienne Defendi, which she gave to me on a fiftieth-birthday card: a silhouette of trees in mist in which I suppose I imagine some truth about myself lurks. The other is my favorite photo, *Washington Square, 1952* by André Kertész. I carry a copy of this particular photo with me in my journal as well, and my journal goes most everywhere I do. Kertész did more famous shots of the park, but this one—in snow, with bare trees and a pleasing swirl of fence—includes a blurred figure of a lone person walking through the park. When I first saw it, I thought, "That's how I feel when I'm writing." To this day, I'm not sure why, and I have looked at that photo more times than you would imagine. I think it has something to do with trying to capture myself in focus, trying to understand myself completely, and failing, but continuing to put one word in front of the other in the hope I will come closer, at least, to knowing who I am.

Photographers and Photographs Referenced in *The Language of Light*

David Burnett: photo from *Life* magazine, 1972

Robert Doisneau: *Le Baiser de l'Hôtel de Ville*

Dorothea Lange: *Homeless Family, Oklahoma 1938; Back;* the American Country Woman collection

Robert Frank: *Trolley—New Orleans, 1955; Sick of Goodby's*

Jacob Riis: slum children photos

Nick Ut: photo from *Life* magazine, 1972

Henri Cartier-Bresson

Dmitri Baltermants

Bruce Davidson

Mary Ellen Mark

Margaret Bourke-White

To learn more about Adrienne Defendi's work, visit www.adrienne defendi.com

Questions and Topics for Discussion

1. It takes Nelly a long time to start taking pictures, even after she has bought all of the equipment and agreed to photograph the Blessing of the Hunt. Why is she so hesitant? What gives her the impetus to finally begin?

2. Why do you think Nelly chose to move her boys to Maryland after Wesley's death? Do you think she had different expectations from the life she ends up starting there?

3. What are some reasons the author might have chosen photojournalism as a focal point of the story? How is photojournalism different from other forms of photography? What about it appeals to Nelly? What about it scares her?

4. Why did Emma wait so long to tell Nelly about her relationship with Nelly's father? Do you think she was right to withhold that information?

5. Discuss Willa's relationship with Davis. What impact did it have on Emma? On Dac?

6. Nelly doesn't get the professional reception she hoped for in New York. Were you surprised by this? How does this change the direction of her work?

7. Discuss Nelly's relationship with her brothers. Why do you think they aren't a more prominent part of the story? What influence have they had on her relationship with her father? How, if at all, do you think her feelings about family changed after the insinuation that Dac might have been her half brother?

8. Why do you think Nelly wants to follow in her father's professional footsteps? What about him does she admire? What does she dislike? Do you think he supports her choices?

9. Compare Nelly's relationship with Dac with what we know of her relationship with Wesley. In what ways do you think her marriage affected how she relates to Dac?

10. Emma went to great pains to ensure that Mai and Yvonne were no longer in Dac's life, though she, too, was an outsider when she first married Davis. How do you think her experiences as a newlywed affected the way she dealt with Dac's situation?

11. Emma is a morally complex character, at once extremely generous and extremely selfish. Discuss her work with the Hannah Clark Home. Ultimately, why do you think she founded it? Do you think it was right or wrong of her to do so?

12. All of the major characters—Nelly, Pat, Emma, and Dac—have lost spouses in complicated ways. Compare how each has grieved. Does Nelly's grieving process change over the course of the book, and if so, in what way?

13. What do you imagine the future holds for Nelly and Dac? Why do you think the author chose to leave it unresolved?

14. Why does Pat ask Nelly to burn his photographs after his death? Do you think Nelly makes the right decision about whether or not to do so? What obligations does a photojournalist have regarding the privacy of an individual subject? What, in your opinion, takes precedence, individual privacy or the public's right to know?

15. Discuss what the title *The Language of Light* means. In what ways does the author explore images of light throughout the novel? Did this underlying motif enhance your understanding of the characters' experiences?

16. At the beginning of this Reader's Guide, the author has included an essay discussing some of the photographs that inspired her. What photographs—either personal or professional—have you been inspired by? Have you ever encountered a photograph that has made you uncomfortable? Did you look up any of the photographs mentioned in this novel and, if so, do you feel the author was able to capture them in words?

Read on for an excerpt from

THE FOUR
MS. BRADWELLS

Mia

Betts is sitting alone at a table with two untouched water cups, the pen I gave her the day we graduated from law school, a clean legal pad, and a microphone. On the dais, one of nineteen senators talks his way toward a question he hasn't arrived at quite yet. Cameras whir mercilessly as photographers on the floor between them vie for the better angle, capturing the small fatty deposit on Betts's freckled face, her perky mouth and shattered-crystal eyes. The chair she sits in is poorly chosen; her square diver's shoulders, in a suit the washed driftwood gray of her hair, fail to top its leather back. Still, she looks impressive as she leans toward the microphone, listening in the same intent way she has always listened to Ginger and Laney and me—the way we all need to be heard.

The senator's voice booms, "You were born in an Eastern Bloc country, Professor Zhukovski, a communist child of communist parents," as if this is something she might not have realized. The photographers edge closer on the journalistic racing pit of a floor, none pausing for fresh batteries or different lenses. Television cameras, too, peer down from booths in the side walls, relentlessly recording each intake of breath. "At least the TV cameras are shooting me from above," Betts had joked over the phone a few nights ago. "The still photographers are shooting right at my crepey old neck."

My own crepey old neck feels warm and moist as I stand at the back of the room, behind the computer-laden tables of reporters. Betts has already answered a week's worth of questions, though, sticking to the script. She praised *Brown v. Board* and deplored *Dred Scott* and *Korematsu,* uttered "right to privacy" and "*stare decisis*" while avoiding "abortion," "gay rights," and "guns." She's managed to appear to answer every question without actually stating a single view, all while demonstrating that she has great judgment without ever having been a judge. And the committee vote is scheduled for Tuesday, with the full Senate expected to confirm.

"How are we supposed to believe, Professor Zhukovski," the senator asks finally, "that a communist child of communist parents is the best person in this whole free country to be the arbiter of our laws?"

Betts smiles warmly. "My mother, a doctor in Poland, scrubbed floors here . . ." she responds, her voice rolling gently against the senator's snap. A softer sort of self-possession than she uses in her classroom is called for here, where the minds she is working to win over are still overwhelmingly older, and white, and male.

Scrubbed *toilets,* I'd suggested—words met with a long, expensive, overseas-line silence before Betts had responded, "You'll be surprised when your mom dies, Mia, how much her dignity means to you."

She's taken my advice, though, I realize with a small measure of triumph: she's gotten a friendly senator to ask about the Widow Zhukovski fleeing Poland with Baby Betts in a way that doesn't seem friendly. And the gang back here in the press gallery is taking copious notes.

"My *mother* actually would have made an amazing justice," Betts says. "A fact she would *not* have hesitated to tell you."

The senators laugh easily, as does the audience, the stenographer, and even the press.

I was on assignment when Betts called to ask me to come for this weekend; we'd practically had to shout to be heard over the rickety line. "So let me get this straight, Betts," I'd teased her. "You want me to fly back from Madagascar? *Madagascar,* that's off the coast of Africa, you know that, right? To hold your hand while you worry over a Senate confirmation there isn't a shred of doubt you'll get."

"My crystal ball must be murkier than yours, Mia," she said, her laugh as cozy as the room we'd shared in N Section of the Law Quad our first year, as comfortable as the couch on the porch of the house we'd shared with Laney and Ginger our second and third. I'd slipped my camera strap over my neck and set the Holga aside, laughing with her. Betts, the Funny One. Ginger, the Rebel. Laney, the Good Girl. And me, the Savant.

"Or else . . . Hmmm," she said, "maybe *no one* is exactly a slam dunk for the Supreme Court?"

Laney had told her I'd be back home that week anyway. "They want to meet in D.C. for the hearings and then train up to New York for the weekend," she said. "I told them they could come for the last afternoon. The part where my supporters make me sound like Superjudge." And she laughed again. Betts is always the first to laugh at her little jokes.

"We're thinking *Les Miz* Friday night," she added.

"No doubt we'll be seeing something about a bad mother on Saturday if we let Ginger choose."

"Maybe not, now that Faith is gone." Then, with a crack in her voice, "God, Mi, I wish Matka had lived to see this."

"Matka," Betts always called her mom, the only Polish word she was allowed outside the songs she sang in church, and in church she usually played her zhaleika. Here in front of the Judiciary Committee, though, she calls her "my mother." I stick my hands in my pockets, feeling the cut of waistband, the little roll mushrooming over the top of my slacks as I head for three open seats in the back row. I settle into one of them, imagining Faith and Mrs. Z both cheering wildly together in whatever mom-heaven might exist.

Betts is finishing speaking in her short, straightforward sentences—her "rehearsed immigrant-widow speech," she would call this, although she's avoiding hyphenating here—when the click of high heels sounds. A young woman edges through the crowded room to whisper to a senator we in the press call "Milwaukee's Finest" for his professed love of his home state's Blatz Beer over the Russian vodka he really drinks. I'm reminded, oddly, of the Wizard of Oz as he turns toward her, his gaze as dull-eyed as my editor's—my *ex*-editor's, now that he "let me go," as if I'd just been waiting for his permission to lose my job.

My ex-editor. My ex-paper. My ex-husband and my ex-almost-fiancé. What a fool I am not to have made time to see Doug this weekend.

At the dais, Milwaukee covers the chairman's microphone and whispers, the creased lines around his narrow eyes leaving me wondering if my own eyes are as lined as his are, as lined as Betts's, too, above her pearls. Leaving me wishing my budget allowed for Ginger's expensive facials and creams—a smell trigger, I realize, as Ginger throws her arm around me, not a hug so much as a coach's arm drape. The soft fabric of her quilted winter white wool jacket tickles against my skin.

I turn back her collar to read the label: Kamila.

"I love the buttons," I say.

Her slight overbite disappears into a double-wide grin. "Found-ebony wood chips," she says. Fair trade. Eco-conscious. Fruit of the gods. "You can borrow it this week-end." Evoking memories of the four of us sharing medium-sized Fair Isle sweaters, raiding each other's closets before parties and dates.

Laney slides her long legs gracefully into the empty seat beside Ginger, whispering, "Mi," and reaching across her to grasp my hand.

I pull us all into a three-way hug. "If you two had been much later," I say, "you'd have missed the whole show."

The guy in front of us shoots me a look.

"God, it's so good to see you both!" I say more quietly, try-ing to tuck my rush of joy at being with them again into a smaller voice.

Ginger presses a folded scrap of paper into my hand—a faded old Juicy Fruit gum wrapper. I extract my reading glasses, a bamboo frame that cost next to nothing in China, and examine the tight loops of blue ink on the backside, Ginger's angular, almost illegible scrawl. Laney takes the gum wrapper and reads without the need of glasses as I remember the four of us studying together in the Law School Reading Room, the hush unbroken but for the occasional *thwick* of a page turned in frustration, the scrape of a metal chair, the hushed *swoosh* of the revolving doors, and, if you listened closely enough, the *tick* of a small folded gum-wrapper note hitting the table in front of Laney or Betts or Ginger or me, like a spitball hitting home. Gum-wrapper humor-fortunes like this one, which reads:

LAW QUADRANGLE NOTES, September 2018: Elsbieta ("Betts") Zhukovski (JD '82) has been appointed Chief Justice of the Supreme Court, the first woman and the first foreign-born justice to be appointed to the country's most important legal post. The line to kiss up to her forms outside N-32.

"She's already missed first woman justice," Ginger whispers. "By decades."

The chairman announces a five-minute recess, and the photographers reach for new batteries and memory chips while, behind us, reporters tweet quick recaps.

"You're forgetting the 'Chief' business, Ginge." Laney's Southern accent soft and warm and proud. "Betts could still be the first lady *Chief*. She's got years before that silly gum-wrapper 2018."

I swallow against a scratch in my own throat, envy too stingy to voice. I've always been as jealous of Betts as Ginger is. Not of her smarts so much as her discipline, her courage to imagine she might actually get what she wants.

"*Female* Chief," Ginger says. "Let's not be expecting proper, ladylike behavior from Betts when we don't require the male justices to be gentlemen."

"A real-life Justice Bradwell," I manage finally. "Not made of stone."

Laney's dark fingers smooth the folds in the wrapper. Fifty-some-year-old fingers, fifty-some-year-old hands, but her short nails unbitten now, there is that. Her teeth aren't as white as they once were and she has a few smile lines at her eyes and mouth, but the only place she shows her age in a real way is in her hands, bony and unevenly colored, lighter splotches against her African American skin where I have darker spots on my own Irish pale. I suppose she's imagining, as I am, what a real *Law Quadrangle* magazine alumni update might look like after the full Senate vote:

Elsbieta ("Betts") Zhukovski (JD '82) has been appointed to the United States Supreme Court, following in the steps of Ruth Bader Ginsburg, for whom Ms. Zhukovski clerked on the D.C. Circuit.

One of us would write the note for her. We've written every one of each other's alumni notes ever since Isabelle was born and Zack died in the same few short weeks and Betts, who'd somehow managed through it all, broke down over the writing of this irrelevant announcement. "How do I do this?" she wanted us to tell her. "How do I announce in fifty words or less that my daughter is born and my husband is dead?" The bones of her wrists as fragile as Zack's had been, as if she'd gone through chemotherapy with him: an aggressive form of non-Hodgkin's lymphoma, dead at twenty-nine. It had been, surprisingly, Ginger who had put her arm around Betts's shoulder and said so soothingly she might have been reading a favorite poem, "Let me, Betts. Let me do this for you, this one small thing." It's something we've done for each other ever since, too: set out the words to announce each other's joys and sorrows to the world.

Or joys, really. Only joys, not sorrows. Betts would never have thought to submit a class note about Zack's death if it hadn't so closely coincided with Izzy's birth. We don't ever announce bad news in the alumni magazine. Ginger didn't submit anything the fall she was passed over for partner, any more than I did when I divorced. And I sure don't plan to submit a class note announcing I've been fired. If I find a new job—*when* I find one—Laney or Betts or Ginger will compose a note that makes it appear I've moved up in the world, even if I haven't. That's the way of alumni notes.

"Betts is wearing your mama's black pearls," Laney realizes in a whisper—"your mama" being Ginger's mom and the pearls not really black so much as unmatched shades of gray tinted silver-green and blue and eggplant, with a looped white-gold clasp now resting at the base of Betts's throat. They're the good-luck pearls I wore to the Crease Ball our first year at Michigan, and Laney's "something borrowed" on her wedding day. " 'Next to my own skin, her pearls,' " Ginger says in what Betts calls her "look-how-well-I-quote-poetry voice."

I don't remember ever seeing the pearls on Betts, but they look better on her than on any of us; it's the hair color, I think, the echo of gentle gray.

She's too thin again. She could stand to participate in one of those paczki-eating contests from her childhood—those celebrations of the Polish jelly doughnut Betts swears is not a doughnut. It's the stress, of course: the months of interviews and background checks, and the worry she'd lose the nomination to someone with judicial experience—not that she regrets having stayed in Ann Arbor for her daughter's sake. Then the weeks of holing up in a windowless room at the White House, crafting answers to every question the staffers could imagine, then practicing them again and again and again. And now the daily hearings, the cameras and questions, the news clips, a short few words taken out of context, replayed at 5:00 and 6:00 and 10:00, and then again on the morning shows. Betts's confirmation may very well be as secure as I think it is, but that doesn't make good press.

"We should make Betts color that hair this weekend," Ginger says as she smoothes the cowlick at my right temple into submission. *Let me do this for you, this one small thing.* "That gorgeous auburn it was before Zack died."

"I'm liking the gray," Laney says, and I agree. Betts's refusal to color it is an odd form of penance, as if colorless hair could make up for not having loved Zack enough to keep him alive. Ginger needs to let her be.

"So you both like the gray on Betts, but not on your-selves?" Ginger says.

"Betts beats us all the way to heaven at being smarter," Laney says. "Surely she'd allow us prettier, Ginge."

I reach across Ginger to touch Laney's hair, which, after twenty-five years of being chemically straightened and shoulder-length, has been allowed to reclaim its natural spring. It frames the curves of her jaw in loose rings of dark curls her face has clearly wanted all along. "I love this," I say, meaning the hair, I think.

"Betts isn't smarter," Ginger says. "Just more disciplined."

Laney and I lean our heads on Ginger's quilted winter white shoulders.

"You're right. You're right," Ginger says. "Smarter, too. I can admit that now: Betts is smarter than me."

Laney and I each pat one soft, black-wooled knee of our dear, not always so humble friend as Milwaukee's Finest re-quests and receives permission to ask one last question.

"But not you two. I get to be second smartest," Ginger says, fingering an ebony button. "Damn, Betts is really going to do this, isn't she?"

"Mrs. Zhukovski," Milwaukee says.

Ginger, Laney, and I all whisper, "*Ms.*" in unison and smile at each other as if the shared thought is a shiny penny found heads up.

"*Professor,*" I whisper.

The cameras, as quiet as they are these days, snap off each moment as though any single shot might capture the whole of what's happening here, rather than distorting it. The TV cameras roll on, delivering every blemish in detail so the folks at home can wonder why Betts doesn't have that little fatty deposit removed. The thought crosses my mind that Justice Sotomayor might never have been confirmed if her "wise Latina woman" comment had been caught on film. Visuals are so powerful, even when they're untrue—or only a piece of the truth that, taken alone, is a lie.

I sit up straighter, leaning forward, wanting suddenly to warn Betts to be careful here: Milwaukee is sporting an expression like the one she'd dubbed "Professor Pooley's you're-about-to-be-called-on stare," but without the humorous underlay. My hands go icy, my neck and my feet, too, my spine. Like the shock of that first plunge into the Chesapeake all those years ago.

"Mrs. Zhukovski," Milwaukee repeats, "I'd like to ask you what you know about a death that occurred in the spring of 1982, at a home in Maryland where I believe you were a guest?"

"*Oh, shit,*" Ginger says—mercifully not before the silent blink of the crowd absorbing the question gives way to a collective murmur, the photographers surging forward as even the senators exhale their surprise.

I take Ginger's hand and squeeze it. She looks startled, but if she was going to say more, she doesn't. She links hands with Laney, and we watch as Betts, oddly, unlatches the clasp at her throat and lets the pearl necklace slide into her hand. Every moment of the gesture is caught in a shutter snap: a single manicured nail flipping the catch; her competent fingers opening the necklace; the gray globes of pearls following the white-gold loop into her palm. She fingers the dark blue-gray end pearl, worrying it between thumb and forefinger as if saying a Hail Mary over rosary beads.

The adviser sitting behind her looks like he's praying for divine intervention, as does Senator Friendly up on the dais, but Betts looks unfazed. She doesn't even seem to realize she's removed the pearls. For a moment, I think she is going to stand to answer the senator's question, the way we were required to stand to answer in law school. I think removing the pearls must have something to do with this.

She doesn't stand, though. She remains in her chair. She leans forward from the seat back that is higher than her shoulders, moving closer to the microphone. She smiles the way she smiles when you stumble upon her doing yoga on her screen porch in the morning: a little embarrassed, but somehow more for you than for her. And in the same soft, self-possessed voice she and I rehearsed again and again over the telephone—a voice even I almost believe—she says, "Senator, I don't believe I have anything to add to the public record on that."

MEG WAITE CLAYTON is the author of the nationally bestselling novel *The Wednesday Sisters* and *The Four Ms. Bradwells.* Her first novel, *The Language of Light,* was a finalist for the Bellwether Prize. She is a graduate of the University of Michigan Law School, and was a Tennessee Williams Scholar at the Sewanee Writers' Conference. A former attorney, Clayton currently lives in Palo Alto, California, with her husband and their two sons.